The Importance of Extracurriculars
& Other Assumptions

Found Families Series Book Five

Kelly Elizabeth Huston

Watermount Publishing

edited by Ash White | cover and format by Watermount Publishing

ISBN: 979-8-9877885-8-5 (e-book) | ISBN: 979-8-9924281-0-0 (paperback) | Library of Congress Control Number: 2025903000

Visit www.kellyelizabethhuston.com for author information

To everyone who needs the reminder that life is short. Eat the cake, buy the shoes, see the world, and most importantly, try to leave it better than you found it.

One

"NOT GONNA LIE, MAX, because you know I don't do that. This hurts." I waited a beat before deciding *not* to indulge his moping and hurried past him to prepare to leave. Sure, he'd given me the silent treatment before, but he wouldn't make me feel guilty—not this time. *Life rule: Don't capitulate to petulance merely for the sake of petulance.*

Max sat on the sofa, a colossal brown leather Chesterfield with a permanent dent that marked "his spot" closest to the television. Perturbed eyes, a similar chocolate color, tracked me around the room as I adjusted the window shutters to cut Atlanta's morning glare, then dug between the couch cushions to fish out the flat screen remote. My guess was he hid it to slow me down or irk me, probably both. He refused to budge even an inch to let me slide my hand in the seat crack to get the TV clicker, and then dared an exasperated sigh, like the inconvenience in all the drama belonged to him. Little did he know, his sulky stunt would delay me just enough that in mere minutes I'd find myself lip-locked with a total stranger in the back of a taxi. Actions have consequences.

I bustled around the apartment, making certain I left everything in its place, yet again skipping the coffee I never took time to enjoy mostly because I didn't make it right. Despite my best efforts, I am an awful cook, and yes, brewing coffee *is* cooking.

Maybe on another visit, but not today. *Life rule: If you're on time, you're late.*

Rules are good. Schedules are important. TV remotes belong—well, not buried in sofa cushions. They say, to be a good leader, start by being a good follower. That's not just Buzzfeed click-bait or fortune cookie wisdom. Serious people have written important books about it and I've read them. And *I* am a *follower* of rules.

I grabbed my weekender bag, my prized, new-to-me Burberry coat, and a cumbersome box of work that wouldn't wait beyond the three-night getaway to be read. Work never waited; not for me, anyway.

"There's plenty of food," I shouted from the front door, but knew Max wouldn't acknowledge me. Just as well. One more pathetic pout, and I might have rolled over and called in sick. *Ha. No.* That wouldn't happen. Couldn't. But I'd feel worse if I got "the look" again. Leaving on Max's favorite channel with a *Hot Guys with Hammers* marathon playing, I fumbled with the hefty bolt lock and brass doorknob, buried under the weight of the carton of early-decision college applications. I'd schlepped the work from my campus office last Friday, knowing I'd treat myself to a rare cab ride come this Monday morning.

A glimpse of my reflection prompted one more smoothing stroke of my routine tidy, low ponytail over the Burberry Check, and a frequent wish to eradicate my freckles. The freckles I got from my mother. My blonde hair too, but I hated the pigment stippling my nose and cheeks. Still, the genetic likeness played a reminder to be better. Better at my job, a better person, just—better. I assured myself that today's pantsuit ensemble was on point for me—Amelia Kanaan, consummate young professional, doing righteous work while rubbing elbows with academic elites and wealthy donors. The name Kanaan has roots in the Middle East, so a disconnect sometimes occurs when I show up with light hair, gray eyes, and a freckled face. One might assume my maternal side's Swedish genes take the lead. My mother's surname is Andersson, according to her driver's license, spelled with two SS, and ranks one of the most common names in Swedish society. But the Middle East includes three continents and a rich history of travel, trade, and immigration. They are a biologically diverse people. I'd read all about it. Even so, when I detect confusion during introductions, catch a quizzical look, I deploy a standing joke about how I'm "more meatball than falafel," and my ABBA karaoke is legendary.

Well, one fib down. Righteous work? I shrugged it off, chalking it up to a little Monday morning encouragement—plus that Max would forgive me for abandoning him. *Dang it.* That made fib number two, and two white lies exhausted my daily allotment, even to myself—a strict rule I established when a certain "untruth" had gotten out of hand long ago.

On second thought, that last one wasn't a lie. Max *would* forgive me. He always forgave me; why would this time be any different? No, one fib left for the day. But only one, and *only* a fib. Again, rules.

I closed and locked the door, then rested my head under the scrolled metal *12A* that decorated it, contemplating my choices—like I could fool myself into thinking I had any. But when I heard—and felt—the rumble of The Midtown Mews timeworn elevator, I adjusted my bulky load and dashed for the call button to avoid missing what might be the slowest residential lift in all of Atlanta. Most often I took the stairs, walking all twelve flights rather than waiting for the sluggish contraption. Hoisting the box on one knee, I appreciated my lucky timing as the cables and gears groaned closer, and I hit the down arrow's dim glow once more for good measure.

A reminder flash of Max's adorable pout tightened my chest as I glanced down the hall to the apartment I'd just left. "Amelia, stop it," I chided under my breath. "He's a *dog*, for goodness' sake."

With a noisy *clunk*, the elevator ground to a grumbling stop, but the doors remained closed for a dramatic pause. Over ten years of many visits, I'd grown accustomed to the posh but dated apartment building, with all its quirks. Locals call it *The Mews* and the residence overflows with them. A prime example stood beyond the elevator doors. The unmistakable high-pitched born-and-bred southern drawl of Mrs. Rose Bimah from the sixteenth floor bled through the sliders' divide that often stalled, only opening an inch or two.

The wealthy widow's name was a happy accident as she'd married into it, but she held forth whenever she found a captive audience. Her long-held favorite topic was her niece Matilda, Tilly for short, and how smart, tidy, and available Tilly could be if anyone sought to make a love match. I waited for the big reveal of today's poor, hapless hostage.

"I'm telling you, *Sonny*. She cooks, she cleans, and irons, too. She can stiffen a collar like—*hmm*, maybe you're not the sort to enjoy a stiff collar, having only ever seen you in your Notre Dame t-shirts and athletic shorts." Despite her small stature, Mrs. Bimah possessed the uncanny ability to look down on a person, even while looking up. "Don't you think you're a tad long in the tooth for such everyday—" She paused. "Informality? Do you even own proper trousers?" Her cattiness carried so much contempt, yet dripping in southern sweetness, leaving anyone in earshot a jumbled mix of pity and envy that the woman took the time to dole out the playful barbs in the first place.

"Oh, thank God," the man muttered when the doors finally opened wide. A smile stretched across his face, accentuating the crow's feet that framed his eyes peering over the well-coiffed head of Rose Bimah. Cornered in the burled wood-paneled elevator car, he reached toward me. "There you are." Another set of chocolate brown eyes landed on me. This pair lit up with the uncontained joy Max had denied me moments earlier, and despite what their owner said, I'd never seen them before that moment. He continued, "I wondered where you'd gotten off to."

To be clear, I don't subscribe to Cupid's arrow or love-at-first-sight plots. I stick to facts and figures. Statistics. But facts are, this man's kind face, his tousled curls, and the tenor of his voice did things to me. Biological, chemical, physical things. I jerked my head to glance behind me, confused by this total stranger's comment, nearly dropping my box in the hasty move.

"Aww, let me get that for you, *hon*." Mr. Fighting Irish squeezed by the curious widow and snatched the carton from my slipping grip.

I grunted an elegant, "Huh?" but Mrs. Bimah was already reeling, jumping to the conclusions her beyond-casual captive intended. It wouldn't be the last time I'd regret not taking the stairs.

"*Sonny.*" A mock-scolding tone tinged his name. "Do you know our Mimi here?" She called me by the nickname most anyone outside my work circles used. "Though it shouldn't surprise me. A hunky fella such as yourself."

"Know her? Well, I oughta." The hunk winked at me. "She's my girlfriend."

An indelicate noise oinked out of me, and I smacked my mouth in the embarrassing aftermath. The two elevator passengers shared a chuckle.

Sonny nudged Mrs. Bimah with a gentle elbow. "You'll have to excuse—*uh*, Mimi, Mrs. B. It's new. Us. Mimi and me. We're kinda new."

"*Kinda* new?" I stepped on board, eager to get to the ground floor and out of this bizarre scene I had no bandwidth to navigate, no matter how charming I found those crinkly brown eyes. I pressed the lobby button, then twice more. With only one fib left for the day, but no reason to blow up the poor guy's storytelling, I simply nodded. Obviously, he only meant to stymie the matchmaking epidemic making its way through the building. Who could blame him? I changed the subject. "Where are you off to this morning, Mrs. Bimah?"

"It's Mahjong Monday, sugar," she explained. "The Chen sisters in *7D* are hosting," she clutched her purse to her chest, "and I'm feeling lucky."

"It's not even eight o'clock. You ladies don't fool around. That's some real dedication to the game."

"Well, it's like they say… you can't play all day if you don't start in the morning."

The next animal-like noise came from our new friend Sonny, but he cut his laugh short when the old woman and I snapped our gaze his way. He coughed into his fist and furrowed his brow. "Oh, no, right, I've heard that," he hurried to agree, with a sincere head bob when he must have realized Mahjong Monday was no joke.

As we neared the seventh floor, the elevator slowed further from its gradual descent.

"Well, you ladies have fun. Good luck today," I said, fighting a grin at the ride-along stranger.

"None needed. The game's not only about strategy but also superstition, you know. And today, I'm wearing my charmed bloomers. This gal can't lose while sporting these granny panties."

As she declared her crucial gaming tactic, I shot the man a warning glare, but, evidently a quick study, he swallowed all signs of amusement. It won him instant bonus points in my book, and my glare morphed into a satisfied smile. When he returned it, my stomach rose and fell like the initial steep drop of a roller coaster ride. I caught the smooth brass handrail to steady myself.

Mrs. Bimah adjusted her purse as the lift finally stopped. We waited through the pregnant pause before the doors inched open, but she didn't waste a second of it. "Now you listen, Sonny. I know you are new to town, but Mimi here is a good girl. A real catch if you know what's good for you. Don't mess it up." She patted his cheek, a pat that might have carried a bit of sting. "But if you do—mess it up, I mean—pop back up to *16C*, and I'll arrange a little get-to-know-ya-time with Tilly if she's still available. And she will be..." She sighed that last bit. "*Tootle-loo, y'all.*" She waved over her head as she exited.

I considered hopping off to avoid the awkward ride down the remaining six stories, but Sonny still carried my box, and the doors slid closed with unusual speed, or so it seemed. "She's sweet once you get to know her. She means well. Let me take that." I reached for the lidded carton.

"I've got it. Least I can do for saving me from the female Chuck Woolery." He switched arms, holding my weekend workload away from me.

"Actually, I just read a fascinating book about the rise of mid-twentieth-century television game shows and whether we should consider them the first generation of reality TV. At least those shows were live on the air, automatically making them more *real* than what we get from the genre today. Anyway, Jim Lange hosted *The Dating Game* first and longest." I caught his mystified side-eye in the elevator door's hazy reflection, but I kept my focus defiantly front-facing, too late realizing my habit of sharing useless knowledge in uncomfortable social situations rearing up in all its geeky glory.

Sonny played along without missing a beat. "*Huh*. Who knew my girlfriend was such a well-read game show enthusiast? Isn't it great how we can still surprise one another like this? Keeping it fresh after all this time?"

Wishing I'd taken the time for coffee, I vowed not to engage with this enigmatic man, no matter how cute his dark blond curls or quick his wit. I pursed my lips, then bit the top one, fighting the urge to defend myself. "I read a lot." Vow broken. "Non-fiction, mostly." It sounded casual and steadied my confidence.

"Pretty gross concept when you think about it," he added. "The game show, I mean."

"*Yes*. So much worse than the arbitrary swipe right or—say, stealing a stranger's things while she's confined to an elevator, then claiming she's your romantic partner for the sole purpose of duping a dear old woman innocently searching for a mate for her sweet niece who happens to possess exceptional ironing skills." I kept my eyes forward, willing the elevator to move faster. I might have gone too far. Sometimes I do that too.

"Wow. Okay. Touché, but I just—"

"No. No, no," I interjected, softening in case my counterpunch had landed too harshly. "I'm teasing. No apologies. No explanation. I don't know you, I don't *need* to know you, so I don't need to hear your story, Sonny."

"Actually, it's not—"

"Really. It's unnecessary." I waved him off, relieved to feel the firm landing depositing us into the white marble lobby full of palm trees and some of Atlanta's oldest residents. "I'm sure you're a great guy. And while I'm not a fan of pulling one over on a senior citizen,

I don't blame you. Mrs. Bimah is—a lot." I took what should have been one last look at him. "Now, may I have my box, please? I need to catch a cab."

He shook his head, grinning with a tickled squint. "Nah, I think I'll see this through to the end. Please." He head-gestured for me to exit. "After you."

Two

I figured enduring another minute of Sonny's company wasn't worth a fight. "Hello, Mr. Colby. Think I could get a cab this morning?"

The uniformed gentleman with wild, white hair under his navy-blue cap met us on the sidewalk as we spun around the revolving door. He tapped his visor that couldn't hide his fat caterpillar-like brows and offered me a small but kind smile. "Could be a moment at this rush hour with all this rain, Miss Mimi, but I'll flag one down for you."

Sonny squinted toward the clear blue sky, then at the street with very little traffic.

I shrugged. "You never know what Mr. Colby is going to say. We just roll with it. Please, let me take—"

No sooner had I made my third attempt to free my weekend work from the clutches of the questionable Samaritan than an unexpected and unfortunate wail, *"Mimi,"* came at us from half a block away.

My wide eyes met Sonny's grinning version as The Midtown Mews treated the new guy to *all* its eccentricities that Monday. "Shoot," I mouthed, making a slow turn toward the fast-approaching Geneva Spieler, the seventy-something resident of *12A* and owner of the lovable, even if moody, Max.

"Something wrong?" Sonny peered over my head at the woman coming our way.

"It's Geneva. Max's owner."

"Owner?"

"I'm Max's sitter. *Dog* sitter. Ten years now. Since he was a pup."

Geneva loved Max more than just about anything or anyone, including her travels, and she qualified for Diamond Medallion's frequent flyer status many times over.

"Max, huh? Sounds like a big dog's name." Sonny's dubious reaction didn't surprise me.

At first and even second glance, most would guess the glamorous Ms. Spieler owned a miniature something or teacup something-or-other, some handbag-sized pet she could take with her wherever, whenever. Alas, no. Max was a coffee-colored Portuguese Water Dog with a smattering of cream coloring his chest and feet.

"Oh, he is. As Porties go, Max more than qualifies as a big boy. Two feet to his shoulder and probably staring down the barrel of sixty pounds of fluffy goodness—thanks to too much bacon and his fur mom's indulgent ways." I couldn't help but gush. I loved Max, too.

Geneva's fancy pooch-purse loss was my gain when my first of many post-undergrad side jobs came via *Oodles of Poodles*. The premier pet service offered everything from dog walking to in-home pet-sitting. And though I'd given up the daily dog walking gig when I earned my master's degree, I was the only one Geneva trusted to stay with Max on her frequent getaways.

Max and I hit it off at once, priority one for Geneva. But she and I got on well too. We even socialized at times, with her waxing on about her surprisingly wild youth through to her even wilder last Tuesday, while I shared the mundane details of my career-centered life. Yes, she was loud, pushy, and eccentric, but generous more than anything. But when she took to the skies, or the road, or the open seas, texts were best. She appreciated my quick replies, day or night, no matter what her time zone, and I enjoyed having a dog, even if only part time.

"Careful, Sonny," I confided. "If you think Mrs. Bimah is—*assertive,* Ms. Spieler makes her look like an amateur. Rose only peddles the one niece, but Geneva carries an unending roster of Old-World oligarch progeny, UAE royals, and the latest stepchildren of Hollywood elites."

Though widowed and divorced many times, the woman loved married life. Six trips down the aisle proved it. Seven, if you count the man she married twice. Both number three *and* lucky number seven, Moishe Spieler was the great love of Geneva's life. Rumor had it he also played a role in some questionable business dealings. Geneva swore he'd gone straight, which was why she married him again. Since his death, she endeavored to see almost everyone else take that love leap too, but her marital meddling was one more Midtown Mews quirk I didn't have the time or interest to bear.

With a quick pleading glance toward Sonny to "play along," I spun into Geneva's tall frame. She rocked me side to side, repeating my name before she held me at her long arms' length for careful examination.

"Geneva. Hello. What's with the long walk?" On my tip-toes, I scanned over her shoulder. "You keeping someone on the down-low?" I teased, but for a split second, her eyes said I'd stumbled onto something.

"Don't be daft. You know I like to get in my steps. But would you look at you? *Tres belle,* Mimi. That coat. Fabulous."

Her noting my classic fashion statement provoked a prideful smile even though I'd bought it second hand, but the moment faded fast.

"It has been a while since I've laid eyes on you. Too long. But I've been thinking." She tapped a bright, fuchsia-painted nail to her matching mouth. "Do you know who would be perfect for—"

"Geneva," I rushed to interrupt again. "It is so lovely to see you, but I have to get to work."

"Yes, yes. *Masochist Mimi*, all work and no play. But speaking of playing—" she practically purred.

I ignored the amused snicker from the box-carrying pack mule, Sonny.

"No, we were not. We were speaking of working. *Me* working. Specifically, me getting to the place where I work." I kept my scolding lighthearted with a wagging finger.

"All right, all right. But this evening, come back over. I picked up a little something for you on my whirlwind tour of Majorca, and I met the most charming family with the most delectable son, *two* sons, in fact. *Available* sons."

"Sonny!" I half-shouted over my shoulder. "Geneva, have you met Sonny yet?"

"Who, love?" She looked past me at the man. The two shared a confused expression.

"It's the weirdest thing. We ran into one another in your building, and *bam*. A couple of walks with Max, and one thing led to another." I hooked his arm, nearly dislodging my box of early decision applications from his grasp. "He's my—boyfriend." I almost choked on the word and my last fib for the day. *Darn it.*

"Who?" she asked again.

"Hi, Ms. Spieler. Ethan Ledes. Welcome back." He pulled from me to shake Geneva's hand.

"*Huh?*" The confusion bug spread, and I caught it.

"Yes, I know, Ethan. I'm on the condo board. My vote put you over the top. You settling in all right?" She cocked her head, looking skeptical.

"Of course, ma'am. Getting there." His affable smile flipped a switch as he continued to schmooze the willing septuagenarian. "I trust you enjoyed your trip. The island is perfect in October. Gorgeous days and cool at night. But the crowds are mostly gone."

Whatever his name, he whisked Geneva right back from whence she came with wistful, recent memories of the Spanish island. A place, it seemed, he knew well.

"So, so right. It was divine but far too short a trip," Geneva sighed, lost in the recollection.

"Um, Sonny? I-I mean, Ethan?"

"Aww, come on, Meems." He gave my arm an affectionate elbow bump, calling me by a new nickname I wasn't sure I hated. "You and Mrs. Bimah will never get that pet name to stick. Besides, I think she only calls me that because she doesn't remember my real name." He winked. "And you've got to get to the office so—" Ethan adjusted his load to flag down an approaching cab. Mr. Colby backed up the gesture with a whistle. "And don't forget we have that thing later, so not sure you'll be back this way tonight. Remember?"

"The thing?" It was like the opening night of a play, with everyone knowing their role and the lines to say, but I'd never even read the script.

"At the—place? Where you work?" He urged me to remember our *non-existent* plans.

"At Chastain?" I asked.

"That's it." He bumbled to open the taxi's door, and I hurried to the curb.

"Another time, Geneva. Okay? Max did great, by the way."
I tossed my travel bag in the cab's backseat, then crawled in after
it.

"Fine, fine. Far be it from me to get in the way of you doing
something fun for once. Even if it is work-related. I take it you
didn't try the coffee."

"I forgot again. Sorry. Next time."

"Sure, sure. We must catch up, though. And soon.
Obviously." She ogled poor Ethan and his faded Notre Dame
t-shirt and matching gym shorts in a way that made me twitch.
"Go, Irish," she cheered with her raised bejeweled fist.

Ethan grinned, then bent to place the box in my lap.

Frazzled by the whole encounter: Geneva's spirited
backward retreat while pantomiming "call me," Mr. Colby with
his wiggling bushy brows and exaggerated goodbye salute, and
the crisp alpine smell and baffling closeness of Ethan's face
inside the taxi, I kissed him. On the mouth. Chaste, but far too
long. Ethan banged the back of his head on the car door frame in
his escape. Geneva yelped, giving an eager fuchsia thumbs-up,
and spun on her Louboutin heel before trotting inside on Mr.
Colby's burly arm. I gasped at the mayhem of it all.

"Oh, my goodness. I am *so* sorry," I said, only for my
accomplice's ears. With my lap full but one foot on the curb
again, I tried to scramble from the cab.

Ethan rubbed his curly head. "Nope, just a minor bump."

"No, I mean the—I didn't mean to—you leaned into the
car and—"

"To put the box on your lap," he explained.

"Right. Of course. I got a bit flustered with the names and
the plans and the—"

"Yeah, way to level up in the Boyfriend Game."

"Hey, wait a second. You started it. Don't complain when you—"

"Who's complaining?" He looked around and shrugged. "Not me. I like a job with benefits."

"And what job is that?" I asked, genuinely curious about who I'd kissed.

"The Fake Boyfriends of Hotlanta—trademark pending, of course."

Embarrassed, I shook off a laugh. "Well, you really must be new to town. We don't say *Hotlanta* here. At least not unironically, anyway. But speaking of jobs—I need to get to work."

"Sure. Me too. Nice to—meet you—" He pressed his lips together, making me wonder if they tingled like mine.

"Mimi," I filled in the blank and offered a handshake.

"Right. *Meems*. I heard. And I'm *Ethan*." He nodded hello, and his warm grip enveloped mine.

"Right, Ethan, *not Sonny*. I heard," I mimicked with a head bobble. "Nice to meet you, too." I slid my hand free of his, reluctant to close the car door. We both hesitated, like more needed to be said in the awkward moment.

"Bye," we finally said in unison.

He shut the door and gave a motionless wave. I returned the gesture, pondering the *thud* that echoed from my chest to my ears.

Three

"CHASTAIN, HUH? THAT'S A fancy school." The cabbie's ID swayed on a steel-ball chain in front of me, hypnotic in its back-and-forth.

If I could have reached the phone buried by my box and bag, I'd have employed the universal signal for "Don't talk to me." Of course, my job in undergraduate admissions centered on talking about Chastain University, so it seemed my workday was off to an early start. Somewhat of a relief. A distraction from the morning elevator and sidewalk debacle.

"Fancy? It's a good school, if that's what you mean. I'm proud to say I'm an employee and also a graduate."

"Oooh." The man raised his brow with a look in the mirror. "I meant pricey. Takes a good bit of coin to go to a place like that. I guess for that kind of price tag, it best be a *good* school, too."

"I attended on a full scholarship. That's why I do what I do now. I'll be forever grateful to the generous donors who make it possible for young students without great means to attend Chastain. I do my best to make sure those opportunities exist for the next generation of worthy, if not wealthy, scholars." If my mini-speech sounds canned, it's because I'd spoken the words more than once. That's not to say I am always so forthright about my penniless upbringing.

"That's right fine work, Miss." The driver's approval reflected in the rearview. "It seems to have worked out well for you, too. Ritzy Midtown address."

I didn't detect any sarcasm or disdain in his false impression, but my nature wouldn't let it go uncorrected. I fidgeted with the collar of my treasured Burberry, realizing its overkill on such a mild October day. "Well, I was pet-sitting at that Midtown address, but you're right. Chastain has done me well."

Fifteen years ago, I received that overstuffed envelope announcing my yearned-for acceptance, and the university monopolized the bulk of my days ever since. None of that would have happened without my academic diligence, but even more so, other people's charity. Even at thirty-two, I hadn't shaken the notion that I wasn't quite up to snuff, and I didn't think I would ever absolve myself of my long-ago indiscretion, no matter how young I was at the time.

The shoulder strap of my unwieldy bag slid down my arm as I balanced the box of printed applications, struggling to heave open the enormous wood-carved door to the old gothic building that housed my office. No doubt, someone somewhere had nicknamed me *Tree-killer* because of my penchant for printing the deluge of digital submissions I could read on a screen. To be fair, I didn't print all of them. Only the truly viable candidates' pages went to the printer, a small percentage of those who opted to hit *submit*. Even fewer earned an acceptance letter, both a congratulatory email and one on embossed, fine linen stationery. I'd framed mine.

Georgia's Chastain University is a Southern Ivy, as some like to say. A small, elite school with a rich history and tight-knit alumni that includes generations of well-known, well-off, and (mostly) well-regarded families. But there are other attendees like me, and I aimed to make that number grow. I oversee "special" cases. The reasons some candidates warrant this exclusive label vary, but those particular applications find their way to my desk after the initial reads by the selection committee.

"Amelia, you have a call with President Cromwell at eleven-fifteen this morning; the latest application numbers are here." My assistant Nora Okafor fell in stride as she slapped a sticky note atop the carton I carried on the walk from her desk to my office down a short, wide hall. "The development office has some questions about five-year-and-under alumni and probable capital campaign contribution expectations. They'd like to send over a new-hire to ask those questions, and I'm guessing to get you to give that poor lamb the once over," she paused for the briefest chuckle, then continued bustling around my office, depositing unsealed mail on my desk, opening the blinds, and giving a cascading philodendron a splash of water. "As I said, it's a new-hire, so I can make that happen in the next hour or after lunch. They'll come when I—I mean you—say so.

"And then there's the matter of making the first-round of second cuts in early acceptance applications, and if you have any hope of staying on track, you need to decide by the end of business today. Oh, and Mr. Pembroke's office called first thing this morning. I have him at the top of your call sheet, and the development office will no doubt want to hear about that chat, too." She passed me a stack of messages, each labeled by her hand with the date, time, and her initials underlined in the bottom corner. Efficient as always. "Other than coffee, can I get you anything right this minute?"

Nora runs my office like a German train and had been there long before me. To call her my assistant seemed a gross understatement, but it was the title she preferred. If you overheard a conversation, you might wonder who worked for whom. We each had our strengths, but I'd never get done all that was required in my job without her. Her brusqueness frightened away more than a few staff-members before they could witness her gooey center. Their loss, but it kept our office small, and that suited me fine.

Another check in her win column came by her good rapport with students. I remembered her from my candidate interview almost fifteen years ago. She knew the best, most reliable ambassadors to choose when we needed undergraduate envoys to perform welcoming duties for those recruits with expectations of a little extra hand-holding. When she called, they came, primed with background information I assumed she'd gleaned from reading the essays and applications. Current students would bring up those personal highlights when greeting them to help make the newly accepted students and their families feel seen. Nora Okafor called it the "fawning treatment," much to my dismay. Nonetheless, the woman was invaluable.

I smiled. "Good morning to you too, Nora. Yes, I enjoyed a lovely weekend. Hit the Beltline with Max, binged that Netflix show you recommended—good stuff. Then finished a book, non-fiction about the history of television and its impact on social norms, and ate way too much Thai takeout. Sweet of you to ask. Oh, wait, you didn't." I tossed my load onto my desk and thrashed out of my coat. The iconic wool plaid might have looked the part, but sweating through my pantsuit would not.

Nora stared with a cocked head as I hung the Burberry on a brass hook of a walnut hat stand.

"Max is still a dog, right? Because if he is, I have work to do. But, if this Max is a man, I will put the phones on *do not disturb* and sit my old lady bones down to hear all about it, but my guess is I'm getting you coffee and heading back to my desk and the phone that will ring non-stop until next March."

"Make it the big mug, please," I hmphed, then plopped into my desk chair to take in the view of a campus courtyard below, full of rare, cultivated chestnut trees turning color. The change in leaves promised cooler breezes, and that led my olfactory sense to spark with the memory of that crisp alpine scent and the ridiculous start of my day. I must have smiled again.

"What are you grinning about?" Nora returned with my café au lait, extra hot, like I liked it. She made it better than I ever could, so, long ago, she decided I shouldn't bother to try. Lean into your talent, she'd said.

I took a careful but immediate sip of the scalding coffee to stall my answer while wondering if, since I only *thought* one of those earlier fibs, maybe it didn't count. Then again, if I wouldn't hold myself accountable, no one would. I shrugged, "Something that happened this morning, an odd start to the day, is all." I left it there. "Nothing from Briana Johnson?"

"No, not yet." Nora's disappointment reflected my own. "It's not been a week yet. And who knows what her email access is like? Maybe she hasn't seen your message."

Some might find it hard to imagine a teenager without easy access to email, but it was a reality, and not only in rural areas. But when I discovered a potential student, a special case for admissions to consider, I looked for every opportunity to reach out to the candidate to make sure that young person got due time. Briana

Johnson was that student in this submission round. I didn't know her, but her application rang familiar. I recognized a background of hard work, little money, and having to navigate a system built on a deck stacked against her.

"Let's not let this week go by without making contact, okay? And be thinking of at least two alumni for interviews and three current students for introductions. I think Rashida Turner is an obvious choice for the alumni interview if she can carve out the time. She's young, local, quasi-famous."

"You think a high school student is watching CNN?" Nora didn't give me a chance to reply. "And let's be sure we pair Ms. Johnson with more than token black interviewers and students." It served as a gentle nudge, not a reprimand, but as I scrolled through the other names of alums and current undergraduates I'd considered, they all had one thing in common. I chided myself, simultaneously thanking the universe for the guiding hand of the seasoned Nora. My list of names to meet with Briana required some tweaking.

"Of course not, Nora, and none of our alumni or current students are *token* anything. We're all Mighty Roosters."

"She's the one, huh? Briana is the lone basket you are placing all your *rooster* eggs in this year?"

Rooster eggs. I wouldn't let Nora's *punny* dry humor sidetrack me. "She's a smart, diligent, young woman who has scraped her way to this moment. I'll try to help her level up, if I can. I think she deserves it. I see myself in her."

"Yes, I know. You see yourself. But she is lacking some—"

"Some of us didn't have the luxury of interning at Daddy's hedge fund or volunteering summers at the dolphin sanctuary on Mr. Branson's private island." I'd snapped with more bark than intended, but it was Nora's raised brow that made me apologize. "I'm sorry."

Nora nodded her forgiveness, but her pursed lips hinted she had more to say. She would share it another time. "I'll give it a day or two for her to reach out. In the meantime, I'll make a list of names for you."

"Mr. Pembroke called? Who is *he* championing this year? More importantly, please tell me the applicants are qualified."

Meriwether Pembroke, a deep-pocketed alum who'd turned *his* father's millions into billions in the energy business, had an annual tradition of picking two applicants to bestow his unwavering support. One for early acceptance and one for the "regular season." These young people were the fortunate offspring of a country club crony or big business ally of the powerful Pembroke at the top of Pembroke Industries. Two lucky teens would see their Chastain dreams fulfilled, if the energy titan had anything to say about it—and as far as I knew, he always did. I couldn't say the same for the likes of Briana, even with me at her back.

"I've already highlighted them in the latest report, but I'm sure Mr. Pembroke will tell you exactly how qualified the two are." Nora winked as she backed out of my office. "Oh. How's your mother?"

"Fine." The syllable came out too fast and too sharp. With a quick inhale, I smiled. "She's fine. Thank you for asking."

Nora often asked about my mother. Strange, since the two had never met, but I guessed it was Nora's way of connecting with me. Who else would she ask about?

I shook off Nora's personal concern and the lack of a reply from Briana Johnson to steady myself before I punched in the ten digits that would connect me to Mr. Pembroke, ten digits my job dictated I know by heart.

An hour and seventeen minutes later, Mr. Pembroke gave me my marching orders and then snarled his more terrifying than charming dismissive laugh when I gently reminded him of improprieties and appearances in elite academia. For a man at the helm of a billion-dollar company, he squandered an inordinate amount of time chatting on the phone. As a busy woman of lesser means, I knew I'd lost an hour and seventeen minutes I'd never get back.

But before I could delve into the next item on my growing to-do list, muffled but raised voices interrupted my progress. Nora's unmistakable tenor snapped again, and I bolted out of my office to find out which unfortunate soul stood on the wrong side of my formidable gatekeeper down the hall.

"...and as I've said, *three times now*, Ms. Kanaan does not take walk-ins. She's a busy woman—"

"Aww, come on, Ms. Okafor. We're *all* busy. Okafor. I met a family in Nigeria with the name Okafor. Are you or your ancestors from—"

"I'm from Macon, sir. My people are from Macon, Georgia."

Something about that "aww" brought me to a hard stop before I rounded the corner to the reception area and Nora's grand mahogany desk. I'd heard it recently, more than once, but couldn't imagine how it found its way to my office. As I peeked around a potted Weeping Fig tree, two questions got answered. Ethan Ledes dared to challenge the recalcitrant Nora, and he did, in fact, own a proper pair of trousers.

"Ethan?" I interjected before Nora leveled the unsuspecting man.

The visitor jerked straight, more rigid than the crisp crease that ran down the back of his dress pants. His head took its time, swiveling to meet my eye, and I wasn't sure who looked more startled, Ethan or Nora—or me.

"Mimi?" he whispered, like the sight of me caught him off-guard.

Heat crept up my neck. "What are you doing here?" I asked.

"I—"

"I mean, how did—did you know I worked here?"

"I didn't. I swear I had no idea—" he stammered, but I didn't let him finish.

"Nice pants."

"What?" He looked at his legs, took a deep inhale before he met my grin with his own. The same grin that caught my breath at the Mews. *Kapow!* "Thanks. Be sure to tell Mrs. Bimah for me, won't you?"

I could only nod but found my way back to the moment when Nora let loose an exaggerated cough. "No, really, who told you I worked here?"

He opened his mouth, then closed it with a head tilt before I steamrolled over him.

"It was Geneva, wasn't it? Or poor Mr. Colby?" I rolled my eyes, knowing Geneva Spieler likely recruited the sweet doorman to join her geriatric cabal of matchmakers.

"And now that I think about it—you mentioned it too." He grimaced to himself with something like frustration as he seemed to replay our earlier ruse to avoid more of Geneva's antics.

"Did I?" The morning's jumble of events was just that, so I took his word for it.

"Barely," he mumbled.

"Why don't you come back to my office—"

Nora swooped in. "Mr. Ledes didn't make an appointment, Amelia, and you know appointments are the linchpins that keep the trains running on time." See? Even Nora embraced the Teutonic rail comparison.

"That's okay, Nora. This drop-in is personal, not business," I hurried to say.

"*Personal*? You don't say."

More heat climbed and my cheeks radiated.

"You did say your name was *Ethan*, didn't you? Not Max, right?" One brow disappeared behind the elegant side-sweep of Nora's gray bangs.

I glared at her impish grin.

"Isn't Max a dog?" Ethan's gaze bounced from me, to Nora, and back again.

"This way, Ethan." I spun on my heel and then batted away a face-full of Ficus leaves before darting down the hall, hoping he would follow.

Four

FROM MY OFFICE DOORWAY, I forced a smile through my nerves. Catching myself reaching to twist my ponytail, I intercepted my anxious tell and ushered Ethan across the threshold.

"Your name is Amelia?" He hesitated, standing close enough to allow that woodsy scent to daze me again.

"Yes." The word caught in my throat, but I rallied with a hard blink.

"Amelia Kanaan?" he asked again.

I pointed over my shoulder to the name stenciled on the frosted glass. "Vice Dean of Admissions, Chastain University. Go Roosters!" I reminded myself this office was *my* turf. Ethan was the interloper and his sudden uneasiness, so different from his earlier confidence, signaled he found himself out of his depth. I didn't understand it, but both personas appealed to me.

"Not a lot of people know this, but the term 'rooster' is relatively new." More of my arsenal of non-fiction burbled up. "The word didn't appear until 1772. Still well before Chastain opened its doors, but we think it a good fit for what we hope happens here, a symbol of new beginnings, vigilance, and courage. Of course, there's the whole masculinity aspect that no longer applies since we're a co-educational institution now, but that will have to be another generation's fight."

"What? Oh, right. Of course, I just mean, I didn't imagine—a name like—uh, Mimi, I never thought of that as a nickname for Amelia." Not the first time my eggheaded commentary went unappreciated. Something preoccupied him. He struggled to find his poise and his way into a chair. Something I took for a shy sweetness glimmered in his kind eyes as he inexplicably focused on nicknames.

I slid into my seat with all the reclaimed confidence I could muster at the same time Ethan bounded to his feet again.

"You know, this was a—a bad idea." He spun toward the exit.

"Was it?" The abrupt one-eighty from flirting to fleeing was a surprise. I tended to be the one making hasty retreats in social situations.

"Pretty sure. Yeah." Ethan pulled his phone from his pocket like it had rung. It hadn't. In the dead quiet of our awkwardness, even if it vibrated, I would have heard it. I didn't. With eyes only for his phone screen, he said, "Sorry, Mimi—Amelia! I need to—" He gave me one last glance. "Thanks for the mini treatise on roosters, though." Then he bolted from my office.

What just happened?

As if on cue, like she read my mind (something she did often), Nora appeared at my door. "What just happened?"

"I don't have a clue," I sighed. But in a count of three, I decided I'd frittered away enough time on the once-charismatic Ethan Ledes. Time to get back to work.

Nora's suspicious gaze lingered on me, but other than that, she kept her thoughts about the incident to herself. Small favors. Better still, she closed my door again and left me to the day's agenda. I worked without a break, nibbling the sack lunch I always brought. And other than an afternoon visit by a nervous neophyte from the development office, I only saw Nora when she brought me a second café au lait. The pick-me-up helped me get through to the end of the day and the latest crop of "special case" early submissions that came with it.

My eyes crossing for the third time, I focused out my window on the fading sky. Fall days turned to night with speed, and I preferred not to walk home in the dark. That stroll was the only exercise I got most days. Now that we'd survived Georgia's Hell's Front Porch season, the trek home through Chastain's ivy-covered campus and Freedom Park was a pleasant escape from the stuffy surroundings of my work life.

Working at the university came with perks, aside from changing the lives of a chosen few. Many of my more established academic colleagues owned homes in the tony environs neighboring the campus. Those gorgeous old residences often included small outbuildings, former carriage houses renovated into cozy apartments, perfect for one. Seven hundred square feet, nestled behind a grand Craftsman in Druid Hills, held a living room, a generous kitchenette, a bedroom with a full bath and a walk-in closet. Furnished.

My landlord, Reginald Jaspers III, taught American History at Chastain for so long, many joked his vivid Civil War lectures were based on first-hand knowledge. If his resemblance to Black Colonel Sanders with a white suit and black string tie didn't catch you in a snicker, you'd likely get snared by his Foghorn Leghorn voice. The funny part? It was all a charade, a character he'd played in front of students for years. He made history come alive and decades of Mighty Roosters adored him for it.

The scholar wrote books too, fiction and academic. I met his literary agent at a garden party years ago. A spitfire of a woman from Manhattan who loved his southern persona, she'd insisted he double-down on the caricature to sell more books. His home made clear his success, and thanks to him, my version of home was close, quiet, safe, and sparkling with pristine charm and embarrassingly low rent. I knew my luck in calling it mine.

My walk home gave me the time to consider the odd hitch in my typical Monday, the gatecrasher, who showed up without warning but then disappeared without explanation. And all of it happened in a cloud of confusion, as if it wasn't my gate he'd meant to crash—like I wasn't the person he'd come to see. More likely, he had second thoughts when he got a second look and heard my ridiculous rooster trivia. He was the adult equivalent of a "cool kid" and I didn't warrant a seat at his lunch table.

Twilight's chill jolted me out of my silly speculations, and I relished the feel of cool air. The rustle of downed leaves at my feet seconded the reminder that fall had arrived. I hurried inside for a quiet night with a glass of red wine and a new book—non-fiction, of course.

Alas, it was Monday, which meant I had one more to-do to do. On cue, my phone rang.

"Hey, Mama," I answered with all the pep I could manage. "How was your week?"

"Can't complain. I mean, I've got one of those catches in my neck. I'd say I slept on it wrong, but I haven't been sleeping much lately, and since winter decided to show up today, my rickety bones are talking to me, but what are you gonna do?"

I squelched my laugh. "Your bones are barely sixty, Mama."

Obviously my mother Livia *could* complain, but her tone said she was actually having a good day. She deserved it, too, having raised me alone, working the gigging-life long before it was cool. She cleaned houses, babysat neighbor children, worked catering jobs during the busy summer wedding season, and retail throughout the hectic winter holidays. Whatever she could find to keep a roof over our heads and food in our bellies.

She still worked in the housekeeping business, an industry that reached into the homes of middle-class America now more than ever. But she no longer did the scrubbing. She managed schedules and trained and organized cleaning teams for a local chain popular in the exurbs.

My father never played a role in my life. I'd been in grade school when I learned never to ask about him. To look in the mirror, it seemed obvious the only thing he ever gave me was my name. Save a couple of inches I had on her, and the years she had on me, Mama and I were the spitting image of one another. Mama made it clear long ago we were alone in this world. No father, no other family. I don't even recall asking about them, though I'm sure I did. My thirst for knowledge began early, but as luck would have it, a library filled in as childcare in my younger days. Once I could read, the need for questions ended.

My mother continued our Monday evening catch-up. "Speaking of old, and I know you explained this to me already, but I got an alert on my phone from Elmo, and I'm not sure what to do with it now."

"Who's Elmo?" I asked.

"Velma? No, that's not it. The money thing you set up for me?"

"*Venmo*, Mama. It's Venmo. And I've been sending you money that way for more than a month now. You need to transfer that cash to your bank account."

"Whatever it is, I don't get it. You make things so complicated. I also don't understand why you insist on giving me money every week like I'm some sort of child in need of an allowance, and why can't you give me a check like you used to?"

"Because no one uses checks anymore, Mama."

"Then put cash in an envelope."

"It's my busy season, so I'd have to mail it, which means stamps. And I'm pretty sure stamps went the way of checks. Plus, it's not secure—or the freaking twentieth century."

Her exasperation whooshed into my ear in a forceful exhale. "I don't care for your sass, young lady." One more thing I inherited from her. Despite her sometimes-salty language, she forbade me to use any. Ever.

"I make plenty, and I like to share, and Venmo makes it easy. Particularly this time of year when I can't get up your way regularly."

"You could if you took a better job and bought a car and moved out of the god-forsaken city and—"

"So, Mama." Mondays were always a two-glasses of wine night. "First you open the Venmo app..."

Five

THE SECOND GENEROUS POUR of wine and the engrossing book *Triumph and Turmoil in the Desert: The Rise and Fall of Ancient Egypt* I'd enjoyed the night before made for a sluggish morning. But the cool air, carrying a surprise crispness Atlanta couldn't usually boast about, put some pep in my step. Landscape crews nodded polite hellos as they waited for the appropriate hour to blow the fallen leaves into piles to be bagged and twist tied. Heaven forbid we allow nature to remain scattered on the ground. Not when noisy equipment and industrial-sized plastic sacks could cart them to a landfill like God intended.

Crossing a street to enter the university campus, I kicked at colorful leaves the college's groundskeepers would, no doubt, scoop up by the end of the day. Memories flashed of students jumping into mounds of the stuff, laughing and making leaf angels because snow was a rarity. Back in the day, I watched the frolicking from a library window, never having the time to take part.

Lost in thought, with another playful punt of fallen autumn color, I nearly face-planted in the damp grass, startled by a baritone shout, "Amelia!"

With the sunshine on my face, I raised a hand to shield my gray eyes. A figure jogged toward me, and I stumbled again, losing my footing on the edge of the bricked campus walk.

"Whoa, careful there, Meems. You almost fell—*twice*." Ethan eclipsed the sun, replacing the direct sunbeam with his beaming smile.

"Ethan? What are you—"

"Coffee?" he interjected, handing me a cup from my favorite local roaster.

"I don't drink coffee," I lied.

"Sure you do. You had a mug on your desk yesterday. A *big* mug."

"Aren't you observant?"

"I'm a details guy. Details are important."

I spun to head toward the admissions building, embarrassed he'd caught me in a fib and miffed that I'd wasted half my daily allotment on something as silly as coffee and Ethan Ledes.

"Aww, come on. Take the peace offering." He skidded to my side. "Yesterday got off to a wonky start, and then I made it worse. Got ahead of myself. Sort of ambushed you at work."

I kept a swift pace, but he met me stride for stride until I unwittingly shared my self-doubt . "More like a hit-and-run situation. You bolted like—well, I guess I thought we were vibing, but then we *definitely* were not—"

"*No*." His abrupt stop forced me to do the same. "We *were*. We *are*."

The sun haloed his sand-colored curls, glinting off a touch of silver-gray I hadn't noticed the day before. Angelic with a cup of coffee in each hand. But when I squinted to focus on his face, a questioning look stared at me.

"Wait. Vibing is a good thing, right? I'm not always great about keeping up with the vernacular, but I swear, Amelia—"

"Mimi," I interrupted, keeping our eyes locked. "My friends call me Mimi. You can—call me Mimi." I swallowed hard. "And I'll take that coffee. *The Peachy Bean* is the best shop." In his shadow again, I relaxed into a sip.

"Whew. I'm new to town and haven't had a lot of scouting time yet. I travel a lot. Lived in many places and like to stake out the three Bs early on in my stay."

"The three Bs?"

"Bars, brews," he lifted his coffee cup, "and barbeque."

"Oh, that last one will take some thoughtful exploration. There's Fox Brothers, of course, and Fat Matt's. Rubs n' Suds is good. Then you've got The Pickled Pig, The Tipsy Chicken, The Soused Cow," I ticked off a few area favorites. "Obviously, some went all in on a theme. The list goes on and on." Atlanta doesn't joke when it comes to smoked meats.

"You pick then. Tonight?"

"I'm sorry?" I coughed on another coffee swig.

"Didn't you just ask me out for barbeque?"

I laughed. "No. I don't think so."

He sipped his coffee with the mischievous eye I'd seen him employ in the elevator the other morning. "I'm pretty sure you did, and if you back out now, you'll call into question the whole notion of southern hospitality, and that's quite the institution to attempt dismantling, particularly on a Tuesday when you're already late for work."

"*Shoot*, I'm late for work." I spun and hurried to the huge wooden door.

"I'll take that as a yes, then?"

"Maybe," I called over my shoulder, grabbing the forged iron handle. "Hey, why particularly on a Tuesday?"

He shrugged. "I've always considered the toppling of long-held social conventions to be a weekend activity. How about your number?"

I rattled off the digits without the usual thought I gave when asked for personal information, then peeked to see if he wrote it on a scrap of paper or the palm of his hand. He hadn't.

"Are you going to remember that number?"

He tapped his forehead with his index finger. "Details. I always remember the details."

Holding the door open for a rushed backpack-toting student, I said, "Hey, Ethan. Thanks. For the coffee, I mean."

He lifted his chin in reply but then followed up, "*Hey, Meems*, have a great day." He turned with his cup raised in the air like he toasted the few stragglers headed off to the dreaded eight a.m. class.

No, I definitely didn't hate the new nickname.

"You stopped to buy coffee?"

Was it a sixth sense? A hidden camera? An otherworldly olfactory system? Because Nora never looked at me before she spoke.

"I didn't. And good morning, Nora." I fought the giddy urge to skip to my office, playing nonchalant for decorum's sake, but my outer office despot followed close at my heels.

"Care to explain the cup in your hand?"

"I ran into Mr. Ledes this morning." My casual tone and inspection of the potted plant on my windowsill impressed even me. I waited for a favorable response, but it didn't come. "The man from yesterday," I reminded her. Still nothing. "What? Nothing to say to that?"

"No. I was thinking how disappointing it is to know you weren't driving at the time. You know, because you don't own a car." Sometimes Nora's wicked sense of dark humor concerned me.

I gave a blank stare.

"Oh! *Did* you buy a car?" A smile cracked wide across her face.

"Nora. Do you not like Ethan—Mr. Ledes?"

"I don't know the man, so I couldn't make a fair judgment of him." Like that ever stopped her.

"But you could get behind his vehicular homicide?"

"No, of course not. But a scrape might knock his outsized confidence down a peg. No man should be that pretty." Nora straightened chairs that didn't need straightening.

"I'll have you know he was quite contrite earlier. Apologized and brought an olive branch in the form of coffee. Good coffee. He asked for a do-over."

Nora's spine drew up straighter than even her usual proud posture. "There is something off about that man. I haven't sniffed it out yet. Might be good, might be—not good. Jury's still out. She exited, holding her rigid stance. "Messages and schedule on your desk," she hollered from the hall, leaving me to my day. Or so I thought.

A few minutes later, Nora returned with an expertly steamed café au lait in a big mug. She snatched Ethan's peace offering from my desk and dropped it in my office garbage can with a *thunk*.

"Was it better than mine?" Her expectant stare bore down on me.

"Not even close," I frowned. And there went fib number two for the day. Nora let slip the start of a smile before closing the door behind her. The oddest Fairy Godmother there ever was.

Lunchtime arrived, and as usual, I pulled my insulated sack from my messenger bag to eat at my desk. Later in the year, lunches often included rubbing elbows with wealthy donors or wooing potential students and their parents (who, fingers crossed, would become wealthy donors) at white linen-clad tables in a dining room that rivaled something out of a movie, minus the floating candles. By March, my pants might be tight, but my team and I would confirm a distinguished class for the next academic year. For now, I'd eat last night's leftovers and a mealy apple.

Midday also meant freeing my phone from the locked drawer at my side, but only for twenty minutes. I set a timer to be sure. A string of texts glared back at me. A long string from a number I didn't know, but a New York City area code my job made familiar.

> **917-555-3815:** Ethan here. Hope I remembered your number correctly.

> **917-555-3815:** Hello?

> **917-555-3815:** Hmm. I called. But no answer. I'm guessing you are 1. Busy, and if so, I apologize for the interruption. 2. This is some sort of playing hard-to-get, in which case, BRING IT. I like a challenge (but not in a creepy way), or 3. You are stuck under something heavy, and dinner is probably off.

> **917-555-3815:** Huh. Still, nothing, and now I'm starting to look desperate.

> **917-555-3815:** Ok, getting a little concerned, but I'm holding out hope this is situation #1, and you'll reply when you can. For now, I'm planning to meet you on campus so we can walk to Rubs 'n Suds, more for the nearby address than the name of the place, but what a fantastic name. Right?

Mr. Ledes walked a tenacious line, but I appreciated the effort. Still, as I hit the callback icon, I knew I had to cancel.

"Meems, you called. Didn't think young people did that."

"We don't, but it seemed the least I could do to give your old man thumbs a rest." I hoped my reply sounded like banter and not real condescension. He rewarded me with a sexy laugh, which would only make my next move harder.

"So, what time tonight?" he asked while I prepared to give him my regrets for his dinner offer.

"To be clear, I never gave a definitive yes to your *not quite* an invitation. I'm afraid I'll have to say no. It's a busy week and the start of a demanding stretch that will last several months. I really need to focus on my work and while I appreciate the offer and your kind attention, you should find someone better suited to introduce you to all Atlanta has to offer." An unexpected silence followed. I looked at the phone, wondering if the call dropped. "Ethan?"

After an agonizing pause, he asked, "How old are you, Mimi?"

"Not sure you're supposed to ask me that, but I'm thirty-two. Why?"

"That makes you almost ten years younger than I am, but you talk like you're—well, so polite and measured. I'm just a guy asking you out on a date. For fun. You know about fun, right? Don't you eat during this busy work season of yours?"

Taken aback by his boldness, I focused on the question. "Oh, yes. I eat." I tugged at the waistband of my dress pants.

"And what do you plan to eat tonight?"

"I hadn't gotten that far. It's not even one o'clock." It was true, but I imagined the frozen burrito I'd likely buy from Trader Joe's on my walk home. I also had no more fibs for the day.

"Great. Why not make it some dry rub and a beer or whatever else might be on the menu at Rubs 'n Suds? A couple of hours to take a breath and relax might be the thing to save you."

"Save me? From what?"

"From yourself, Mimi."

It was my turn to keep quiet.

"Aww, come on. Let's have dinner. You might find you like me."

"I *do* like you." Heat sprang to my cheeks when I spouted off that truth nugget.

"Even better. Starting off strong out of the gate. I like you too. Six-thirty?"

"If I had another fib for the day, I'd use it. I'd make it a good one, a doozy, but I'm out. So—"

"I'm sorry. Did you say you're out of fibs? I don't even know what—"

"I get two. Two fibs a day. Nothing significant, but only two."

"*Hm*, not sure how to take that. I'm only worthy of an *insignificant* lie?"

"Not a lie. A *fib*. But I'm out, anyway."

"Because—you only get two."

"Correct."

"And who keeps track? I mean, who holds you accountable to this very strict rule of yours?"

"Accountability is important, Ethan. I do it myself."

"You fascinate, Mimi Kanaan. I'm utterly captivated. Six-thirty. Say yes."

I sucked in a gulp of air and did something very un-Amelia-like. "Yes. Fine. Six-thirty."

"It's a date." He sealed the deal.

"Is it?" Was I going on a date? With an older man who hinted at a Peter Pan complex? A handsome, carefree, world-traveling...

"You bet your sweet freckles, it is."

More warmth radiated off those freckles to my fingertips. "Six-thirty. See you then." I pressed my lips together to stop a goofy grin and ended the call before he could say another word that might push me to a full sweat. Slipping my phone into the desk drawer, I turned the skeleton key and plowed ahead, shaking off the schoolgirl silliness and on to important matters. Matters like Briana.

My call went straight to voicemail. It wasn't the first time I'd called the promising candidate, but it was the first time her voicemail box wasn't full. I chalked it up as a win and left a message.

Ms. Johnson, this is Amelia Kanaan calling from the admissions office at Chastain University. I was hoping to set up a time for us to chat, meet even, if that suits you. I'm happy to work around your schedule if you give my office a call at this number and arrange something with my assistant, Nora. Hope to hear from you soon. Go Roosters!

Six

By SIX-TWENTY, A FLURRY of some of my worst life choices bombarded me. The night I ate spaghetti pie at the county fair before riding the Tilt-a-Whirl. Every time I thought, *Oh, one shot of tequila won't hurt.* The COVID-19 lockdown-induced "bangs incident" of 2020. And most recently, when I agreed to a date with a leprechaun-wearing charmer named Ethan Ledes.

I had concerns.

What if Ethan was unapologetically late? Or rude to the waitstaff? What if he put ketchup on the dry rub? Even worse, what if his kind eyes were even more beautiful in the nighttime light and he made me laugh? What if he asked to see me again? What if he didn't?

I found the man difficult to say no to, and that was over the phone. He showed signs of being a bad influence—or at least someone who might coerce me to cross lines, finding myself out of my comfort zone. The kind of thing the Geneva Spielers of the world lived for. I thought Nora might appreciate it, too. Or maybe not.

"How did you meet this man?" It sounded like the start of an interrogation that would not help my nerves already running riot, but Nora wore a determined look I couldn't ignore.

"The elevator at Midtown Mews," I confessed while examining a pen I pulled from the sterling cup on Nora's desk. She swatted at my hand when I replaced it and reached for another.

"That's a slow elevator."

Apparently, I'd complained about it in the past. "Mm-hmm."

"And he's a fast talker."

"Mm-hmm." That's when I realized I wanted Nora's approval, and it didn't seem like I'd get it.

"A Yankee, I'm guessing."

Ethan's 917 area code said that might be true, but that tidbit wouldn't help sway the strong southern woman sitting in front of me to go my way. I kept quiet as long as I could. "It's a step up from a mopey Portuguese Water Dog." I beamed with hope.

"That remains to be seen."

My face fell, and I shored up the bag strap on my shoulder.

"Then again, a little barbeque might be a good way to find out. He gets points for having respectable taste in food. And women."

It wasn't a gushing endorsement, but I'd take it. "Hey, how'd you know we were going out for barbeque?"

"Amelia. When will you learn? I know everything that happens in this office. And who's doing it. Now go. Have fun."

"Nothing from Briana yet?"

Nora only shook her head.

Glancing at the clock, I reminded myself tomorrow is another day. "Walk out with me?"

"No, thank you. The last thing you need is an old woman horning in on your time with a gentleman-caller. Scoot. I'll close up here."

"There she is."

The sight of him surprised me, and I expelled a small plume of breath in the chilly twilight. His smile made it impossible not to respond in kind.

"You're early."

He raised a shoulder. "You strike me as a 'If you're not early, you're late' kinda girl."

He wasn't wrong.

"It's a Midwest punctuality thing, actually."

I set aside the Manhattan area code. "Midwest? Where abouts?"

"Indiana."

If the *aww shucks* routine didn't give it away, his Notre Dame wardrobe should have. "Ah. Of course. The Hoosier State. Crossroads of America. Popcorn capital of the world." My encyclopedic brain flaunted itself.

"That might be more than the locals know. But my parents raised me never to keep a woman waiting, but also to give her all the time she needs."

"Wise parents." I couldn't pull my gaze from his.

"Mitchell and Constance Ledes were—*are* the best." Ethan offered me the gentlemanly crook of his arm, and I played along, taking it. We strolled a brick pathway. "They're retired now—I'm the baby of the family, the youngest of four. Ellie, Evie, and Emmy. Three older sisters, so I didn't walk until I was two or talk until three and a half."

"Why?" I'd missed the joke.

"Didn't need to." He smirked. "But I've made up for it since. My childhood was pretty much a Norman Rockwell painting. Mitch and Connie have been in academia all their lives, so they'd love what you do. My sisters are all educators too. Which makes me an utter disappointment. Not that they ever say as much. Luckily, as the youngest and the only son, I guess I get a pass. You?"

"Can't say I relate to the Rockwellian life, but I know how to disappoint my mother." What about this practical stranger had me sharing too much?

"Now, that I can't believe."

"Oh, believe it. I don't know. Maybe I'm too harsh. Mama just wants—*expects* more of me, I think."

"And your dad?"

I tripped. It must have been a sidewalk crack I missed in the growing dark. Ethan caught me with his other arm, bringing us face to face under a streetlamp guttering to life. His gentle brown eyes and the slight shag of curls called to mind a dog. But it was the sweet expectation on his face that sold it.

"My father?" With a slight head jiggle, I grimaced. "He's never said a word about it. Not to me, anyway." I didn't lie, but shame burbled in me, and I knew Ethan read the discomfort. I shivered.

"Ah." His single syllable could have signified many things, but I couldn't focus on what he might have meant with his nose inches from mine. He let go of his grip on my elbows, but now his hands tugged at my lapels like he meant to help me get warm. It worked. "I've got a tough follow-up if you're game?"

I wasn't, but a hard swallow prevented me from refusing. So long, comfort zone.

"What kind of barbeque do you prefer? Sweet? Vinegar? Mustard? I'm not saying there's a right answer, but—there might be a right answer."

A laugh gave way, and with it, a smidgeon of my tension. I stepped back from the silver-tongued flirt, out of the harsh light. "If you believe I'll show my cards this early in the evening, you'd be wrong, Mr. Ledes. Besides, I was born and raised in these parts, so I have nothing to prove. You with your Midwest alma mater, your Manhattan area code, and an as yet unspecified job, you're the one facing scrutiny tonight." I winked and nudged his chin before walking away at my usual swift clip. "I mean, we haven't even ventured into your taste in pie."

"Are you saying there will be pie tonight?"

"I'm saying we have all kinds of things to explore."

He caught up with me. "Mimi?"

"Hmm?" I kept my eyes front, avoiding his tractor beam stare.

"You should know—next to pie, exploring is my favorite." He laced his fingers in mine as if he'd done it a hundred times and kept my pace.

More heat billowed under my layers, but the tang of cherry-wood smoke mixed with the sweetness of honeyed hushpuppies wafted toward us and kept my feet headed south. The prospect of fresh-baked pie made it all the more worth hurrying.

What you need to know about Rubs 'n' Suds is, well, it's a thing to behold. Originally, the place was an auto service station with concrete floors, garage doors, and cavernous holes in the floor for old-timey mechanics to do undercarriage car stuff.

The next owners covered the holes and installed large, galvanized tubs with overhead water hoses when it became a dog grooming spot (pre-*Oodles of Poodles*), and called it *Belly Rubs 'n' Suds*, so when the next proprietor moved in, he dropped the *Belly* and saved a good sum when he didn't replace the rest of the signage. A fine example of business smarts.

"Wow. Well, I know it's true because I assume your, um, *candor clock* doesn't reset until midnight. What a piece of history, though. Someone should write that down." Ethan tore off another handful of paper towels to wipe tangy sauce from his hands and mouth, at ease in the unique surroundings.

"They did. I read it. In a book," I spoke with my mouth full, nodding with my excitement.

"You really love your non-fiction."

"Sorry," I mumbled into my wad of paper towels, wondering if my cheeks were as red as the as yet unused ketchup bottle between us.

"No, it's infectious. Unabashed delight is a thing to behold. And there's not enough of it in this world."

I tempered my enthusiasm, slowing my nod and taking my time to swallow before I spoke again. "So, speaking of non-fiction and history—what's your story?"

"Well played, Meems." He sat back and took a palate-cleansing swig of beer. "*Hmm*, where to start?"

I caught the first glimpse of something I read as apprehension. I couldn't be sure, but I thought I'd help keep the conversation light.

"Whatever landed you here can't be too shabby. You live at Midtown Mews. It's an upscale address, and you are definitely bringing down the average age of its residents."

His confident toothy grin returned while I wondered if I had collard greens stuck in my teeth.

"The Mews folks are good people. And I'm their handyman."

I flashed to Geneva and her mention of the condo board and voting for him. I assumed she meant as a resident, not an employee. "You mean, like the building super?"

Ethan Ledes morphed before my eyes.

"Not *like* the super. I *am* the super. Comes with a very nice, very affordable apartment in a great neighborhood in a city that's new to me. The hours are flexible until there's an emergency, but I'm only a text away. It's one of my better gigs."

"*Gigs*? Plural? You have more than one?"

Did he hear the words coming out of his mouth? Who would choose this? It's like he's willingly living the life so many are trying to escape. My struggling special case students. Myself.

"Not currently. Not exactly. But I've been all over the world. Walked on all seven continents, waded in every ocean, watched the sun rise and set over more countries than I can count." His head bobbled, then tilted like he wanted to tell me a secret. "That's not true. Seventy-three."

"Seventy-three *countries*?" I fumbled for my beer and drank it too fast. Even if he included Disney's EPCOT, that was an impressive number.

"Waited tables here, shined shoes there, sculled a gondola for a month once, but that was in Las Vegas, so it lost its appeal pretty quickly. Whatever gets me to the next city or ranch or seaside village where I can learn about different cultures, people's traditions, all the different ways to live."

The busy restaurant's white noise ricocheted off the concrete and stainless wash tubs as his account of a drifter life stunned me. The adventure and romanticism flew over my head, leaving nothing but instability and a kind of chaos in a nightmarish wake. "Then what?" I stammered.

"Then what?" As if he didn't understand the question.

"Then what do you do? After you shine shoes and wade into oceans and watch the sunset? Then what?" I leaned in, not proud of my tone, but that didn't stop me.

"I don't know, Mimi. What do you do when you finish a book of non-fiction?"

I scoffed at the comparison, and the conversation crumbled.

"I move on to the next new experience. Find another story to tell. No judgment, but I bet all I have in my wallet that the real thing is better than anything you'll read in a book. Of course, there's often not much in my wallet. Trade-offs." He forced a laugh, but his gruffness told me he felt slighted—like *I* was the one making poor choices.

"Trade-offs? An obviously intelligent, educated man who happened to win the genetic lottery and chooses to play—hobo, dabbling in food and shelter insecurity—for what? Fun? Talk about the height of privilege. Privilege that too many will never experience."

"Whoa—"

"You're forty and living like a teenager on summer break, and you wonder how you've disappointed your parents?" As soon as the words fell from my mouth, I gasped. I'd never flung an arrow like that. Never berated another human being, a person sitting right in front of me. My regret hit fast. "Oh, God. I'm sorry. I—"

"I'm forty-one for the record, but don't worry, I've got enough to cover dinner." He pulled his wallet from his jeans, jerking it out of the way when I reached for his hand. "You Chastain folks are something else."

"*No.* You don't have to buy dinner. Let me buy dinner."

"That's not gonna happen."

"Please. Ethan. Let me pay. My half, at least."

"I'm buying the damn dinner, Amelia," he barked, then his whole being got smaller, quiet. "Let's drop it." He crumpled the strip of paper that tallied our order before throwing an uncounted wad of cash on the wood-slat table. "Ready to go?"

Patrons nearest us gave side-eye looks at our obvious quarrel. Straddling the bench seat, I only nodded, too embarrassed by my behavior to speak. My apologetic gesture to the young woman at the next table went ignored when she looked away. Stress throbbed all over me as I scooped up my things and followed Ethan out the heavy metal door to end my worst first date ever.

Gravel crunched as we walked toward the street corner, away from the noisy restaurant. Maybe no one heard the uncomfortable back-and-forth. Not the specifics. Regardless, Ethan needed to hear my apology now.

"Ethan, I am so—"

"Should I walk you back to campus?"

"No. That won't be necessary."

"Well, I can't let you walk alone."

I pulled my phone from my bag. "I'll order up a ride."

"You're going to get a car to take you to your car? I'd heard Atlantans were car-dependent, but that's just—"

"I don't have a car. My ride will be to home." I busied myself with the phone app.

"No rail station near your place?" His tone lightened some, and we met each other's eyes.

I struggled for a grin that wouldn't take hold. "Not in my neighborhood. No." I caved to the cold and slipped into my coat. "Ethan. Please let me apologize."

He waved me off, uninterested in anything I had to say. And while I only waited a minute for the Lyft to pull to the curb, that minute dragged on longer than any I could remember.

"Amelia?" The woman at the wheel stretched the seatbelt to talk out the passenger's side window.

"That's me." I spun to see Ethan again.

"Goodnight, Amelia." The dismissal came with a curt nod that stung, and I couldn't move fast enough to get in the stranger's backseat, out of the dating nightmare, and home to Druid Hills.

Seven

By Friday, anyone could have mistaken me for a zombie—pale, bumping into door frames, with a lusty craving (for caffeine, not brains), while communicating in inarticulate grunts. *Life rule: Guilt and sleep don't mix*

The week included reading dozens of essays, coordinating alumni/applicant interviews, and schmoozing phone calls to donors. I also squandered too much time on a seating chart we would tweak ad nauseam up to the moment the doors opened at the annual Fall Ball less than a month from now, and hours helping the new hire in the development office write her first official grant.

At home, I tossed and turned, scolding myself for my deplorable date behavior, and distracting myself with Egyptian history. That part I liked. Five o'clock couldn't arrive soon enough.

Trader Joe's teemed with shoppers. Friday night happy hour. Instead of congregating on barstools with adult beverages, young professionals bustled shoulder to shoulder in narrow grocery aisles chock-full of quasi-healthy, organic, pre-made sustenance to go with their polite small talk. Clutching at a frozen cauliflower-crusted pizza (for one), I dropped it, startled by my ringing phone. That's when I spotted the oxymoronic "vegan cheese" label and closed the freezer case, leaving behind the abomination.

"Hello?"

"Max needs you. Cocktails. My place. Eight o'clock tonight." Geneva skipped the pleasantries.

"Really?" I grinned. "And what is Max drinking these days?"

"Don't worry about that, my sweet. I'll provide the libations. The contents of my liquor cabinet have been known to shock a Saudi oil baron," she bragged.

Empty-handed, I squeezed through the crowd to the end of the aisle and headed for the grocery's exit. "I imagine so, since Saudis don't drink alcohol."

Geneva possessed a loud laugh, a single "*HA*" accompanied by what sounded like a walloping knee slap. Her bangles jangled. "It's so adorable you believe that's true."

"But I read—"

"Eight o'clock, Mimi."

"What can I bring?"

"Bake me a goddamn pie for all I care but be here at eight. Ciao."

Geneva flung open the door to *12A*. "Goodness gracious, Mimi. You baked me a goddamn pie? And you look like a ghost."

"Not exactly, and um, thank you?" I placed the still-warm pie on the foyer table. Truthfully, her sarcastic mention of pie shamed and inspired me, and with two hours to fill before the visit to Midtown Mews, I set to work. A frozen pie crust, a couple of jars of peaches my mother canned in the summer, brown sugar, lemon juice, cinnamon, and cornstarch, and a pie was born. Even I couldn't mess that up, but I probably did. Cookbooks are some of my favorite non-fiction. And I enjoy the precision of a recipe. This pie was for the Midtown Mew's new super. The time came for me to make amends. I shared an abbreviated version of my poor behavior with a captivated Geneva.

"Oooh." My hostess danced a jingling, jazz-handed jig. "I knew tonight would be full of scandalous clishmaclaver. But who knew it would involve you and the tool-belted Hotty McIrish? Come, come. This calls for some Jameson Bow Street. Whiskey from Dublin. I *do* enjoy a theme night. And you must tell me every detail." She twirled toward a Tansu tea chest that housed the best booze with her colorful caftan flowing in her wake.

That beautiful, lacquered furniture piece was one of many treasures to find a new home in Atlanta—keepsakes that, along with her comically jumbled foreign vocabulary, drew a haphazard map of her years of globetrotting.

An hour later, with a lap full of Max, a belly full of smoked cheddar and apricots, and a head half-full of Irish whiskey, I appreciated Geneva's call and the narrow escape from vegan cheese. "Oh, and I should confess, I didn't know Ethan on Monday when I said he and I were—"

"Yes, *a ghrà*. I figured when you didn't know the man's name. Not that I haven't enjoyed a dalliance or three when names didn't come up, but I knew that wasn't quite your speed. But sometimes telling a little tale can be fun. An escape from the monotony. Just be careful not to let the fiction take over."

She spoke like she knew from experience. I, too, had firsthand knowledge of such a thing and vowed never to fall victim to that again.

"Then again, ever since my Moishe left this, well, this existence, I've imagined what starting over might look like. Shed the trappings of life and create a whole new fiction I could make real."

A sadness Geneva scarcely indulged in came over her as she fiddled with the huge canary diamond on her left hand. I caught a rare glimpse behind her flashy façade, her voice fading into the quiet of her glorious but, perhaps, lonely home. Solitude wasn't for everyone.

"Geneva? You okay?"

She threw her hands into the air, reborn. "Always, love. And before you go, speaking of *your* speed." She stood, waking Max. He watched her every move, and when she disappeared down the hall, he rose like he should follow, but settled when she returned. She carried a small burgundy velvet pouch and sat next to me. "For you."

A short strand of pearls slipped from the uncinched bag and curled into my palm.

"Every young woman should own a string of pearls. They're often a family gift from one generation to another, and I know that isn't probably going to happen in your case."

"No, but I could not possibly accept these. It's far too—"

"Ah, ah, ah." She wagged a fiery red talon at me. "I knew that too. But these are *Majorica* Pearls. The most meticulously *manufactured* pearls you can buy. They are fake. But no one ever needs to know. And should the day come when you receive the real deal, you can pitch these without a thought." She beckoned for me to face away so she could clasp the necklace at my nape.

"Fake?"

"Mm-hmm."

"You promise?"

"They are as a fake as my hair, and my nails, and my—"

"Yes, I get the picture. Still, this is generous, Geneva. Thank you."

"You are worthy of more. So—much more." Eyes welled with tears, she sniffed and whipped around, her silken robe gliding toward the door. "Now, do me a favor."

A windstorm of a woman, Geneva flitted around a room like she bounced around the world. I never knew what to expect or even what to believe about her madcap tales of her wild life. But I never doubted our bond.

I followed. "Is this about the coffee? I still haven't tried it."

"No. Let's not get into the coffee tonight." Her glassy eyes gave away weariness. The hour had gotten late.

"What then? Name it."

She helped me into my coat, then handed me the pie. "Go get you some Irish," she whispered, with a gentle hip-check out the door.

The Jameson provided enough liquid courage that not even the slow elevator ride to the ground floor had me second-guessing. But the long hallway Geneva assured me led to Ethan's apartment seemed longer with each step, and I couldn't muster a deep breath. I knocked before my feet took over and ran, wishing I'd convinced Geneva to share her still untested coffee. She made it clear the time for coffee had come and gone.

A slow shuffle of footsteps sounded, then nothing. Realizing the security fisheye gave me away, I lifted the pie to its level.

"I brought pie." Stating the obvious wasn't getting me in the door. "Did you know the first baked pies date back to the year 6000?" I circled the dish around, hoping the sweet aroma might seep through to Ethan's nose and help. "B.C. clearly." I waited. "Egyptians. Visionary architects *and* pastry chefs. Who knew?" Still no answer. "See, I read a—"

The door opened but only a few inches.

"A book? Yeah, I know." Ethan's monosyllabic interruption came dredged in more cold exasperation than a warm welcome, but he didn't deter me.

"You knew about the Egyptians and their pioneering baking skills?"

"No, Mimi." Serious brows furrowed in the narrow door opening. "I knew you read it in a book."

"Oh, right." I smiled, but mostly because he called me *Mimi* and not the dreaded *Amelia*. "Plus, I bet you've probably been to Egypt."

He didn't confirm or deny, but his nose wiggled. "What kind of pie?" The door opened farther, and he leaned against the frame, arms crossed over the faded shamrock of his navy t-shirt. A model of indifference.

"Peach." I offered him a closer sniff.

"Of course. When in Georgia, right?"

"Actually, Georgia only ranks third in U.S. peach production. Behind California and South Carolina, and you probably wouldn't believe me if I told you who was number four."

"Well, now you gotta tell me."

"New Jersey."

"*No.*"

"Yes, I read it—"

"I believe you, Meems." With one nickname, the ice thawed. Still, neither of us moved. "Is Georgia number one in anything?"

"Oh, sure. Watermelons in South Georgia and wall-to-wall carpet north of here, but those make lousy pies."

Ethan caved with a laugh, opening the door wide. "Get in here."

I ducked under his arm and into his apartment before he changed his mind.

Eight

ETHAN'S APARTMENT INCLUDED ALL the fine features of Geneva's *12A*: gleaming dark hardwoods, arched doorways, and over-the-top crown moldings, but that's where the resemblance stopped. A pub table with stools sat in a corner, and matching tweed club chairs faced the painted brick fireplace on an exquisite, well-worn Turkish rug. He owned more boxes than furniture, though that wasn't saying much. To say the apartment was spartan might have been overselling it with nothing hung on the walls or anything covering the windows. The place echoed in all the emptiness.

"I'll take your coat in a sec." Ethan gestured for the pie and trotted with it to the kitchen, returning before I pulled from the second sleeve. "I have a closet, and I've been eager to try it out. Now, before you ask, because I recognize the concerned look on your face, no, no one robbed the place."

I found some courage to speak. "No, it's—tidy." I hesitated to say more, for fear of ruining the tentative detente we'd established in the hall.

"Aww. Someone's reverted to polite and measured speech. I'm just not a big collector of things. On the go like I am."

"Sure. Makes sense. What's in the boxes?"

"Books, mostly. But don't get too eager, it's all fiction, so you wouldn't have any interest."

I crossed to a window, smaller than those on the upper floors, with a view of a side street marred by shrubbery. "Got me all figured out, huh?"

"Not yet. But I'm working on it." The coy look suited him.

"You can fit the contents of all these cartons on one little device, you know?"

"What can I say? I'm old school."

"Me too." I nodded. "Well, I think before—well, before anything else, I need to say something."

His solemn face returned. "All right."

"I'm sorry. My dinner behavior was unforgivable. Rude. I don't date much. Busy with more AARP members and teenagers than anyone my age. And my job has shown me how difficult it is to navigate this world for people who—who don't look like you. People who get by with little, not by choice, but because it's all they have ever known. But that's no excuse. I have no excuse for the way I spoke to you. I don't mean to justify it. Truth is, I'm probably a little jealous of your freedom. Your ability to go, do, see. Again, not an excuse. But I am sorry."

"I should probably clear something up here. I'm not really a professional vagabond, you know."

"*Hobo*. Pretty sure I called you a hobo."

"Yeah, ya did," he exhaled in a laugh. "I'm not that either."

"No, of course not. Whatever. Follow your bliss, right? But please know how sorry I am."

"Do you feel better?"

"Me? I don't know yet. How do you feel?"

"I feel *great*." Hands to his hips, he puffed up, chest broadened with a deep breath.

"Great? Really? Why—great?"

Ethan started a playful swagger toward me with that impish glint in his eyes. "You brought me pie."

"Yeah, I should warn you. That might not really be edible."

He stopped close enough that I raised my chin to keep his gaze. "It'll be the best pie I've had all day. You also consider me 'your age.'" He air-quoted. "So, my week has taken a significant turn into positive territory."

Pressed to the ornate window casing, I looked down, stifling a grin. I couldn't move, but I wasn't looking for an escape. Ethan's knuckle grazed my jawline and lifted my chin, putting us face-to-face again. A tingle buzzed through me as his finger followed the line of the new necklace draped across my collarbone.

"Not sure I've ever kissed a woman in pearls." Confidence never looked so sexy.

Hearing Geneva's "wise" words, I swallowed the urge to confess they were imitations and instead countered with boldness of my own, "Would you like to?"

One corner of his mouth rose, and he nodded, inching closer. "You smell like whiskey."

"Yes." More air than sound came from me. "Irish Whiskey," I said, fingering the shamrock on his chest.

"Irish Whiskey *and* pie? Good *God*. Marry me." His grin unraveled all the way to his eyes, eyes that wouldn't break free from my mouth. "I think I have a new thing for freckles, too."

I squinched my nose at the compliment I found hard to believe. "I should tell you—I'm not the marrying kind."

"What does that mean?"

"Just what I said." My hand crept up to his stubbled cheek, my thumb winning the first touch of his lips that go around.

"We'll see." Another inch closer.

"Maybe," I whispered. "Maybe not."

In slow motion, our heads tilted in sync, his one way, mine the other as his palms cupped my cheeks, and I inhaled his dreamy scent. Our lips stopped a breath apart when his phone's loud ring shattered the quiet, jolting us out of the moment.

Ethan backed away, fumbling for the blaring phone in his back pocket. "Sorry. Uh, I should take this. Excuse me."

I only nodded.

"Hey," he answered, walking toward the bedroom hall. "Pretty much the worst..." A door clicked closed, and all went silent.

A legion of butterflies rappelled from my chest to my stomach, then ricocheted up again. I enjoyed this heady sensation I hadn't experienced in a long time. Or maybe ever. When I found my legs, I peeled myself off the window frame and peered into an opened box stacked on two others. The fiction Ethan told me to expect sat spines up, all the titles clear to see. Popular writers like Asher Cray didn't surprise me, but somehow seeing Guy de Maupassant and Henry James didn't either. Women authors like Calliope Jones pleased me too. I enjoyed learning this nomad was an equal opportunity reader, especially after noticing a novel by a local politico, putting Ethan over the top. I might not have been into fiction, but I was becoming a fan a particular world-traveling reader.

Etiquette kept me from opening any cartons, but the minutes ticked by, and an awkwardness took hold as I sunk into a deep club chair, eyeing the antique hand-knotted weave of the colorful rug underneath me. But it got worse. I rushed to my feet when the door Ethan had closed opened with an ominous creak. It took another few seconds for him to round the corner to the living room. Something was wrong, and I kept still expecting an explanation—an explanation Ethan struggled to give.

"Uh, I'm gonna—have to—call it quits here, Mimi." The slow, clunky muttering didn't include eye contact.

"Oh?" I waited for more.

"Yeah. Sorry."

Ear-piercing silence returned.

I cleared my tightening throat, desperate to fill the void. "Do you mean tonight or—?"

More quiet and more avoiding my eyes. All that sureness gone.

"Oh." Reality crash-landed. Confused and mortified, I scrambled for an escape, but Ethan stood between me and my dearest garment, and I was *this* close to bolting without it. "May I get my—please?" Trembling from the inside, I tried to keep a steady tone.

He sprang into action, pulling the Burberry from its hanger and offering to help me into it. I snatched it from his grasp with force and lurched for the door.

"It's just—something's come up, Mimi. The timing's bad. Couldn't be worse, actually. I thought I took care of it, but—I didn't mean to—"

I didn't stick around to hear the rest.

In my flustered state, I pushed by Mr. Colby in the Midtown Mews lobby and knew I'd owe him an apology the next time we met. My head appreciated the cool glass as I leaned into the backseat window of yet another stranger's car. A perk of city living included a rideshare at almost a moment's notice, and if you're lucky, that driver wouldn't burden you with conversation.

As far as Mr. Ledes was concerned, this felt like a third strike situation. Athletics didn't play a big part in my life, despite Atlanta's pro-sports successes, but I'd remember the analogy if Ethan and I had another run-in. It seemed like a comparison he would appreciate.

The weekend passed like most any other, but I didn't venture far from home. A walk for coffee each day let me enjoy the late October air. Sweet muskiness floated in wood smoke, and I imagined the roaring flames lighting up large logs in the grand fireplaces of the old stately homes of my neighborhood. Back in my cottage apartment, I lit candles for extra heat and a glow to ward off the gray skies, cool damp, and even gloomier thoughts that clouded my brain.

I remembered the mix of shame and confusion in Ethan's living room, a similar feeling I had in college whenever I left my comfort zone, getting caught trying to be something I'm not. In one case, a misunderstanding had snowballed, resulting in the loss of friends, my dignity, and almost my mother. That's when I'd vowed never to be dishonest again.

Of course, no one likes one hundred percent honesty either, but that realization came with its own learning curve. I settled on the strict two-fibs-a-day rule and, for better or worse, stuck to it. The return of that remorse and humiliation brought the reminder of a life rule: *Stay in your lane, Amelia Kanaan.* Venturing off course only asks for trouble with a capital T and that rhymes with E, and that stands for...

Non-fiction, a healthy stack of special case admission applications, and the New York Times crossword kept my silly downward spiral at bay, and by Monday, I readied for work early, like the mortifying Friday night never happened.

Ethan didn't help matters with two texted pleas to call him "ASAP" on Sunday and a *third* before dawn Monday morning. I ignored them, making sure not to allow Ethan Ledes to sidetrack me. While I often worked longer, later hours than Nora, I never beat her to the office, but with the early start, today would be the day.

It wasn't.

Nine

A FLUSTERED NORA BOUNDED to her feet when I entered the office. Her desk stood uncluttered, framed by massive, draped windows. The sun hadn't inched above the horizon yet, and with little natural light, her murky pallor stood more pronounced. My optimistic mood after a brisk walk in the purple dawn disintegrated in an instant.

"I am so glad you got in early this morning, Amelia. I hesitated to call at this hour. Has anyone called you? This weekend? Anyone?"

"What's wrong?"

"Maybe it's nothing."

"Nora? Why would you need to call me? Why would anyone call me?"

"It could be nothing. Let me take that, dear."

Brisling at the rare pet-name, I shed the coat as she came toward me with her arms outstretched. Without stopping, she took it and headed to my office, me not far behind her.

"You have an hour before you need to head to the president's office. Eight-thirty meeting. In person."

"Was this on the books?"

She shook her head.

"Was there an incident on campus this weekend? Is someone hurt? Worse?"

"No, nothing like that. It's more of a—public relations issue, I guess you'd say. Some allegations of—well, it's not like other institutions haven't fallen victim to gossip."

"Nora. Words like allegations, victim, gossip—these are not Monday morning words. Certainly not Monday-morning-without-coffee words."

"Yes, coffee. I'll make your coffee."

"Forget the coffee. What's happened? Who accused who of what?"

She straightened, her hands twisted around each other. "It's an admissions scandal."

The words hit, and I flinched at the impact, the shock knocking me into the doorframe. A surge of bile rose, and I swallowed hard, forcing myself not to cover my ears to guard against the buzzy whir that bombarded them. No one else could hear it. Nothing to be done but to endure it.

"No. No. That's—that's not possible. I mean, wouldn't I know? I would know. Sure, I don't admit every student. I don't personally admit *most* of the students. I'm the special case officer, but even so, wouldn't I know? Who is accusing us? What's the evidence? I need to sit down." I fell into a wingback but sprang up like I'd landed on a tack. "This is impossible. Chastain would never—Why? I'm the one who makes sure everyone gets a fair shot. Well, everyone who's qualified, so if someone wasn't qualified, I would know. Wouldn't I know?"

"*Amelia.*" The moment might have called for an attention-grabbing face slap, but Nora's harsh snap did the trick. "I'm sure you'll get answers to all of your questions at the meeting. For now, you don't know anything. Nothing at all. Isn't that right?" Her pointed stare hinted it was time to use one of my allotted fibs, but it wouldn't be necessary. I was clueless, but if any of it was true, ignorance seemed worse than negligence, considering the title on my door. The no-confidence vote I read in my office manager's eyes didn't help matters.

"Where's Dean Rayburn? I'm assuming he'll be in this meeting, too. I'm the number two. Sure, he's a hands-off guy but—"

"Last-minute trip. A family matter. Gone to the St. Simon's house."

"Now?" My head flopped back. "You know what, Nora? That sounds about right." Dean Rayburn had been at Chastain longer than most and to say his tenure was more *ceremonial*, at least behind closed doors, is a kindness I'd learned to live with since the earliest days in my job.

"I'll get your coffee." She sidestepped the pair of chairs to exit.

"No, thank you. I'll go without today." My heart rate had to be triple digits.

A moment of silence followed, then, "What a start to the week, huh, boss?"

I groaned and slid a few inches down the buttery leather without looking her way. "Could you close the door? Please."

She obliged.

In an hour, I buttoned up on my route to the president's office, housed in a more majestic building at the dead-end of campus walk. The brick and limestone structure loomed against a backdrop of gray clouds. The dark green of Hedera ivy climbing the pillars remained year round, clinging like a stranglehold, overgrown and creepy in my current mood.

Janice, the pin-curled, blue-haired receptionist outside the president's office, was straight out of central casting, Hollywood circa 1962. Yet somehow she hadn't aged in the decade and a half I'd been on campus. The horn-rimmed glasses perched on the end of her nose magnified her piercing eyes. Her scowl broadcasted she knew why I was there. Then again, she always scowled.

Whatever had gone wrong was worse than I thought, and if Janice had her way, all blame would fall on me. I stretched my torso, trying to combat the kinking in my colon.

I skipped the morning niceties Janice wouldn't have returned anyway. "I'm here to see—" I gave my best impression of confidence.

"Have a seat." Not even a courtesy glance.

"Dr. Cromwell summoned me."

"And who do you suppose does the actual summoning around here?" Pearly pink polished nails flicked toward a neat row of straight-backed chairs.

I took a seat.

The *clang* and *hiss* of century-old radiators groaned their displeasure at waking to Atlanta's version of cold weather. Humid heat swirled the grand foyer like the city's outdoors in August, the way I presumed the chancellor's immortal gatekeeper liked it. Maybe that was her age-defying secret—one of them, anyway. Without so much as an intercom squawk or tinkling bell ring, the watchdog barked, "Dr. Cromwell will see you now. Hang your coat." She pointed at the standing hat rack outside his door, and I was thankful to shed the Burberry.

Here's a life rule: *Never back into a room, no matter how quickly you try to hang your coat or how much side-eye someone's executive secretary might deserve.*

Dr. Cromwell welcomed me before I saw his face or that of the other man who bounded to his feet, taking several steps toward me before I turned to the room.

"Amelia Kanaan, this is Ethan Ledes, a reporter from *The Public Eye*, an investigative journalism unit with the Daily Independent out of New York City." Dr. Cromwell's raised brows and rushed but wordy introduction were all the warning he could give me. Of course, he didn't know what made it all so shocking.

A mere two steps across the threshold before Ethan shook my hand like the professionals we were, proclaiming, "Good to meet you, Ms. Kanaan." Then whispered with a slight head shake, "You really should have called me back yesterday."

"I really should have taken the stairs last Monday," I mumbled in return and forced a tight smile.

"Please, sit. Both of you. No need for this to be confrontational." Thatcher Cromwell, Chastain's president, rarely appeared so humble. I'd seen him play a raucous, back-slapping good ol' boy and a high-nosed academic elite—all in one evening, but no sign of alpha-anything showed in his demeanor with this reporter.

"No, not at all." Ethan ushered me to the wingbacks set at angles in front of another grand mahogany desk. "As I explained to Dr. Cromwell, one of *The Public Eye's* latest probes involves corruption in higher education admissions. We've been at it several months now."

"At Chastain?" My angst spat out with the question.

"*No.*" He reached for my hand that white-knuckled the chair arm but must have realized the inappropriate gesture before he made contact. "Well, yes, but not only Chastain. As a matter of fact, I've just started—"

"Nosing around here?" I couldn't hide my contempt.

"Ms. Kanaan," Dr. Cromwell interjected. "Let's go easy, young lady."

I'm not sure which offended me more, my boss's patronizing reprimand or what happened next.

"That's okay. We've blindsided Ms. Kanaan here this morning. She has every right to—"

My glare stopped Ethan's attempt to defend me. Like I was some damsel in need of a shield. Ethan took my disdain and rerouted his talking points. Talking points, I had every intention of interrupting.

He continued. "We've investigated some of the best colleges and universities in the country and—"

"And our number is up?" I did it again. "Chastain's turn under the microscope?"

"Something like that, yes. Think of it as an opportunity to prove Chastain's admissions is a scandal-free zone. All legitimate. A chance for transparency," the reporter offered.

Dr. Cromwell faded into the wainscoting leaving Ethan and me the only two in the room.

"Every institution has its own admissions policy, Mr. Ledes. The formula varies—the secret sauce is different everywhere, and we guard that recipe. Strictly. Surely, those Yankee Ivies told you the same." There she was. The Vice-Dean of admissions got her bearings. Finally.

"Look, Mim—Ms. Kanaan. I'm here as a courtesy. I rarely divulge my investigation to a subject before I reach out for a comment on my findings. Actually, I *never* have. Not once. People alter their behavior when they know they are—under the microscope, to use your words. The truth gets twisted, difficult to see."

Dr. Cromwell reappeared. "Well, Mr. Ledes, Ethan—may I call you Ethan?" While he sounded chummy, the president didn't wait for a reply, the first sign he meant to put this uninvited guest in his place. "That certainly raises the question. Why are you telling us?"

"Excuse me?" Forced to acknowledge the third party, Ethan wrung his hands and stalled with an inhale.

Cromwell pressed harder. "To what does Chastain University owe the never-before extended courtesy of a heads-up, Ethan? What makes us special?" My boss kept his tone friendly, but the crease between his brows simmered with scrutiny.

For a moment, the potential answer scared me.

"I've been an investigator a long time and a journalist even longer. What separates the good from the best is the ability to think on one's feet. Change one's tack. Recognize the best way to get a story and shift accordingly. That's what this is." Ethan stood, handing each of us a business card. "That's all I have for the time being, but you'll be hearing from me. Both of you."

Ethan's second pair of proper trousers exited the sweltering office, and I waited for the door to latch before giving Dr. Cromwell my full attention. I slumped, allowing myself brief relief before expecting coarse demands to right the wayward ship and shouts to get Dean Rayburn back to Atlanta.

"Well, he seems nice enough. For a Yank and a journalist." The twenty-first-century war against the press was unfortunate and not one I subscribe to, but the issues of North versus South began two hundred years ago; nevertheless, they persist. "I don't expect we have anything to fret about, do you, Amelia?"

"Uh, no, sir." Fib number one and the clock hadn't struck nine in the morning. My boss Franklin Delano Rayburn's hasty exodus to the coast unnerved me. That he did it while a storm brewed made me sick to my stomach. Add Ethan's involvement, and I could have retched on Cromwell's desk.

Downstairs and steps from the door to outside, a *psst* caught my attention. No one appeared until a door inched open. Ethan stood in a dark cloakroom used for storage nowadays.

"You've got to be kidding me." I scanned the hall, but we were alone.

"Come on, Mimi." A flash of his sly grin made me *tsk* as I stepped into the dim space. Light seeped through a small, frosted oculus at the end of the long, stale hidey-hole. "I'm sure you have questions."

"Questions? You bet I do." My mind chose that moment to go blank.

Ethan's puppy dog eyes didn't help.

"Hi."

"Hi." I inhaled, then walloped his shoulder. "Don't '*hi*' me."

"Ouch," he chuckled. "Aww, come on, Meems. We were doing so well."

"Were we? When? When exactly were we doing so well? When you ambushed me in my office and then bolted for no apparent reason? Or when I insulted you and your vagabond ways at Rubs' n Suds—which doesn't even seem true anymore. Or how about Friday night, when out-of-nowhere you practically shoved me out of your apartment without an explanation? An explanation which I guess isn't necessary anymore, given our recent and oh-so-enlightening chat with President Cromwell upstairs."

"It *is* true. I've traveled the globe, worked all kinds of jobs—*for* my job. A job I had every intention of telling you about."

"Oh yeah? At what point did you plan to tell me?"

"Probably—right after I kissed you. I swear. I was about to. And in my defense, at the time, all I could think about was kissing you. So, let's be fair. I'm not sure this is all on me. But if I'd had one more minute, I'd have confessed. And I didn't shove you out. I didn't even *touch* you."

"*Ha.* Oh, you touched me." I flinched at the memory of him fingering my pearls, then realized how close he'd stood and what must have been a coat hook poking between my shoulder blades.

His grin returned. "See? That part was going pretty well. Plus, you brought me pie. And you took an evening out of your busy work life to go on a date with me? Or how about the time when—out-of-nowhere—you kissed me in the cab? That's a moment I've played on repeat this last week. And I bet you have too."

His overconfidence grew, but why did I find it so attractive? Too much time elapsed while I stood mute. I didn't want to use fib number two, and I certainly couldn't admit it. Silence was my only option.

"You're thinking about it right now, aren't you?"

Another life rule: Never be at odds with a mind reader. It's not a fair fight.

My palm pressed to his chest. I replayed the Friday night tracing of the three-leaf clover stretched across his admirable pecs. The memory, mixed with his crisp scent, worked like catnip and made the tiny, darkened room tilt. I pushed him away before things got out of control.

"I don't imagine either of us thinking about it amounts to much good. Don't you journalists take some sort of 'do no harm' oath? And since I'm apparently the subject of your latest investigative pursuit, we should forget any notions of you and me."

"First, it's a creed, not an oath. 'Do no harm' is for physicians. Two. I'm investigating Chastain, not you, and my pursuit—for the moment—is for the truth. Something I figure you'd appreciate given your penchant for all things non-fiction. And three, I'll be keeping any notions of you and me to myself for the time being because of number two. But once this ethical dilemma is no longer barring our way, I have definite plans to kiss you again. So, let's both try to look on the bright side because if we had kissed on Friday night, it would be a whole hell of a lot harder not to kiss you now, and since I can still feel the heat of your hand on my chest and can't stop wondering what you taste like, that's saying something. Are we clear?"

Even in the low light, I eyed his clenched, clean-shaven jaw before forcing my gaze to the shadowy floor. For someone who *wrote* for a living, he sure used a lot of out loud words. "Yes," I whispered. "It's a creed, not an oath. Got it."

Something like a growl came out of him.

"Why is it you?" *Dang it.* I meant that as an inside thought.

"What?"

"Why does this have to be you? I know *The Public Eye.* I *read The Public Eye.* It's a *group* of investigative reporters. A whole bloodhound gang. Why can't you go harass the good folks in Cambridge, Mass? I hear it's lovely this time of year."

We both exhaled in defeat. The answer didn't matter. Even if we separated our connection with six degrees *plus* Kevin Bacon, we couldn't fraternize. There were rules. Appearances. Heck, he'd already labeled it an ethical dilemma.

"Look, Mimi, when you walked out of your office that first day, and I bolted, it was because I expected someone *very* different from the Amelia Kanaan I met at that moment. Chastain's website should really include more staff pictures."

Chastain was old-school like that.

"Certainly not the beautiful, freckled, blonde *Mimi* I'd flirted with earlier that morning. Not the smart, feisty woman who saw through my bullshit but played along anyway, only to reward me with her well-read, dry sense of humor and a kiss. But when I realized the conflict, yes, I took off and immediately pushed the team to skip Chastain, move on to another school in our southern swing. I thought I'd handled it. But Friday night, my editor, with her impeccable timing, called to say I got vetoed, but she'd put someone else on Chastain if I had an issue. I said no."

"Agree to disagree on the freckles and how the events unfolded that morning—but why?"

"Why what?"

"Why did you say no to your editor?"

The whites of his eyes widened in the darkened hideout. He shrugged and frowned like I asked a silly question or he failed to know his own reasoning. "I don't know. Maybe because I don't back down from a story. To make up for suggesting the group give Chastain a pass in the first place. I'm not that guy. Well, I'm not that journalist. Maybe because I thought there might be a way I could—I don't know, protect you—maybe?"

"Wow," I gasped, fumbling for the doorknob.

"Wait, Mimi." Ethan held the door closed.

"No. You wait, Ethan. I have never and *will* never ask for your protection from anything. And if you thought that answer would win some kind of pass or praise from me, think again. And maybe, just *maybe*, you should have asked me if I've done anything wrong during my time in admissions here at Chastain. You could have just asked the darn question."

"Really? Do you want to go there?"

"I don't know what you're talking about."

His breathing strained against his willingness to continue. He couldn't upset me anymore than he already had, so I goaded him to speak his mind. The man didn't know me, so whatever he said was sure to be rich.

"Fine. I've only scratched the surface. Hardly looked at all, and you know what I've already discovered?" He paused. One last chance to abort.

"Please, enlighten me, Ronan Farrow."

"I like to think I'm more Bob Woodward, but I'll take it." He stepped back again, as far as he could in the close quarters.

As my eyes adjusted to the dim light, he avoided my face. With a deep inhale, he prattled on, looking anywhere but at me.

"You come from nothing. A mom who, until ten years ago, never held a full-time job and no sign of dear ol' dad anywhere to be found. You finished both undergraduate and graduate school at a private—and when I say private, I mean *expensive*—university. You stand there in a three-thousand-dollar strand of pearls and a flashy plaid everyone knows costs as much or more at Bergdorf's. And it's no knock-off. I saw the label. Your address is a six-thousand square foot house that sits on more than an acre in Druid Hills, and here's the kicker. You have zero debt. None. And I don't know what one has to do with the other, but your boss seems to have suddenly skipped town, and for the last month, you have Venmo-ed one account with the suspect handle *The Cleaning Lady* five weeks in a row. But your bank account, while in the black, is kind of paltry by comparison. I don't care how big your house is, no one needs that much cleaning help."

"Whoa. How do you know that?"

Immediately sheepish, Ethan stuttered, "I-I know a guy."

"You know a guy who hacks bank accounts?"

"That's your response, Mimi? You've got no defense? Nothing else to say?"

My first thought went straight to my mother and her unfortunate brand of funny when we set up her Venmo account. She even joked how *The Cleaning Lady* might make her sound like a mobbed-up fixer or money laundering service instead of the lifelong housekeeper she meant to imply. "Yeah, I have something to say." I opened the door and stepped into the bright light of the lobby. "Thank goodness *I'm* not the one you're investigating, but for someone who has been 'an investigator for a long time and a journalist even longer,' you are *awful* at your job." It didn't matter how my mocking tone or the career critique landed. I borrowed a move out of Janice's playbook and left without so much as a glance.

Ten

AFTER A LONG, FRUITLESS day of watching leaves fall to the courtyard grass, I grabbed the $91.00 Burberry I'd outbid four others to win on Goodwill's auction website, and headed for the door.

Besides composing a terse email to the staff regarding *The Public Eye*'s latest investigation and the coincidental absence of our department head, I didn't get much else done at my desk. Nora spent the day giving me space, then slipped out without saying goodnight. The former was typical; the latter was not, but this day had tied me in too many knots to be bothered about it.

At home, I pulled the cork with my teeth and poured a glass of wine as my phone rang. I paused, then kept pouring. It didn't matter who called; the cabernet would be a blessing.

I took a healthy swig and answered, "Hey, Mama."

"Happy Monday!"

"Yup," I squeezed out after another gulp. "Oh, before I forget. Have you gotten the money from Venmo into your bank account?"

"Yes. Why? *For cripes' sake.* Did I do it wrong? Because if I did do it wrong, blame the teacher, not the student. I followed directions."

"No, just checking. Keep doing it, okay? Every week." I considered reverting to mailed monthly checks or making the Venmo transactions private but remembered *someone* had mentioned how people alter behaviors when under scrutiny. That *someone* didn't need more ammo than he'd already collected—no matter how off his assumptions. "Now, tell me about your week. All of it." I emptied the wine bottle and eyed another cradled in a wall-hung rack.

I didn't mention the impending exposé to my mother. She'd learn about it eventually, but I didn't want to hear how I'd fallen short yet again. Though not lofty enough for some, my career was my pride and joy. But it seems that disappointing my mother was my superpower.

I'd always considered my direct supervisor, Franklin Delano Rayburn (yes, he liked to be called FDR), more of a *macro*-manager. He'd been at Chastain for decades and implied he had everything to do with me getting hired as an assistant admissions officer right out of undergrad. He showed little interest in day-to-day operations but fostered my steady ascension in a small environment. Many employees move on quickly in the admissions field. The money isn't great, the pressure, if you are at all empathetic, can be taxing, and in a unique, small, private university setting like Chastain, personnel often wear multiple hats.

But I liked what I did and still felt a debt of gratitude, if not tuition loans, for the opportunity the school provided. I had a plan. Ten years. I would give ten years post-graduation to the university. Of course, I'd thought little beyond that mark, and if I looked at a calendar, I'd see that date fast approaching. Plus, I earned an advanced degree. Shouldn't that warrant a reset on my obligation timetable?

Still, some staff members were lifers. The Janices, Noras, and even FDRs walked the halls before me and would likely be there after I left, but they were the ones who showed me the ropes, made those trains run on time, the ones who knew where they buried the bodies and who hid the shovels. I shook my head at the dark metaphor, dumped my third glass of wine in the sink, and went to bed.

The rest of the week trudged along with little noise. Too little noise. FDR still hadn't reached out, so Nora kept me on task with the last of the early applications marked "special case," and I chose photo art for next year's admissions advertising campaign. What might that marketing promotion look like in the shadow of *The Public Eye* story—whenever that landed? I also doubled down my focus on the annual gala committee work. The *tick, tick, tick* of the scandalous time bomb warned us we needed to elicit as much as possible from our benefactors before the press destroyed the university's name. Desperate times forced me to arrange a lunch date with the energy titan and alum Meriwether Pembroke for the following week. My nightly showers grew hotter, longer, and included vigorous scrubbing as the stink of something rotten grew.

Friday evening candles glowed, my Peggy Lee playlist crooned in the background, and, to mix things up in my humdrum routine, I plopped three olives into a martini.

"Here's to you, Mama," I called out to no one. "Thanks for raising me to love cool jazz singers." I lifted my drink to salute her but sloshed it when a rap at the door startled me.

Setting down my glass, I swiped at the dribble of gin off my fuzzy pink robe lapel. The candlelight and music were obvious, so I knew I couldn't avoid my landlord, Dr. Jaspers, the string-tie-wearing history professor who played golf with the president. Maybe he'd heard about the disgrace about to befall his beloved alma mater and wanted to know if he'd be in the market for a new tenant soon.

Safety first, I peeked from behind the drapes before unlocking the door. Imagine my disappointment at not seeing the good Dr. Jaspers. I retreated to the coffee table, downed the rest of the martini, minus the olives, and dragged my sleeve across my mouth as I marched to greet my unexpected visitor.

The porch light caught a flicker of a grin before Ethan lowered his head to examine his shoes. He appeared shy, with fists deep in his jeans pockets and shoulders around his ears. Then again, maybe he felt ashamed.

"Hi, Mimi."

"I think, under the circumstances, we should stick to Amelia, don't you?"

He winced but kept my gaze. "If you prefer." Our locked eyes lasted too long. "*Uh*, are you—alone?" He glanced over my shoulder. The lowlight and sultry music gave the wrong impression, but I didn't correct it. The reporter had gotten so much wrong already. What was one more thing?

"What do you want, Ethan?"

"Loaded question," he mumbled.

"Excuse me?"

"Nothing." He cleared his throat. "I wanted to apologize. As you can see, I discovered where you really live and some other aspects of your life that didn't present themselves at my first *very* cursory glance. I made some assumptions and connected dots that weren't there, and I am deeply sorry. It is not at all the way I do business. I'm good at my job, but you've got my head spinning, doing things I would never ever do. Changing the direction of an investigation. Revealing an inquiry to the subject before—"

"So, this is my fault?"

"*No*. God, no. Of course not." His hands escaped, pleading surrender with wild eyes and exasperated exhale. "I'm also not normally such an ass, but I am *killing* it on that score these days."

"*Huh*. Nice that we can agree on something."

My snark didn't even garner me a pity laugh. He just nodded, then refocused on the toe of his upturned shoe. "The story is moving forward."

"Okay."

"Here. Including Chastain."

"Okay."

"So, you might see me around. On campus."

"Terrific," I oozed sarcasm.

"And I definitely won't protect you from any of the fallout."

"Don't need you to, but I appreciate the heads up." I wished I could temper my disdain. I wished I had another martini. And more than anything, I wished those brown eyes didn't rake over me like they did. Despite the cold, heat rippled under my robe. "Anything else?"

He ignored what I intended to be his dismissal. "Are you listening to Peggy Lee?"

"Yes, why?"

"Come on. Not everything is an affront, Meems—Mi—Amelia. She was a talented singer."

"*And* actor, composer, and philanthropist. A bit kooky too. I read this amazing biography by James—never mind." The nerd girl tripped onto the scene, but I muzzled her.

"No, I want to know."

"You want to know about Peggy Lee?"

"I want to know what you read, why you read it. I want—to know you."

I opened my mouth, but no sound surfaced.

"Jesus, I've gotta go." His quick turn made him stumble down the two short slate steps to a brick walkway that led to the street. Fast feet steadied him, then hurried him into the dark before he turned back to me. "Mimi?"

My voice still paralyzed, I simply raised my brows.

"I really did like you. *Do* like you, and I'm so sorry things went this way. Maybe—" he grimaced with a head shake. "Good night." A resigned motionless wave followed, like the one he offered when I rode off in the cab the morning we'd met, but he was leaving this time.

"Ethan," my voice strained against the tension in my throat, loud in the still November nighttime. Half an octave too high.

He stopped but didn't face me.

"I really liked you, too."

His chin hit his chest, and from behind he looked headless in the inky yard. The rest of him disappeared as he jogged to the street.

The old door needed help closing. The colder the weather, the harder the hip check. Ms. Lee sang her signature song, *Fever*, and, with a hasty mouthful of drunken olives, I grumbled, "Preach, Peggy.

Eleven

"GOOD MORNING, NORA. HOW was your weekend?" My cheery entrance intended to relieve whatever tension grew between us. Maybe I imagined it.

"You're chipper for a Monday."

We walked and talked on the way to my office, almost like normal.

"Sun is shining, we're inching our way through November, and as of now, we are twelve days from surviving the Fall Ball. Any news?" I flipped through the mail at my desk.

"Briana Johnson finally scheduled her interview. I've arranged time with our student ambassadors, and she'll start with her alumni meeting and Rashida Turner. That's quite the *get* there, boss lady. Excellent job."

"Rashida was happy to do it. Particularly when I assured her that Briana wouldn't only be meeting with people that looked like her. So, good call on changing up my original list. Thank you. Won't happen again."

"That's why we make a good team, Ms. Kanaan. On to other matters. You got a call from Mr. Pembroke's office regarding your lunch today."

My fragile, buoyant mood burst. "Please say he hasn't canceled. I'm counting on him to pledge a little extra this year. I hoped I could flatter him by letting him think he flattered me." I shivered at the thought.

"You are getting too good at this." Nora knew her way around a backhanded compliment. "The woman who called asked, or rather *informed* me, the lunch would need to move up by an hour because—" Nora checked the memo in her hand. "And I'm quoting here, 'Mr. Pembroke is playing *squash* this morning and needs a meal by eleven, or he gets cranky.'"

"Mr. Pembroke plays squash?" I shared a dubious look with my office manager. "I'm impressed."

"Also, instead of dining at the Markham, he'll meet you at The Roost."

"You're kidding?"

Nora flashed me the handwritten message, then set it on my desk.

The Markham, short for the Markham School of Hospitality and Tourism Management, provided the best dining on campus. It was a full-service restaurant run by students in Chastain's undergraduate and graduate programs in what most participants called Hotel School. The dining room sat in a solarium with a soaring glass ceiling and window walls with views of a seasonal organic herb garden. Lunching there was my personal incentive for scheduling this money grab meeting in the first place. Very disappointing.

The Gallic Rooster, or The Roost, our mascot-named pub in the student union, provided much of what The Markham did not:

noise, paper napkins, and deep-fried everything, plus the greasiest pizza most students knew to be the best hangover cure in the world.

Mr. Pembroke's restaurant choice made sense when I found him that late morning. The lunch rush would trickle in soon, but the real crowds waited for evening and weekend hangouts. Rather than Pembroke himself, a man my age, and far too tan for Veterans' Day, sat alone, smiling at his phone screen. My hopes for an increased pledge fell flat, and I plodded to meet my revised lunch date.

"Hello, Mr. Pembroke." My formality felt strange, but I thought it was the best approach under the circumstances. "Amelia." I offered a handshake. "Thank you for meeting with me."

Tristan Pembroke, the sole offspring of Meriwether Pembroke and heir-apparent to Pembroke Industries, bounded to his sockless, loafered feet. "Hellooo, Amelia. Didn't this get exponentially more enjoyable? The pleasure is all mine. It is so nice to meet you, not only because you aren't the dowdy old woman I imagined I'd be lunching with today." He hurried around the table to pull out my chair. "But mostly. Please, sit and call me Tristan." When I sat, he took his own seat again. Cradling his chin, he leaned on his elbow with a charming grin and the harmless flirtation I remembered from our undergrad days—undergrad days that seemed to have slipped his mind.

"We've actually met before, Tristan. Several times." Reminding him might not have been the best move.

"No. That can't be. I'd remember you." His bold overture continued, both entertaining and approachable, and so unlike his father. I relaxed my guard.

"I assure you, we have."

He narrowed his eyes like he strained to place me, and I opened my mouth to put him out of his mock-misery.

"No, no." He held up a hand, intercepting my attempt to save him. "Don't tell me. Here's what we are going to do. First, let's dispense with the business portion because business is boring and impedes a good time." He pulled an envelope from his inside blazer pocket and slid it across the table to me. "I'll be purchasing two more tables for the Fall Ball. I'll send the names of those attending. No need to arrange their seating. They're minglers. Put the tables near one another, and my guests and I will manage the rest. I hope none of that is inconvenient for you."

"*Uh*, no. We can arrange that. No worries. This is very generous of you. Thank you."

"That's what I do now. It's like being Santa—if Santa was tall and tan, with boundless charisma." His wink revealed his self-deprecating nature. "At thirty, I inherited gobs of money, and half of it is to be given away. Philanthropy. It's the new black. Also, one party after another, which makes it a job I am exceptionally well-suited to do."

Tristan and I hadn't sat in the same room in many years, but his ability to fill any unoccupied space with his colossal personality had only grown in that time. He lived center stage, his natural habitat, and somehow drew you into the warm and flattering halogens that lit his world and put you at ease. Like you were welcome in that light, interesting, and almost as pretty as him.

"I have to say, for the record, this will in no way influence our decision on your father's special candidates or any applicants for this class or any other." I meant every word, but never felt the need to hammer it so hard before last week. Now I spoke as if someone had bugged the saltshaker, or like Tristan was wearing a wire. Paranoia is an ugly beast.

"My father's special candidates?"

"Yes, his annual 'chosen two.' One for early decision and one for the spring acceptance," I explained with air quotes.

"That isn't something I knew Daddy Dearest did. And of course, my contribution comes with no strings attached, except for the paperwork, charitable rules, tax implications, blah, blah, blah. But now that bit of work is done, let's order a pizza while I scour the recesses of my obviously addled mind to figure out how we know one another, Miss Amelia. It is *Miss*, isn't it?"

"Why don't you order that pizza, Tristan?" I brushed off his facetious leer, unconcerned with his innocuous flirtation. I'd encountered far more truly lecherous men in my days. Besides, when the recollection hit him, he'd lose even his pretend interest in me. I only hoped he wouldn't revoke the extra gala tables he purchased.

"Already did. I'm famished."

Tristan engulfed his first slice before I finished dabbing off the excess grease on mine. Thank goodness for the paper napkins.

"That's the best part, Amelia. You're sopping up the slurry that makes this the best pizza in all the land."

"Oh, I remember, but I can't—"

"Ah-ha! *You* are an alum. We're Chastain siblings, aren't we? Fellow Roosters. That's how we know one another. You must have been some years behind me, though. Why can't I—"

"Same class, actually."

"*No*." His knitted brow and twisted mouth showed a genuine struggle to remember. "It's a small school. Everyone knows everyone."

"Well, yes, for better or worse." I threw caution aside. "Want a hint?"

"Please, but don't make it too easy on me, Amelia. I love a mysterious woman."

I rolled my eyes. "Well, for starters, people didn't call me Amelia. Aside from my professional life, I go by Mi—"

"Mimi! Mimi 'The Con' Kanaan. Good Lord. Of course, I remember you." Tristan crowed too loudly for my comfort. I twisted around to see if any of the growing lunch crowd noticed, but they all brought their own low rumble of conversation.

If the grease-laden food hadn't turned my stomach, hearing the rhyming moniker Mimi "The Con" Kanaan did the job. I returned the pizza to my plate and dug for another napkin from the stainless-steel dispenser, waiting for the fallout of my discovered identity. It wasn't what I feared.

"Well, I'm glad you could put that brief chapter behind you. Ridiculous, really. Blown out of proportion, to be honest, but people can be cruel and unforgiving."

Tristan's last words rang true. Except I knew I'd been the cruel one all those years ago, and I didn't think I would ever forgive myself.

Tristan pulled me from self-loathing with an earnestness I didn't expect. "Really, Amelia—Mimi. Who hasn't—embellished their biography from time to time? And we were kids. Though we sure thought we weren't, didn't we? Clueless." It was hard to imagine someone like billionaire Tristan Pembroke once shared even an inkling of insecurity like the scholarship girl raised on government help, and yet I believed him.

"Not to make excuses, but I didn't. Embellish, I mean. I'm not even sure how it happened. Someone assumed or confused me with someone else, and I desperately wanted to fit in, not be the *subsidy* girl. So, when a guy said his stepsister's cousin's best friend knew me from summer camp, I played along. I didn't correct him, and the story snowballed. No one saw the poor girl raised by a single mom on food stamps and Medicaid. What harm did it do to let my classmates think I was an equestrian, an exotic blonde named Kanaan, and with a name like that, my family must have had ties to oil, right? Kind of a presumptuous leap to make. And for the record, I never told anyone that. But I never denied it either."

Dredging up the past hadn't been on my to-do list for the day, but if I was honest—and I vowed I would be—the past haunted me daily, and it drove my silly two-fibs-a-day rule. It compelled me to send my mother money weekly. Even my career path paid the penance for my errant youth. I suppose an unexpected meeting with a gregarious eyewitness from those bygone days fueled my over-share. Tristan's warm, welcoming glow cracked open my hardened shell.

"No harm, I guess. Until your mom showed up on campus." The pity in Tristan's eyes reminded me why I'd allowed the lies to continue all those years ago, but he was merciful enough not to spew the details of that fateful day.

In contrast, I wanted to purge myself of the specifics. Maybe saying the words aloud would make it easier to breathe.

"Ha," I huffed a pathetic laugh. "Until she showed up at my dorm wearing her 'Dust Bunnies Maid Service' uniform. No harm until, in an act of gross desperation, I pretended she was some deranged stranger. Denied she was my mother. Allowed campus security to escort her off the premises. They manhandled her like human garbage. I publicly rejected the woman who moved heaven and earth to raise me the best she could, and for what? Everyone knew the truth. Anyone could see our resemblance. I was horrible."

Tristan reached a kind hand for mine. A sympathetic act, nothing more. "You were a teenager, a kid." He squeezed my fingers.

"Yes. A *horrible* kid." I grimaced, then avoided his sympathetic look but caught someone else's entering the pub. I pulled my hand from Tristan's gentle grip as Ethan Ledes and I locked eyes. "Shoot," I murmured.

Tristan followed my gaze. "*Hmm.* And just when I thought this couldn't get any more interesting." My lunch date resumed his playtime antics. "What's with the broody silver fox over there, and doesn't he know Notre Dame garb at Chastain is like waving red at a bull to us Mighty Roosters?" No, Chastain University doesn't have the boldest mascot, but the jokes write themselves.

Broody doesn't describe the Ethan I'd known. Not until recent days, anyway. Ethan was confident, quick with a joke, eager to learn anything new. But I noticed his gray more today and liked it more than I should. "It's nothing." I pushed my plate away, determined to ignore this uncomfortable scene.

"It is *not* nothing. That much is obvious. So, is it personal or professional?"

"A bit of both, I guess you'd say."

"Even better," Tristan said and then let go an uproarious laugh, meant to turn heads. The guffaw boomed over the din of the lunch crowd. People stared, lots of them, but Ethan hadn't looked away. Tristan held my hand again, but I ripped from his grasp and placed my hand in my lap.

"What are you doing?" I hissed.

"I'm helping." He grinned and flipped his blond hair the playboy way he'd done so long ago.

"No. I don't want—that's not what this is. Please—"

"The look on his face says different, Miss Mimi."

"Tristan, I do not want you making a scene, or implying anything—we were just talking about the hazards of dishonesty."

"Relax. *Ooh*. The handsome man cometh this way."

"Please, no. No, no, no," I begged in a whisper, but the puckish troublemaker ignored me.

"He's not gonna hit me, is he?"

"What? Why?" I jerked to see the star reporter sidestep his way through the now-bustling dining room. A man on a mission. "No, he won't hit you. I don't think he'll hit you. *Huh*. He looks like he could hit you, doesn't he?"

"I can take a punch. I've taken a few, believe it or not."

"Oh, I believe it. Tristan, please do not do—"

"Hi, Mimi—Amelia." Ethan half-shouted his corrected greeting from a table away.

"Ethan. Hello. I thought that was you." My nonchalance wouldn't win me any awards, but I had to jump in before Tristan took control. "Ethan Ledes, this is Tristan Pembroke. Tristan, meet Ethan. He's an investigative reporter looking into admissions irregularities at some of the country's better colleges and universities." My eyes begged Tristan not to make an unpleasant situation worse. "Tristan is an alum and generous benefactor to our endowment here at Chastain." That was me clarifying the professional meeting and not any sort of romantic rendezvous.

"Not *just* an angel patron. Mimi and I were classmates—and, dare I say, friends? Plus, there's a little devil in me too." He slipped in an exaggerated wink. "Won't you join us? Pull up a chair. We were talking about the little shindig Mimi is putting on for all of us well-heeled folk. I hope we'll see you there."

That's when *my* heel landed on Tristan's fancy leather loafer and twisted. He gasped.

Ethan ignored it. "I'm guessing my invite got lost in the mail, but I'm sure Mimi and her staff will throw a stellar party."

"Well, this must be fate, because I happen to have a couple of seats open at my table. Please, come. Bring a date. My treat."

Mid-sip, trying to relieve my arid throat, I sputtered, "Oh, no, Tristan. That's not a good idea—it's black-tie, and Ethan travels light. Uh, probably. I'm sure he doesn't have formalwear. Not that he doesn't *have* formalwear, just maybe not here, locally, I mean. Probably. We wouldn't want him to feel—"

"I own a tuxedo," Ethan interjected. "And besides, it sounds like an excellent opportunity to ask some questions of the—*well-heeled* folk."

"Does it?" I chugged the rest of my water glass.

"Surely Mimi knows, add a little liquor and the bluebloods will out *all* the skeletons. Well, not their own, but their neighbors, for sure. This is *outstanding!* I love it when a plan comes together. Mimi will get you the details, and I look forward to seeing you and meeting your lucky plus one."

"Oh, I don't mix business with pleasure." Ethan frowned and avoided my face.

"Well, that's your first mistake," Tristan *tsked*. "I find a little pleasure helps the business medicine go down. Besides, it is a party."

"No, I'm afraid it's a hard rule, inconvenient as it may be, so I won't be bringing a date, but thank you, Tristan. I'll keep an eye on—*out* for you."

"I don't doubt it. Good to meet you, Mr. Ledes." The two men shook hands like they each had something to prove.

"Meems? I guess this means I'll be hearing from you soon. I look forward to it." Ethan backed away before forcing his way through the lunch rush and out the door. Apparently, he decided not to eat.

"I don't doubt that either, *Meems*," Tristan snickered.

"Just stop."

"No, I like it. I think I'll start calling you—"

"No, you will not."

Tristan raised his hands in tittering defeat.

"I could throttle you where you sit." My full attention returned to the wealthy scoundrel who evidently thought himself Cupid.

"You don't mean that."

"You're right." I patted the envelope next to my plate. "First I'll cash this check, and *then* I'm going to throttle you."

The roguish billionaire howled a carefree laugh, reaching for another slice of pizza.

I couldn't help joining him with my own little grin.

Twelve

MONDAY EVENING, I HURRIED home, hoping to beat my mother to the dialing punch for our weekly catch-up chat.

"Hey, Mama."

"What's wrong?"

"Nothing's wrong. Well, nothing that you can help with, so let's not dwell on it." I retracted the fib, so it didn't count. A five-second rule of sorts.

"I shouldn't think so, spending your day in a cushy chair in a fancy office with all the drapes and the plants and ritzy furniture."

For someone who'd never visited my office, not once in my nearly three years as Vice-Dean, Mama conjured a real likeness. I shrugged off her lucky guess. "You sound good. Chipper, I mean." It wasn't the first time I'd clocked a change.

"Do I?"

The tactic worked. We skirted the "something wrong" topic even though the potential scandal certainly qualified, but meeting with Tristan Pembroke served as a pick-me-up with the extra tables he purchased. Digging up old memories also roused the latent guilt for how I treated my mother back then, reminding me to make the time to head north for a visit.

Day trips to see Mama required a planned activity, a preoccupying endeavor to split her focus. Too much attention on me never ended well. Plus, my mother enjoys a challenge, and I had one at the ready.

"How's the Singer doing these days?"

"It's a workhorse, like your mama. Oh, that's right. It's getting to be that time, isn't it? What have you got for me this year?"

"It's a beauty, I think. Simple lines but a floral brocade in metallic. Think you can manage it?"

Every year, in the weeks before the Fall Ball, I lugged a consignment gown I bought for a steal at *Gowntown Y'allywood* and matching threads to my mother's house. One perk of living in a movie-making city: costumes. Mama and her Singer sewing machine worked her self-taught magic to turn any garment into something I could wear.

"I can handle anything you throw at me. I think we've damn-well proven that now, haven't we?" Somehow her comment felt like it had little to do with couture and more to do with that despicable behavior of a long-ago teenager... Or was that my stirred-up remorse talking?

"Yes, Mama. You are a wonder."

We made a plan for the coming Saturday.

Atlanta is only the thirty-seventh largest city in the United States with a population of half a million people, but all of Metro Atlanta has nearly six million residents. Thirteen counties sprawl in every direction. Neighborhoods vary. Communities have their reputations and broad-brush personalities, but the one delineating line is I-285, the perimeter of the city. Residents have potent feelings about living ITP (inside the perimeter) or OTP (outside the perimeter). And while I lived and worked well inside that highly-boasted boundary, my mother lived outside—*way* outside.

Living a car-free existence made getting to Mama's a convoluted trip. The most economical route includes a seven-minute walk to catch fifteen minutes on a bus, followed by a twenty-minute train ride to Doraville of the famed 1974 song. A LYFT drove me another half-hour further out to the exurbs. If I made it to Blossomy Bough in an hour and thirty minutes, it was a lucky day.

The once cow country had grown exponentially with excellent schools, affordable housing, and every big box store known to retail. Mama owned a car but driving into the city with sixteen lanes of Atlanta's notorious bumper-to-bumper traffic was not an adventure that interested her, so traveling to see one another fell to me. I owed her that much.

"Let's see it." Mama answered my knock and led the way through her small entry to the intended dining room. Two sewing kits, a hanging rack, and a handheld steamer joined the decades-old Singer sewing machine ready and waiting on the oblong dining table I'd known for years. She rubbed her palms and stretched her fingers, watching me hook the hanger and begin the great unveiling, one unzipped inch at a time. "Huh. It's not the gaudy mess as I thought it'd be the way you described it, and that silver might brighten your drab gray eyes."

"*Our* drab gray eyes, Mama. Mine are just like yours."

"Do you want my blasted help or not?"

"Yes, ma'am. Please," I caved to her critique as always.

"Well, obviously, I'll need to take in the waist for a better fit."

I held my breath, waiting to see if she'd followed up what anyone might perceive as a compliment with something less flattering.

"That way—if you don't slouch like you do, people might not notice your weak, slopey shoulders."

I exhaled. There it was. "Is *slopey* a word, Mama?"

"If not, it should be because it describes your poor posture to a tee. You'd think you were raised in a slouch factory. Now let's get this gown on you so I can work my magic."

Elevated by a milk crate, I stood as still as possible to avoid the extra-long straight pins my mother's fast fingers employed to mark her revisions to the thick, forest green fabric brocaded in a silver, copper, and gold floral design. The floor-length skirt was full, appropriate for the university's gala venue and the company attending the event.

Mama spoke with pins precariously pinched between her lips, "I don't know why I bother, but I'll ask, anyway. Are you taking a date to this swanky soiree this year?"

"No. *Ouch.*"

"M'sorry."

I doubted she meant the apology. "It's a work function, not a social occasion. I wouldn't have the time to spend with a date if I brought one. It would be rude to ignore someone for—for what?"

"Oh, I don't know. The opportunity to have a little fun. Sip champagne. Take a whirl on the dance floor. Whoever made this gown, made it for dancing."

"If I want to dance next weekend, there will be plenty of takers. Trust me."

"Sure, but they'll all be twice your age."

"With wandering eyes and grabby hands. Yes, Mama, comes with the job." I meant it as a joke, but every year at least one incident made me uncomfortable.

"I guess it doesn't sound all bad."

"Mama," I scolded. My thoughts wandered to a certain older man. Only ten years older, not twice my age, but the vision of him in a tuxedo did things to me. Physical things. Perched in high heels on the latticed plastic carton, I teetered too high for my dizzy state.

"There. All pinned. Let me undo you so I can get to stitching this mammoth into shape."

I navigated a slow turn for her to pull the tab on the bodice-long zipper.

"Good God almighty, Amelia. You're sweating."

Yes, yes, I was.

Thirteen

THE WEEK PRIOR I had avoided Ethan, mostly by sticking close to my desk. After our run-in at The Roost and his good-news-bad-news invite to the Fall Ball by a wealthy, conniving donor who enjoyed playing matchmaker, I deposited the reporter's business card on Nora's desk, asking her to manage delivering Ethan the details.

"Would you like it to slip my mind? Should I misspell his email address? Maybe send the wrong time and place? It's never happened before, but there's always a first time."

An image sprang to mind. Nora and Tristan Pembroke in a boxing ring. Two schemers at odds, going head-to-head, both on my behalf.

"Mr. Ledes will attend at the behest of the Pembroke family." My words indicated all business, but my widened eyes and curled lip let Nora know the recent development made me salty.

That news wiped away the mischief on Nora's face. "I'll see to it directly." No one messed with the Pembrokes.

But somehow, Monday came around again, and Mondays seemed to be "our" day. Ethan's and mine. Since our first introduction, we had yet to avoid one another at the start of a week, so to think this one would be any different seemed another good-news-bad-news scenario. But the clock wound down on the day, reporter-free.

"Last chance at the guest list by table assignment before I send it to the printers for the place cards. Care to peruse it?"

I met Nora's raised brows with a smile. "Nope. I trust you. Nothing to do now but drink champagne and collect the checks."

"And the Oscar goes to—" She applauded my attempt at happy-go-lucky, setting the pages-long list in front of me. "Let's cross our "i"s and dot our "t"s, shall we?"

Nora's insistence included a wink and unusual softness. I guessed the background scrutiny of our department manifested itself in different ways for different staff. Did Nora doubt her administrative skills? Hard to imagine. Yes, the investigation gnawed in the back of my brain, too, but I put faith in my staff, faith in my alma mater. We are Chastain and Chastain doesn't cheat. Still, my assistant's change in demeanor caused me concern, even if unwarranted. I deployed more lighthearted needling.

"Do you think you left someone off the list, Nora? Are you concerned we've snubbed some dignitary? Mistaken someone's mistress for the wife? Did we seat dueling divorcees at the same table? Siblings mired in probate, perhaps?" In truth, any of those catastrophes were actual possibilities. Still, my efforts to remain cheerfully blasé shouldn't be so difficult. Who knew a carefree attitude could be this hard?

"*Hmmm.* Someone needs a vacation."

"What's a vacation?" I deadpanned, but then noticed her serious face. "Speaking of. Any word from FDR?"

She shook her head, then pointed to the list, and I scanned it. Everything appeared in order until the end of the last page. I opened my mouth, taking in a quick, noiseless suck of air, then adjusted the page to be sure sleep deprivation wasn't messing with my vision. Instead, I let the glaring addition toy with my faith in the universe, my faith in my always-accurate office manager, my ill-advised faith in a certain man's word. Apparently, I ran on nothing but faith and caffeine now.

"*Uh*, there is an error." Shuffling through the pages another time, too fast to do any more actual reading, I tapped the paper stack on my desk and handed the list back to Nora.

"Is there?" she mumbled as she slid into one wingback.

I reverted to business speak. "You have Mr. Ledes sitting with a nameless plus one. But that seat will be empty because he won't be bringing a plus one. The younger Mr. Pembroke was generous to offer him the second ticket, but Ethan refused because, like me, this will be a work function, on-the-clock."

Nora sat, wordless at my rambling, so I continued as my professionalism slipped.

"Plus, he's lived here—for what? Six weeks? A couple of months? How'd he meet someone to take to a black-tie affair in so little time? I mean, you don't take just anyone to a formal event."

"He met you, didn't he?"

I grimaced, annoyed at how heartsick it made me. "It's not a mistake?"

She shook her head.

"He's bringing a date?"

Nora nodded.

"A nameless date?"

She shrugged. "I'll look into it."

"No. Don't. I only hope, whoever it is, they bring a generous donation." Even the thought of an added hefty tax-deductible gift didn't make it better.

"What's wrong with you tonight?" Mama and I were a few preoccupied minutes into our weekly call, even though we just saw one another on Saturday. *Life rule: When you have a schedule, keep to it.*

"Mama." Exasperation huffed out of me. I should have appreciated her interest, but somehow her curiosity read like an invasion of privacy and usually came with a zinger attached. Mothers and daughters.

"Is it work? Or maybe something personal? Something to do with your social life?"

"What social life?"

"Exactly."

And *zing. Ouch.*

"Fine. Both. If you must know, both work and personal. I'm not going into the details, but I have a bit of a crush, no big deal, which is good because a work affiliation makes a personal relationship impossible—at least for the time being."

"Hell's bells. Please tell me he isn't a student. Oh, my. He's a student, and you are waiting for him to graduate. Only you would make such poor choices. That's it, isn't it? You are cradle robbing some damned, immature student—"

"Mama!" I needed the laugh, even though she likely meant every word. I poked the bear. "Graduate students attend Chastain. Lots of them. Perfectly age-appropriate grad students."

"Oh, stop. If he's your age and still in school, he'll be one of those perpetual learners. Bouncing from one degree to another, never settling down in any sort of career." She was half right. Ethan's wandering ways, always chasing the next story, certainly didn't agree with my rooted at home lifestyle. And *boy*, was I getting ahead of myself.

"He's not a student," I confessed, and more truth tumbled out too. "He is the opposite of younger than me, and he is a non-issue. I just liked him. And he liked me, and that hasn't happened in a while. I mean, like *kapow,* and—actually that's *never* happened. Not for me. But the truth is, we are an unsuitable match. Total opposites, so it's for the best things ended before anything began because it would end, eventually. Probably. We saved ourselves a whole lot of trouble." I never spoke with my mother like this. My social life scarcely existed, one more way to disappoint.

"Ever heard of good trouble? It's real, you know." Not a hint of humor or teasing shaded her remark.

"Not really."

"Yes, *really*, and since you've never so much as mentioned any interest in someone like you just spat out, it makes me think this might be another example."

"Of what? *Good* trouble?"

"Exactly."

"Another example? Name one more instance of good trouble, Mama? A personal experience."

She kept quiet for a moment, and I figured it was time for the punchline, but the silence lasted too long. Too long for it to be anything but a well-thought-out reply.

"You, Mimi. *You* were the best kind of trouble. Now it's late. Get some rest." Mama ended the call.

Fourteen

THE GOWN FIT LIKE a comfortable glove, and Mama added pockets, a must for a woman working while dressed in formalwear. When she finished her stitching, and I slipped into the dress, she offered a lackluster, "It'll do." But even days later, as I dressed for the formal work night out, her words about "good trouble" bounced in my brain.

"Well, well, well, this must be the place." Tristan Pembroke spun in shiny shoes and a burgundy velvet tuxedo that only someone with his panache could make work so well. A mix of Fosse and Astaire. A blond Michael Jackson.

"What gave it away?" I gestured around the room. "The music? The festive but elegant lighting? Your last name inscribed over the door in front of the words *grand* and *ballroom*?"

"You know I have nothing to do with that, don't you? That's Daddy Dearest and my Granddaddy's influence. When it's my turn, I'll have them renovate this gargantuan room and rename it the Immersive Intergalactic Bar and Safe Space Lounge. Nothing but velour sofas and lava lamps with a variety of ASMR piped through the sound system. And puppies. There should *definitely* be puppies. The kids will love it."

I yelped a laugh, almost spilling the champagne glass I held for show. "How on earth did you get in here and out of here, with such a serious degree, too?" I joked.

"Don't let my good looks fool you. I'm not just a pretty face. Plus, I'm sickeningly rich. What money can't buy—well, I'll let you know when I find out." Tristan's quip couldn't have been more untimely.

I don't know what clued him into the change. My saucer-sized eyes? My ashen complexion? The barometric shift accompanying the lightning strike? He twisted to see what seized my attention. A stoic Ethan Ledes stood breathlessly handsome in classic black-tie attire.

"Good lord, did you feel that?" Tristan staggered like he sensed the earth quaking too.

I treated his question as rhetorical. What choice did I have when rendered speechless?

The billionaire looked Ethan up and down with a grumpy frown, strangely reminding me of Mama. "It'll do, I suppose. If you're into that sort of thing. Conventionally dashing. Predictably, urbane sophistication. Whatever." He swiped at his claret-colored satin lapels, then leaned into my ear. "Have some fun tonight, Miss Mimi. You deserve it. Don't be such a Virgo."

"How'd you know—" But before I could reply, he let fly his signature hair toss and bellowed another attendee's name with his arms outstretched, strutting away to do what he claimed to do best.

The low thump of a Cole Porter tune played by a student jazz quintet added to the hushed chatter of a party getting underway.

"Wow." My raspy exclamation took everything I could muster to push it from my lips, not that I should have. My goal was twofold: to stay upright and not snap the stem of my champagne flute.

"Back at ya," Ethan replied.

"What?"

He cleared his throat. "You are—beautiful."

I wished I could let those few words hang. Ring in my ears forever. But my inner child stepped up to deflect the compliment.

"This old thing?" I curtseyed like a coquette at court, then gave up the playful ruse. "No, really. It's secondhand and altered."

"Aww. Mine too," he confessed as his palm glided down the front of his fitted dinner jacket.

I feigned a gasp. "Busted. You said you *had* a tuxedo." I relaxed, finding our banter groove.

"I said I *owned* a tuxedo. It happens to be in a climate-controlled storage unit in Hoboken, New Jersey, but I own it. And I sure as hell couldn't let that stand in the way of me coming here tonight. And seeing you—in that dress? Worth any price paid. Plus, my date insisted."

The moment of calm ended with another abrupt tilt of the earth, but I kept steady on my feet at the mention of Ethan's nameless plus one. She didn't stay anonymous long.

"I'm thirsty. Who does an old broad need to cuddle up to for a drink around here?" Plumage in regal violet rounded the corner. I gasped, for real this time. That noisy inhale included awe and relief and a smidgeon of glee. Geneva Spieler knew how to make an entrance.

"I think that's my cue." Ethan gave the slightest bow to me, then sidestepped, offering the crook of his arm to the statuesque owner of *12A*. "What can I get for you, Ms. Spieler?"

"I thought we agreed you would call me Geneva—for the evening, anyway." She patted the man's lapel with something like pride, as if she admired her own creation. A moment of silent stares lasted a beat too long before Ethan brought us back to the cocktail question.

"Okay, what can I get you to drink, Geneva?"

"Ah, yes, right. I'll take a Manhattan. But skip the vermouth. And the bitters. And please, for heaven's sake, no cherry." She winked.

"So, straight rye."

"Oh, how I adore a mixologist of a man." Geneva shivered, even more pleased with her handsome companion.

"Did you know the term 'mixologist' isn't really a recent one? Sure, it's trendy now, but it dates back to the late 1800s." I recognized my nerves getting the better of me as I twisted a lock of hair, but that didn't stop me from spewing some of the trivial nonfiction socked away in the corners of my overcrowded mind. "Names like 'mixologists of tipulars' or, even better, 'mixologists of fluid excitements.' I read an interesting book on the Gilded Age, and the writer devoted an entire chapter to the profession. With the rise of industry came money, of course, and wealthier patrons expected a different sort of experience than the booze slinging of the savage Civil War days." I shrugged and nodded as I sucked down the now-warm champagne. Drinking my prop seemed the only way to keep the flustered nerd-girl from nattering herself into further embarrassment.

"Wow, you must be a hoot at parties, *ma chérie*."

A grinning Ethan interjected, looking around the grand ballroom. "I think she's fascinating. And isn't this a party?"

"Not yet," Geneva groused, releasing his arm, "but as soon as you get me my drink, we'll take care of that. Make it a double." She nudged him toward the bar on the far side of the hall, then took a breath before turning to me. "Are you okay? Did you take a fall? Are you concussed? Don't get me wrong, you look fabulous aside from the deer in headlights face you're wearing. But I've never seen or heard you blather on like some idiot savant."

"I'm pretty sure that's not a term we use anymore, Geneva."

She snatched away my empty glass and placed it on a passing tray, seizing two full flutes in one smooth move. When she followed my gaze to her 'date' at the bar, her faux lashes snapped back to me. "*Uh-oh.* Bottoms up. I didn't realize how dire this situation was until now. Fear not, I'm on the case." She clinked her glass to the one I magically held and sipped.

"Please, Geneva. Thank you, but no. I don't need—"

"*Pish posh.* You *do* need, and I shall provide. It's what I do."

Feeling anchored to the earth again, I recalled Mama's critique of my 'slopey shoulders,' inhaled, and straightened my spine. I had a job to do, but my success depended on stopping this relentless romance conspirator in her Jimmy Choo tracks.

"I have never once taken you up on your many offers of moneyed bachelors, Geneva. Why do you think I would cave to a handyman?" I despised my tone but thought it might be the only way the matchmaker might cease and desist.

Her loud, single-syllable laugh barely dented the growing throng of the gala. "Oh, Mimi, I couldn't possibly name all the reasons, so I'll list two. One. He looks at you like he could devour you for dinner. And two. You look at him like he's your own personal dessert cart. And don't think for a moment I'm buying your haughty, judgmental act. It's not you and never has been. Besides, I think we both know there is more to that man than his tool belt."

Heat rose out of my strapless gown and with it a stomach rumble that coincided with a guttural noise from Geneva's throat as Ethan approached. He clutched a triangle of three different cocktails. I glanced at my old friend, wondering what her last comment implied. Did she know about Ethan's real 'gig' or could she see beyond his purported workaday lifestyle to the kind, quick-witted, curious traveler, working for the greater good? How much did she know about her building's new super?

"Rye for you, Geneva. It's local, apparently."

"And divine."

"Another champagne?" He offered me the glass despite the full one Geneva had placed in my hand moments earlier.

"I'll be switching to club soda after this, so no thank you. Work function, remember?" I eyed the third drink he carried, a highball with clear fizzy liquid and a lime. He lifted it and gave me a wink. The subtle gesture prompted a *thunk* in my chest. How on earth did no one else hear that?

"Oh, you two. Don't mind if I do." Geneva drained the three fingers of dark liquor, scooped up the champagne flute from Ethan's grasp, and replaced it with her empty rocks glass, all with the grace and flowing feathers of a Purple Martin. "Now, let's get down to business, shall we? You, Mimi, need to add to the university coffers before a scandal hits the wires, and Ethan, you need intel to cement your scandalous story so it can hit the wires. Money and scandal happen to fall right within my wheelhouse. Tonight, everyone wins!" she crowed with a raised fist.

"Geneva," Wide-eyed, Ethan and I hushed her enthusiasm in stereo.

"What? Was I not supposed to let each of you know that I know what the other one knows about all this *mishegoss*?" The smirk flickering across her face contained not an ounce of regret. "Oops. Ooh la la, is that Tristan Meriwether Pembroke? Why I haven't seen that boy since Cannes, three years ago..." Geneva Spieler fluttered away to enjoy her evening, doing what *she* did best, leaving Ethan and me floating in a vacuum, as if she sucked up all the air, the sound, the gravity from our little spot.

Ethan filled the void. "Now that I bought you a drink, care to dance?"

"The drinks are free. You didn't even buy your own ticket. And don't you have a job to do? I know I do." Avoiding his eye, my gaze bounced around from guest to guest. I nodded, smiled, and mouthed vague greetings from a distance in the crowded room, a model of calm and in control with enough enthusiasm to hide my spiraling dread.

"My paper will reimburse the Pembrokes."

"Really? And how will that look when your story breaks? One of the country's leading newspapers giving money to one of Chastain's biggest donors?"

"*One* of the leading papers? We *are* the leading—never mind. I don't give a damn how it looks. It's the right thing to do. And looks don't tell the entire story. Someone might live in Druid Hills, but that doesn't mean she—"

"Why are you arguing with me?" I snapped under my breath, then reverted to my plastic smile, lifting my glass to no one in particular.

"Because I can't do anything else with you." He uttered those words through gritted teeth, his chiseled jaw flexing as he clenched it.

The frustration ran a two-way street, but Ethan's implication had me spinning figuratively and literally, just in time to catch the speedy approach of President Dr. Cromwell.

"President, incoming, twelve o'clock."

Ethan's focus shot over my head, squinting.

"Shoot. Six o'clock. Your six, my twelve. *Smile.*"

"Ethan Ledes," the hulking Head of School bellowed his cowboy-esque charm. "I didn't realize you were joining us this evening. This little lady must have been keeping you as a surprise."

"He was on the guest list, sir."

"No, no. What better way to prove the veracity of our program than to let the fox into the henhouse? Complete transparency, isn't that right, Ethan? The truth, the whole truth, and nothing but..." The amalgamation of scholarly doctor, down-home party host, and irate boss made for an unsettling confrontation. Add the liquor on Dr. Cromwell's breath and I found myself in uncharted territory.

"Dr. Cromwell, good to see you're making the most of the night. I was saying to Ms. Kanaan how impressive she is and how sorry I am to have sprung this on you all so last minute. My buddy Tristan invited me. I'm fairly new to town and he can be very persuasive. Downright formidable if you find yourself on his wrong side. Of course, you've probably witnessed his staggering persistence. Like a dog with a bone, that guy. So, here I am."

"Tristan? Tristan Pembroke?" Dr. Cromwell unmasked personality number four, money-grubbing sycophant.

"The one and only. Broke the mold with that one."

"Yes, quite right. I'll have to thank him for broadening the tent. I'm sure if there is anything you need, Amelia will be on the case. Nothing but candor from this one, guaranteed."

"Aww, she's been candid with me so far."

"I wouldn't expect anything else. Enjoy your evening." He tipped an imaginary hat, then took my arm as he pressed his ersatz grin to my ear. "Don't let this wanna-be muckraker out of your sight." His grip tightened, but then he moved on to a cheery crowd where Tristan Pembroke held court. It seemed I'd been let off the hook for inviting Ethan, but now I hung on another, virtually handcuffed to the one man I needed to escape.

"Your buddy Tristan?" I *tsked*, thankful Ethan diverted Dr. Cromwell's ire.

"Sure. Watch this." The journalist waved and shouted, "Hey, Tristan!"

Tristan tossed his beachy hair and a toothy grin in our direction, raising his glass.

"See? We're pals now."

"Hate to tell you, but he'd give that attention to anyone who said his name. An indiscriminate puppy dog, that guy."

"Wait. What are you saying? Tristan Pembroke and I aren't on the verge of becoming besties? Say it isn't so, Meems." He frowned, patting his supposed broken heart.

I laughed. The warm champagne bounced from my empty stomach to my brain. Embarrassed, I pinched closed my lips, fingers pressed to them to ward off further outbursts.

"God, I hope I get to hear that sound again and soon."

"I need you to stop saying things like that." I handed the champagne to a passing cater-waiter with my thanks.

"You're right. I'm sorry. I will." His earnest apology made him even more appealing.

"And I've been told to shadow you tonight, but I also have other responsibilities, so to show you I have nothing to hide, I'd just as soon have you join me on my rounds than try to be wily about it. I'm not nearly that clever."

"That—that sounds great."

"Shall we?" I didn't wait for a reply, crossing to an elderly couple nursing glasses of wine. "Hello, Mr. and Mrs. Ronsfeld. So, pleased you could make it. How are you this evening?"

"Oh, Ms. Kanaan. You never cease to impress. This event gets more elegant every year. We wouldn't miss it. Such a lovely walk down memory lane for us old folks," Mrs. Ronsfeld gushed.

"Thank you, and how are the kids? I seem to recall Jonah and Patrice were expecting this time last year."

"Oh-ho, let me show you." Mr. Ronsfeld's slow, knobby fingers fumbled for his wallet, and I assumed dog-eared photographs were in our future.

"Let me introduce you to Ethan Ledes." The lull provided the perfect entry. "Ethan is an investigative reporter. From New York. Guess that means whatever we say tonight is on the record. Who knows? He might have a mini recorder hidden in his pocket." I said the words as if I was both impressed by his occupation and *perhaps* jesting about the tape recorder, all while making certain everyone knew where they stood in the conversation.

The gentlemen shook hands. "Nice to meet you. And I assure you, I have no hidden recorder or agenda this evening, and no one is on the record." He gave a playful wink to the glimmering Mrs. Ronsfeld. "Let's call it deep background." In mere seconds, Ethan charmed the awestruck couple. His confident flattery lacked all the heedless bombast of Tristan Pembroke, leaving only a sincerity that no doubt made him a success in his field. He had the wealthy donors entertained with rapt attention.

As we moseyed to our next round of chit-chat, Ethan whispered, "That wasn't necessary, you know? The whole 'on the record' thing."

"Oh, I'm sorry. Was it the wrong thing to say?" I may have batted my lashes with my innocence routine.

He chuckled, "It's unnecessary, that's all. But no, don't worry. You haven't hurt my feelings or anything."

"Good. Cuz you'll be hearing it with every single introduction I make tonight. So, get used to it." I tugged his knotted bow tie, foolishly locking eyes. A beat longer, and those whiskey-colored irises would strike me drunk. Lesson learned. "Ready to meet the illustrious Reginald Jaspers III?" I juddered from his tractor beam pull.

"I'm on your six." Ethan's palm grazed the small of my back. The touch was brief, inappropriate, and likely unnoticed by anyone but me. I'd have given anything to feel it again.

"Dr. Jaspers." I leaned to kiss the man's cheek.

"Well, I do declare, Miss Amelia. If you aren't prettier than an Easter bonnet on He Has Risen Sunday."

"Too kind, sir. Allow me to introduce you to Ethan Ledes. He's a re—" I didn't get to repeat my spiel.

"Oh my. *The Public Eye.*" My landlord bowed, using his natural voice for only us to hear, "I am a rabid fan of your work, young man. The detail, the time you must devote to a subject. So much time. Months and months. Nothing short of superb."

"The feeling is mutual, I assure you, Dr. Jaspers. I have read all your books, well, your *fiction.*"

"Good." The professor character returned. "They're the best ones," he crowed. "If I dare say so myself."

Another budding bromance, except this one I believed.

"Dr. Jaspers is also my benevolent landlord. Has been for years."

"I say, Ms. Kanaan is the finest tenant a man could ask for. Quiet as a church mouse and tidy as a Swan House topiary." Reginald and I shared a wink at his over-the-topism.

The humble glad-handing continued for hours. My coerced companion kept at my side with every encounter. He engaged with everyone we met, asked interesting but benign questions, laughed at jokes, and told some of his own, sharing stories of his childhood and South Bend, Indiana days. Best of all, he took the ample Mighty Rooster ribbing in stride. He even flagged down a server to deliver me a club soda and lime as my tongue thickened with thirst. Ethan was the perfect company for what quickly became the best Fall Ball I'd ever attended.

Fifteen

THE CLANK OF SILVER, glass, and fine china jangled in the background. Chandelier lights burned brighter as the waitstaff cleared away the remnants of the party. For the first time all evening, Ethan and I sat alone at a large round table, sipping a glass of leftover champagne to save the staff from pouring it down the drain. Geneva left an hour earlier, insisting Ethan stay to enjoy the night and that he see me home.

Slipping off my shoes under the table, I flexed and pointed my aching feet with silent curses at the makers of beautiful shoes that could not withstand hours of pain-free wear.

"That was fun." Exhaustion and relief loosened my lips, and I sipped my drink to keep from blathering on further.

"More than I thought it would be. *You* are amazing, by the way." He raised his glass in a toast. "You knew every single person's name. Their children's names, some other noteworthy mentionable. Golf handicaps, Civil War reenactment rank *and* regiment, the stargazer's preferred telescope. How do you keep all that information in there?" His finger tapped my forehead. "Plus, Ancient Egyptian baking trivia."

"All in a day's work, but thank you." The earnest complement didn't help my waning professionalism. Coupled with Ethan's sexy Rat Pack vibe, with his shed dinner jacket, rolled sleeves, and undone tie, my exhaustion found it difficult to fight off his appeal. Thankfully I was also too drained to do anything about it.

"I am a little disappointed though."

"Why? Didn't land the scoop of the century?" I teased.

"Didn't get to dance with the prettiest woman in the room."

I stiffened, finding some resolve. "What did I say about talking like that? We are two professionals with jobs that are at odds with one another. And the fact that we're apparently going to find ourselves thrust into one another's circles in the coming—who knows how long—as Dr. Jaspers made clear, will not make it any easier. So, do us both a favor and quit with the charming compliments and suggestive remarks." I stumbled to my feet, toeing under the tablecloth's edge to find my discarded shoes.

"Mimi."

"What?" I snapped, finally sliding my foot into a strappy high heel. "No, please don't apologize. Just don't, because it will come off as genuine and kind, making you that much more attractive, and I swear I have never met anyone who could persuade me to bend a rule, much less break one, but I'm on thin ice with you. You and your easy way and captivating stories, those glints of silver at your temples, and the way your eyes crinkle when you smile. It's more than—"

"I meant Geneva. I didn't get to dance with Geneva." He stood, stoically pushing in his chair. "But good to hear where I stand with you. Almost makes up for the missed dancing. Now, why don't you let me see you home?"

"Home?"

"If I said I'd rather stay here and rub your aching feet, drink more champagne, and talk all night, I'd bet you'd give me another scathing earful, so yeah, let me take you home."

I stared, too flummoxed for words, but with wits enough to reach for my glass and down the rest of the sparkling wine. Hoisting my gown, I beelined to the ballroom's foyer in search of my evening wrap, the lone garment hanging on a coat rack at the entry. Ethan arrived in time to slide the stray end of my cloak over my shoulder. His hand never touched me, but in the wake of my mortifying gut spillage, the laughter he tried to suppress snuck out, and I had to join him.

I sighed, "She was stunning, wasn't she?" Cold crept through the drafty old doors leading outside, and I bundled up tighter, smiling at the memory of the glamorous woman in all her plum-colored pomp and plumage.

"The belle of the ball," Ethan agreed, pulling keys from his pocket. "And she left me her car. Ready to go?"

I nodded, sad for the first time that the Fall Ball had ended.

An odd mix of mercy and agony swirled inside me with the quick ride to Druid Hills. Ethan kept a slow speed, beyond cautious, and I hoped he intended to stretch the trip because of me and not because he drove Geneva's brand-new Bentley. Geneva never drove, yet she got a new car every year. The perk of an ex-husband, as she put it. She not only married well, but divorced well, too.

Ethan pulled to the curb in front of the long walkway to my carriage house apartment and reached to turn off the ignition.

"Oh, you don't need to walk me back there. It's not like this a date or anything." I gathered my wrap around me, preparing for the cold. Still, I didn't reach for the door handle.

"Right. Work function. Seemed to be a success. To me anyway. Not that I know what the barometer for success is in these things. You'd know better, I guess. It is your job and all. Did you think it was a good night? For Chastain, I mean. I had a good time. A great night," he babbled, his words all over the place like the bouncing butterflies in my stomach.

"You okay there?" I hurried to put him out of his word salad misery, flattered he could get flummoxed too. "It was a great night. Better than I hoped." And I didn't mean the money raised, an amount I wouldn't learn for weeks.

"Good. Good to hear it." He gripped the classic woodgrain steering wheel.

"*Uh-oh*. Was that on the record? *Fat Cats Fill Chastain Coffers at Fancy Fête.*"

"No," he said. "Not at all. Nothing about tonight was on the record, Mimi. And I'm with the Daily Independent, not the New York Post."

Then came my first mistake, touching his arm. "I was kidding." That's when I should have said my goodbyes and scurried down the shadowy path to my home, but I didn't move. Neither did he. The lull thickened, making it difficult to breathe. I'd stalled long enough and reached for the door latch.

"So, this is a beautiful neighborhood," he sputtered as he leaned toward the windshield to see what he could in the dark. "Wide streets, great landscape."

My teeth found my bottom lip as I took in the familiar surroundings, obscured by the nighttime light. "You should see it in the daytime." Biting back my grin, I let my inner geek swoop in for an unnecessary rescue. "Frederick Law Olmsted, the father of landscape architecture, planned it."

Ethan's eyes fixed on me, but he gave no other reaction. The nerd girl kept talking.

"You might have heard of him. He and his sons designed countless other developments. Neighborhoods. University campuses. Park systems. The surroundings of the U.S. Capitol and Central Park, to name two. Berkley and Stanford out west. Ironically, he never graduated from college. He attended. Yale. But couldn't graduate because of weak eyes. Poison sumac. Ironic. Taken down by the thing you love most? Plants, in his case. Wow, and that's more than you ever wanted to know about—"

"No, I could listen to you all night. I'd watch you read the phone book."

I swallowed hard, trying not to fidget in my seat. "Careful, old man. You're showing your age. No one uses phone books anymore."

Our combined airy laughter faded.

Then I did the unthinkable, asking, "Do you have any plans this week?"

"Plans?"

"For the holiday? I'm guessing you don't know many people in town, and I wouldn't want you to be alone. My mother and I have a long-standing tradition. We meet at her place and eat every traditional Thanksgiving food item from a can or a box. Canned green beans, canned cranberry sauce, instant stuffing, Stovetop. We splurge for the good stuff nowadays. Top it all off with canned pumpkin pie filling. No crust for us. I've taken to bringing some sliced turkey the last few years, but it wasn't something we could ever get when I was a kid. But discounted dented cans and boxes with crushed corners we could do. We watch the National Dog Show and eat straight from the aluminum. Mama cleaned enough for other people in her work life. She didn't want to do dishes on her day off."

"Well—that sounds—"

"Awful? Yeah. Yeah, it is. I don't even know why I brought it up." Another inappropriate over-share, this one personal and humiliating. Why would I tell him? What about Ethan made me so open when I'd told no one else? "I just thought you—anyway. I've got to—"

"Hold on, Mimi." He touched my cloaked arm, keeping my nerves from launching me into the darkness. "I'm off to Indiana. To see my folks and sisters and all the rest of my wild extended family."

"Oh, nice. That sounds fun." I meant every word. "I've seen that Norman Rockwell painting. Not the artwork itself, but in a book. Of course. But I bet you and your family do it big in real life." The iconic holiday dinner scene flashed in my mind's eye, remembering how he described his upbringing on our date before I wrecked it. The differences between the man on my left and me couldn't be more profound. Our professional obstacles were the least of our worries.

"*Freedom from Want.*"

"*Hm*?" The cloying tension returned, and words stuck in my throat.

"The Rockwell painting. With the turkey. The family 'round the table. It's called *Freedom from Want.*"

That irony tipped the poise I'd been struggling to keep. I grabbed the cold handle to find fresh air and my escape.

"Mimi—" His hand clutched mine, warm and firm. Safe, yet so unsafe.

"I should go, Ethan."

"Should?"

"I need to—"

He gave a slight head shake and held tighter.

"I *want* to go."

He let go. "I don't think you do."

"You're wrong." And I bolted down the dark walkway after slamming the tank-weight passenger door behind me, thankful I had those two fibs at my disposal when I needed them most.

Sixteen

THE FOLLOWING WORK WEEK was short, as the Thursday holiday stretched into a long weekend. With the Fall Ball in the record books and the early application deadline passed, I found myself in another brief respite before the rush of holidays and the opening of the regular admissions enrollment window.

I had one item I swore to accomplish in the following three days: set eyes on Briana Johnson and convince her that, though she would not receive an early acceptance letter in mid-December, her Chastain dream wasn't dead. When she failed to show for the alumni interview with Rashida Turner, I had no choice but to sideline Briana to the dreaded waitlist.

"Hey, Nora?" Phone in hand, I scrolled, taking slow steps from my office to her grand desk. "Is there some kind of road construction or major sewer work going on in the city? I can't get a ride to where I need to go. I mean, the app seems to work, but no driver will pick up the fare."

"Where you headed?"

The day was winding down, and if it hadn't been raining, the sun would have made a hasty exit too. I tried putting in the destination address again. "West side of the city. Darn it. What's going on?"

"West side of the city or West End, Amelia?" Nora's tone hardened.

"I'm headed due west. Not quite to Grove Park."

"Oh no, you are not," she chuckled like I'd told a joke and continued typing.

My silence stopped her.

"Oh no, you are not," she repeated. "One, we do not go to an applicant's home unless there are extenuating circumstances. And two, if Briana Johnson doesn't want to meet, then you are going to have to let it go."

"Maybe there *are* extenuating circumstances, and we don't know it yet. I need to speak to her before she gets that waitlist letter and she gives up on us entirely."

"Gives up on *us*? I swear, child." Subordinate assistant Nora faded, and sage Obi-Wan (southern edition) came to the fore. "I thought after your second year when that young man from Lakewood Heights—"

"Javi."

"Yes, when *Javi* broke your bleeding heart, I hoped you'd learned your lesson. Do not become attached to these candidates. I know you feel a kinship with them, but they will never look at you or buy what you're selling when you look the way you do."

"That's not fair. I *do* relate to them, no matter what I look like now, and it's why I do what I do."

"Amelia, I appreciate you. I respect you, I know you mean well, and I understand your past makes you feel you have something in common with them, but I think you need to be careful about throwing around the word *fair* when you're talking about young people like Briana and Javi."

I took a quick inhale and tightened my jaw, knowing this woman I held in the highest regard had cause to admonish me. No sense in defending it. Nora was right. I knew it, and now I had to sit with it.

"You're right, Nora. I apologize."

"I know, but I also don't need you taking unnecessary risks. I will see that Briana Johnson is here tomorrow, Wednesday, latest."

"How? How will you get her to come?"

"Don't you worry about it. Never underestimate an old, determined woman of color. *Any* color."

Images of Geneva, Rose Bimah, the Chen sisters in *7D*, and even my mother joined Nora in my mind.

"I would never. I've had a host of fine examples—"

"And maybe Ms. Johnson has not. So, let's see if we can remedy that. But here, in a professional setting. All proper-like, okay?"

"Yes, ma'am." I gave a small, gracious grin before returning to my office, tail tucked slightly between my legs.

As promised, Wednesday noontime, a knock interrupted my lunch and a mouthful of Tuesday's dinner leftovers.

"Yes?"

Nora's scowl peeked through the few inches she'd opened the door, her speech more rigid than usual. "I am sorry to interrupt, but Ms. Briana Johnson is here to see you. She did not confirm a time per my instructions, and I know it isn't our—*your* routine to accept walk-ins, but—"

"No." I straightened, almost hopping out of my swivel chair. "I mean, yes. Please, send her in." My excitement threatened to get the better of me, but Nora's pointed look said I shouldn't encourage improper office etiquette with my eager hospitality. In the Good Cop/Bad Cop Act, our roles were clear. I flattened my grin and pushed my day-old Trader Joe's lentil loaf aside, standing ready to meet Ms. Briana Johnson.

Briana hardly looked at me, but kept a close watch on Nora, who remained at the door. There may have been some telepathy at play with Nora, insisting Briana return my welcoming gesture. Even her hunched shoulders couldn't hide that she had a few inches on me. Glossy curls hung down her back, and the only thing I envied more were the long, dark lashes outlining her makeup-less eyes. When I finally caught her focus, a beautiful girl took a quick seat like she couldn't wait to make herself smaller, fidgeting with a coiled lock of hair in a nervous tell I recognized.

"Hello, Briana. I'm Amelia Kanaan. So nice to meet you, finally." I reached across my desk to shake the young woman's hand.

"Can I get you anything? Water? Coffee?" I hoped to put her at ease.

"No. No, thank you." Briana cleared her throat when her words carried little sound.

Nora cleared *her* throat, prodding in an overbearing, motherly fashion. Tension strangled the room.

"No, thank you, *ma'am*," Briana spoke louder this time, with direct eye contact, and adding an apologetic nod.

I smiled. "Thank you, Nora." I took my seat with a slight head jerk toward the door to let Nora know I had the meeting well in hand. "May I take your jacket? You're welcome to hang it." I gestured to where mine hung.

"I'm fine to keep it. Thank you."

"Like I said, it's nice to meet you and put a face to the name."

"It's my understanding you could request a picture from the College Board from when I took the SATs."

Briana's first statement of genuine conversation surprised me. She spoke politely, without a hint of uncertainty. None of the jittery speech I'd expect from any prospective student sitting in her seat. Not at all the anxious young woman I misjudged had entered my office. She'd flipped a switch. The youthful connection I thought we might share morphed into a more self-assured adult likeness of someone with something to prove.

"That's true. But I didn't make that request."

"Just as well. I wore braces then. And my acne has cleared up. Plus, I wear contacts now. You probably wouldn't have recognized me." She straightened in her chair and took in the room as she talked. Pride resonated from her, and I was glad to see it. In person and on paper, Briana's self-esteem was justified. "Some schools ask you to upload a photo with their application. I'm glad Chastain doesn't. I suppose you can see how some might perceive that practice as problematic. The request for a picture." A small, sweet smile followed Briana's keen insight.

Surprise number two, but I took her frankness in stride.

"Full disclosure, Chastain did, for a time, include a photo request. Nothing nefarious about it, I don't believe, but yes, it wasn't—a good look—as the kids say." I grinned, hoping we could both take a breath and relax, that my language bridged any perceived divide. But Briana seemed more interested in friendly sparring.

"The kids," she repeated, using air-quotes. "Funny how challenging the *kids* are these days. Demanding equity. Our openness to diversity and inclusivity."

The room warmed by degrees, and the view of the young woman still in her outdoor winter wear made it even more stifling.

"Funny," I chose her word. "That's a big part of my role. It's why I took this job after I graduated from here. My aim is to meet those demands—I mean, my goals, Chastain's goals, include DE&I." I used more of the vernacular of the day but wondered if I sounded as defensive as I felt. "And the application photo thing was before my time." Yep, more defensive than a linebacker. I shuffled through the small stack of printed applications to my right while I got my bearings, ready to shift the dynamic.

"So, do you want to attend Chastain, Briana?" I kept a kind tone. "I mean, you applied early but then didn't follow through with the requirements for December acceptance. Even if you meant to apply as an *early action* student rather than early acceptance, your missed interview with Rashida Turner, at best, gets you moved to the regular admissions pile for the Spring announcement. At worst, denied outright." I swallowed some frustration, hoping the latter wouldn't be the outcome of her case. "I'm less concerned about the current student meet-and-greet you didn't attend, but Ms. Turner is a distinguished alum and busy woman with a high-powered job at a leading global news organization that we're lucky to have headquartered in our backyard. Her availability is—tight."

"Plus, she looks a lot like me," Briana interjected.

"Does she?" Even I couldn't believe those two words came out of my mouth. Huge and instant regret.

Briana's dubious stare bore into me.

"Yes. Yes, she does. That was a stupid thing for me to say. I apologize. Interestingly enough, Ms. Turner said the same of you when I asked her to take the meeting. She was a bit more generous about it, at least over the phone. But she also agreed to the interview because she thought it was important for you to see that people like her could be successful here at Chastain and beyond." *Shoot.* I'd done it again.

"People 'like her?'" Briana's question contained a whiff of exasperation, but I knew she wasn't to blame. She warranted the irritation. How had I done this all wrong?

I tried to rally with my true intent. Focusing on how *I* related to her, whether or not she knew it. "Yes. People with smarts. Driven, tenacious, talented women, born and raised here in Atlanta."

Briana's face softened, but she kept quiet.

"Why did you miss the meeting with Ms. Turner?" I asked without judgment. No accusation or reprimand.

She played with her fingers, and for the first time since she sat in my office, her confidence slipped. "That day, I needed to help my mother." Briana's jaw clenched with a noisy exhale.

I didn't remember Briana's mother mentioned on her application, but I felt validated in the instant kinship I recognized weeks ago when I read her submission, even without knowing the whole story. This was how we could connect. "I can relate. I grew up with a single mom. Right here in the city. Because it was only the two of us, she often needed my help."

"Oh? Was your mother a thirty-eight-year-old grad student, clerking at a law firm fourteen hours a day and then spending the other ten studying for the bar?"

Surprise number three. "Uh—no. She was—" I scanned Briana's paper submission, fumbling with the pages and with my words. "My mother cleaned houses and uh—babysat and—why—so, none of that is on your application. Your mother, law school, clerking." I continued searching the application I had memorized backward and forward, to be sure.

"I didn't include it. Didn't think it was relevant. It asked about legal guardianship. My grandmother is my legal guardian. She's unemployed. Retired, I guess. Besides, I want to get into school on my merit, not my mother's late great success."

I nodded, reordering the pages, tapping them on my day planner into a neat pile, unsure how to respond.

"Yes, of course. I want you to get in on your own merit, too. And I happen to think you have great qualifications. I hope to help ease some stumbling blocks. If there are any. I didn't know your mother's circumstances. How could I?"

"Did you assume why?"

That was the $64,000 question. I did assume. For a time, I assumed Briana and I lived a shared experience.

"I assumed the conflict to be immovable, considering we require such a meeting as a component of the process. I assumed you needed help, and I took steps to give it, but I meant no disrespect to you or your privacy. Still, I can't help but think you must hold some appreciation for what your mother is doing now."

"She works very hard, but it has been a long time coming. She wasn't around much when I was younger. She's still not." That short statement marked the first time Briana mumbled. "Have you ever wanted to succeed at something not only *for* someone but also *despite* them?" The young woman fiddled with a button on her well-pressed cuff, looking no more than her seventeen years. A young woman intent on carving out her space in the world on her own terms. A young woman battling much of what I did and then some.

"Wow, Briana." I leaned across my desk with a brief but fake scowl. "Get out of my head."

We shared a laughed. Short-lived, but real.

"I apologize for missing the appointment with Ms. Turner. That was rude. I'd be happy to reschedule if she's open to it. I understand it's a condition of acceptance, even for the regular submission window. Chastain is still very much in the running, maybe even more so after this visit, believe it or not. But other schools have expressed interest, and it's become clear options exist for me out there. Options that are—not in our backyard, to use your phrase."

"Yes. Sure, of course." Apparently, banal affirmations were all I could articulate. But it was no surprise to hear other schools were courting her.

"Getting out and seeing the world might show me things I can't find in a book. And I've read a *lot* of books. Also," she paused, "my mother casts a long shadow these days. In lots of ways."

Our similarity reared up again, and I never felt more envious of a teenager.

"Me too. The books, I mean. And I certainly understand the desire to flee the backyard. No matter how big it is on paper."

"Why didn't you?"

"Flee?"

"You said you grew up here. Went to school here. Now you work here, too? What happened?" Nothing hits one's self-esteem quite like the spot-on observations of a child.

"Well, I'm not dead yet, but I'm not sure. I suppose I thought I had responsibilities. Ignorant of what my options might have been. Fear?" I hesitated, considering the question no one had ever asked me. Of course, I had a mistake to atone for, but that wasn't a story for Briana. I stood and offered my hand, knowing the young woman already had more going for her than I did. "What do you say? We reset the clock? A do-over?"

"I'd like that, Ms. Kanaan. Thank you." We shook hands.

"No, thank you, Miss Johnson. It's clear from your transcript, the application, your essay—you are everything we here at

Chastain want to see in our students. And I am certain we can make it worth your while to attend."

"Kind of you to say."

"If you have any questions or concerns, you have my number."

"I do."

"I'll leave the meeting with Rashida up to you two. No need for me to be involved any further. And for what it's worth, I didn't mean to take on the role of the nice white lady swooping in to save the day. Don't get me wrong. I recognize that's exactly what happened, but it wasn't my intention."

"'Nice white lady saving the day.'" She air-quoted again with a knowing sigh. "Your words. But I appreciate you using them. Thank you for your time and the effort—and the epiphany. I think we both had it wrong today. Like *really* wrong."

"We can only aim to do better."

We both stifled a more uncomfortable laugh that stopped short. I imagined we both held out hope that someday institutions would evolve rather than banking on individuals to plug those holes. Someday soon.

"I hope this isn't the last I hear from you, Briana. Chastain would be lucky to have you. I'll see you out."

Nora stayed at her desk as Briana and I walked into her space and said our polite goodbyes before Briana left.

"That was sort of quick. Did you pick the wrong basket for all your eggs?" Nora asked as I closed the door to the hall.

"Not exactly. It's a good basket." I leaned against the frame, the old cut-glass knob at the small of my back. "Just happens her basket is good and full. Lots of possibilities for her."

"Is that right?" Nora continued her work. I knew she only *appeared* disinterested.

"Yep. Briana Johnson is going to be fine. No doubt about it."

"Is that right?" my assistant repeated with a tinge of mocking sarcasm.

"Even without help from little ol' me."

"You don't say," she snickered.

"Lesson learned, Nora. Thank you for that."

"We all have lessons to learn. You, Briana—well, not me. I know everything." The twinkle in her eye said she jested, but the doorknob pressed to my back turned in my hands, startling me as I moved to get out of the way of the opening door. "Mr. Ledes," Nora's grin weakened, and her eyes widened while I took a breath, thankful for the frosted glass that offered me a split second to compose myself.

"Hello, Mrs. Okafor. Good to see you again."

Nora nodded.

I popped my head around the door and almost smacked into a foil-wrapped pie plate Ethan carried. It smelled delicious.

"Mimi," he said my name quietly with something like relief. "I was afraid I'd miss you. With the holiday and all. Wasn't sure of your schedule or—"

"Well, you almost did." Nora pushed to her feet. "Amelia was saying how we're likely the only ones left on campus, and we should call it a day. I tried to fight her, but she's the boss. Besides, I've got a ten-pound bag of potatoes sprouting eyes in my pantry that won't be peeling themselves. So, it's mighty nice of her to let me go home early." Nora's neat-as-a-pin desk needed no tidying as she scurried to snatch her belongings.

"Yes, very nice of me—I guess." I had no misgivings about calling it a day, particularly while still smarting from my Briana meeting. But Ethan's unexpected drop-in and Nora's speedy exit flustered me.

"I'll leave y'all here to discuss whatever needs discussing," Nora said. "Give my best to your mother." Nora's sweetness was genuine but spread a little thicker with the reporter in the room. "Happy Thanksgiving to the both of you. Enjoy that long break. Bye now." And she hurried out the door with a wave over her shoulder, lacking even an ounce of subtlety.

Ethan tilted toward the hall to watch Nora's getaway. "Is there a fire somewhere I don't know about?" he joked, but his surprise visit fanned a flame I couldn't think about, much less admit.

We hadn't seen one another in days. Still, one look and a five-alarm blaze took off inside me.

"What brings you here?"

"Your pie plate."

"Can't say for sure, but it looks like more than an empty pie plate. Smells like it too." I leaned closer for a better sniff—of pie, of course. At least that's the fib I told myself. *Darn it.* There's one.

"Aww, see, I'm from Indiana, and in Indiana, you never return an empty dish. Pretty sure there's a law on the books. So—"

"Did you know that even though Coca-Cola started here in Atlanta, the bottles are from Terre Haute?" I beamed, sharing useless Georgia-Indiana-related facts.

Ethan merely smiled in return.

"Terre Haute, *Indiana*," I clarified.

"Yes, I know where Terre Haute is."

"Right. Of course, you do. What kind of pie did you bring me?"

"It's not pie."

My turn to reply with a dumb smile.

"It's Connie's famous corn pudding. A Thanksgiving mainstay of my youth."

"You know your mom's corn pudding recipe? By heart?" It sounded like teasing, though I wanted it to be true. But the reality was even better.

He stalled after an emphatic, "Nooo," then, "I, uh, I called her this morning, and she walked me through it. It was remarkably simple, actually, and it's delicious, I promise. Just heat and scoop. A little change-up from your tradition. Well, not a change, an addition, really."

I tried to ignore what might have been pity, silently reprimanding myself for sharing our pathetic custom of the Andersson-Kanaan scratch-and-dent Thanksgiving.

"You called your mom?"

This man grew more endearing by the minute.

"I call my mom every week—every week I'm somewhere with phone reception. Which is most weeks, but sometimes—well, she likes to know where I am. That I'm not someplace dangerous or—"

"I call mine every week too," I interrupted. He was rambling, like his confession embarrassed him, but I didn't want him to feel uncomfortable. Certainly not about anything as sweet as calling his mom for cooking advice. "Did you tell her about me?" It was an earnest question that seemed to stump him.

"Maybe." His eventual reply sounded more like a question, and the ruddiness of his cheeks deepened.

I punched his arm like a fifth grader on a playground might or during some serious car ride Punch Buggy gameplay. The only way my addled brain could think to touch him. "What did you say?"

"I told her your name, and that you were funny—and smart—and a real ball-buster, making my job more challenging than it ever has been before."

"Right. Your job." Recess was over. "How's that going, or shouldn't I ask?"

"Oh, it's going."

"What's that mean?" My hand went for my ponytail.

"Look, Mimi. We're not law enforcement. Prosecution isn't what we do. We find the truth, tell the public, and let the people decide. I'm not saying anyone broke the law, but people have paid money, falsified resumes, ignored test scores. And it's happening at universities all over the country."

"Not here, though."

"Yes. Here."

"Well, not by me. Not with my knowledge, and certainly not with my permission, or even my looking the other way. I have no—"

"I believe you."

"You've got it wrong, Ethan. FDR is coming back, and he'll explain all this and clear it up. He's been here since before I was here, before Nora, before—"

"FDR?"

"Dean Rayburn."

"Do you mean Franklin Rayburn?"

"Yes, Dean Rayburn took a few weeks between the admissions windows. He'll be back Monday as a matter of fact and—"

"No. No, he won't. Monday, you're going to hear that Dean Rayburn is retiring effective immediately. Staying on St. Simon's Island with his lovely wife, Cookie. Seems his impromptu vacation made him realize he wants to spend more time with his family."

Bile rose in my throat, burning with my hard swallow. "Why am I hearing this from you? Why hasn't this come from Dr. Cromwell?"

"Mimi, you *didn't* get this from me. You understand that, right? I haven't told you anything. When Cromwell informs you on Monday, it will be the first time you hear it. Save up your fibs. You're gonna need them." If he meant to be funny, he failed, but his stern stare told me none of this was a joke. "I'm sorry. This isn't how I meant to leave things, but I have a plane to catch."

"You're leaving? Like forever? You're done here and—"

"No, just for the holiday in Indiana. I'm coming back on Sunday. I'm not done here. Not by a longshot. I promise you that." He handed me the wrapped pie plate, the aroma of Connie's corn pudding less enticing than it had been earlier.

I wanted to believe his promise was a well-meant vow of sorts rather than some dire warning. Ethan didn't look like a threat or sound like one. But I didn't know who or what to believe about the world I'd lived and worked in my whole adult life. Chastain was my home, and now Ethan Ledes believed members of my Chastain family had been working against the very thing I'd been trying to make it. And with the help of *The Public Eye* megaphone, people would see me as a fraud. Again. But this time, on a global stage.

Seventeen

WITHOUT A CLOUD IN the sky, my exhale wafted white against the bright blue. I took one more therapeutic deep breath before knocking on Mama's door. I always knocked.

"You're late," Mama squawked. "You're about to miss the beginning of the parade, Mimi. The top hat guy with the big scissors is making his speech." Mama laughed, not looking away from the television. "They've got the weather guy squished into something like a sidecar attached to a Segway, tooling around the crowds. He looks like a—"

"Mama," I cut her off before she said something I'd regret hearing, but found her in good spirits, a new pattern I cautiously enjoyed. "I've got my hands full of—"

"The kitchen's that way." She flicked her hand; eyes still fixated on channel eleven.

I settled in the small kitchen. The room took up more space than my city version, but my appliances were of this decade. Mama's weren't from this century, but everything stood in working order, tidy as ever. I'd be sure to leave it the same way.

"I'm changing it up a bit this year. Well, not changing so much as adding some extras," I amended. Change sparked trouble.

"Don't tell me you cooked," she called back, still content to watch her annual tradition.

"No. Not exactly. But someone cooked a dish for us, and I picked up a small, pre-cooked turkey breast to heat and slice ourselves. Not the pre-cut kind this time. Plus, I brought paper plates. The sturdy kind." I preheated the oven to warm the feast improvements.

"All that sounds sort of fancy. Don't forget where you come from."

I snorted with my whispered, "Like I could."

"And don't mumble, Amelia. It's unbecoming." Nothing wrong with the woman's hearing. "Well, I'll take the turkey, but you can keep the stranger-made whatever. Who knows what someone might put in their home cooking?"

"He's not a stranger, Mama. He's a friend, and he's kind, and he went out of his way to make it. For us."

"A friend, huh?" She appeared at my elbow.

I dropped a can of green beans mid-turn of the handheld can opener. "Jeez, Mama. When did you get so stealthy?"

Ninety-eight pounds in a bathrobe didn't make much noise.

"What? I walked from there to here. Not my fault if you're all dreamy-eyed and distracted, thinking of your *friend*. Finally, something interesting is happening in your life."

"Why don't you start the boxed potatoes." If I kept her hands busy, she'd be less likely to come at me with her mouth.

"I'll miss the parade," she groused on her way to her armchair view. "Tom Turkey has probably already gone by."

I knew I'd have some peace for the next hour.

I sat back from the TV tray in front of me, swallowing another bite of corn pudding. The casserole, along with the real roasted turkey breast, added something special to our less than joyful ritual. Even Mama couldn't muster a negative word to say, and no word from her qualifies as a glowing five-star review. She saved her praise for the furballs prancing and preening on the television to the dulcet narration of John O'Hurley.

My silenced phone lit up at my side.

The Reporter: Did you see Santa ride down 6th Ave?

Mimi: Mama doesn't really like that part. We always turn it off before then.

The Reporter: Oh. Sorry.

Why would I tell him that?

Mimi: No. I'm sorry. I should have fibbed.

The Reporter: No

I chastised myself with an eye-roll at my stupid mouth—er, fingers.

Mimi: ...

The Reporter: ...

Mimi: Did you know the parade route used to be 6 miles and now it's just over 2.5? If that isn't a commentary on the country today, I don't know what is. On the flip-side, they've never canceled the parade because of cold weather, which is pretty amazing considering they cancel school down here if too many leaves fall, so…

The Reporter: Lol. I guess you read a book, huh?

Look at that. Nerd-girl to the rescue.

The Reporter: Since we're through the Best in Breed and Best in Group rounds, I figured you'd had time to try Connie's pudding. How was it?

Mimi: Wow. You're either a quick study or a closet dog lover. And I like to think of it as Ron Burgundy's mother's Corn Pudding. It's delicious. Thank you.

The Reporter: You're welcome, but Ron Burgundy? I've been called by more journalist names in the last month than I ever thought possible. You're scraping the bottom of the barrel.

The Reporter: Hey, sorry to lay all that at your feet yesterday. Rayburn and all that.

I wished I hadn't heard any of it, but the Monday surprise would have been worse.

> **Mimi:** No, I appreciate it, but I'd rather not dwell on it now.

> **The Reporter:** So, who do you guess takes Best in Show?

> **Mimi:** Given the chance, I always pull for the Portuguese Water Dog. I'm a diehard for Geneva's Max, and all dogs like him.

> **The Reporter:** Hmmm. Care to make it interesting? A little wager? I say the Scottish Deerhound has it in the bag.

> **Mimi:**...

"Mama?" I deferred to the expert. "Who is going to take Best in Show?"

"Mimi, I swear. It's like you aren't even paying attention. That Scottish Deerhound is trotting away with it. It's not even close." My mother never pulled her focus from the television.

"Oh."

> **Mimi:** No, that's ok. I'm not the betting sort.

> **The Reporter:** Good. I'd hate to take your money. I mean, I would, but I'd feel bad about it.

The slightest chuckle snuck out of me, enough to make Mama look my way. I straightened my posture and my grin, sliding the phone into my lap underneath the TV tray.

"What's going on over there?" A raised brow spied over her shoulder.

"Hm?"

Laser eyes zeroed in on me as she raised the remote and muted the dog show and the melodious Mr. O'Hurley.

Mimi: Uh-oh. Busted. Gotta go.

"Is that the too-old student, who's a non-issue anyway, making you giggle like a schoolgirl?"

"I told you he's not a student, and he's not too old, but yes, he is a non-issue. And I didn't giggle." Did I?

"Sounds like an issue. And what is he then, a professor? If he's a professor, he'd better be a full-fledged tenured professor and not some associate. At least tell me he's tenure-tracked, Amelia."

"Mama, lots of associate professors are associates because their careers go beyond teaching. They write or do research, work in their field—and it doesn't matter. Ethan isn't a professor, and I don't care to talk about it. The obstacles are currently insurmountable, so none of it matters."

"What does that mean? *Currently* insurmountable? Like someday they won't be insurmountable?"

"Things are going on, things to do with work, with Chastain. Things to do with me that I'm apparently blind to—that call into question how I do my job. Look, I'll face it all Monday. Can't I enjoy a holiday with my mother without getting raked over the coals?"

"What did you do now, Amelia? What mess have you gotten into? It's always the same with you. If you want to be on top, you need to do a little extra, be a little more, but you—"

"I know, Mama. I never quite do it well enough. Whatever it is, I inevitably miss the mark. I *almost* do it right."

"Don't be melodramatic. What's any of this got to do with—Ethan? Is that his name?

"Don't tease me, Mama. Not about this. Don't use my words against me."

"Fine. I won't tease. This is new, is all. You've never acted like this before. I kinda like it. We've never talked about boys. With you it's always some rare bird migration or a documentary on eighteenth century labor laws. Talk about all those old game shows *almost* held my attention, but not really. A secret crush, though. Now we're talking."

"Somewhere, Alison Bechdel is crying right now."

"Who?"

"Never mind, Mama."

"Then tell me what this Ethan has to do with your screw up at work."

"Jeez, Mama." I flew from the sofa, catching the flimsy mini-folding table I'd hit with my thighs. What little clutter I left in the kitchen would get my full attention.

"Fine. What does Ethan have to do with your work?"

"You want to do this?" I smacked the latex gloves against the sink, startling even me, but I spun to face my mother, anyway. "Why the hell not? Are you familiar with *The Public Eye*? The investigative journalist group under the umbrella of the Daily Independent? They—"

"Amelia Louise, watch your mouth. And I may not have gone to college, but I'm not an idiot. I've read *The Public Eye*. And you damn well know it."

I gripped the counter, white-knuckled its edge to avoid mentioning every time my mother called me on the carpet for assuming she knew something when she didn't. The reminders that the frivolous factoids bumbling around in my brain weren't anything she had the luxury to collect with all the toilet scrubbing and furniture dusting she did all those years. My cleansing breath did its best to calm me.

"I don't wanna fight with you, Mama. Ethan is a journalist. A journalist with *The Public Eye* and the organization is doing an in-depth piece on higher education."

"Well, that can't be good," she sneered.

"Why do you say that?" Always straight to the negative with her, not that she was wrong.

"Your attitude aside? *The Public Eye* doesn't do feel-good stories. It's police corruption, it's pedophile priests, it's Hollywood big-wigs and D.C. politicos caught up in prostitution stings. For the life of me, I can't imagine what my daughter has to do with anything scandalous enough to catch the eye of—well, *The Public Eye*."

"You're right, I'm in a bit of a mess of someone else's making, but a mess nonetheless. This is my point, Mama. I've done nothing wrong, except maybe been oblivious, which is its own crime, but you know what people say—stink rolls downhill."

"No, Mimi, that's not what people say," Mama laughed. "So, this Ethan and you are on opposite sides of some brouhaha on campus, making relations sleazy, huh? This *is* interesting."

"I prefer the term unethical—"

"Same, same. Is he accusing you of something?"

I huffed, eyes-rolling. "Not anymore."

"Then problem solved. You can make the biggest mound outta nothing at all."

Jaw clenched, I spun back to the dirty pie plate and utensils. "It's not 'problem solved.' Chastain could be in trouble, and it's not just Chastain. Colleges and universities all over are—Never mind. While *The Public Eye* is working this story—a story that might take months, a year or more to get out—"

"What story? What did the academic elites do?" Mama must have grown tired. Out of sight, her questions were now coming from the living room and the armchair she'd settled into again.

"Believe it or not, they—we, but not me—managed to make themselves even more elitist," I sighed.

"There's a good a trick. And how did *they*—you but not you—do that?" She knew how to slink to the tenderest part of me, zero in on my weakest spot, and push. Her superpower.

"By actively working against everything I've tried to do in my time as Vice-Dean of admissions. Which is to level the playing field." Steam from the rush of hot water spewing from the spigot rose, fogging the window view to the deep backyard. "Do you know there are families, families with generations of attendees probably, who pay for their child's spot at tier-one schools? Sure, mommies and daddies have ponied up big bucks for auditorium seating or building names, overt contributions by the über-wealthy. That's a tale as old as time—and odious, by the way, but *now* people have ringers who take standardized tests for their kids, lie about summer internships, Photoshop them onto polo fields or a kibbutz, or a Central American dental clinic."

After Ethan's bombshell the afternoon before, I went home and did my investigating via Google. I wished I hadn't.

"They pay professionals to create dossiers an FBI analyst would have to scrutinize to swear to their illegitimacy. And now the practice has made its way to Chastain, if Ethan is to be believed. And I do. I believe him. One more example of privilege, separating the haves and have nots." My fingers ached, and no pie plate had ever been so clean.

"That one exam point, the one award, that one photograph of Mitzi Von Uppington-Smythe feeding a baby bald eagle with an eyedropper against a green-screen of the American flag and Jackson Hole, steals a spot from some brilliant kid in the projects bagging groceries or scrubbing fast-food restaurant toilets to help put food on the dinner table."

I snapped out of the yellow gloves that clung to my sweaty hands and wiped my brow. "Nothing? As someone who has scrubbed her share of toilets in her day, I'm surprised you, of all people, don't have an opinion here. All the groceries I bagged? Are you kidding me?" Nothing but silence met me as I grabbed a dish towel and stalked toward the living room. "Mama?"

"Now, Mimi, we missed Best in Show." She avoided my eye and turned on the TV's sound, upping the volume on a Purina pet food commercial.

"Do you seriously disagree that this is abhorrent? Why would you take the opposing view just to—what? Just because? This atrocious behavior that my alma mater, my *employer* evidently sanctions?" Exhausted, I leaned on the doorframe, rubbing the deep lines between my eyes. Lines I thought I'd adopted way too early for my age.

"I'm not disagreeing with you. I'm ignoring you. Your naivety about how the world works isn't as charming as you think it is. Why do you think I have always pushed you to be better, do better? You get more stuff if you're at the front of the line. The more stuff you've got, the more options you have. You won the golden goose, and instead of hightailing it out of this place, you turned right around to give golden gooses to other snot-nosed kids."

"Geese, Mama." I should have swallowed the knee jerk correction.

"*Bah.*" She dismissed it with a wave of her hand.

"Yes, to help snot-nosed kids and their families like us—without a single box of tissues. And you're so willing to shrug and say that's how the world works? Even after all we went through? Particularly that last year?"

She avoided my face.

"Jeez, Mama. We were hungry. *Really* hungry. I showered in the school's locker room. I studied by flashlight. We almost froze that winter, sleeping in layers of clothes, *other people's* donated clothes. Remember sleeping in the car at least twice that winter, so you could run the heat? Then sweating like pigs later that summer? No money to run a fan, much less air conditioning—"

"Criminy, Amelia! Where the hell do you suppose that money went?" she barked.

The last words I heard before my world took another discombobulating turn were an ironic sing-song of, "Purina Pet Food, keep life simple."

Mama clicked off the television and slammed the remote on her TV tray.

"What money?" The question whispered out of me like I didn't mean it for her—like I'd meant to use my inside voice.

"What money? Your grocery store money. The money I scrimped and saved, the money I scrubbed until my fingers bled to earn. And yes, I sold some of our EBT bought food. Sue me. Kinda screwed us, going from paper to the debit card, but I found a work-around. And you're all right now. What money," she grumbled.

I understood the words, heard her exasperation, but couldn't make sense of it—or didn't want to.

"What did you do, Mama? With the money?"

"I did what was necessary. Exactly what needed to be done. So, it's not only the wealthy that finagle their kid to the front of the line. Just because we were poor didn't mean I was dumb."

My vision blurred at the same moment my mother's meaning became clear. The instant mashed potatoes, the canned green beans, plus the special turkey and Connie's corn pudding, all turned to stone in my stomach. I clung to the slim moldings between the kitchen and living room with my forehead pressed to the frame, hoping to stay upright as everything crashed down around me.

"Don't get all dramatic about it. It was nearly fifteen years ago. There was only so much we could do back then."

"We? Who is *we*?"

"Mimi. That hardly seems relevant; none of it seems relevant. Forget I said anything."

"Forget it? Forget the most important turn in my whole life is based on—on—on lies? My biggest accomplishment wasn't my accomplishment at all. The one achievement that has shaped my *entire* being—"

"Oh, stop. Who knows? You might have gotten in on your own. You tried, no question. But I didn't want to take the chance that you weren't—"

"I wasn't—*good* enough?"

"Well, I don't make the rules, Amelia."

"No, you break them."

Mama tsked. "If it's any consolation, I bet it would have been a very close call. You getting accepted into Chastain."

"Somewhere in there, I'm sure you actually believe that's a nice thing to say but guess what. It's not. And now we'll never know, will we? We'll never know if I was good enough." I pulled my head from its resting spot, a test to see if I would stay standing in this new reality. With a burst of panic, a desperate need for air, I grabbed my pie plate and coat before I tore out into the fading daylight to find a way home.

Eighteen

ATLANTA INTERSTATES ARE TYPICALLY slow-moving parking lots, but a midweek holiday helped matters. Despite an ill-advised stop at Blue's Spirits and Wine, I made it home before dark. Frankly, it surprised me that Mr. Azul was open, but the steady stream of customers proved he met an obvious demand.

"Busy evening, huh?" I placed my liquor order on the high counter when I reached the head of the queue.

"Thanksgiving, man. Always is," the cheery man chuckled. "Ms. Kanaan. How are you?" Despite the line, the neighborhood shop owner took the time to chat. Mr. Azul made the effort with any regular any day of the year. "I see you've got your usual. You good on olives? We've got those blue cheese ones you like so much. Ah? Give that vodka a little extra something." He gestured to a display behind him. Small businesses survive on the upsell.

"Sure, thanks." A glimpse around the bustling store didn't find anyone judging me with the proprietor's obvious knowledge of my drinking habits. He made it sound as if my "usual" purchase happened far more regularly than it did. At least to my ear.

"Hey, now. And what have we got here? Bow Street? This is a nice bottle of Irish Whiskey. Very nice." Mr. Azul rubbed his fingertips together, eyeing me from his raised perch. "This for you or—"

I caught the fib before it hit the air, tight-lipped to keep it from breaking free. He slipped the dark liquor into its own paper bag and leaned down to whisper, "I'll give you the friends and family discount. Tis *officially* the season, right? You have a good night." His wink had a sadness to it, like he recognized some sorrow in me and silently wished me a speedy recovery. But with the electronic *ding* of the shop's door, his jolly smile returned, and he shouted, "Happy Turkey Day! Gobble, gobble!" to all those waiting behind me.

Years of catering to a clientele on the brink of celebrations or the verge of despair likely honed his sense of moods. Then again, how difficult could it be to decipher the festive drinks of enthusiastic revelers versus the tear-drowning liquor for a solo night of lament?

I hugged the brown sacks to my chest, wondering what that ratio looked like. How good-time purchases stacked up to bad. But one snapshot of the drawn faces and furrowed brows of my fellow booze-buying patrons told the story, or at least the overarching theme of that Thursday's stressful holiday, coupled with the compulsory joy of the coming month.

A dozen pillar candles of varying heights lit the otherwise decorative fireplace boarded up and painted over long before I'd moved into the cozy carriage house. I'd sooner run the air conditioner on blast at peak summer than spend money on heating those far fewer wintry days of the year. I could always drink steamy tea and huddle under another blanket with a hot water bottle. Living out the distressing memories of cold from my youth provided a strange sort of comfort in adulthood. A questionable reminder that things weren't so bad when it was probably much worse. But I'd sworn never to sweat through another summer night again.

That night my favorite teacup with delicate flowers and a gold-painted rim and handle contained zero Darjeeling but plenty of Irish whiskey to help keep me warm. Too much.

Hours ticked past, and the candle flames blurred thanks to equal parts alcohol and angry tears, but I could only blame the Bow Street for my next mistake.

Mimi: You awake?

The Reporter: Barely. It's late, and I'm full of turkey.

Mimi:…

The Reporter: U ok?

Mimi:…

The Reporter: Did your mom get on you about texting at the dinner table?

Mimi: Let's not talk about my mom.

The Reporter: Ok

Mimi:...

The Reporter: Mimi?

Mimi:...

The Reporter: You texted me, right?

Mimi: Ask me what I'm wearing.

The Reporter:...

Mimi: Come on, Walter Cronkite. Show me what those clever thumbs can do.

The Reporter: Cronkite? Big shoes.

Mimi: You know what they say about big shoes.

The Reporter: Whoa. Ok, Mimi.

Mimi: What? Do you prefer the big bustle of Nellie Bly?

The Reporter: lol This is the nerdiest sexting I have ever read.

Mimi: Is this a sex thing?

Mimi: Sex thing?

Mimi: Sex thing?

Mimi: Argh. SEXTING? Darn auto-correct! Let's start over. Ask me what I'm wearing again.

The Reporter: I didn't ask the first time.

The Reporter:...

The Reporter: Is this a good idea?

Mimi: No. Ask anyway.

The Reporter: At least you're honest.

Mimi: Ask!!

The Reporter: What are you wearing, Mimi?

I peeled back layers of blanket to see the fleece of my oversized one-piece footie pajamas. Candlelight glinted off the metal zipper as I took another swig of dark liquor.

Mimi: Lace and not much of it.

Fib number one. A good one, I thought, but then came radio silence.

The Reporter:...

> **Mimi:** Hello? Is this thing on?

> **The Reporter:**...

Too much radio silence, except for the occasional yelp of drunken hiccups that grew in intensity. Finally...

> **The Reporter:** Do me a favor?

> **Mimi:** K

> **The Reporter:** Answer the phone when it rings.

Ethan didn't allow me time to text a reply. My phone vibrated in my hands, and I stared, thumb hovering over the red *decline* icon, but then changed my mind.

"Hello?" I sucked back a hiccup.

"What are you doing, Mimi?" Not an ounce of playfulness mingled in his question.

"Well, I thought maybe I was doing the *sss*exting thing, *hiccup* but it seems *hiccup* I can't even do that right. But in my defense, it was my first time." More of those angry tears surfaced, but I fought them and swallowed another hiccup.

"Mimi? Have you been drinking?"

"Yesss, sir. But only a lot." No sense using my last fib.

"Are you home? Your home? Druid Hills home?"

"How many homes do you think I have, Anderson *hiccup* Cooper?" An unfortunate snort oinked out with my laugh, but Ethan didn't join me.

"Hold on a second, Meems." The scratch and scuff of a phone receiver pressed to someone's chest obscured a conversation on the other end. A moment later, Ethan's clear baritone returned, and it didn't seem fair that the universe blessed him with a face for the movies and a voice for radio. "I'm back. You still there, Mimi?"

"Meems," I repeated. "I like it when you call me Meems. It makes me sound fun. *hiccup* Meems. Meeeeeems."

"Aww, you are fun. And funny. God, you make me laugh."

"Not tonight, apparently. I'm sorry I—"

"Please. Don't apologize," he interrupted. "It'll come off as genuine and kind, making you that much more—"

"Hey. *I* said that to *you*. Are you making fun of me?"

Ethan's teasing gave me a momentary second wind.

"Wow, that is the second time someone has used my words against me today. I'd expect taunting from *hiccup* Mama, but you? We don't know each other well enough—"

"To be sexting? Yeah, call me old-fashioned, but that's more of a third, or maybe *fourteenth* date activity. We barely survived the first one."

"*Shoot.* What was I thinking? I knew I'd be terrible at it."

"No, I disagree. You've got real potential there, Miss Kanaan. You might have overdone it with the liquid courage, that's all. Anyone with a heartbeat would appreciate the effort." His soothing tone mixed with my last sip of whiskey.

"But I don't want just anyone. I want—"

"Mimi," he sighed into my ear.

Ethan was right. I overdid it but conjured enough sense not to make matters worse. I kept quiet, listening through the phone to his breath as the candle flames hardly wavered in the stillness. If I closed my eyes, sleep would have taken over, but his voice coaxed me awake.

"You still with me?"

"Mm-hmm."

"Good. I'm going to hang up and call you back in one minute."

"One minute? *hiccup*"

"Thirty seconds. Answer, okay?" The call ended.

My heavy head flopped to the sofa cushion, but bounded upright with the loud ringtone, followed by a quick wrap at the front door.

"Hello?"

"Answer the door, Mimi."

I scrambled out of my blanket burrito, phone in one hand, empty teacup in the other, looking around the dim room.

"How d'you know someone is at my door?"

"Meems. It's me. Hurry, it's cold out here."

"It's cold in here." I missed whatever he said next as I ended the call and tossed the phone onto the coffee table. Re-wrapped in a blanket, I scurried in the dark to the door, my fingers still knitted through my prettiest teacup's handle.

I unlocked the door but tugged one-handed, to no avail.

"Mimi?" Muffled concern came through the old wooden door jamb that shifted on the coldest of days.

"It's stuck. It sticks sometimes." I yanked again. "Yep. It's stuck. *hiccup* You push, I'll pull."

"Okay. Count of three. One, two—"

"Wait. Pull on three or three and then pull?"

"Three, Mimi. Pull on three. One, two, three."

I wrench the door, but my hand, draped in the blanket, slipped off the worn brass knob. The door swung open with startling force as my hands flew overhead, followed by the tinkling crash of shattered porcelain on the cottage's tiled entryway floor. To top off the middle of the night mayhem, my feet sailed upward too, and I found my whole body off the ground, Ethan cradling my backside like a real-life, blond, no-glasses-wearing Clark Kent.

"What are you doing?" I gasped.

"I—I heard breaking glass and didn't want you to step on any—to cut your feet."

"My very own Superman slash Clark Kent." I squeezed tighter, holding on to him around his shoulders. "No worries, though." I straightened one leg, kicking up a foot. "See, footie pajamas. Thick socks inside, too. All safe," I bragged.

Away from the fireplace, the small-scale foyer stood shadowy, but my eyes adjusted enough to recognize the sexy grin of my newfound hero.

"Lace, huh? And not much of it?"

My chin dipped, my eyes following the line of the zipper that ran from my chest to one ankle. "Oops. Okay, I fibbed, and I counted it, but I thought it was a good one as far as little white lies go."

"Oh, it was a very good one. Grade A, but I think it'd be better if I focused on what got broken and not on you in fictitious lace. Where's your sofa? I'm gonna set you on the sofa."

"My teacup. Darn it. It was my favorite."

I pouted, pointing toward the couch and the warm candle glow.

He settled me on the couch and stroked my cheek with a warm hand, but my eyelids grew too heavy to fight. I took a deep inhale of his nearby skin.

"Oh my God. You're killing me, Smalls."

"Who? *Hey*, listen to that. My hiccups are gone. Must have scared 'em outta me."

"Don't suppose you've thrown up yet." He patted my cheek, keeping me awake.

"Yet? What do you mean yet?"

"Oh, you will. Got a bucket nearby?"

"Trash can under the sink," I mumbled, flailing an arm in the right direction.

"Want to tell me what happened today, or at least why it's so cold in here? Is there something wrong with your heat?" Ethan stroked my hair. The sensation carried me away on his alpine bakery baby scent.

"No. It's penance. And a reminder of where I come from."

"Where's that? Greenland?"

"Isn't it funny how Greenland is mostly ice and Iceland is mostly green? They are both ruled by the same king, you know? The King of Denmark. I bet you've been there, haven't you? Someday, I would love to go there."

"I'd love to take you there someday."

"Take me where?"

"I'd take you anywhere, Miss Kanaan. Anywhere you'd let me. Say the word. Any day. Anytime."

"Ethan?"

"Yeah?"

"I'm sorry I lied to you."

"About the lace? I'll get over it. Eventually. And you know I didn't come here for the lace, right?"

"I know. But I'm not talking about the lace. I mean about Chastain. About me."

Ethan exhaled, then fidgeted in his seat to adjust the blankets up to my chin. "Let's not talk about that now. Another time would be better."

"Okay, but I am sorry. I didn't mean to. I didn't know."

"Not now, Mimi."

We sat in silence, except for the ticking clock on the fireplace mantel.

"Ethan?"

"Hm?"

"You didn't come here for the lace at all?"

His brief snicker sounded far away. "The lace might have played into it. But only a little. I am a man. With a pulse. But I was concerned about you."

"That's nice to know. I like that you like my imaginary lace." My sigh morphed into a moan. "Oh, no." My hand covered my mouth. "About that other thing?"

"Meems. Really. You'll regret it tomorrow."

"No, I—"

"Please don't put me in this position. We'll talk about you, lies, and Chastain in the morning—with clearer heads—and very strong coffee."

"But I need—" I groaned.

"No, you don't need to clear your conscience tonight. Not like this."

"But—"

"Shhh."

"*Ethan.*" I bolted upright. "I'll take that bucket now."

Nineteen

No one needs the details of the ensuing hour, but I learned two things. One. Ethan could somehow hold a cool, damp cloth, a garbage can, and my hair all at once, without so much as a disgusted eye roll. And two, I would never ever drink whiskey again. Ever.

When I emerged from the bathroom, washed, brushed, hydrated, and changed into sweats and an oversized sweater, I contemplated my welcoming bed. But movement in the low light of the living room reminded me of the visitor still in my home. When the burn in my nose reminded me of what that visitor witnessed, another wave of shame-flavored nausea roiled inside me.

Ethan lay on the sofa underneath a blanket, eyes closed.

"You asleep?"

"Nope." He sat and spun for his socked feet to meet the floor, pressing the heels of his hands to his drowsy eyes. "You better?"

"Better," I nodded. "Thank you, and I apologize—"

"We will never speak of this again. Promise." His impish grin didn't fit the solemn-sounding vow. My soused brain struggled to navigate the inconsistent messages in the wake of the high-priced Bow Street and the sight of the handsome man sitting in candle glow on my sofa in the middle of the night. He patted beside him. "Want some blanket?"

Did I? You bet I did. I wanted a full-on weighted blanket made of one-hundred percent Ethan Ledes, but my feet wouldn't move.

"For heat's sake. Nothing more." He unfurled one side of the wooly covers.

"I'll turn up the heat if you'd like. If I'd known to expect company..."

"It's up to you. If a chilly house is how you grew up—"

"What?"

"You said the cold reminded you of where you're from. And I asked if you were from Greenland. And then you treated me to a civics lesson on—"

"Oh my goodness," I grumbled, rolling into a ball at his side. "I'm—I'm from here. From Atlanta. Born and raised."

"I know," he murmured.

"My childhood might have been more southern-fried Dickensian than your Midwest Rockwellian version."

His arm slid around me. A gentle squeeze to his warm frame soothed me. My head rested on his chest, and I enjoyed the mix of our heat. He spoke just loud enough to hear, his cheek grazing my head. "The cold home and dented canned goods paint a shockingly distinct picture. A bleak one. And now I feel like an ass for bragging about my idyllic upbringing and life as a professional sightseer. Your comment about food and shelter insecurity at Rubs 'n Suds is particularly worrisome in retrospect. My childhood anecdotes were pretty disgraceful. I see that now and I'm sorry for it."

I pulled from him, peeling out of the cocoon we made, a cozy nest that felt safe. Like no home I'd ever known. "I didn't share to make you—well, I didn't mean to share that, but I certainly didn't do it to shame you, and I sure as heck don't want your pity."

"Pity? No, Mimi. You'll get no pity from me. Look at this place. Look at how you live, how you work, what you do. I don't pity you. I am in awe of you. You work hard, are gracious with everyone you meet, whip-smart, fast on your feet, and funny, and I'd never seen anyone more beautiful than you at the gala the other night. But then you walked in here, stood in the candlelight in that enormous sweater and ratty sweatpants, and I swear I forgot how to breathe for a second."

"Wow." I digested that for a moment, then returned to my usual humility with a side of sarcasm. "You should consider a switch to writing fiction."

"No fiction here. Nothing but the facts." Those earnest brown eyes caught some reflection of the fireplace pillars, drawing my face closer to his.

With my lips a whisper from his, I asked, "Why are you here, Ethan?"

"Hm?"

I pulled back an inch. "Why are you here?"

"You texted. Then I thought something seemed—off, so I called to hear your voice, and sure enough, you were drunk. I was in a cab, pulling into the Mews. I rerouted the driver to here."

"Yes, I remember all that. Vaguely. I also remember you were supposed to be in Indiana. But you're not."

He sighed a laugh. "One night was enough. Did I mention the whole family gathered? That's a lot of people, and I love them, but my sisters are all married, with kids, so... I gotta say, when the young ones were little, it was pretty great. I was the cool uncle, and they told me the funniest stories, asked questions until I thought my head would explode. Now they're teens and tweens with eye-rolling skills they must practice because they are world-class eye-rollers, but they do it glued to their phones, tablets, laptops." True disappointment oozed from him.

"Tell me their names."

"Whose names?"

"Your family's. Tell me all of them."

"You don't want that."

"Yes, I do. I have no family. An enormous family fascinates me. Tell me. I want to know. More than anything." I burrowed back down into his side and entwined our fingers, admiring the union in silhouette.

"More than anything, huh?" He gripped my fingers tighter.

I sandwiched his hands between my two—rough hands that spent days doing more than typing column inches. His strength and calluses told other stories. Not just those fit to print, but how Ethan Ledes immersed himself in a community to learn their ways, how he worked alongside locals to meet them at their level, in their everyday lives, to gain a better perspective for the story he'd later tell.

"No. Not more than anything, but I'll take what I can get."

An instant before I placed a foolish kiss on his fingers, he pulled from my grasp, saving me from my near misstep.

He barreled into the innocent talk about family. "So, you know Mitch and Connie and I've mentioned Ellie, Evie, and Emmy. Ellie is married to Evan. No, I'm not kidding. Evie, thank goodness, is married to Natalie, and Emmy and Stuart round out the marital pairings. Ellie and Evan have three: Mitchell the second, Anthony, and Joseph. Evie and Nat are our nature lovers with the oldest Constance Lily, but she goes by Lily, followed by the twins Daisy and Poppy. While Emmy and Stu have Stuart Jr, poor kid, and Calliope, she's named after Emmy's favorite writer. We breathed a collective sigh of relief when they had a girl, otherwise we'd know little Callie as *Tex*. The beloved main character of a book series you might know."

I laughed, at least on the inside, but my weighted eyelids couldn't stay open any longer. "I'm familiar with the influx of

Bellas, Aryas, and Harrys in the world thanks to popular fiction. Thousands of college applications make the trends obvious. But Tex isn't one I've seen yet. But with the TV show now, it's only a matter of time."

"Probably so. Needless to say, my family is a lot. And this time, with the news of my corn pudding gesture, news that spread absurdly fast, there were questions. *Lots* and lots of questions. Questions I didn't know how to answer. Or didn't particularly like the answers. *Anyway*, maybe that's why I chose a solitary line of work. An escape. One where I ask the questions."

I faded as whiskey and sleep ganged up on me. "Hmm. It sounds wonderful to me. The holidays must be the most beautiful chaos. I can see the Indiana snow and Christmas lights now."

"Plus, a menorah. Natalie's Jewish. And a kinara. Stu is Black."

"Even better," I sighed. "And you? No one for you?"

"I guess that solitary life isn't conducive to having a—someone."

"That's a shame, Mr. Ledes. Cuz, I think you're a real catch."

"Yeah, well, you're drunk. Funny though. Suddenly, I'm feeling kind of caught." His thumb stroked my hand.

"Hm?" I lost my battle to stay awake.

"Nothing."

"Ethan?"

"Yeah, Mimi."

"I think I'm gonna fall asleep right here. You okay with that?"

"Nothing I'd like more."

"Huh. Nothing?" I nestled down for good.

"Well. I'll take what I can get. Good night, Meems."

"G'night, E—"

Twenty

I KEPT MY EYES shut. My nose poked from blankets I knew were not my usual bedding, but the cold air hinted I was home. With a groaning stretch, I pried open my gritty lids to see what might have been the most beautiful sight: a tall glass of water with two aspirin beside it. But when I raised my head to reach for the liquid salvation, the real beauty came into focus. Across from me Ethan slept in a cushy chair, legs outstretched, socked feet resting on the coffee table. The modern wingback supported his head at an odd angle and his wool peacoat draped him for warmth.

The water and pills went down fast, and I appreciated the caring gesture from the man who was probably going to wake with a terrible kink in his neck. I couldn't help but wonder why he'd settled feet away when, last I remembered, we'd been cuddling, enjoying each other's heat—platonically, of course.

Pushing past that letdown, I rested my head again to take stock of my physical state and found it in good condition, all things considered. Some collegiate resilience must have stayed with me in my extended time surrounded by university students. I knew I'd survive without a slice of The Roost's greasy pizza.

I perked up, holding my breath at the first sound from the adjacent chair, but my stare met with closed eyes.

"Are you staring at me?" Ethan kept his lids shut.

I wouldn't start the day with a fib. "Yes," my first spoken word rasped from my raw throat.

"Am I drooling?"

Was I? I wipe my mouth, just in case. "Not that I can see, no."

He smiled before he shared his drowsy brown eyes with me. A delectable, crooked grin I thought would make any morning worthwhile. A chest-rattling *thud* went off again as I hugged a couch cushion tight to keep my heart from escaping. I sat balled up, unable to stop gawking or, apparently, use my filter.

"Why are you in the chair? Over there, in the chair, I mean. Not here, on the sofa. Closer, uh, to me?"

His smile grew. "Self-preservation."

"Oh." Then it hit me. "Did *I* drool?"

"You wiggle."

"I wiggle?"

"Yes, Mimi. You wiggle in a—let's say—in a sleep-depriving sort of way."

"I'm sorry. I didn't mean to—"

"No. No apologies. More memories of this—thing to play on repeat." He gestured overhead. "Whatever you and I have going on here."

We might not have a name for it, but he certainly grew braver talking about it. Ethan didn't even try to pretend we should ignore the electricity crackling between us. Why deny it?

"I'm just saying I've slept better on a crowded, open-air school bus, circa 1971, rollicking through the Mexican rainforest in one-hundred-ten-degree heat, with a crate full of chickens on my lap, than with you and your—"

"Wiggling?" I couldn't help my grin, enjoying every word. The way he roused every sense.

"And now we have to stop saying that word."

"What word? *Wiggle*?" I teased.

"Mimi," he growled my name, sending the thudding in my chest to a more southern region.

I clenched and bounded to my feet as I threw off the unnecessary blankets. "Coffee? I'm terrible at it. Making coffee. But I'll try."

Before I passed him on my way to the kitchenette, he snagged my hand. A mini fantasy flashed in my mind, him dragging me atop his lap. Warm hands sliding under my sweater as our ravenous mouths crash into one another. Sighing each other's names as our tongues meet, teeth nibbling, and eager fingers exploring.

"Make it strong."

"Hm?" I jerked from the daydream to see his serious face and slipped free of his grasp.

"Very strong coffee."

With those three words, the events from the day before came hurtling to the present. What I'd learned. What my mother did so many years ago. What I needed to tell Ethan and how it would end this *thing* we had before it ever got a chance to start.

"Did you know that instant coffee has been around for over two hundred fifty years?" I beelined to the kitchen, eager for a distraction. Any distraction. "Surprising, right? 1771 in Great Britain, but it didn't really come around to the States until the 1850s. Civil War time. Some people credit George Washington with a version of the creation. Which is true, except it was another George Washington. An American inventor and businessman in the later 1800s, not the *cannot tell a lie* Founding Father." My mouth moved faster than my brain. In trying to maneuver us through a minefield, I'd inadvertently circled back to the notion of truth-telling.

"Mimi?"

I ignored him—or tried to, focused on the coffee-making task. But with one spin, the small kitchenette shrunk by half as Ethan entered the nook. With my hands each holding an empty mug, I avoided his eye, trying to sidestep the sudden mountain of a man standing in my way.

"Mimi?" He repeated. "Hey, look at me."

I dared to obey but kept mum.

"Please tell me," His head shook as he paused; apprehension flickered across his face. "Please tell me you have something other than instant coffee."

The mood lightened, but I nudged the cups into Ethan's hands and him out of my space, hoping for a deep breath that wouldn't include his scent.

"A choosy beggar, huh?"

"Not really, no." He gave me the room I thought I wanted.

"Surely you've sampled all sorts of exotic beans around the world." I rolled my eyes, unsure if I'd confused coffee beans with something more—female.

"I've drunk a lot of coffee on my travels."

I bet he had. "Well, maybe you should scoot on back to the airport and catch a flight to one of those faraway places instead of enduring the local brew." My intended lighthearted teasing sounded like anything but.

"Why are you doing that?"

I pressed the button on the coffee grinder. The gravelly whir drowned out the end of his question. Lifting the appliance in his direction, I assured him I wouldn't serve him some freeze-dried variety.

He didn't allow a beat to pass when the little motor stopped. "Mimi. Why are you pushing me away?"

"I'm not," I scoffed at the involuntary lie.

"That's one." He raised a finger, counting my first fib that was bigger than I knew. "You are. And you do. A lot. With a joke or far-out factoid. It's a great tactic. Entertaining. So much so that I almost miss the next layer of brick you placed in the wall you've built around yourself. But why? Why now? Are you embarrassed about last night?"

"Should I be?" I thought I had a clear enough recollection, but one can never be sure.

"Aww, no. You were an adorable drunk with stellar aim, which is really the more valuable skill, but you managed both. You overachiever, you." His word choice mocked me, whether or not he knew it.

"I think you should go." The dismissal burst from my insecurity. Again, my mouth bested my brain when his joking praise missed the mark in ways I'd only just discovered. But one more line of Ethan's midwestern-aww-shucks routine and the bricks would crumble.

Then it all changed. His warm brown eyes darkened, heated by degrees. The new sharpness of his stare and the edge in his voice gripped me. Thrilled me. Frightened me.

"That's two." Calling out the second fib played more like an aside, breaking the fourth wall for those keeping a tally at home, but then he soldiered on with, "And go where, Mimi? To Costa Rica, Sumatra, Saturn? There's no amount of exotic coffee or a place on the planet—this solar system, even—that is far enough away from you. Cards on the table? No distance will stop how I feel about you. Or keep me from trying to knock down that darn barricade. And I'm pretty sure you feel it too." He stepped back when I didn't agree. "I'll grant you, I'm in unfamiliar territory here, not only because I've never faced a conflict like this with a story subject, but because I've never felt like this about anyone.

Ever. In a month and half, you have turned my world upside down."

Thank goodness for the sturdy counter that held me upright as my knees buckled. My ears roared. Blood rushed, pounding through each limb.

"I'm also a professional and more gentlemanly than I let on, so you don't have to worry. That said, you are the most head-spinning, brainy, clever, captivating, and frustratingly beautiful woman I've ever encountered, so, one nod, one *syllable* in the affirmative, and I'm tossing you over my shoulder and—"

"Ethan, stop."

"Chastain and journalistic integrity be damned."

I'm sure I gasped, not that any air could move in the taut scene. And while his boldness provoked my initial reaction, the reminder of our situation kept me rigid, paralyzed by the reality that we were more at odds today than this time yesterday, occupationally speaking. Before I knew I'd benefitted from the very corruption *The Public Eye* tasked him to expose. Before I knew every compliment he'd laid at my feet, who and what he thought I was all spewed from a tainted well, a false narrative claiming me worthy when the newly discovered truth said Ethan Ledes had it all wrong. Again.

Silence dragged. With both fibs burned for the day, I only had honesty to offer, and telling Ethan the truth, the whole truth, when I hadn't processed it myself, proved to be more than I could face. I'd be holding *my* cards close for now.

For the first time, his gaze dropped. His tone changed again, softened. And I feared I'd made him self-conscious by denying him even the slightest sign the feelings were mutual.

"I know the truth is a big deal for you, Mimi, so I'll never give you anything but, and that confession should prove it. So, while you're grappling with some lie you've evidently told me, I can tell you two things. I'll find out eventually, so you might as well fess up, and I swear on my mother, I don't give a damn. Whatever it is won't change how I feel about you, how I see you. And whenever you get your head around that, come find me, own up to it, and then maybe you'll let me help you figure out a solution." He walked to the armchair, his bed for the night, and swung his travel bag over his shoulder. "Keep your coffee. You know where I'll be."

The front door squawked its disapproval when Ethan's firm yank opened it, followed by a hollow clunk as he slammed it closed.

I barely managed one breath before my phone rang. My grunted answer didn't qualify as speech. The next wave in the tsunami currently wreaking havoc on my life suddenly crested.

Instinct, nothing more, had me running for the door. Adrenaline opened it with little effort. At the same time, the stress hormone spike squeezed my throat, so my shout, "*Ethan!*" sounded as strangled and desperate as it felt.

Ethan had traveled the fifty yards to the street, but he stopped at the second frantic cry of his name. "Ethan!" I held up the phone as his wide eyes met mine. "Something's happened to Mama!"

He tore back up the walkway, catching me before the tidal surge dragged me under.

Twenty-One

GROWING UP, IT HAD only been Mama and me. I can't speak for her, but in my case, I chose solitude. From a young age, I opted to fall into books rather than friendships. Besides, they didn't allow talking in the library. Maybe I fooled myself with my non-fiction picks. I didn't delve into fantasy or try to get lost in make-believe. No, I absorbed facts and figures, real knowledge, and that made the choice a wise, worthwhile one.

By high school, everyone was wise. Wise to my situation, anyway. At least that's how the narrative ran in my head. Each student knew where they belonged and who didn't belong at all. What John Hughes's canon explained, the wizarding world's magical sorting hat perpetuated. Heck, I'll even throw Jane Austen and her have-and-have-not stories under the bus. Yes, I've read my share of fiction too.

But somehow, I'd missed the classification before high school, only to find myself on the outskirts of teen society. Of course, those fringes were a category on their own. Still, I had work to do, and no after-school club or Homecoming dance ranked higher than an acceptance letter from Chastain University. Not for me. I had zero regrets.

College proved to be a whole new world. A time for reinvention, a place to be reborn. It didn't take long for me to realize I missed some lessons in people skills, but then I got lucky—and I never get lucky. Someone mistook me for an old friend's babysitter's cousin's bunkmate at some unknown international equestrian camp, and in a blink, I had a group of friends. Smart, wealthy, world-wise friends. My first ever. Of course, we know how that cataclysm ended.

The incident grew legs, not unlike the earlier misunderstanding with the horses, but I ignored it. Instead, I returned to my old spot on the periphery with my head in books. That discipline would provide the escape to my next life chapter, but also doomed me to the old days of loneliness with my critical mother as my only companion. That, and my new steadfast truth rule.

Now, I sat in an uncomfortable waiting-room chair, bombarded with overhead squawks of urgent-sounding messages in number and color codes I didn't understand, doubting that, despite everything, I could face a world without my mother in it. Afraid what true solitude would mean, even though the outcome would be of my own making.

"Drink this." Ethan swirled a paper cup under my chin.

The steamy heat and acrid aroma of subpar coffee replaced the smell of sick and antiseptic taking up residence in my nose. None of it appealed to me, and I mumbled an *uh-uh* like a cranky toddler.

He wedged the cup into my hand and urged it to my mouth. I drank and gave an equally immature face of disgust—almost in jest.

"Thank you. Thank you for coffee and for—"

"No need. Glad I was there. Glad you let me be—"

I squeezed his hand, filling in the blanks with my touch instead of words. Another encrypted wail, sounding like God herself, hit the airwaves, and I pulled from Ethan's grip and leaped to my feet.

"Seriously. What is taking so long?" I stomped toward the closed double-wide doors emblazoned with NO ADMITTANCE in bold, red letters. Another sip of the bitter brew sent a spastic flinch down my body as I spun toward the administration desk to demand answers they likely didn't have.

Ethan swooped in between a hapless hospital employee and me, snatching the coffee while redirecting me from my ill-advised confrontation.

"On second thought, I'll take that. Who knew a little caffeine would wake such a monster?" The cup landed hard in a nearby trash can. "Let's go for a walk." His hand at the small of my back guided me toward a Seussical-like botanical art installation. That hand remained, and I stopped short, twisting to see his face. The physics of it all put us too close, but neither gave an inch.

"Did you just call me a monster?"

His chuckle delivered his warm, exasperated breath to my temple. "You know, I've said many things about you today. Too many, probably, but it totally tracks *that's* the one bit you heard."

"I—I heard them. I did. All of them," I stammered, wanting to allay any regrets he had about what he said.

He tucked some errant wisps of hair behind my ear. I closed my eyes and tilted into the tickling caress.

"I heard you," I repeated, "but right now—"

"Of course. There's a bigger story here. I get it."

"*Not* bigger, maybe more—*pressing* at the moment, and there is more I need to tell—"

My name boomed above us. *"Amelia Kanaan, please report to the second-floor admin desk. Amelia Kanaan to the second-floor admin desk."*

I gasped at the thundering summons, tripping over my feet as I bolted toward the staff seated behind a glass partition. Reaching back, I found Ethan's hand, or he found mine. Either way, I knew I wasn't alone.

"Can I prove it? I don't carry around a birth certificate, but have you met the woman? She looks like me, or I look like her, except older, or—younger."

"Yes, ma'am. All I can tell you—"

"Ma'am?" I jabbed Ethan with my elbow, a reflex brought on by his snicker.

"Yes. Because you have different last names according to your driver's licenses."

"Well, thanks to the patriarchy, my birth certificate also shows a different last name than hers, so I'm not sure what good that—"

"Hi, Birdie Lou." Ethan gestured to the woman's name tag through the glass wall separating the lucky patient relations specialist and my ratcheting anger. "Please excuse Amelia here. It's been a long day, and now that we know her mom is apparently going to be all right, that earlier stress is looking for a place to spew. I'm sure you see this all the time. Can I assume if Amelia brings around some insurance paperwork, medical power of attorney, that sort of thing, we can get all this squared away tomorrow? Since they're keeping her mother overnight, anyway." His calm demeanor and friendly bordering-on-flirty tone were just what Birdie Lou ordered—if patient relations specialists could order such things.

"Darlin', *you* bring me anything even close, and I'll make it work." Birdie Lou smiled for the first time, and Ethan rewarded her with one of his own.

"There you go. Birdie Lou will see that everything's right tomorrow." Like a member of the diplomatic core, he nodded to her while raising his brows at me. My cue to speak up again.

"Uh, thank you, Birdie Lou. I'll be back tomorrow with the necessary documents."

"*We'll* be back tomorrow," Ethan added with a wink.

"I look forward to it." Her lipsticked grin spread wider, but she only had eyes for the sweet talker standing beside me. "Next."

Ethan guided me away, smirking at the hard side-eye I gave him.

"Don't get all bothered because some people find me charming. I am honey to flies, Mimi. Honey to flies."

"Ever been to a North Georgia pig farm? I'll tell you what flies like."

He placed his arm around my shoulders. "There she is. The wisecracking smart aleck I adore. Glad to have you back."

I allowed the one-armed hug to continue and tried to ignore the word "adore."

"Thank you for stepping in. I'm usually better than that. With people, I mean. Then again, I've never known my mother to panic about anything, and here she is, in a hospital, because of a severe panic attack. At least that's what they're saying. So, I appreciate you helping back there."

"Well, someone needed to stand up for the patriarchy." His joke came with a gentle squeeze before he released his reassuring hold. "All bets are off when it comes to family. Don't give it a second thought. Speaking of family, *do* you have the necessary documents?"

"Yes. I mean, they exist. The papers. Putting my hands on them? That, I'm not sure about. Next stop for me is Mama's house. So, I'll let you be on your way. I know you must have Midtown Mews super duties to attend to." I didn't dare mention *The Public Eye* work.

"Don't tell anyone, but all my employers think I'm out of town until Sunday. I came back early, remember? I can spare some time."

"You certainly don't need to babysit me. I'm a big girl."

"You know who is awesome at scouring old files and overstuffed desk drawers and shoeboxes in search of usable intel? This guy."

"Really? Because I'm particularly adept at ordering takeout food."

"Winning combo."

Twenty-Two

ESTABLISHED POST-CIVIL WAR, BLOSSOMY Bough, Georgia boasted a train depot that connected Atlanta to Charlotte, North Carolina. That rail station still stood, providing a quick stretch-your-legs visitor spot with a small museum and a caboose exhibit. Suburban sprawl stretched its limbs to the exurbs with discount stores, strip malls, and more traffic than the old country roads could manage, and the small town didn't always live up to its flowery name. But when I graduated from college, it offered a far more affordable life than living in the city.

Now, given a push for a more quintessential hometown feel for folks with families, the tiny, old, dilapidated town center evolved into a cozy downtown, including a tea and scone cafe, a knitting shop, and remarkable farm-to-table dining. Everything old was new again on those two blocks, with a promising future of further rehabilitation.

Lately, many moving to town had knocked down the sturdy, minimal, mid-century homes to build bigger and, some thought, better residences. Improvements like those hadn't reached Mama's side of the tracks, but the writing was on the wall. Bermuda grass lay dormant, and Mama's flower boxes hung empty given the cold. I couldn't help but wonder what the world traveler thought of this drab scene as he followed me up the cracked concrete walkway.

"Festive," Ethan remarked, gesturing to the holiday wreath with faux berries and an oversized red bow.

Most years, Mama and I decorated together after our canned food feast, but yesterday, I bolted before we got to "haul out the holly." Guilt churned again, and with an empty stomach recently abused by fancy whiskey, it made for a precarious combo. I should have been there when Mama had her panic episode. And who knew? My hasty exit probably contributed to it.

I knocked.

"Are you expecting someone to be here? The landlord?"

"Ha. No, habit, I guess. I always knock. It's not my house." I shrugged. "And the landlord is here." I put out my hand to shake in an introduction. "Nice to meet you. I'm the landlord."

"So, it is your house?"

"Well, I guess technically—"

"No, not technically. You bought your mom a house?"

"I did. I owed her." Given what I'd learned the day before, my gratitude now had a conflicted feeling, and I needed to come clean sooner than later about that to the handsome man leaning on the wrought-iron railing, who only saw the festive and not so much the forlorn. With a jagged breath, I unlocked and pushed through the door.

The clean, herby scent of Meyer lemon wafted in the warm air. The mix of the two would tell me where I stood even if I wore a blindfold. Absolute Mama. The Swedes' minimalist sensibilities also fit my mom to a tee. She abhorred clutter. Dust magnets, she called it, and if one thing riled her more than clutter, it was dust. Besides, things cost money, and until the last decade, money had been in short supply. One more reminder of the new albatross choking me. I paused, feeling the weight of it.

"You ok?" Ethan's hand squeezed my shoulder in support, I'm sure, but I flinched from him to keep from burying my face in his chest.

"Yes, hungry, I suppose." *Life rule: When in doubt, blame a dip in blood sugar.*

"Then let's eat before we get to work."

"I owe you dinner. No doubt about that, but the rest is on me. Mama is beyond tidy, as you can see, so how hard could it be to find insurance paperwork and legal documents? You don't have to stay to help."

Removing his coat, he shook his head. "You're doing that thing again. The pushing me away thing. I'm here to help. Let me. If my nose in your family's affairs bothers you, put me on dinner detail. I'll stay out of your way. I'd hope by now this goes without saying, but we're off the record here. Now. Always."

"It's not that. You've caught me at an awful moment, a lousy day."

"Yeah, I gathered the solo whiskey binge wasn't about holiday cheer."

"Please don't say the W word. I don't want to think of it, much less let it pass my lips ever again. Coming or going." Something swirled in my stomach, enough to have me press a palm to my middle. I blamed Ethan's lingering stare at the lips I'd just mentioned, not the booze. Like my feet sunk in wet cement, I spun toward my mother's kitchen. Slow-motion until I escaped the pull of his eyes. I plucked takeout menus from a drawer and hurried back to the man.

"If you're having second thoughts...?" I focused on the carpet in case he decided he should leave.

"Aww, no." He waved off the awkward moment. "We're grown-ups. Right?"

"Right. I mean, one of us is practically middle-aged."

"Ah. And one of us acts like she is, which makes us quite the pair, don't you think?"

I saw the potential, but knew our circumstances called for keeping level heads and our hands to ourselves. No sooner had those simple but well-thought-out rules crossed my mind than I broke one, pressing the handful of takeout menus to his firm chest. He covered my hand with his.

"What do you want? To eat, I mean. For dinner. What do you want to eat for dinner?" If he'd said me, I'd have climbed him like a tree. If he'd said me, my fingers would be laced in his curls, and I would have done anything he asked. If he'd said me... "These places all deliver. You pick. Then take a load off. You must be tired." My fingers slid from under his after I contemplated their warmth a beat too long, then hurried to the safety of a spare bedroom that stored Mama's sewing, out-of-season clothing, and a file cabinet I hoped contained the important papers.

"Any luck?" Ethan leaned in the doorway, rumpled with drowsy eyes. Beautiful.

I found the first drawer locked without a key in sight, but I combed through the second without success.

"Not yet. Nora has spoiled me. Not only does she file everything for me, but most everything is digital, and if I need anything, a file appears on my desk before I even know to ask for it. I like hard copies. The feel of paper in my hands." I kept digging in drawer number three.

"You must be in heaven elbow deep in reams of the stuff." He smirked, raising a brow at the overstuffed file cabinet.

"If only I could crack Mama's sorting system." Her organization was as much an enigma as the woman herself. "I swear, if she kept a folder for bananas, she'd file it under Y for 'Yellow *comma* fruits that are.' I will not be deterred. I'll figure out the method to her madness, but I've yet to decipher it."

"Take a break. Food's here. You'll think better on a full stomach."

Walking into the living room, the pungent aroma of Indian food wafted. My mouth watered at the same time I imagined Mama's reaction to the overwhelming odor later. Oh well. I'd face that fight tomorrow.

"Uh-oh. Your face says I ordered the wrong thing." Ethan sat on the floor at the coffee table he arranged with plates and spoons. "You told me to pick."

"No, I love Indian. Mama won't love the lingering scent, but I'm too hungry to think about that now."

"Phew. I saw the menu and got a hankering. I spent close to a year in New Delhi not too long ago. An extraordinary culture."

"I read *The Private Eye* series on commercial surrogacy in India. That you?" I sat while he spooned up a plate and gave me a piece of garlicky naan as big as my head to serve as my utensil.

"We're a team. We each take a facet of the subject to investigate and write." Ethan showed a rare moment of modesty, as attractive as his bravado.

"You drove a lot of change with that work. An industry built on the wombs of voiceless young women is abuse."

"The change is slow, but it also harmed the livelihoods of poor families and broke the hearts of loving couples with fertility issues desperate for children. Like most issues, not everything is clear cut, black or white. Those are the harder topics. It's easier when right or wrong is more obvious. I can only hope I helped more than I hurt."

"Of course. You know you have, right? That you've been a force of good. You don't doubt that, do you?"

"I'm doubting *this* story."

"Don't," I replied faster than I intended.

"Easy to say if we held the bad seeds accountable. I'm finding more and more that isn't the case."

"Some will. Some already paid in similar instances. A celebrity perp walk is some comeuppance. Jail time is real punishment."

"I'd bet if those *perps* hadn't been famous, it might have gone away in those early cases. It wouldn't have made as big a splash as it did. That's why *The Public Eye* took it on. To see how widespread the practices go."

"People need to be held accountable." I pushed my plate away, my appetite ruined. "Some things are a moral right. And access to better education merely because someone found the wherewithal to buy a seat at that table is wrong."

Ethan tossed the wad of paper towels he used as a napkin. "Don't take this the wrong way—"

"The phrase everyone likes to hear before they're about to be insulted," I chuckled with zero humor. "Please, continue." I sat back, cross-legged, resting on my palms.

"Your naivete is a bit frustrating, Mimi. It's like you don't even see the semi-truck barreling straight for you at a hundred miles an hour. Except I can't believe you don't know what's coming. You're too smart not to."

Ethan was right. I knew what headed my way, and even before my mother blurted her confession I'd had concerns about getting tagged with blame, but now it all seemed right. Meant to be. I, too, would face my comeuppance. I deserved it.

"Please. Don't lose any sleep over it."

"How can you say that? Who the hell do you think will get pinned with this mess? The dean that has been at Chastain for decades? The president who allowed that dean to slink off to the coast and a quiet retirement? No, it'll be the underling. A university's version of middle management they can hold up for the cameras and make an example. Regardless of the truth, a public firing can ruin a career. You get that, don't you?" Ethan scrambled to his feet like all the pieces of a puzzle fell into place, and he needed a new vantage point to see the big picture.

"Only now Chastain has gotten ahead on this one. They will elevate you to the role of dean on Monday, but only long enough to get toppled when *The Public Eye* runs the story sometime next year. You'll be the face of it, and all that's because I couldn't keep my mouth shut in some—I don't know—chivalrous attempt to spare you. My rule-breaking, going to Cromwell, has given them enough time to put the target on your back."

I stretched my legs and sighed, "Actions have consequences."

"Come on, Mimi. You can't be trite about this. My actions, Cromwell's, Rayburn's—*our* actions will land the consequences on *your* doorstep. True or not, the university will make a big show of lopping off the head of the diseased snake, and that'll be you."

"Don't take this the wrong way, Mr. Pulitzer," I mocked. "But maybe you're the naïve one."

His fidgeting stopped, stunned into a motionless calm when the scenario coming into focus surprised him. "Why are you covering for them?" The first hint of anger came as a glare.

"I'm not. I have no idea what they've done. Or even who 'they' are, but what goes around comes around."

"You *are*, Amelia. You're willing to take the fall for this, but you've done nothing wrong. Believe me, I've looked."

That admission spurred anger in me, too, and brought me to standing. Sure, the investigative reporter needed to investigate me, but I didn't want to hear about it. More importantly, I needed to end this squabble before it escalated into a full-fledged fight. "Ethan. You've barely slept, and you're wearing the same clothes you flew in yesterday. Go home. Back to the Mews. Rest. Shower."

His shoulders slumped as his chin hit his chest. "Tired? You bet I am. You are a whole new level of exhausting, Meems." The sweet nickname had lost its allure, and a pit of sadness burrowed in me.

"Would it help if I said I deserve whatever is coming?" Our eyes locked.

"If you did, it would make for lie number three for the day, so—" He took two long strides toward me, still holding my gaze.

"It wouldn't be, though."

"I don't believe you." We stood toe-to-toe. His squint begged me to cave, to tell him he was right, that I broke my two fib rule, and somehow we'd find a solution.

"I guess that's why I like you so much. Because you think so highly of me." I sucked in a mini gasp when he grabbed me by the shoulders. But just as abruptly, he released me and spun, looking for something. "What are you doing?"

"The right thing. I'm going back to the Mews to shower, sleep, and then I'm going to fix this because—I—I want you, for a hundred different reasons, I want you in my life, but somehow, you think you're *un*-want-able. You deserve nothing but good things, and I'll be damned if I'm responsible for keeping you from getting them."

I snorted; the mix of exhaustion and shock of his words made me giddy. "Way to manage my expectations."

He rewarded me with a reluctant grin but followed it with skewering accusation. "You say you prefer facts over fiction. Honesty above all else, and yet, here I am, telling you the truth and all you do is doubt. Not only that, but you aren't being honest with me. Or yourself. Why?"

"I'm honest with myself," I whispered. But the truth said out loud would change how he saw me and losing his admiration would crush me. It was like college all over again. My first friendships were based on lies. I knew what would happen when—if—*when* Ethan learned the truth. Of course, I recognized, either way I'd lose. Until I knew more—until Mama explained what she did—I'd keep the secret. *Her* secret. See? It wasn't even my tale to tell. Regardless, I'd protect her. I owed her that much.

"Give me some time, Ethan. I need a little time."

He nodded, rubbing the two-day-old scruff on his chin. "Don't suppose I have any choice."

"Don't you? You could walk away."

"From you—or the story?" He raised his hands, waving off any reply. "Doesn't matter. I won't do either. Someone let you down, broke you a bit. Maybe a lot. I'm not saying I can fix it, and God knows you'd never ask me to, but I'm not about to pile on by walking away. I'll give you time. I don't like it, and I don't want to, but the call is yours." Ethan left, thumbing a ride on his phone as he walked out the door.

Pushing aside the lasting image of his fraught face and darkly circled eyes, I searched for the paperwork that would satisfy Miss Birdie Lou in the morning.

Twenty-Three

ANXIOUS, I CHECKED AND double-checked Mama's house before taking off to see her at the local hospital. I bumped up the heat to sauna-like and slammed closed all the windows I'd opened, hoping the telltale smell of curry had mellowed when mixed with the fresh, frosty late November air.

With paperwork in one hand and a spare ring of keys I'd snagged from the garage in the other, I stared down the next challenge of the day. My mother's car. I could drive, but I didn't do it often. I took solace that lighter traffic north in the backwoods made it easier than city driving.

I squeezed into the driver's seat, my chest inches from the steering wheel. A brief thought of changing the position of Mama's setting crossed my mind, but I knew better. "Driving Gods, don't fail me now," I begged, trying to find reverse with the stick shift. I'm not sure what scared me more: the lurching vehicle, the grinding gears, or the jarring *thunk* when the compact car stalled.

I should have guessed, given the late hour the day before, that Birdie Lou wouldn't be at the administration desk when I returned the following morning.

"Hello. Good morning," I greeted the shift's gatekeeper, determined to be kind and patient. "I've brought all the documents I could find to prove I am who I say I am and that my mother is who she says she is and that we are—well, we come as a pair, so I can take her home today if that's what the doctors say can happen." I took a deep breath while I doled out my evidence: my driver's license, Mama's insurance card, the Power of Medical attorney, a mortgage statement that bore Mama's residential address, but my name as the borrower, my birth certificate, and my valid but never used passport, just for good measure.

"I'm sorry, Miss Kanaan. I'm not sure why you put yourself through all this trouble. You and your mother are in our network system. We're aware who you are, who to bill, and Mrs. Andersson was merely kept for observation because she said she lives alone. She's a sweetheart." Charlotte, today's Birdie Lou, offered a sympathetic smile as she stacked one hard-sought item on top of another and slid the pile toward me.

"*Ms.* Andersson? Livia Andersson? A sweetheart? I don't understand. Yesterday, Birdie Lou said it'd be best if I went home—or to Mama's home to collect—" I quit mid-sentence, my steadied brain clearer than the panicked version spinning out-of-control yesterday. I forced a smile and asked for my sweetheart mother's room number.

"There you are. Of all mornings to sleep in, Amelia, you pick the day I'm getting discharged from the hospital? And what are you wearing? Did you sleep in those clothes?" Mama sat in a chair, dressed and holding a plastic bag in her lap. The snippy criticism played like music to my ears. Mama was okay.

"Mama? Did you tell the staff *not* to let me see you yesterday, and then send me on a wild goose chase looking for unnecessary documents?"

"I knew that Birdie Lou was good people. Hand me my pocketbook off the shelf there."

"Mama. I spent all last night hunting through your ridiculous filing system for—for what? Why?"

"You're always calmer with a task, Mimi. I know you. Without a distraction, you'd have paced the halls and harassed the nurses and doctors. Who knows who else? This way, you got to solve a problem, and the rest of us got some peace. Well, as much peace as one can expect in a hospital." Unperturbed, she fumbled around in her oversized purse, finally locating her Tic-Tacs. "Want one? You look like you could use it."

"An imaginary problem. What good is an imaginary problem?" I tugged the sheet and blanket tight to the hospital bed's top edge, smoothing, then turning down the two layers and fluffing the unfluffable hospital-grade pillow.

"If this little back and forth is any indicator, it did a whole lot of good. Now let's get outta here. Too many sick people."

"Are you all right? I mean, the doctors say you can go home? No follow-up? Nothing?"

"I've got everything in hand. There is nothing wrong with me. I got a little worked up, felt some heartburn. I blame your friend's corn casserole."

The mention of Ethan stopped my tidying routine, but I kept quiet.

"I heard he was here with you. Yesterday. Birdie says he's quite the looker."

"I love that you've made a new friend, Mama, but gossiping about *my* new friend isn't the best use of time. Besides, he's more than good-looking. He happens to be pretty brilliant and noble and affects actual change in the world. Plus, he's funny. A dry wit—the best kind—and he cared to wait with me and help solve imaginary problems for my ailing mother."

Mama's raised brow and smirky mouth let me know I should keep my thoughts on Ethan's scent to myself. I'd over shared plenty.

"Toot toot. All aboard." A twenty-something aide in red scrubs rolled in a wheelchair. The crimson uniform made me afraid for his survival. Like a fabled Star Trek security officer, his perky attitude would have the monstrous Livia Andersson strike him down where he stood. "You ready to blow this joint, Mrs. Andersson? Your chariot awaits."

Mrs. Andersson? Mama despised anyone mistaking her for a *Mrs.*. I cringed for the unsuspecting Redshirt, hoping it would be a quick death at least.

"Now, Ricky. I told you to call me Livia. I also said I don't need the wheelchair." My mother couldn't have sounded kinder.

"Rules is rules, ma'am. I don't make 'em, but you gotta follow 'em. Besides, don't you want a few more minutes of alone time with me?"

Mama laughed, then cooed, "Oh. See, Ricky isn't just a pretty face either, Amelia. He's a big flirt, too." She settled herself in the chair while Ricky secured her feet on the footrests.

"Only with you, Miss Livia. Only with you." Ricky winked and crossed his heart.

"Careful now, Ricky, or I'll find a reason to stick around this place."

The twosome headed out of the room toward the elevator, keeping up their banter while I followed, wondering if Mama had hit her head or suffered a mini stroke. Maybe a sweet-talking alien body-snatched her.

No sooner had Ricky closed the car door on my mother than she returned to her usual grouch mode.

"Did I tell you about the hospital's excuse for chicken fried steak?"

"Why is a hospital serving fried anything to patients—or visitors, for that matter?"

"I don't know, Mimi. I don't set the menu." Her diatribe about the failures of medical center cuisine rambled on until the last two blocks before we reached her home.

"Mama. I don't want to get you upset again, but we need to talk about it."

"About what?"

"About what you did before I got accepted at Chastain."

"Ancient history, Amelia," she sighed. "Don't make up your own imaginary problem now."

"It's not so much that you did it; it's why you—There's a man standing on your stoop."

Mama dove into her purse again, scrounging for another Tic-Tac and avoiding my eyes. "What?" she asked.

"There is a man on your doorstep. Oh, look. He has flowers." I turned off the ignition, and Mama bolted from the car, leaving me to scramble out of the tight driver's seat set for her driving habits.

The elderly gentleman smiled, waving a fedora he'd removed in the sweetest act of senior citizen gallantry I'd seen outside a Nancy Meyers movie. Mama marched up the driveway and across the dormant lawn like Patton taking Palermo, but the old man's expression never wavered. He presented the flowers still in the grocery store cellophane with such flourish I couldn't help but giggle while my surly mother stood, hands to her hips, looking up at the cardigan-clad suitor. I hurried to not miss one word of the confrontation.

"Now, Miss Livie, don't give me your sour face. I know you told me not to come, but I was worried about you, so here I am.

And I brought you flowers. The white alstroemerias you like so much. You know, with a touch of yellow in the center."

"I know what flowers I like, Winston." She snatched the bouquet from his grip. "And sure, you listen about that, but not when I tell you to stay put until I called you."

My brain met a new whirlwind. A whirlwind that included a kind gentleman bringing my mother her favorite flowers and calling her Miss Livie. No one familiar enough to use her first name called her anything but Livia, except for the one day a longtime bagger at the corner grocery store called her Liv. I always wondered what happened to him. Poof. Disappeared, never to bag a single piece of produce again. Coincidence?

"Hi, I'm Mimi. *Miss Livie's* daughter." I grinned at my mother's scowl and shook the man's hand.

"Miss Mimi. Winston Bonmanos. You *do* exist. The way your mother goes on and on about you, I couldn't be sure you were the real thing. So nice to meet you, finally."

"Likewise. Although I like to think my mother's grumblings about me are—"

"Oh no. She sings your praises—"

"What are you doing here, Winston?" Mama interrupted.

Mama singing my praises? Maybe the alien possession took place long before today. I had noticed her mood improved these last weeks.

"Invite the man inside, Mama. It's cold out here, and he's only wearing a sweater."

"Ah, I'm from Buffalo. Ran my own business almost forty years, much of it outdoors." Winston re-donned his hat, and I couldn't help but notice his large, calloused hands before he slid them into his pants pockets. Hands that suggested long days of work with rough materials, in cold weather. "This is a spring day up on Lake Erie."

"And I'll be deciding who I let into my house and when, Mimi. Thank you very much."

"Whose house?" I mumbled. Ethan had a point. I'd never considered the house mine before he mentioned it.

"Let's not stand around making a scene on the front lawn for everyone to notice," she groused, pushing past the adorably smitten Winston to unlock the door.

"Have a seat, Winston. I'll go put these in some water."

"I'll help," I yelped, scurrying behind her. "Who's your boyfriend, Mama?" I whispered as low as my excitement allowed.

"He's not a boy, Amelia. Have some respect."

"Okay. Who's your *man* friend, Mama?"

"Now you make it sound creepy."

"I don't think it's creepy. I think it's nice."

"For goodness' sake, he moved here from Buffalo a few months back. Lives two doors down. The Browns' old place. Turns out they'd leased that property from Winston. Made it easy to go when it came time for assisted living. He bought it fifteen years ago as his daughter's starter home, but she married and moved out soon after. They'd turned it into a rental."

"Still no one next door, huh? That place has been vacant. What? A year now?"

"Closer to two, I'd say," she replied, snipping the ends off stems and placing them in one of her canning Mason jars.

"And Winston owns the Brown's house?"

"That's what I said, so you can see I'm not alone." She lifted the fresh floral arrangement. "Someone's nearby if I need something, so you can go back to your city life. I'll be fine."

"Jeez, no need to be so pushy. I can see I'm not needed here. But maybe be a little nicer to the man. Don't be so bossy."

"Oh, he likes it. Besides, he takes his bossy turn, believe me." The corner of her mouth quirked, and I'd swear I caught a twinkle in her eye.

Before I could do the math, I asked, "What's that mean?"

"Birds and bees do it, Amelia. I at least taught you that much."

"Mama!" I may have sucked all the air out of the room.

"I'm sixty, not dead." She carried the vase to the living room like she hadn't just blown my mind. "I'm glad you two got to meet, but unfortunately, Amelia has somewhere to be. Pressing work duties or some such."

"That's a shame. I hope maybe we can do dinner sometime. I'm sure Miss Livie told you I cook for her more than a couple of times a week these days."

"A c-couple of times a week?" I wasn't thinking about his cooking.

"The one thing that brings me pleasure these days." His grin glowed, both endearing and rakish at once, somehow.

"I bet."

Mama shot me a glare, and I bit my lip, realizing I said those two words aloud.

"Nice to meet you—Winston. I look forward to getting to know more about you." I omitted the fact I'd known nothing of him until ten minutes ago. "Talk Monday, Mama?"

"Don't we always?"

My telepathic stare said, yes, and isn't it strange how Winston never got a mention during any of our regular Monday chats? Mama encouraged me toward the door, evidently eager to end the introduction.

"Good to meet you, Mimi," Winston said, stepping away to give mother and daughter some privacy in the small living room.

"We have things to discuss, Mama."

"If you mean him, that'd be a big ol' no thanks."

"Not him. Your health. Your panic attack. Your dubious chickens coming home to roost with my employer. My job. But yes, also—*him*." My phone signaled.

"Monday then, sweetheart," she cooed with all the syrupiness of Miss Livie and not an ounce of my typically cheerless mother. As far as Mama was concerned, I was already gone.

Through the closing door I heard, "Winston? Did you eat curry last night?"

Twenty-Four

I CLUNG TO THE blankets left strewn about my sofa—where I'd slept two nights ago, before fleeing to the hospital. Burying my face, I hoped for any lingering scent of Ethan, but came up empty. An exasperated sigh exhaled from me when a text alert interrupted the storm of emotions swirling through my head, heart, and gut. Too much new information, too many new people, and I doubted I took much of it in stride.

> **Geneva:** Last-minute invite to some place fabulous. Too fabulous to share where and too fabulous to turn down.

> **Mimi:** Max needs me? I'm assuming this isn't an invitation.

> **Geneva:** You make me laugh. Available? Of course, you are. You're always available. Pack a bag, be here in an hour.

> **Mimi:** I'll be there.

To be honest, Geneva's gallivanting came right on time. I wanted a change of scenery and the unconditional love of a curly-furred dog. Okay, love was more than Max would offer, but he'd allow me to heap affection on him until he'd had enough.

"Oh, dear, you look a mess." Geneva gaped in her version of casual travel wear. She loved her Lululemon, and it hinted her travel might be long and definitely private; otherwise, it would call for something more formal.

"Why, thank you, Geneva. This week has been a month. I could use a nap."

"Maybe a shower first. Better yet, a soak. Enjoy the tub. Enjoy the fridge. Enjoy everything life throws at you." She took me in a bear hug, holding tighter and longer than anytime I could remember. "And drink the coffee. The can on the top left shelf. Au revoir, my *petit fromage*. Be good to yourself."

"Your little—cheese?"

"Yes, my sweet. You carry the stink of fetid Limburger, but not in the good way. Love always, Max. Promise. *Mwah*." She sailed out the door without a look back.

"Stinky cheese?" I sniff my armpit, catching Max's patient eye at my side. "Do I smell like cheese to you?"

He nudged my thigh, then sneezed an affirmative before he walked away.

"Wow, bath time it is."

An hour later, fresh as the daisy print on my camisole and matching shortie bottoms, I snuggled down on one end of the sofa. Max sat in rapt attention on his end, watching a real estate show as a pair of professional birdwatchers decided between a three-million-dollar fixer-upper or a three-and-a-half-million-dollar move-in-ready to buy on the

Gulf Coast. Married thirty years, the duo always wanted a waterfront vacation spot.

"I don't know about you, Max, but I'm in the wrong line of work."

He nestled in the crook of my legs, resting his head on my bare thigh, and closed his eyes. He liked to lead by example.

"Yeah, yeah," I yawned. "Less yapping, more napping." Sliding a Kantha quilt around my shoulders, I fell asleep before Max's first inevitable snore.

He moved first, lifted his head from my leg, and let out a muffled *ruff* that made his collar jangle.

"Not yet, Max," I groaned, only half conscious. "A few more—hours. Please?" Rolling to my back, I freed him from my legs and drifted off to sleep again. This nap proved less restful. Pictures flashed. Black and white. Not the sort of dream that played out like a story, but a frenzied slideshow of spinning old-timey newspaper headlines detailing the Chastain admissions scandal, my fraudulent acceptance, and Mama's sex life. I shot up with a gasp that strained my throat and pressed my eyes to rid them of the frightening images and sleepiness.

When I focused on reality, the day had faded to dusk. I'd slept for hours. And Max had left me to it. His absence brought the first pang of concern. Max would never leave his post. Sticking close to his caretaker had always been the Portie's M.O..

Bath time, mealtime, and sleep time. Max played the vigilant sentinel.

"Max?" I called. "Hey, buddy, where are you?" Panic swirled. Where would he go? I recalled a time when Geneva joked that if she ever found herself in the bathroom free to do her business alone (her words), she would know Max was dead. Nothing else would keep him from accompanying her, even on her most personal tasks. He was almost as attentive to me.

I crept from room to room, terrified I'd find a motionless Max or not find him at all. I didn't know which would be worse. The latter came true. I scrambled to the guest room—my usual sleeping quarters when I stayed overnight. I ransacked my weekender, searching for the sneakers in the bottom. My heels crushed the backs of the black and white Chucks, and I hopped down the hall, attempting to finger the canvas onto each foot, trying not to fall over in the graceless rush to the front door to go hunt for the dog. I groped for the drawer handle of the vintage bombe chest that housed Max's leash and treats. No leash.

Another whirl of dread caught my breath. Did I sleep-walk the dog and abandon him somewhere along the route? I looked at the daisy pattern on my camisole and skimpy, matching sleep shorts. Was that even possible? I darted back to the sofa to find my phone, pleading with the universe for some answers in a message, text, voicemail, anything. Nothing. With one more digit to go in my 9-1-1 call, the soft rattle of keys and creak of the door opening stopped me. In toddled Max with a skulking, head-down, hooded man in tow. I saw the dukes-up leprechaun before the wearer's face, and my mix of relief and fury spewed.

"You stole my dog?" I barked. "Come here, Max." How I would have appreciated a joyful scamper to my side, but in Max's Eeyore-fashion, he looked up at Ethan for a beat, then lumbered to me, no doubt expecting his customary biscuit. Ethan reached for the second drawer of the chest where a crystal bowl of dog treats lived for that sort of occasion. "Don't even think about it, Ted Baxter. Here you go, Maxi." I offered not one but two bone-shaped cookies I'd pocketed before making the call for reinforcements. Geneva had them baked especially for him at *The Pooch Patisserie*, and I hoped they would ensure Max remembered where his allegiance lay.

"Aww, come on now. First of all, you startled me. Second, I didn't steal Max, and third, he's not your dog. And Ted Baxter? That one really hurts, Meems." Ethan sounded off his list as he tucked away the Gucci leash.

I stood while Max crunched his second treat. "How'd you get in here? And why?"

"I'm the super. I have all the keys, and when Geneva caught me back in town, she asked me to check in on Max. Take him for walks. Keep him fed."

"Why do you think I'm here?" My worry and wrath morphed into righteous indignation.

Ethan walked past me, carrying a reusable grocery tote. "I figured you were on some kind of couch tour. Seeing how many sofas you could sleep on this holiday weekend. By my count, this makes three. And Max and I didn't want to wake the sleeping beauty."

Damn the charmer's wit and flattery. I swallowed my laugh and caravanned with Max in the rear, following Ethan to the kitchen. "Sorry."

"What for?"

"For startling you. For hurling accusations of theft. But mostly for the Ted Baxter crack. That was over the line."

"Wanna make it up to me?" He kept busy, unloading the groceries on the island in Geneva's enviable kitchen.

Boy, did I. Max settled on his kitchen bed, one of many custom designed with each room of the apartment in mind. Tuckered out from his long walk and sated with two treats, he made two spins before settling in his spot like he assumed we'd be in the kitchen for a while. "Uh, sure," I wheezed with little confidence.

"Stay for dinner. I'm cooking."

"Stay? I *am* staying here. While Geneva's off, wherever it is she's gone."

"You don't know? Hm." He grinned but kept to his task. "Is that usual?"

"It's not *un*usual. Geneva is a mystery. Elusive. It's part of what makes her so wonderful. We all could learn from her spontaneity."

"So that's a yes to dinner?"

New life rule: When a man offers to cook you dinner, the only correct answer is, "Yes. Yes, to dinner." Just ask Miss Livie of Blossomy Bough. I leaned across the island for a better look at the ingredients he'd bought.

Ethan grumbled, "Jesus," under his breath, then scooped up the produce and headed to the sink to wash dark leafy greens and twine-tied herbs. His back to me. "Hey, do me a favor."

"Sure. I'd love to help."

"No help needed, but I'm gonna need you to put some clothes on before I—before anything else."

I peered at my matching cami and shorts. Perfectly appropriate for the balmy seventy-five degrees Geneva kept the apartment (because that's how Max preferred it) but not so much for the platonic company. The realization he'd barely looked at me since our run-in at the front door made sense. Good sense. Totally admirable, flattering, swoon-worthy sense. "Back in a flash."

"Take your time." His voice cracked like an adolescent boy's. In jest, of course, but it supplied one more example of subtle sweet talk I'd never get used to and didn't want to.

"What am I smelling?" A meaty aroma mixed with earthy herbs and mouthwatering garlic tantalized my nose. A sauté pan sizzled while water bubbled in a large pot. The greens cut in strips, minus the stems and spines, lay on a wooden cutting board, ready to be called to epicurean service. A pile of fresh, wide pappardelle joined the spread.

"A simple, rustic wintry pasta with chicken sausage, garlic, sage, and kale with fontina."

"Were you a chef in one of your many gigs?"

"I washed dishes in Aosta, Italy, but I learned some stuff and not by anyone who would call herself a chef. Few ingredients, but the freshest you can get your hands on, and don't overcook them."

"Despite the distance between the two, Swedes make Fontina too. Something about traveling monks in the twelfth century, if I recall. I might have been seven when I read about it. Of course, it's made in other places too nowadays, Wisconsin included, but the Swedish version has the traditional red waxy rind." I retrieved two glasses and poured each full of water while I shared my cheese knowledge. The anecdote didn't start from a place of discomfort or nervousness, and I appreciated no embarrassment followed. I'd found a new comfort zone.

"Aww, you read a book about cheese when you were seven?" Ethan asked without a hint of condescension. Like he found it endearing and maybe a little sad.

I sipped my water and sat on an island stool, enjoying the quiet conversation with unknown music wafting in the background, adding another layer for the senses. The leathery soapstone under my palms, the savory smells of the pan-sauteed meal, the beautiful man responsible for the cooking. "I read a book, well, *lots* of books about Sweden. When I learned what little I could about my lineage, I camped out at the local library and read every book I found—and could understand—about Swedish and Middle Eastern culture. Dear Mrs. Fitz—the librarian helped me do all kinds of research, for years. The second one, the Middle East info, was a lot. Broad brush strokes and assumptions don't suit much of the region, if you know what I mean. I guess you do. First-hand."

"I couldn't tell you about the twelfth-century anywhere, but I know how people work, how they celebrate, how they mourn. Who sits on the floor to eat, who never shakes hands. The things that make a people unique and yet all of us utterly the same."

"Hm. I never saw blue like that." I rested my chin in my palm, marveling at all Ethan must have seen.

"What's that mean?" He pulled me from my reverie.

"Just something I say to myself when I learn something new about anything commonplace. The unexpected found in the ordinary."

"I might have to steal it."

"Nope. Public domain. I'm sure I heard it somewhere, or read it probably. I don't remember. Mrs. Fitz, maybe."

The room hushed. Music still played, but the sizzle and bubbling of supper prep faded while the intimacy of the scene grew. Ethan cleared his throat for both of us.

"Glass of wine? I bought red and white. Boy scout motto and all that."

"Boy scout, huh? What's your plan here, Ledes?" I leaned back, squinting in mock alarm.

"Uh oh. She's using my real name. That can't be good."

"You planning to ply me with delicious food and wine to get me—"

"No," he calmly interjected. "But I sure do like where your head's at, Meems. I'm just hoping for more of this. More get-to-know-you time, as Mrs. Bimah calls it."

"Probably too late to invoke off-the-record status, huh?" I joked, but his body contracted. A jolt that altered the mood.

"You know that's not—that we don't—"

"I know, Ethan. Sorry. I was kidding. Didn't mean to touch a nerve."

His shoulders lowered, jaw relaxed. "No. Just a reminder of who we are and *what* we are. To each other, I mean." He pulled two pasta bowls off an open shelf while I wished I had a clearer definition. Who and what we were to one another. Whatever the classification, wine wouldn't help. When he pulled his sweatshirt over his head, I glimpsed taut skin, a trail of hair down his torso, and a teasing peek of a tattoo. Then I knew it for sure.

"I'll stick to water. Thanks." I guzzled mine and poured another.

"Good plan."

"Hey, what's that?" A saucer-sized plate sat next to the large, fancy range.

"A few bits of s-a-u-s-a-g-e for M-a-x."

Max's collar clanked when he jerked his head up, ears twitching.

"Playing hardball, I see." The battle for Max's fidelity began in earnest.

Kneeling at the dog bed, Ethan rubbed Max's coffee-colored curls and scratched the cream of his chin. "Nope. I just think Max needs a man in his life. Isn't that right, boy?"

I clenched my thighs together and released a long slow breath, thinking, *Same, Max. Same.* What is it about a man with a dog?

We humans ate side by side at the island, deciding the formal dining room's modern take on Rococo made it unsuitable for casual diners like us. Conversation flowed. He told me he'd learned never to cut bread with a knife, only tear it apart by hand, and other superstitions and traditions in Italy. I recalled reading the number seventeen meant bad luck for many Italians, and we laughed when he shared a story about betting on black seventeen at a roulette wheel in Milan and winning. Everyone gave him a wide berth the rest of the night. He'd wondered why. Now he knew.

After brief bickering about who would wash the dishes, we settled on more hands made for less work and washed and dried together. But we deferred the real quarrel until we moved to the living room, Max following to that room's bed but changing course to sit with me on "his" sofa spot. Ethan took an armchair a coffee table away.

"Are you prepared for Monday? Have a plan for how to react when you hear Rayburn won't return?"

I grimaced. "You sure know how to ruin an evening. Doesn't he, Max?"

Max lifted his head from my lap, offering a small sneeze of agreement. I doted on him for a beat, delighted he chose me over the hunky reporter who fed him sausage.

"Can't say I haven't thought about it, but I think the best course is to go into it unrehearsed, for appearance's sake."

"Unrehearsed? Mimi, you can't take the job, but you know they will offer it. Not only that, but they'll make you feel like they're doing you a favor."

"I'm guessing it will be an offer I can't refuse."

"Of course you can refuse." Exasperation shot him to his feet. "Just say no. It's a powerful word. A full sentence, even."

"I can't say no and risk losing my current position."

"They won't fire you. Not from Vice-Dean. Not now."

"They could."

"They won't."

"I don't know that."

"I know they won't leave your department leaderless in the middle of application season."

"I can't be sure of that, and I can*not* put myself or my mother in danger."

"Danger? What kind of danger?"

"Unemployment. I can't take that chance. No matter what." The argument escalated to a full-throated row. "For someone with so much insight into how people live, you keep getting caught with your privilege showing. I don't have the safety net you do."

"I'll catch you."

"That's not your job, Ethan."

"I *want* that job, Mimi."

His ability to infuriate me while also making me weak in the knees made for an unfair fight. The shouted declaration lingered in a silence I didn't have the words to fill, but he didn't leave it hanging long. A hushed, more level head continued.

"Were you even listening to me the other night? They will pin this on you. Make you the sacrificial lamb. They will eventually fire you. Publicly."

"You don't know that either."

"I *do* know it. It's the way the world works. I've seen it too many times." Ethan grabbed the sweatshirt he'd discarded earlier.

"And there he goes," I sighed, patted Max, who sat up in the hubbub.

"Meaning?"

"Meaning you tend to make an exit when things get—confrontational. When you can't control the narrative."

Ethan wrenched his neck, freezing in a moment of thought. "I do?"

"I cannot be the first person to make this observation. The first morning in my office. The time when you brought me corn pudding. Yesterday morning at my place? At Mom's last night? Probably whatever happened in Indiana that made you hop a plane to escape family on a *family* holiday. And now you're standing, sweatshirt in hand, ready to skedaddle."

"Skedaddle?" His grin sparked as his figure relaxed.

"Skedaddle. Scoot. Make haste for an exit. I'm surprised you don't know it. A newspaper invented it in 1860-something to describe the hurried evacuation of Richmond—"

"I know what it means. I'm also pretty sure I've never heard it used by anyone under the age of—never mind." He tossed his sweatshirt back to his chair with the torn look of someone waging an internal battle.

"What? Use your words, newshound. No sense clamming up now. Lay out your defense," I insisted, getting to my feet.

"Okay, that first time you genuinely shocked me. I never imagined you—my brain couldn't figure how you could be—you. The corn pudding incident? I had a plane to catch and on the busiest travel day of the year, by the way. Yesterday morning—well, I came right back, if you'll recall and at your Mom's last night, well you—you provoke me, Mimi."

"Provoke you?"

"Yes, you irk me. You're doing it now. You aggravate me. *Vex—*"

"I know what the word means, and back at ya, old man. *Vex,*" I scoffed.

"Not in the bad way or a grating way, but in a *trying* way that makes me want to—to do things."

The inquisitive kid in me still existed, and couldn't help but ask, "What things?" I shouldn't have.

"Inappropriate things."

"Oh." The "oh" sounded like the wheeze of the wind getting knocked out of me. The sensation was similar.

"So, I find walking away is the better thing to do, given the situation."

Max nudged my calf. I guessed he only wanted to remind me of his presence, but it felt like coaxing to close the gap between Ethan and me. The insistent Portie crossed the rug to sit at Ethan's feet when I didn't move. Leading by example again?

I found enough air and courage for, "What sort of inappropriate things?" The brave question came with an even braver step toward him.

"Like kissing the hell out of you, for starters."

Uh-oh. Someone else discovered a bit of nerve too.

"Yeah?" I wondered what monosyllabic oaf possessed me, but she kept moving toward the handsome man, and I was okay with that.

"Definitely."

While his four syllables impressed me, his phone ring shattered any momentum, forcing us to retreat from one another like the Chastity Police caught us doing exactly what we were about to do.

"Yes, Mrs. Bimah. What can I do for you?" Ethan paused for her answer. I heard her distress from across the room—the safe distance Ethan and I put between us again.

"Did you turn it off?" Ethan asked. "Okay, I'll be there in a minute. Well, Mimi Kanaan will be there in a minute. I need to—uh, find my toolbox. Hold tight, Mrs. B. Help is on the way." He pocketed his phone. "Something about the kitchen spigot and water. You head up? And I'll hurry down to grab some tools."

"Yes, of course. Go."

When he reached the door, he turned. "Hey. For the record, I'm not—skedaddling."

I gestured to the door. "*Go.* I'll meet you on sixteen."

Twenty-Five

I KNOCKED UNDER THE scrolled *16C* but then pushed through the door Mrs. Bimah had left ajar.

"Hello, sugar," she called out from her living room. "Is that yummy fellow of yours with you?"

I would have thought Geneva had outed 'Sonny's' and my ruse by now, but maybe not. Perhaps Mrs. Bimah played along, anyway. She sat on a baby pink tufted sofa with a crossword puzzle book, a large magnifying glass, and a pencil in hand. A gigantic, distorted eye startled me when she peered up at me through the lens. Her gaze traveled from my head to my toes and back again. I couldn't help but notice the air of panic one might expect amid a plumbing emergency didn't exist.

"He should be here in a few. He went to get his—"

"Hello?"

"In here, Sonny," she called with her sweet, if loud, lilt.

A deep breath and a glint of perspiration at his temple gave away his effort to get to the woman's top-floor apartment. A vein that ran down his forearm bulged from exertion and the weight of the old metal toolbox. It flexed as his grip on the handle gave and tightened again.

"My, my. Did you run all those stairs? Sixteen flights? All for little ol' me?"

"Not to worry, Mrs. B. I had some—energy to burn. Besides, anything for you."

I couldn't tell whether he meant to wink at the aging belle or me.

"I see you have yet to find yourself some proper trousers," she *tsked*. "Mimi, certainly there is something you can do to get this man out of those athletic shorts."

I snorted and coughed to keep a yelping laugh from escaping, and I knew my cheeks bloomed three shades darker than the living room's upholstery.

"Didn't you say there's a problem with your kitchen faucet, Mrs. B?"

"I did, didn't I? This way."

We followed her through the apartment, the mirror opposite Geneva's layout with décor like a 1960s time capsule. *16C*'s straight lines and pastels couldn't be more different from the earth tones, mounds of pillows, and broadleaf botanicals of *12A*.

A visitor would be hard-pressed to tell if Rose Bimah had renovated the kitchen in a vintage style or if it all dated back to the original decade. Regardless, given her frantic call, no one would have expected to find a dry room.

"Did you mop up already, Mrs. Bimah?"

"No, sugar," she tittered. "My niece comes in to clean on Wednesdays. Have I mentioned my niece Tilly, Sonny?"

Ethan stood in front of the sink, looking for evidence of a problem, even sticking his head in the cabinet underneath to find the leak. He found no sign of a crisis, except a shiny wrench within easy reach, still bearing its price sticker.

"Well, Mrs. B, I don't see any water. So, what would you like me to do?"

"Oh, silly me. You're right. I was supposed to turn on the spigot."

"Supposed to?"

No sooner had he asked than Mrs. Bimah stretched her arm past Ethan and lifted the lever. Water spewed. I lunged out of the way, leaving Ethan to take the brunt of the spray from the chest up before he slammed off the sink handle.

Wide-eyed, the old woman and I held our breaths until we couldn't hold back the laughter. Ethan blew droplets from his lips and wiped the water from his eyes.

"And there's the cold shower I needed," he grumbled, just loud enough.

"What'd you say, Sonny?"

"Uh, it seems the spout O-ring and the aerator are loose. A little righty-tighty and problem solved."

I offered him a hand towel as he opened the rusty-edged chest.

"There's a wrench under the sink, dear. I think you'll find it fits perfectly."

Sure enough, the adjustable wrench needed little adjustment and Ethan fixed the faucet with a simple twist. Without trying to appear rude, Ethan and I excused ourselves after a minute more of polite chit-chat. After playing Mr. Fix-it, he seemed as eager as me to leave.

The elevator lurched open for us on sixteen. A pleasant surprise. He gestured for me to enter and followed, pushing the button for the ground floor. His floor. We waited through the long-drawn-out pause for the doors to slide shut.

"Weird, right?" he asked.

"Little bit, yeah."

I couldn't help but recall the day we met in that very elevator and all that had happened in the weeks since. Not a day passed that

I didn't think about how I'd kissed him in the cab, wondering what it would be like to do it again.

He set down the toolkit between us, and we leaned, backs against the wall, hands braced on the brass rail hung on three sides. Neither of us spoke, but my breath caught as his pinky brushed against mine. I returned the gentle touch as the sliders inched to a close. Another long pause followed before a jarring clunk signaled the start of the contraption's sluggish descent.

"So, how slow do you guess this old bucket of bolts goes?" His hand covered mine, still gripping the rail.

"Slow enough, I think."

"Yeah?"

"Uh-huh."

"Is this—a bad idea?"

"Yep."

He huffed with a hint of his sweet chuckle. "You couldn't have fibbed?"

"Not about this. Definitely not." I dropped my chin, cursing my honesty.

"Do you care?"

I tilted my head to meet his eye. "Do I care that it's a bad idea? At the moment, not even a little."

"Thank God," he sighed as he spun. The *clank* and *scrap* of metal sounded as he kicked the tools out of our way, and his lips crashed into mine.

In the split-second ahead of impact, I gasped. Not in surprise. Not in fear, but in complete awe. The moment I'd craved since the day the autumn sunshine haloed his curls as he offered me coffee and an apology. Finally. Ethan kissed the way he talked, like a man who knew what he wanted and didn't mind telling you. His hungry lips took mine with powerful need. A want I'd never encountered, a desire that fanned the fire that smoldered for weeks.

His hand slid from my cheek to my throat, my pulse hammering against his fingers. But when his mouth softened, easing into a gentler kiss, I might have panicked, thinking it was over too soon. My hands skimmed up his thumping chest to meet at the nape of his neck, a tight hold to say, "Don't stop." To underscore my longing, I nipped his bottom lip. A slight pull with my teeth let slip how starved I'd been, too.

He pulled from me, his eyes dark and stunned, and I feared maybe appalled, but his grasp dropped to my hips. With one squeeze, he hoisted me onto the elevator's protruding handrail, settling between my thighs, pressing me to the dark burled wood of the old lift.

I murmured, "Yes," into his mouth as his velvet tongue found mine. They swirled to explore while his fingers pulled at the roots of my hair, half-fallen from its ponytail. My hands double-fisted the back of his t-shirt, holding him close, desperate for more.

"God, I've wanted this," he groaned. A demanding tug on my tresses raised my chin, and he nibbled my jaw on his way to my ear and then down my neck. Slow, greedy kisses trailed along my collarbone to the shoulder exposed by my old-school sweatshirt.

My goodness, the man knew what he was doing. Of course he did. He'd been doing it a lot longer than I had and in seventy-three countries on seven continents. All those exotic "beans" to sample. I didn't care. As a matter of fact, I wanted to thank each and every one of those lucky and likely beautiful, worldwide women for giving Ethan Ledes a fine cultural education in how to do kissing right.

"Mimi," his beautiful mouth seized my lips again, torn between talking and taking more of what we both wanted.

"Hm?" I clung tighter, my ankles locked around his hips.

"The elevator. It—it dinged."

"No." I hadn't heard it. I heard lots of things: the whistle and boom of blinding fireworks, a choir of angels singing in joyous praise, raucous cheers from what I could only guess were my tragically under-used lady parts, but the elevator ding? Nope, didn't happen. The car came to its usual sudden hard stop, slamming us together in a way I didn't hate.

"Shoot," I whispered into his chest as I slid from my perch.

"Not the word I'd use," he grumbled, settling my feet to the floor. "Wow. You're beautiful. Your mouth all..." He placed an agonizingly chaste kiss on my tingling lips before he stood next to me, our backs to the wall the way we'd started the journey. When the doors jerked open, our eyes met one of the Chen sisters, Lei, the older and more dour of the two. Our gazes, in sync, rose to see the lit number seven above the elevator doors, then back to Ms. Chen.

"Mimi? Are you all right? Were you stung by a bee?" Worry etched her stony face.

"A bee? It's almost December." I couldn't connect the dots.

"Your mouth looks swollen, like a bee sting, and your hair is, well, it's—" Her fingers wiggled over her head as she frowned.

My hand met my head, recognizing the lumpy wreck of tousled hair pulled loose but still partially tied. I pulled at the elastic that failed its one job, determined to smooth the locks without letting go of the nervous laughter tightening my chest.

"Never mind. Mr. Ledes, I was just coming for you. Hurry! We have a problem with our kitchen sink." She grabbed Ethan's forearm to urge him from the elevator.

He snatched the recently abused toolbox and allowed her to guide him down the seventh-floor hallway. "The *kitchen* sink?"

he asked me with skepticism. His furrowed brow. "What are the odds?"

I followed to find out.

The Chen sisters shared a lovely apartment, if more austere than Rose Bimah's or Geneva Spieler's. A small table off-center of the door in the entry welcomed us, adorned with three stalks of Lucky Bamboo and a grouping of lit white candles. The smell of vanilla hit my nose, but Ms. Chen had us at a near-jog through the tidy living room. I glimpsed a low-profile suede sofa perpendicular to the large, undraped windows, and matching chairs at precise angles flanking the fireplace, but noticed little else in my pursuit of Ms. Chen and Ethan, with the younger Ms. Chen, Susu, the sunnier sister, appearing from nowhere to bring up the rear.

Not a pot, pan, dish, or small appliance decorated the kitchen. The countertops were devoid of any clutter. Any *anything*, except water. Not a lot, but enough to say there had been some sort of incident. An incident not unlike the one we witnessed in *16C*. Lei reached to turn on the faucet with Ethan in the line of fire if we knew what would happen next. Déjà vu with an alternate cast.

"Uh, uh, uh." He waved her off, uninterested in playing the fool twice. Water dribbled at the seam of the spout and the aerator when he lifted the handle a fraction. Ethan spoke his line, "Huh. It seems the spout O-ring and aerator are loose."

"Ooh," the sisters chimed in stereo.

"Kind of interesting, actually." He kept a stern face, taking his time to open the toolbox for his own adjustable wrench to make the easy fix.

"How so?" Again, the siblings spoke as one.

"Mrs. Bimah on sixteen—you all are friends, aren't you?" He didn't wait for an answer. "Mrs. Bimah in *16C* had the *exact* same problem."

"No," Susu peeped. "Rose was supposed to take the batteries out of her TV remote, not loosen the thing from the thing. The sink was our—"

"*Ān-jìng!*" Lei snapped at her sister. "*Hm*, interesting," the older one continued in kinder, gentler English, still side-eyeing the chastened Susu who looked about to confess all. Who stole the Lindbergh baby? Where was Jimmy Hoffa buried? Did Carole Baskin do it? I had my suspicions on all three, but we can get into my binging True Crime books another time.

"Ladies? What's going on here?" I applied an ounce more pressure to see if Susu would break.

Susu opened her mouth before Lei shushed her again.

"*Tāmen zhīdào, Lei.*"

The younger Chen rolled her eyes at her sister's scolding.

"Yes, we know," Ethan added.

"You speak Mandarin?" Stereo turned to surround sound when all three of us women asked in unison.

"No, but I understand enough to be dangerous. What is this? I'm all for a little harmless hazing, but I've been around for a while. Seems a bit late in the game to be razzing the new guy."

Lei Chen often carried an aura of exasperation about her, and that moment was no exception. Exasperated by the overall ruse? Its failure? Or Susu's quick caving with so little coercion? All three seemed likely. Her irritation morphed to full-on annoyance with a knock at the door.

"*Yoo-hoo!*" Rose Bimah's noisy drawl carried from the apartment's door. "I did it, girls. Sprayed him right good. Probably should have tried it out first to see what would happen, but it worked like a charm." Her tickled laugh came to an abrupt stop when she rounded the corner to the kitchen. "Oh, *fiddle.*"

"Aww, Mrs. B, glad you popped in. Now we can get to the bottom of this." Ethan's sweet smile worked like truth serum for the over seventy-set. If only you could bottle it.

"It was all Geneva's idea." Mrs. Bimah saw the bus coming and threw the absent Geneva right under it.

"Ms. Spieler, huh?" If he meant to appear perturbed, it didn't work. And those midwestern manners read plainly with his respectful use of her formal name.

"She wanted us to keep an eye on you. And busy."

"Busy? Busy with what? From what?" If anyone other than Lei Chen let slip her irritation at the situation, it was me, miffed at the elevator disruption. My testy tone had me backpedal. "I mean, what's she got against this big lug here?" I punched him in the arm like that was something a grown woman would do. "Does she think y'all are giving him an easy go or something?"

"She's always got some scheme going, Mimi. You know that. And we're always looking for a way to pass the time."

"So, it *is* hazing?"

"No. She meant to help." Susu came to Geneva's defense. "Help Mimi, I think," she clarified.

Lei took the reins. Her no-nonsense character wanted an end to this foolishness and fast, no doubt. "She was light on the details, as she is about most things, but she claimed Mr. Ledes presents a—shall we say, *problem* for you, Mimi. Between dog walks, leaking sinks, and—*ahem*, 'broken' television remote controls, we could run some interference. But also give him a reason to stay around." Done with the silly episode, the older Chen pushed her way out of the crowded kitchen. The rest of us followed her to the living room.

Ethan must have read my mind. While, in my head, I groused that I'd gone from one meddlesome mama to four, he quipped, "You all know Mimi already has a mother, right?"

Susu tittered. A puff of pink sprang to her cheeks.

"No, no. Not *that* kind of interference." Mrs. Bimah said to me. "*Never* that kind. Something about his job. His *other* job. Paul Pry, she called him. With all her foreign slang, I don't understand half of what comes out of that woman's mouth, and frankly, I'm not sure I should even believe the other half."

"Oh, stop," Lei Chen barked. "You love Geneva. We all do."

"Of course I do. Love her like she's my own sister. Melanie, not Kitty Ann. Kitty is a real—"

"Okay, ladies," Ethan quashed what could have devolved into a wordy tell-all from the chatty Rose. "I think you have more than lived up to Ms. Spieler's instructions..." Ethan continued to charm the meddlesome faction of the Midtown Mews mafia while my worlds collided. My interfering mother, Ethan's obligation to *The Public Eye*, the skeletons in my closet that connected the two and would surely end what we'd barely started.

"Excuse me, everyone. I need to see to Max." In my usual gracelessness, I bumped into a coffee table, one Chen sister, and a wall, stumbling to make my getaway.

Ethan said my name, but I cleared the door to the seventh-floor hallway with the Chens' door closing with a slam I hadn't intended. Refastening my hair, I bargained with the universe that I'd stick to a *single* fib a day for an entire week if only the elevator would still be there. Desperate pecking at the lit arrow produced nothing but a grinding gear noise too far away for a quick escape. I offered the fib deal with an upgrade to one whole month if the elevator gods sent the car at warp speed, but again, they denied me.

"Mimi." Toolbox in his grip, Ethan closed the door I had banged shut and took an easy pace to meet me.

"This *damn* elevator," I murmured.

"Whoa, Meems. What's the problem?"

"Hm? Problem?"

"Aww, come on. You just swore at the elevator. I've never heard you swear." He reached for my arm with his free hand, but I side-stepped away from his touch. "No. Wrong."

"What do you mean, 'wrong'? I didn't say anything."

"I mean, you don't get to call me out for quick exits, then pull away from me after making one of your own. And definitely not after the best kiss of my life."

"That was a mistake."

"Wrong again. You're not very good at this game."

"Game? Is that what this is? A game? My career? Yours?"

"No. But this isn't about the knee-buckling kiss, either."

"You *really* need to stop saying things like that."

"What? The truth? It's what I do. And so do you—usually. But you didn't, did you? You lied. To me. Or at least you're hiding something and it's eating you from the inside."

The elevator opened.

"You're right. We might as well get this over with, but not here. I need to see Max." *Life rule: When something stinks, blame the dog.* I stepped into the car, expecting Ethan to follow. He didn't.

"I'll meet you there. Geneva's. I'm taking the stairs." The resignation in his voice made my eyes sting.

Why hadn't *I* taken the damn stairs?

Twenty-Six

ETHAN AND HIS TOOLBOX waited for me in the hall, leaning in the doorway of *12A*, arms and ankles crossed, eyes to the penny tile and carpet.

"I read a book about the psychology of body language, and you are a textbook example of someone who wants to block out what they are about to hear, putting distance between them and another." The useless knowledge packed in my brain had to go somewhere.

"It can also be a self-soothing pose that helps one concentrate and focus on an arduous task. It makes use of both your left and right brain, creating a higher functioning cognitive ability to better solve a complicated problem. If you think I haven't learned a thing or two about body language in my investigative years, think again. Plus, I got a B.A. in psychology before going to J-school."

I'd never heard a nerdier comeback to my own dorky habit, and it only made me fall more in—harder. I fell harder. "Oh." So much for volleying with more witty banter.

"Might be a friendly reminder to keep my hands to myself, too. I'll sit on them when we get inside."

The idea of his hands on my body made me fumble with the key to open the door. It would be a fond memory to replay many times, but it was his humor, his self-assurance, his quick mind

I'd miss most. I'd already jumped to the part where he left after learning the truth about me. It was inevitable.

"Hey, Maxy boy."

Max lay on his foyer bed, waiting for my return. Or anyone else who would give him a biscuit. I gave him two.

"Glass of wine?" I pointed over my shoulder, walking backward to the kitchen.

"No. No thanks."

"Right. I get it. You're on the job now."

"Mimi—"

"Joking. Sort of." I gestured to the sofa while taking a chair. Necessary distance. "I won't say the off-the-record thing because it will only make you angrier and more disappointed than you will be when you hear what I have to say."

"I'm not angry, Meems."

The nickname. Yeah, I'd miss that too.

"Hear what?"

"*I* am your story," I blurted. "One version of it, anyway. I am proof positive of longstanding corruption in Chastain University's Office of Admissions."

Confusion played out on his face. His jutted chin, the sweet crinkle at his eyes deepening to something more ominous while his mouth opened and closed, then did it again. When he stood, I sank into the plush cushions of my rattan seat. It snapped and crackled with my preemptive flinch from whatever would soon erupt from the strangely silent reporter. But nothing came.

"Say something, Ethan."

He paced with slow steps, hands to his hips, creases migrating from his eyes to his brows and forehead. "No. You say more."

"More?"

"How many times?" he spoke in a near-whisper, steady and too calm.

"I don't understand the question."

"How many times have you perpetrated fraud, Amelia?"

Ouch. My formal name and the legal vernacular made it all worse.

"Once." I couldn't look at him anymore. My fingers twisted together, the same with my insides, and I feared I'd be sick. Twice in one week. In front of Ethan.

"One time? When?"

Quick math gave me a moment to catch my breath. "Fifteen, no, sixteen years ago."

The pacing stopped, his back to me. Those shaggy curls fell forward with his slumped head. But when his ah-ha moment hit, he spun, showing a more rutted face. "Mimi, that would have made you sixteen, maybe seventeen years old."

"Yep. But really, I suppose that one time still makes for years of deceit. Everything since then. *Half* my life has been a sham."

"Let's be clear. Are you saying you cheated your way into Chastain as a student?"

"I'm saying I worked my butt off to get into Chastain, but chances are, none of that mattered because it's likely I was unqualified for admittance. And yet, here we are." My knees met my chin, and I hugged my shins, making myself as small as possible.

"How?"

"What? When? How? You take this journalism thing down to the bare bones, don't you? Are the details important?"

"I'm a details guy, remember?"

"Fine. I don't know the details. Someone got—paid, and I got in."

"Who? And, dear God." His fingers entwined, rested on his head. He blanched. "Please tell me the payment was monetary."

"Ethan. *Ew*. She wouldn't—" I swallowed the rest of the statement.

"She?" He unclenched. "She. Now it all starts to fall into place. This wasn't you. You were a kid. You wouldn't have had a clue how to do such a thing. So, some teacher—no, your librarian friend you mentioned? Mrs. Fitz was it? Someone else did it. Someone else did it and you found out."

He worked the puzzle aloud, but talking to himself, not me. That big picture he liked to step back to see appeared in front of him as he placed one piece of the puzzle after another. "Oh, my God. You *just* found out. Your *mother*. That woman..." His hand rubbed the scruff on his chin. "You found out on Thanksgiving Day that your mother interfered with your application. You pulled a *Ledes-like* exit on her, and she had some kind of attention-grabbing panic episode."

"Hey. Whoa up there. Mama had a real emergency."

"Explain to me—no one gets admitted to—how did she get admitted to the hospital—a private hospital without the proper insurance information?"

"Okay, that part wasn't real, but she sent me on the snipe hunt to keep me busy, so I wouldn't worry. She says I always need a task."

"So, she manipulated you—"

"Ethan," I launched from my chair. "Say one more word against my mother. I dare you. I can badmouth her all I want, but not you. Not anyone." Family was family, and Mama was all I had.

He exhaled with raised hands, taking a seat on the sofa. Truce.

"It's not even that she did it. Which is awful, but if I'm honest, it's *why* she did it. One more example of me falling short. I was *almost* good enough. *This* close to success." I flopped back into my seat. "In elementary school, I *almost* had perfect attendance, but no, chickenpox, fifth grade. The number of times she said, 'If only you had gotten them over the winter break.' I won *runner-up* in the Geography Bee in fourth grade because I mixed up Tuvalu with Palau. Alani Fiva won. Know where she's from? You guessed it. Palau. It didn't matter that we couldn't afford to celebrate with ice cream. Ice cream was for winners." I bounced out of my seat again, pacing the living room on my walk down memory lane.

"Even earlier, I sold the *second*-highest number of girls scout cookies. Sure, Leia Snodgrass's dad worked at Dewey, Cheatum, and Howe or some such and made every intern, assistant, paralegal, and lawyer at the firm buy five boxes. And don't get me started on the shame of graduating high school salutatorian. Salutatorian. *So close.*" I flailed in full chaos mode.

Ethan stared, wide-eyed, probably as aghast at my litany of failures as Mama always had been.

"Frustrated by my constantly disappointing her, she took matters into her own hands. Fed up, I guess. But now, I'll never know if I could have succeeded. All I know is that I didn't. Not really." I sat again, disappointed that no relief came with the confession.

"Wow." He finally broke the laser beam stare, but his exclamation left a bit to be desired.

"Yeah, well, now you know. And I'm sorry. But I understand you have to do what you have to do."

"Jesus, Mimi." The reporter rested his head in his hands; fingers tugged at the adorable curls that had grown unruly since we first met.

I unfolded in my chair, wrenching back, unsure what fury I had released. Ethan bounded to his feet but stopped short and spun one-eighty, headed toward the door.

"Please don't go." My words flew into the atmosphere with zero warning. I'd rather face the man's ire than his absence, and it terrified me to think what that said about me. Any reprimand would be better than silence.

"Go? Where would I go? How could I go?"

I flung my arms in his direction. "But you—"

"I just gotta move. Get some distance to keep from throttling you, but I'm not going anywhere. Not until I get you—"

"On the record? I told you this is fair game. All of it. Except Mama. Please don't get her involved. Can you leave that part out?"

"God, Mimi." He sat again, pinching the bridge of his nose and shaking his head. "Can you forget *The Public Eye* for one damn minute? Can you forget that I'm a journalist for one *bless-ed* moment, or at least recognize I'm more than that? That I'm a man who's—who's mad about you. Like—bananas—nuts for you. Grab our passports and the next plane to anywhere kind of wild about you. I'd pitch it all to show you the world; show you aren't runner-up to anything or anyone. Deprogram you from this goddamn bullshit you've taken as truth your whole life." Midwest met Manhattan with coarser language than I'd ever heard him use.

"I know you're angry."

"Angry? Hell yeah, I'm angry. *Angry* is an understatement. But not at you."

Silence followed, but I liked the plot twist.

"Bananas nuts?" I asked.

He shrugged. "Yellow *comma* fruits that are."

I looked at him askance, unable to flatten my grin.

"It's—uh, it's a Midwest saying."

"No, it's not."

He huffed with a frown. "No. It's not," he admitted.

I stood and closed the distance between us, kneeling in front of him on the sofa. My next breath bloomed. Deep and cathartic, filled with Ethan's magical scent, that gentle intoxicant that relaxed and excited me all at once. With my hand to his chest, near enough that I needed to lift my chin to meet his eye, his arms wrapped around me, urging me into his lap. We couldn't forget the obstacles between us, but for one damn minute, for one *bless-ed* moment, we could ignore them.

"I see you," I whispered. "And I'm bananas nuts for you too."

"I *know*."

"You are the most—presumptuous man I have ever met."

"Well, I'm no Tristan Pembroke." Ethan made a good point.

"You are the *second* most presumptuous man..."

"It comes from being raised by a mother and three sisters who thought the sun rose and set on my command." He cocked his head, still holding me. "You could use a little doting like that. Let me."

"Let you what?"

"How about a kiss to start?"

"Thought you'd never ask." I moved an inch closer.

"Those freckles. And your gray eyes. I've never seen any like them. Light and dark at the same time."

A quick snort snuck out of me. "What are you doing?" The heat of a blush spread like fire.

"It's a little pre-kiss doting."

"But you said, 'how about a kiss to *start?*' So, get started."

"So literal—and bossy. I kinda like it."

Now it was my turn to shrug. "It comes from being an only child. I want what I want when I want it. So, kiss me."

Ethan eased into the kiss. Tender brushes tickled, softer than the bruising version in the elevator. No need to rush. No fear of interruption. All the time to savor and stroke, explore and enjoy. When he wrapped his hand in my ponytail, the gentle tug lit a new spark. I squeezed tighter, losing myself in the thrill of his touch. He broke apart the shortcomings I saw in myself. Plucked out every imperfection and filled the spaces with silent praise I'd never experienced. A single kiss, an adoring look, and already my weaknesses bled from me. What a little nourishment could do for the soul. I never knew.

"Wait." He kept close. "Why *couldn't* you ever know if you were good enough to get into Chastain? I've done a deep dive into qualifications for lots of elite schools. Not as far back as your undergrad days, but surely that data exists."

He'd rested his chin on my head, and I held him around the waist, my ear to his chest, reveling in his warmth and the strong, steady beat thumping through him. Was it the excitement of our kiss or the possible remedy for a problem?

"Thank you for trying to help. Brainstorming a solution to fix—me. But that's not your job either."

He'd said I was "broken a bit. Maybe a lot." No one forgets hearing that, no matter who says it or why. Even if I knew it was true, I'd hoped no one else noticed.

"It's not. But that's not my intention. The fact you even think you need fixing proves my point. I want you to see what I see. Hold up a mirror. Not some funhouse distortion. A truthful reflection. Facts. That's what I do. And I'll bet real money you'll find that you were every bit as qualified. More so, given your situation."

"My situation?" I rolled off his lap.

He wasn't wrong. Not about the circumstances. I thought about the Brianas and Javis I tried to help. The kinship I feel for them and the shared frustration of clearing hurdles that most people don't talk about in the application process. No one brags about housing and food insecurity. Young candidates don't write about feeling neglected by single mothers trying to keep a roof overhead. The "bootstraps" mentality touted by many in elite circles, Chastain circles, is little more than rhetoric for most. For many, *most* even, if the applicant owns bootstraps, they're the finest leather, twenty-four-carat-gold.

"I appreciate the sentiment, but you can't know that. You can't know whether I was qualified."

He stood. "No, but you can find out. *We* can find out."

Did I want to know? I didn't even know what my mother had done. What she'd paid or what 'services' she'd provided. But Mama wouldn't revisit her misdeeds. Besides, I'd rather she stayed out of it now. I didn't know how to protect her, but I would if I could. At any cost.

"You're right. I can find out, probably, but I'd rather—"

"Go it alone?" His grimace hardened while the rest of him deflated. It's like he knew not to fight me.

"It's what I do." I tried to joke with lighthearted mimicry as I held him at the waist, but my smile failed. "How I do."

"Yeah." Ethan's frustration bled out in one sighed syllable.

"Ethan, it's my fight."

"It's late. I'm gonna go. You know where to find me if..." He didn't finish his thought.

Max stood and stretched like he'd heard his cue and lumbered to nudge his head between our pressed thighs. He won a loving, albeit short, ear rub for his trouble.

"Go?"

Max let out a rare *ruff*, his nose bouncing from Ethan to me and back again. *I hear you, bud, but get out of my head.*

"Someone doesn't approve." I'd already asked the man to stay once. I couldn't do it again.

Ethan bent to one knee, face to face with the sullen Portie. The curly-haired twosome rubbed noses in an enviable show of affection that tightened my throat.

"I've got a Zoom call tomorrow morning. Early. TPE gang weekly check-in. I need to get my head straight for that, but I'd love to do lunch. Maybe take a stroll through Piedmont Park?" He pulled from me.

And there it was. The reminder we were still professionally at odds made me crumble inside. Like a harsh buzzer signaled our time for ignoring pesky obstacles had run out.

Ethan took a gentle hold of my chin. "Aww, don't look like that, Meems. You can come with us. Can't she, boy?"

I leveled a solid shove to the joker's chest. "Ha-ha."

He didn't even budge but drew me into him again.

"I shouldn't have said that thing I said. At your mom's. When I said you were broken, that someone broke you. You're not. Not by a long shot. If you know anything, please, know that."

That embrace grew tighter, the kiss deep like you'd see in an old black and white film, one that should have taken place on that foggy Moroccan tarmac and all the fiery kisses witnessed on rainy street corners or crowded train stations with soldiers headed off to war. *Kapow!* Despite my muddled mind and weakened knees, the kiss told me one thing for sure. No matter the stumbling blocks, Ethan Ledes could be mine. Someday. In the meantime, so long as he kept kissing me like a Hollywood movie, I'd figure a way to manage.

Twenty-Seven

EARLY SUNDAY MORNING, I journeyed to campus in the quiet before the storm of students heading back to campus for those last grueling days ahead of the end-of-term exams. Sleep eluded me while my brain contemplated Ethan's suggestion of a "deep dive" into old admissions records to learn how unqualified I'd been all those years ago.

You won't find the rules regarding how long universities store records etched on a one-size-fits-all stone. Different schools legislate different policies, and institutions rarely publicize them. Not to say it's confidential, not like the admissions secret sauce I've mentioned. Of course, digital records make storage easier than in centuries past.

At Chastain, the SparkNotes version reads like this: We dispose of applications not accepted, and those of accepted students who choose to attend other schools. That digital dump takes place at the start of the semester, when the student would have enrolled had decisions gone another way. We keep undergraduate applications of enrolled students for "a number of years." If you apply for a graduate program, we keep a permanent digital copy. Chastain's digital record no longer includes my undergraduate application, while they will keep my graduate school application in perpetuity. Lucky for me and my tree-killing ways, I knew a hard copy of my application existed. Somewhere in

Mama's unique filing system, a paper version existed. I was sure of it.

That said, higher education, like most big businesses, loves statistical data. Chastain knows where students are from, household incomes, grade point averages, and test scores dating back years, at least in aggregate form. That also includes percentages of minority or international status, as well as the number of legacy students, those who followed parents and grandparents to our hallowed halls. Information varies from specific headcounts to a range depending on the data. And while no one should discount the subjective part of the decision-making process, those were the numbers I needed, numbers that could bottom-line my own qualifications, at least to make it into the "maybe" pile.

An eerie stillness blanketed my office. Was it foreshadowing? A harbinger as I keyed in the inner-office access codes and clicked drop-down menus to access the details that might make or break me? My mind wouldn't allow the doom and gloom to stop.

The moment I hit pay-dirt, my phone chirped, signaling a text.

The Reporter: Good morning

My stomach *flipped* with an alarm that someone had caught me trespassing, not that I had. Then it *flopped* with a silly schoolgirl giddiness when I read Ethan's message. Those rollercoaster-like sensations made for a strange headspace, and I froze in my seat. My phone chirped again.

The Reporter: You up?

I wrangled my rollicking feelings enough to reply.

Mimi: I'm up, out, and about.

The Reporter: You're an early bird, I see.

Mimi: Easy to be an early bird if you can't sleep.

The Reporter: You either, huh?

To be honest, I'd spent my restless hours contemplating Ethan's "deep dive" suggestion but also his firm hold and sultry kiss. I hoped his tossing and turning included some of the same.

The Reporter: Kinda eager to see you.

Considering his early morning virtual meeting with his investigative colleagues, another pang of anxiety hit me. Was there more bad news?

Mimi: Business or pleasure?

Was that the best way to ask? Too late. I'd already hit send. His stalled answer ratcheted up my nerves.

The Reporter: I'd like to think pleasure.

I exhaled in relief.

Mimi: Afraid, at the moment, all I can offer is the lukewarm affections of a mopey Portuguese Waterdog.

The Reporter: Lol Max does put the *oof* in aloof, but I'll take what I can get. Is it pushy to ask if we can meet you?

Mimi: Is it pushy if I ask you to hurry?

The Reporter: Already out the door. Where am I headed?

Mimi: My office.

The Reporter: Good for you.

From Midtown Mews to Chastain was a hike. Max, with his sniffing and marking, would make it extra. That left me time to collect some data, all I needed to learn about how I'd stacked up against my fellow classmates from years ago. No, it wasn't a middle-of-the-night rendezvous in a shadowy parking garage, but as the printer whirred to life, a clandestine, *All the President's Men* feeling washed over me and I wondered if Ethan got a rush like it from his work.

Speaking of rushes... With my crossbody bag full of ten years of Chastain admissions stats, I pushed open the giant, iron-clad door to exit. Fifty yards away stood a man and his dog. Okay, not *his* dog, but goodness, what a sight. We stopped. All three of us. Staring at one another across a still campus. Signs of life may have shown at nearby residence halls, but there, on the steps of my home away from home, the serene surroundings were the opposite of the bedlam shooting off inside me.

Max moved first. An insistent tug on his leash got the duo walking toward me. I stalled a moment to insist that my legs take a leisurely pace. No sprinting down the brick path like some mythic shampoo commercial. They both smiled. Dogs do, I swear, and Max sped up to a loping scamper. Maybe it surprised him to see me in a new place.

Feet away, Ethan pulled back on the pooch's fancy lead. "Guess I'm not the only one eager to see you." Ethan leaned in for a kiss that I sprang to accept, but his lips diverted to my cheek. My cheek?

Quick thinking had me on my knees where I foisted all my disappointment into an overzealous greeting of Max.

"Hey, Maxy. Have you been a good boy? Who's a good boy? Max is a good boy, aren't you? Aren't you? Yes, you are." I scratched his ears and rubbed his nose, cooing at him like an obsessive fur-lover on steroids.

"If you're trying to make me jealous here, it might be working."

I quit gushing over the dog and stood, bristling. "No. Just being a caregiver. How about you?"

"Me?"

"What are you doing?" The heartfelt question oozed more sadness than I cared to share.

"I don't understand the question."

"This." I pointed to my cheek. The one still burning from his cool greeting. "Is that you acting as a gentleman—or a professional?"

He bowed his head. "It was the wrong call. I knew it as soon as I did it. But we are in public." Stepping closer, he lifted the chin I'd dropped in my bout of insecurity.

Mutual frowns met.

"And I did just come from a work session that reminded me what happens tomorrow. What will happen to you tomorrow. When I'm forced to stand in the back of a room like a professional and watch while your employer sets you up for *your* professional life to take a massive hit."

I tried to interrupt, but he continued.

"Now, I know you can take whatever comes at you. I have no doubt. But as the man who—cares about you and *not* in a professional way—not even in a *gentlemanly* way sometimes, I don't want you to *have* to take it. I'd like to shield you from it. And let's not forget, I'm part of the reason it's happening in the first place. So, yeah, I'm feeling unsure. Which is also new for me, just in general."

"Yeah." I nodded.

"Yeah? Yeah, what?"

"That was a pretty excellent answer." I pulled at the strings of his hoodie, bringing his mouth closer to mine. "Thank you," I whispered before placing a gentle kiss on it. We stood forehead to forehead while Max sneezed his approval, then yawned a sigh, telling us he wanted a change in venue.

"Coffee?" we asked one another and headed toward the city street.

"Plans for the rest of the day?" the reporter asked.

We sat on a patio at the Peachy Bean Café. A balmy sixty degrees and a standing heater made the outdoor setting possible. Max settled at my feet after lapping up a cup of water and dozed in a sunny spot, tuckered out by the field trip.

"I'm facing the music today. Taking ten years of admissions data to compare to my own." I gestured to my bag.

"Ten years? That's thorough."

"Well, I'm new to investigative whatever, but I figured five years before me and five years after should suffice. Unless you have some pro-tips, you'd like to share."

"I'd like to help if I can, but I also know you have that stubborn lone wolf thing going on. Plus, there's the conflict of interest. And please, don't waste a lie trying to convince me otherwise." He sipped his coffee through a grin.

"No *fibs* needed, Seymour Hersh."

Ethan lifted his lidded cup. "Nice one. Impressive. Almost makes up for the Ted Baxter slam."

"Thank you. I'll admit this game is getting harder."

"We could stop. Playing games, I mean."

But no part of our situation felt like a game. The professional stakes pointed to nothing but serious repercussions. We jeopardized both our reputations, but nagging doubt said mine was worth sacrificing. A trip to Mama's would decide it.

"I appreciate the offer to help but—"

Ethan took a deep, exasperated inhale. Whether it stemmed from my ignoring his "playing games" quip or denying his offer of assistance, I didn't know.

"It's not what you think, Ethan." I continued. "I have to go to Mama's to find my original application. I printed it all those years ago and if it still exists, it's there. Well, she printed it for me at the Dust Bunnies office. First time I noticed her taking an interest—" my mind rode along on that new train of thought, my stomach no longer appreciating the coffee I'd fed it.

"The *what* office?"

"Huh? Not important." I pushed my cup away. "The point is, I think it's a little soon to introduce you to my mother. Don't you?" I hadn't realized it until that moment, but the statement was

unequivocally true. *Phew.* Two fibs still in the bank. I stood ready
to get Max home to a more comfortable bed.

"Aww, moms love me, Meems." Ethan and Max followed my
lead.

"Ha. Not *this* mom."

Max sneezed in agreement as we reached a crosswalk, like he
knew.

"See? Even Max knows and he's never met the woman."

I pulled my phone from my bag and dialed as we crossed the
street, heading to Midtown Mews.

"Hey, Mama."

"It's Sunday," she replied.

"Sure is. Wondering if you'd mind a visit today."

"Can't."

"You can't? Why?"

"Do I nose into your business, Amelia?"

"Sometimes."

"Well, I'm not at home. Won't be until late. Gotta go. Talk
tomorrow. Monday. Like usual."

My phone let out three beeps at the abrupt end of the call. I
forced a smile that Ethan didn't buy. Wrapping an arm around my
shoulders, he kissed the top of my head as we picked up our pace.
He seemed to know better than to comment, and I appreciated not
having to defend her.

Twenty-Eight

I RESISTED ETHAN JOINING me, but learning he had a newly acquired rental car parked at the Mews, compliments of *The Public Eye*, I caved. It meant a quicker return to Max, plus some other perks Ethan made tempting. The man possessed a flair for persuasion.

For the second time in a week, I pulled into Mama's driveway to find a stranger on the property.

"May I help you?" I called out, exiting Ethan's leased SUV.

"Yes, ma'am." A young man trotted toward us, looking very official with a clipboard, embroidered golf shirt, with a matching ball cap. His truck, parked in the street between Mama's and the vacant house next door, included the same logo.

When had I become a *ma'am*?

"I'm Archie Clay of Clay and Sons. Are you the homeowner? Al Kanaan?" Archie stepped in it from the word go, directing his question and outstretched hand to Ethan. It wasn't the first time someone had slighted me for my gender, and it wouldn't be the last.

"My mother lives here."

"And *Amelia* owns the place." Ethan didn't reach for Archie's hand, but gestured to me.

"Right." I slid between the two men, offering my hand to shake. "I own the house."

The man referred to his clipboard. "Ah. I see. Initials. I misread. You must be A. L. Kanaan. The county shows you as owner on the property listing." He lifted a page on his clipboard of notes. "Says you bought it nearly ten years ago."

"That's correct."

"Wow, and you got it for next to nothing." He eyed me from under the bill of his hat. "Don't worry, ma'am. I didn't go snooping. These are legally attain—"

"Amelia is fine, and you don't need to explain public records to me, Archie."

Ethan, still at my back, coughed to cover a laugh—like the day he learned how seriously Mrs. Bimah took Mahjong Monday.

"Great. My dad, brothers, and I are developers." Undeterred, he tapped the insignia on his shirt with a pencil. "Things are getting hot here on this end of the county. A lot of longtime locals are selling at top dollar."

"And going where?" It seemed an obvious question.

"Where?"

"Yes, where are the longtime locals moving after selling for top dollar?"

"I really couldn't say, ma'am."

"*That* you can't explain to me. Hmm?"

Maybe the young Mr. Clay could read my frustration. His eagerness to cut short our impromptu meeting said so.

"If you are thinking about unloading the property, we'll give you a fair deal. A cash offer, no need for realtors, appraisers, surveyors and what have you." The smooth talker pulled a business card from his pocket. "Give us a call. Even if you just want to ask questions. Someone would be happy to speak with you, Ms. Kanaan."

"Probably not gonna happen, Archie, but I appreciate your effort."

"Never say never. The progress train is coming. Better to get on board than get hit by it." His red, white, and blue business card came toward me again. I took it, and Archie Clay left.

"Wow. Can you believe that? How brazen is he?"

"That guy? Archie? Aww, they'd eat him alive in New York City. Real estate is a blood sport in the boroughs."

I shook my head, choosing to focus on getting in and out of Mama's with my college application paperwork.

We picked through drawers two, three, and four of the file cabinet, as well as the two drawers in an old desk I bought years ago at a surplus store. No Chastain paperwork to be found. My back ached from sitting on the floor, and I leaned back to stretch.

"I'd have sworn it would be here."

Ethan sat sprawled out like me. His foot inched over to tap mine. He jerked his chin toward the file cabinet.

"What?" I asked.

"There is another drawer."

"It's locked."

"You're right. It is." He rolled to stand, willing to let it go at that.

"And I don't have the key," I added, defending myself.

"Guess we're out of luck then." He stretched on his feet.

"We could look for the key, I guess." On my knees, I slid open the center drawer of the desk. Pens, some rubber bands, and paperclips, but no keys.

"Totally up to you. I only came for the Sunday drive and the swell company."

"There's a junk drawer in the kitchen."

"*Welp*," he teased, "junk drawers are notorious hideouts for seldom used keys." He cocked his head with his sly grin—a grin I clocked more than a month ago would make me cross lines.

"Isn't that breaking and entering or something?"

"Come on, this is no Watergate. It's your house. Just ask Archie Clay. He'd be happy to mansplain it for you." Ethan's jokey face straightened as he helped me to my feet. "You already came here to look through your mother's papers knowing she wouldn't be here. You could have told her your plan on the phone, but you didn't. And I know you're protective of the woman, but I'm not sure you owe her anything under the circumstances. She isn't exactly a paragon of virtue in this matter. Not sure you should feel guilty about it. And let's not forget, it is *your* application we're looking for." He raised his hands in surrender. "That's all I'll say."

"That's *all*?"

Ethan's skill for sway showed itself again. Reasoned. Convincing. One slow exhale supplied all the time I needed to decide. I marched past him to the kitchen. He followed.

"That is, without a doubt, the tidiest junk drawer in the history of junk drawers. It doesn't even deserve the moniker." He leaned cross-armed in the doorway, looking over my shoulder. I continued my hunt, making sure everything ended up back where I found it. We might not have had much in my younger years, but what we had we kept neat and clean. Mama took pride in her organizational skills and thrived in the work.

"Yeah, well, there aren't any damn keys in here either." I slammed the drawer.

"Hey," he pulled me into a hug. A place, I soon realized, I'd longed to be all day. "Not sure what I'm going to do with you and that long-haul trucker mouth of yours." We both grunted a tired laugh and held on to one another.

My chin pressed to his chest. I looked up, inviting a kiss. "Thank you for coming here today."

"Thank you for letting me. If only for another solo car ride with you—minus formal wear. Sorry it didn't pan out."

"Me too. But the car made it an easier—" I pulled away. "Wait a sec. One more place to try." With a peck on his lips that felt as natural as could be, I headed out the kitchen's side door to the detached garage. The temperature had dropped, and the cold shocked me to a quick halt. Movement out of the corner of my eye drew me to squint into the fading light.

A Clay and Sons work truck sat in front of Winston's house, two doors down. Archie must have come back or just circled the block. No lights glowed inside the residence, but Archie, clipboard in hand, paced off the property's frontage on the street. He disappeared on the backside of the property when he measured by counting long strides on the far boundary.

I fished my house keys from my pocket to unlock the side door to Mama's garage, but found it already unlocked. How nice to live in a community where you didn't feel the need to lock things. I'd never known that peace of mind. Even in picturesque Druid Hills, people bolted their doors. The spare ring of keys hung on its usual hook tucked behind the door frame. What were the chances? Worth a shot.

"Hey," I shouted on my return to the kitchen. "I found something. Two odd-shaped keys on this ring. With a little of that

Edward R. Murrow 'good luck,' one could definitely be for a—"
I rounded the corner to find Ethan's back to me, his head down, engrossed in the file he held. The top drawer of the file cabinet pulled open.

"What did you do?"

He spun to face me, a baffled look on his face. "Talk about hiding your light under a bushel. Why didn't you tell me you were an international ribbon-winning equestrian?"

Twenty-Nine

"Equestrian?" My stomach lurched. "What did you do, Ethan?" I asked again, voice quiet, trembling.

"I got into the drawer. Not exactly Fort Knox security measures here. A paperclip is all it took."

My feet wouldn't move while the blast of heat after the jolt of cold outside started a prickly sweat. "Why?"

"Why? I'm helping. Saved you a minute or more if that key didn't work."

"You shouldn't have done that." As my anger grew, my voice diminished.

"I shouldn't have helped?"

"You shouldn't have picked the lock to my mother's file cabinet. You shouldn't have opened the drawer, much less any of the file folders inside it. You shouldn't even be here. Put it back. Put it all back. We're leaving."

"Mimi, this is what we came here to do. You'll want to look at it. There's more than you—"

"Put. The file. Back."

"No." He met my ominous demand with defiance. "You need to see this. All of it. It's important."

International equestrian. Adrenaline kicked in, a shock of fear and shame. Of all the embarrassing episodes of my life: inadequate housing, lack of supervision, dented canned meals, constant second-best finishes, my mother falsifying my college application. That incident, the equestrian lie, and the result of it, all leading to a pack of childhood stories I didn't want to share. With anyone. Ever. I launched across the small room, grabbing for the papers in Ethan's hands. My flailing grasp sent a bulky folder flying. Its contents scattered at our feet.

I dropped to my knees in a mix of surprise and panic, frantic to scoop up evidence of my early years for fear Ethan would see and what he would think. But as I looked closer, anger morphed into confusion. My dread lessened with every piece of nostalgia that came into focus. Crayon drawings, report cards, certificates, and red ribbons galore landed on the carpet. Stapled term papers with *A+* scrawled at the top. Photographs I had never seen showed a grade school me with Alani Fiva and a boy I didn't remember in front of a world map, another on a stage dressed in a tree costume, one with me eating a blue snow-cone, sweating on a hot middle school field day. A puddle of papers and pictures, a jumbled view of the "Best of Mimi" strewn about the floor.

"What is all of this?" I didn't mean to ask out loud.

"Amelia Louise Kanaan, this is your life," he bellowed in his best Ralph Edwards (whether or not he knew it), then eased to his knees, more subdued. "Mimi, this is you. Or a collection of you, an analog version of your youth's highlight reel. And it's amazing. You were amazing. Still are but look at this. Every accomplishment, big or small."

"But where did it—how is it—this is Mama's? My mother had all of this? *Kept* all of this? All this time?"

"Apparently. I'm thinking I jumped to some conclusions about the woman. Made assumptions. And maybe you got a few things wrong too."

"What else is new these days?"

"Yeah, no one wants to think it's true, and it's not pretty, but we all exhibit bias. You sure were one heck of a cute tree, though. That is a purely impartial observation. I swear."

He handed me the photograph. The photo of me in a tree costume.

"I begged for that part. It wasn't a speaking role, just singing with the rest of the class, but I had read about the oldest living tree. It's a questionable claim to fame because of the clonal nature—that part's not important, but *Old Tjikko* is a spruce tree dating back 9,550 years in the Dalarna province of Sweden. Mama sewed those swooping branches." My thumb stroked the image on my rambling stroll down memory lane. "She wasn't there to see it. The skit, I mean. I wonder who took the picture, and how she got it."

"This is not the act of someone *not* proud of their kid. You get that, right?" He kissed my cheek.

The rush of emotions threatened to crack me open, but I fought back with a quick shift. "You said something about horses?" No matter the compliment or moment of praise, something clicked in me. Wiring that compelled me to prove an admiration wrong. Mimi's default setting.

"Yes." He bounded to his feet. "Something is off, though. Here."

I stared at a photocopy of a grainy black-and-white photograph that looked like an unfamiliar newspaper clipping. The only thing I recognized was my name in the picture's caption: *Amelia Kanaan, aged 9 (above) "reins" supreme with a blue-ribbon win at the International Young Equestrians Federation, Abu Dhabi.* The blurry distance shot showed a child in a tailored jacket and jodhpurs atop an Arabian with its distinct bone structure and high tail. A handwritten note in the lower right corner read *NO* in capital letters and underlined twice.

"Something's off?" I settled onto the floor, keeping my eyes on the obvious-to-me fake. "What kind of something?"

"Well, it looks like a news clipping, doesn't it? There's no article—no big deal—but the caption is incorrect, for the medium. There's a strict format for such things and this one doesn't read right."

I huffed a short, sad laugh. "You think?"

"I do. First there's no date. A photo caption in print media should always include the day and date. Also, there is only one person in the photo, so the directional *above* in parentheses is out of place. No professional news organization would include it. The photo credit reads the photographer's name: Miles Blumenthal *slash* Associated Press photo. It should be AP Photo *slash* Miles Blumenthal. Plus, you never told me you rode horses, much less in the UAE. I'm sure you have all sorts of things left for me to learn about you and I can't emphasize enough how much I'm looking forward to it, but somehow, I think you'd have mentioned this."

Even when showing off his professional know-how, he made me feel wanted. And sad. Sad, because the next thing he would learn about me had *deal breaker* written all over it.

"Ethan, I don't know who's in this picture. I have never been on a horse or out of the country, much less competed on one in the United Arab Emirates, much to Geneva's chagrin. But it points to misconduct and the origin of my eventual social undoing at Chastain, and my fib rule." My mind swirled with the new data, and I couldn't understand it. Who could do this? Who *would* do it? It certainly wasn't a skill in Mama's wheelhouse. I'd keep any conjecture to myself until I knew more.

I continued to tell him the ugly truth about my mistaken identity when someone's friend's brother's girlfriend's sorority sister confused me as their campmate. How I never set the record straight and what happened the day my mother's inopportune arrival on campus made the whole charade fall apart, even while I still denied knowing the woman yelling my name on campus walk.

"See? I'm not so amazing after all. If there was any glimpse of my life that I could keep from you, it would be that. My rock bottom. I'd go to bed cold and hungry every night for the rest of my life to erase that moment, the whole thing. Make that nightmare just that. Nothing but a bad dream. But it's not. It happened. That's who I am. Someone who denies her own mother. I don't know if I should feel better or worse learning she had a hand in the confusion in the first place."

Ethan's exhale heaved like the final death knell. I focused on my sneakers in front of me, both desperate and terrified to see his reaction looming above me. I half-expected to see his well-worn shoes step over my outstretched legs on his way to the door.

At last, he spoke. "You were how old when you did this? This unforgivable thing with your mother? Twenty?"

"Nineteen. And totally aware—"

"Nope. You weren't totally aware of anything. My turn to teach you something. Let me give you a brief lesson in the prefrontal cortex. The part of the noggin that, among other things, plans decision-making and moderates social behavior. It doesn't mature until your mid-twenties. So, it's *not* who you are. It's who you were before you were a fully formed human being. No, it's who you were for an *instant* before you were a fully formed human. I'm talking a *physically, mentally, emotionally* whole person."

"Are you kidding me? You're joking about this?"

"Not even a little, Meems. Did you screw up? Yeah, you did. Spectacularly? You betcha. But if we were all permanently and publicly graded by actions taken, things we said or did on our worst day, most of us wouldn't get out of bed in the morning. As far as going to bed cold and hungry, I think you have been. Metaphorically, anyway."

I dismissed that comment with a mature eye roll and grunt.

"You have, Mimi. You have punished yourself for an adolescent lapse in judgment long enough." Ethan met me on the floor again, crawling to straddle my legs crossed at the ankles. Face to face, inches apart. "And apparently, I haven't made myself clear. Which is worrisome, considering my career. But there is nothing I don't want to know about you. I want the good, the bad, and the ugly, with every inch in between. And when I say every inch, I mean *every*—"

My fingers pinched his lips together to stop the poorly timed but much-appreciated seduction.

"All right. Simmer down, Hugh Hefner."

He dropped his shaking head with his laugh. "Aww, that's just wrong."

I lifted his chin and brushed curls from his brow as the air grew still; all the humor evaporated. We stared. Wordless, but easy. Comfortable. A euphoric but foreign feeling.

"We should go. I don't want to have a run-in with Mama right now. Not until I go through all this and—"

"Yeah. I get it." He backed away and got to his feet, helping me to mine.

"Thank you."

"For what?"

"For getting caught in the elevator with Rose Bimah that day."

"Back at you."

"What are you thanking me for?"
"For not taking the stairs."

Thirty

DECEMBER DARK ARRIVED EARLY, which made reading anything in the file a lost cause on the ride home. The equestrian photocopy sat on top of the pile in my lap. I could hardly make out the shapes in the dim car, but moreover, I couldn't guess how it figured into the confusion that happened so long ago. The longhand message of an emphatic *NO* set off more questions. If someone didn't want the fake news clipping used, someone *else* missed the one-word memo. But how did another student know about it?

All my overthinking triggered a headache, and the silence exacerbated the throbbing. I wanted a distraction.

"What are you grinding away about over there? It's dark in here, but oncoming traffic is giving away your clenched jaw." I brushed his stubbled cheek with the backs of my fingers, and he tilted into the touch. "You ok?"

Ethan nodded. "Climate change. It's a real problem, Meems. Too often overlooked. Lily's cat is sick. And the Colts are putting in a new quarterback this season, so a *lot* of pressure there, plus you've got a big day tomorrow and you're insisting on going in without a strategy when you ought to go in with a resignation letter. Of course, what do I know? Except I do know, but you won't let me help."

The rhythmic thumps of the highway punctuated the silence before I asked, "Sick how?"

That earned me a side-eye smirk, but I kept playing.

"Lily's your niece, right? In what way is her cat ill?"

He chuckled and his shoulders relaxed by inches.

"Ethan. It isn't very nice to laugh about someone's ailing pet, particularly your own niece. Have some compassion," I continued to joke.

"All right. I won't press it, but man, you are stubborn. Just know you don't have to accept the offer in the room. You can take time to think about it. Don't let them pressure you."

"So, what is it? Leukemia, diabetes? I read those are pretty common feline ailments."

The heel of his hand banged on the steering wheel. "Fine. What are you thinking about over there?"

I held up the photocopy. "This."

"You gotta let it go, Meems. I bet no one remembers that day but you."

"Tristan Pembroke remembered."

"All right, but he seemed pretty magnanimous with you. Some might say too magnanimous."

"Some, huh? If that's jealousy talking, 'cause I don't hate it." I glimpsed his jaw tighten again in the flash of headlights, but a grin appeared.

"Should I be jealous? Why? Because he's younger? The life of the party? A billionaire?"

I let his questions hang, unanswered.

"It makes no sense to me. I get this sort of 'accomplishment' might play well on an application, but it definitely doesn't get me a need-based full scholarship. How does that happen?"

"Maybe, like the note says, it didn't get used. Maybe whoever your mother hired proposed the fake news clipping as an option, but she said no. N-O."

"But it *did* get used. Someone used it. Someone saw it, read it. And spread it around."

"Or—"

"Or what?"

"I'm telling you, Mimi, the stuff that goes on out in the world, well, it would surprise you."

I didn't like my lack of real-world experience, now more than ever. Nor could I defend it. Ethan had more answers than I ever would. "Stuff? What kind of stuff?"

"You've heard of whisper campaigns, haven't you?"

"Sure, the secret spreading of negative news meant to hurt someone's reputation, but that's usually in politics, right?"

"First, everything is political these days, and second, people will pay to have news dispersed with a positive spin. The ploy negates the need for a public humble brag. This way, the outed party can play modest, self-effacing while still getting props for whatever good deed got leaked."

"Wow, that's—"

"Calculating? Conniving? Utterly Machiavellian? Yep. And more widely practiced than you would think."

"But why me? Who would do it?"

Ethan didn't offer an answer, just a deep exhale.

"Yeah, yeah, I know."

He chuckled. "You know? You know what? Who are you talking to?"

"You. I know you're thinking I need to go to the source. Talk to Mama. She's the only one who can answer those questions."

"I'm impressed you can read my mind. Maybe a little scared. But also, kinda turned—"

"Don't say it."

Mr. Colby and his caterpillar brows greeted us when we entered the lobby from the backside parking garage for residents. He offered no more than a nod with his "G'evenin'," but I guessed he would inform the nosy parkers around the building that Ethan and I arrived together, after dark, on a Sunday, no less.

"Oh, Miss Mimi. Max and I took a stroll about half an hour ago. Had a nice long talk. Well, I listened mostly. I'm sure you know. Once he gets started." The quiet man tipped his hat.

"Thank you, sir. You've saved me. Now I can fall right into bed." I hugged the overstuffed folders from Mama's to my chest like precious cargo, doing my best casual routine. The doorman gave Ethan a knowing wink I tried to ignore as we walked away.

"We should say goodnight here," I whispered. "You go to your apartment, and I'll go up to Geneva's."

Ethan raised his brow.

I tilted my head toward Mr. Colby who grinned while texting at his station near the revolving door. "He's already notifying the yenta brigade we're together. Plus, I have all this to go through. I know you'd like to be there for me while I do it, but I need you to *not* be there when I do it." With a doleful look, I begged him not to argue.

Our sullen and telepathic goodbye ended with Ethan's sweet kiss to my rippled forehead. But before the slow elevator made its first lurch toward the twelfth floor, my phone chirped with a text.

The Reporter: I'll be going to the campus tomorrow morning. Let me take you. Name the time. I'll set my alarm.

Mimi: I'll be going early. But thank you.

The Reporter: You read the part about setting my alarm, right?

Mimi: Propriety matters. I'll see you later in the day. Standing in the back of the room. That's all you can do, and that's all I'm asking.

The Reporter: I'll be there. Please get some sleep. Goodnight.

The elevator doors juddered open with exhaustion that mirrored my own. With my brimming folders held to my chest, I schlepped down the hall to *12A*, where Max's legendary low-key enthusiasm greeted me. As soon as he ate the second dog treat, no longer an optional indulgence, he lumbered away with a brief look over his shoulder to see if I followed.

We hunkered under a blanket on the sofa and stared at the two thick folders I set side-by-side on the coffee table. Despite my early eagerness to compare and contrast my fifteen-year-old college application to the data I'd stolen, borrowed, *legally* obtained for morally just purposes, my hands hesitated to open the files.

We'd both benefit from sleep and a visit to my pre-college past could wait for another day, but I'm not sure Max agreed. For a moment, I'd have sworn Max *bok-bagoked* at me, but I chalked it up to my fatigue and not the cheeky Portie calling me a chicken. Like I said, I was tired.

Thirty-One

FOR THE SECOND TIME in all my years working at Chastain, I dug through my bag for the keys to the Admissions Office. Any other day, I would have reveled in arriving before Nora, but that morning I wished she was there to greet me with her all-business walk and talk to start the week. The *clang* and *hiss* of radiators played the only background noise, and I made a mental note to never arrive that early again.

Determined to treat the day like any other, I locked away my phone and watered the philodendron a little extra while I waited for my computer to reboot. When my phone chirped, muffled in the drawer, my instinct said to free it, but as I reached for the antique key, the far-away sound of Nora's desk phone rang, coinciding with the blinking red light on my office landline. I answered that one instead.

"Amelia Kanaan, Chastain Admissions. How may I help you?" I met a three-count of silence.

"Amelia. You surprised me. I expected Nora to answer. This is Janice calling for Dr. Cromwell."

"Good morning, Janice. Yes, it's a rarity, but I arrived before Nora today. Maybe she's still prying herself out of her Turkey Day coma." I had no reason to think Janice wanted to chit-chat this early in the morning—or ever, but it felt worth the try. "Did you have a pleasant holiday?"

"It's opportune, your early arrival. Dr. Cromwell would like to see you at your earliest convenience."

Nope, no small talk for Janice.

Every inch of me tightened, but I forced a smile for no one but the philodendron. "Sure, I can be there at *his* earliest convenience."

"Then I suggest you start walking, Ms. Kanaan. He'll be expecting you."

"Oh, you mean, now?"

"The very definition of his earliest convenience, yes. Don't dawdle." The *click-clack* of a phone landing in its cradle and the buzz of a dial tone told me Janice had more important things to do than to summon me. Her brusqueness made me grab my coat and bag and hurry out the door.

I cursed myself for the heavy breathing, but I made my trip across campus at something close to a gallop until I noticed a news van pulling into the president's building lot. While it slowed my feet, it quickened my already racing heart. Once inside and out of sight of any media crew, I scurried up the grand staircase.

Peering at me over her glasses, Janice's disapproval of my huffing and puffing needed no words.

I swallowed hard before saying, "Gotta get in that morning cardio, amiright?"

The executive assistant bit back whatever comment she had at the ready and instead replied, "He'll see you now."

"Any surprise visitors in there I should know about this time?"

"Go right in." Janice was a vault.

With one more deep inhale, I enter the grand office with a put-on smile and two fibs at the ready.

"There she is," Dr. Cromwell stood when I entered. "Please take a seat. May I have Janice bring you something? Coffee, tea?" His smile and manners served as quick reminders that the southern gentleman was the most charming and perhaps the most dangerous of all the versions of the president I'd encountered.

I craved water after my morning jog but knew better than to have Janice summoned for it.

"No, thank you. I'm fine."

"Funny. No one ever takes me up on that offer." He sat once I did, in full chivalry mode. "I trust you enjoyed the holiday."

"I went to my mother's. You, sir?" Full fib allotment still intact.

"You know. It's all fun and games until someone gets a black eye in the family football match. We might call it two-hand-touch, but my young nephew learned about elbows this year. My elbow, to be exact. And as an academic, I say it's never too early for an education." A proud grin cracked wide across from me with a silence meant for a missing laugh track. I couldn't muster a substitute.

He sighed, "So, you are probably wondering why I've called you here this early in the morning."

"How may I help you, Dr. Cromwell?" Still two for two.

"I think it's more how I can help you. This year, someone must have been a very good girl, and Christmas has come early."

I kept my mouth shut, waiting for the big announcement and subsequent promotion Ethan warned me would follow. The president was already laying the groundwork, pitching it as though they awarded me something—that I was the lucky winner of some grand prize instead of the role of the eventual stooge in the school's brewing drama.

"First, the sad news. It's the end of an era for us Mighty Roosters. FDR, Frank Rayburn, has stepped down as Dean of Admissions. He plans to step away from the university entirely. Effective immediately. Spend time with his family. His St. Simon's getaway reminded him how important his wife, kids, and grandkids are to him, and—well, it's probably time, right? I'm sure Cookie played a role in getting him to see the light."

I nodded, but any surprise Cromwell read on my face had less to do with what he said than how Ethan called it, almost verbatim. Evidently, *Scapegoats for Dummies* existed, and both Ethan and my boss had studied it cover to cover. A small cough helped me steady my voice. "The timing seems a tad suspect, don't you think?"

The benevolent gentleman act showed its first sign of breaking. "Suspect? How do you mean?" A glimmer of concern flashed across his face. An unfamiliar touchiness.

"Not suspect, I guess, but ill-timed. Given—"

"Given what, Ms. Kanaan?"

"Given we are in the middle of—well, heading into the regular admissions season. We have a class roster to fill, and now we're forced to move ahead without our fearless leader." I chose to lean into the mundane, rather than the impending scandal break.

Dr. Cromwell relaxed in his high-backed chair and knitted his fingers like a Bond villain whose trap had sprung, catching his prey. Did that make me a Bond girl? I wasn't sure that was a club I cared to join.

"I, for one, have no worries on that score, Amelia. With a quick conference call over the weekend, we gathered a quorum of the board, and they unanimously voted you as the obvious choice to lead the team, with little to no delays in overseeing the regular admissions session. We'll call it interim. The department is a well-oiled machine, so I don't foresee any trouble 'gettin' 'er done,' as they say."

A conference call? A quorum? A vote? Had I missed something? Did my boss ask me if I had an interest in taking a promotion, even if only short-term? The hubris that they thought this was a done deal. Sure, I knew this was coming, but I didn't expect it by way of a steamroller.

"Just one bit of housekeeping to do, and then we can return to our regularly scheduled program like nothing has changed."

Ah, here it came. The offer.

"We have some press waiting outside, and we'd like to make a brief statement regarding the staffing change. It will placate the Board of Trustees, alumni, and future applicants, not to mention our donors, of course."

"Ah, but you just did," I quipped. "Mention them, I mean. The donors."

His cocked head said he missed the joke, but he was already on his feet, gesturing for me to stand to meet the firing squad. Er, media gauntlet.

"Now I see that panic on your face, Ms. Kanaan. But don't worry, you look fine."

"You mean now? This minute? I haven't accepted the position." And did he really think how I *looked* topped my list of concerns at the moment?

"Of course you're going to accept the position, Amelia. You, of all people, wouldn't leave us in the lurch like this. Come on now." Dr. Cromwell rounded his desk and beelined out his office door. "And don't feel you have to say anything. Just stand by a few board members and me while we announce the personnel change. Our focus will be more on our absent friend, FDR. His legacy. Followed by a brief mention of you. The reporters just need a sound bite or two. Shall we?"

My vision blurred in the speed of things. I struggled to shove my arm through one wool sleeve, chasing past Janice to catch the president. My second jog of the day, and both in heels. Not ideal.

"Dr. Cromwell. Wait."

He didn't even slow up as I clambered alongside him, my coat half on and my bag caught on the railing to the grand staircase.

"Thatcher," I yelped in frustration, teetering on the steps as I tried to free the snagged strap. "Sir. Don't you think I'm a little young? I mean, a high-level position at a prestigious school. Shouldn't it warrant some discussion at least?"

Cromwell's forced laugh and stern face gave away his irritation. "The board discussed it. And decided. We can work out the details after we assuage the masses. I don't mean to sound indelicate, little lady, but the Board of Trustees, the donors, are who I need to make comfortable. If that means you need to endure some *discomfort* in the short term, so be it. Just smile and keep quiet." He trotted down the stairs, done with the "conversation."

The morning sun highlighted the clouds of breath by all those chatting on the campus walkway. The press event's backdrop, ivy-covered columns and the carved wood door, loomed over me, slanting, seeming to sway in my hectic headspace.

Reporters from various outlets gathered. Again, just as Ethan had predicted, except outdoors, not in a room where his job forced him to stand in the back and watch. Some waited with microphones and camera crews, while others worked solo with handheld recorders. A lectern stood center stage with a plinth microphone. None of it had been here when I arrived earlier, and I didn't see Ethan in the crowd.

"Congrats, Mimi," Tristan Pembroke whispered as he slid out from behind a massive pillar. "Oh, sorry. I should be in pro-mode. Congratulations, *Amelia.*"

"For what?" I gave my ponytail a workout.

"For the promotion, of course. Franklin Rayburn's retirement. That's—"

"*Convenient* I think is the word you're hunting for. And I didn't accept the promotion," I murmured back at him, confirming the fact with myself as much as with him.

"Well, I think you're about to. Thatcher is a bulldozer of a man."

"Yeah, well, I'm not inclined to—why are you here?"

Tristan replied with a low but dramatic, "*Ouch*," then smiled. "I'm here as a proxy for Daddy Dearest..." But his words evaporated when a man in the distance came running up the brick path toward the crowd. Ethan. The closer he got, the more I realized a look of alarm. He eyed the mob, then zeroed in on me after my discreet wave.

Frenzied hand motions gesticulated the question: *Where is your phone?*

With a glance at my messenger bag propped against a column base and a quick pat-down of my pockets, I remembered I'd left my phone locked in the desk drawer in my office when I received my summons.

I shook my head, but then Dr. Cromwell's voice boomed, "Good morning, everyone..."

Ethan's stricken face said he had news. Bad news. News I needed to hear but couldn't decipher in an agitated game of charades played yards and a swarm of press apart from one another. A polite chuckle at whatever folksy joke Cromwell must have told pulled my attention again when the gathering offered a pity laugh.

"But seriously," the president continued. "Good ol' FDR, as we called him around here, well, we'll miss him, but—"

And that's when I did the unthinkable.

"Excuse me, Thatcher." I muscled my way to the mic. "I just want to second that. We will, no doubt, miss FDR, but I want to assure everyone: the public, our students, and our future students. While we will be without our longtime leader, the staff commits itself to a seamless transition for the next recruitment class until the university finds an *appropriate* new hire to fill such a vital role to ensure Chastain's longevity. It may take time but the admissions staff—and that includes me—will support that new director whenever the search committee finds a suitable interim and then permanent replacement. Everyone agrees that the hiring for such an important post is not a processed we can rush. Now, if you'll excuse me, I'll let President Cromwell finish up here. Go, Mighty Roosters!" I cheered with a raised fist, then spun to avoid my boss's eye and find my bag.

Tristan helped the strap onto my shoulder, wearing a wicked smile. "Bulldozer meet bedrock. I'm so impressed by you, Ms. Kanaan. So. Impressed."

"Thanks. I have to run." I slipped by the dapper billionaire, keeping what I hoped read like confidence affixed to my face, then bolted to find Ethan.

Thirty-Two

I SKIRTED THE CROWD, searching for Ethan's mop of curls, cursing my toes pinched in shoes never meant for running. Another courtesy laugh chortled out of the crowd. In my scrambled mind, I gave a fleeting plea to the universe that Cromwell's joke hadn't been at my expense. Finding Ethan was priority one.

My feet kept their pace while I spun in all directions, hoping to glimpse the only reporter I cared about these days, worried about what he'd say when I found him. With a firm tug and another half-turn, I found my back pressed to the rough bark of a broad tree, Ethan's lips lighting up mine. Adrenaline spiked, and I couldn't care less that a three-foot-wide tree trunk offered the only cover from an army of cameras. Warm hands cupped my chilled face, and the rest of the world faded as I clung to the lapels of his peacoat to keep him close and maybe my feet on the ground.

He pulled away, but only a fraction of an inch. "That was amazing. You are amazing."

"Thanks. You're not so bad yourself." I kissed him again.

His mouth curled upward, but not a real smile. Not the kind that showed off his crow's feet. This one never reached his eyes.

"Not the kiss—which is also amazing, but what you did up there." He whispered, our foreheads pressed. "You elbowed old

Thatcher out of the way and said your piece. You didn't take the job."

"Not when he tried to bully me into it. Played on my people-pleasing ways to guilt me into it. No. I wasn't going down like that."

"I don't want to sound patronizing, but I'm proud of you. You took a risk. Now we see where the chips fall." Ethan tilted in for another tender kiss, but my euphoria crashed.

"Oh my God, what did I do? What if Cromwell fires me? What if I lose my job?" I pushed him away, no longer enjoying the breathless sensation.

He reached for me. Sadness emanated from him and it compounded my dread. "You won't. But if you do, we'll figure it out."

"We? Who exactly is we, Ethan? You have a job. And a life and an enormous family, and I've got nothing—and why are you here? Your miming routine made it seem like something dire."

He tried to hold me closer, tighter, but I needed to see him. I'd face whatever came next head-on, eyes open, not buried in a man's chest.

"Ethan? What is it? Mama?"

I insisted Ethan wait outside while I returned to my office to free my phone. By then, my whole body buzzed numb, my feet no longer feeling any pain, but my heart broken. I rushed by Nora to unlock my desk.

"Amelia, what's happened? I heard from Janice—are you all right? What's happened?"

I struggled with the old key in my shaking fingers. "Janice? Yes, uh, FDR quit. I guess you knew that. We'll be fine. We'll get through the spring acceptances. *Dammit.* This stupid key," I spat just as the old drawer let loose. Grabbing my phone, I glanced at the list of missed calls. Another rare *dammit* slipped from my lips.

"Where are you going?"

"I'll be fine but gone for the day."

"Amelia." It was the closest I'd ever heard Nora come to a shout, but my overtaxed brain had no more room.

"If the press calls, we have no further statement beyond what I said earlier this morning. No comment. That's the line, okay?"

"Yes, of course."

I hurried to the door, calling over my shoulder. "Please hold down the fort for me, Nora. I'm depending on you."

Ethan, head down, took the stairs two at a time, coming toward me as I descended them.

"We agreed you were to wait outside."

"Agreed? Who agreed? I love hearing you call us a 'we,' but *we* made no such agreement back there."

"What if someone sees you, Ethan? Sees us?"

"Like I give a damn who sees me. None of that is important now."

"Sorry. I'm sorry. I—" I grabbed the railing to steady myself, wondering if the bombardment of awful news could take a time out. One bombshell after another exploded around me these past months, each with escalating consequences. The universe had my attention, but I couldn't decrypt the code.

Another unrehearsed meeting, but no one can prepare for shock like what came next.

"Miss Kanaan, Moses Pascha. My condolences." The older gentleman wore a charcoal gray suit and clutched a black leather dossier two-handed after handing me his business card. He bowed instead of offering a handshake and the word petite came to mind. Bright light from the Midtown Mews lobby chandelier reflected off his shiny head, obscure by the dozen hairs that made up his near-white comb-over. When I read the stiff card, it included his name followed by the suffix title *Esquire.* Another glance at the man said that word tracked too.

"May her memory be a blessing."

I hadn't been able to utter a word since Ethan and I left the campus in his rental car. Keeping myself from falling apart took all my concentration, and it seemed my grief-stricken silence would continue a bit longer. How could she be gone?

"Mr. Pascha, I'm Ethan Ledes. We spoke on the phone."

"Yes, Mrs. Spieler listed you as a point of contact to gain entry into her home should the need arise. I appreciate your help in locating Ms. Kanaan. I hope it hasn't been an inconvenience."

Ethan and I turned when a prolonged goose-like squawk wailed from Mr. Colby as he exited the mailroom, his face buried in a rumpled handkerchief as he blew his nose. The lawyer didn't move from his spot behind a potted palm.

"No, none at all. Thank you for waiting for us. Pascha. Is that—Greek?"

"Very good, Mr. Ledes. It is. Would it be possible to find a less public venue? Mrs. Spieler's flat, perhaps?"

Ethan did his best to pull me from the fog of sorrow, swallowing me whole. "Would you like to take Mr. Pascha upstairs, Mimi?"

I swiveled into the low-hanging fronds of another nearby palm tree, then brushed away the tickle the long green leaf left on my cheek. I nodded to the two gentlemen and continued to the elevator that stood mercifully open.

"Should I join you, Meems?"

Going alone never occurred to me. What a revelation. If anything had changed in the last month, that reaction might top the list.

"Please," I rasped and stepped aboard the burled wood and brass car for the slow ride to the twelfth floor.

I dropped to my knees to greet Max, finally able to find words. "Hey, buddy. Surprised to see me this soon?" We nuzzled each other as I reached for his treats, but he wouldn't take them. The bone-shaped dog biscuits sat at his feet. "What? No treats? That's not like you."

Those mopey brown eyes seemed even more gloomy than usual. He pushed his wet nose to my ear, letting out a low whimper I'd never heard him make. I craned my neck to see Ethan. "It's like he knows. How could he possibly know?" My first tear sprang, and I pulled Max closer, using his soft curly-haired ear to wipe it away before the men saw.

"Maybe we should take him for a walk. I mean, it hasn't been two hours, but I should take him." I stood to deposit my bag on the sofa. Max crossed to stay at my side.

"Let me take him. Give you and Mr. Pascha time to get to business. Come on, Max. Let's go walk, huh? You and me, big guy." Ethan pulled the fancy leash from the drawer, but Max didn't move.

The rip in my heart tore wider when the Portie's whimper sounded again, louder this time.

"It's okay, Maxy. You can go. I'll be here when you get back. Promise." *Promise.* The last word Geneva said to us before she left on what should have been just another of her frequent getaways. Max nudged my thigh like he remembered, too. His little sneeze and the way he leaned into my leg told everyone in the room his place was with me.

"Aww, no worries, boy. We'll walk later. A nice long one, okay?" Ethan used the sweetest tone as he tucked away the leash.

When I squatted to Max's level, he rested his chin on my shoulder, making no effort to break our embrace. The poor dog would have witnessed the ugliest of ugly cries if I'd been alone. But all of that would have to wait.

Upright again, I removed my coat, determined to get to that business Ethan mentioned.

"So, Mr. Pascha. Why such a rush? What is it that is so time sensitive?" I ushered him and Ethan to the dining room. The large table in the glamorous, bordering on garish, room drew me to sit. The room epitomized Geneva. Sparkly and busy with gilded scrolling curves and histrionic art that didn't take itself too seriously. No wonder she got along so well with the likes of Tristan Pembroke.

"Geneva Spieler left very strict and detailed instructions should this day come."

I appreciated the man's delicate language. Hearing it said aloud a second time would hurt as much as the first time when Ethan kept me upright with the help of a giant tree. I found solace in the cushioned dining chair at the head of the long, dark walnut table.

Pascha continued. "She was rarely more than a voice over the phone, these last years, but our talks often lasted longer than necessary. She liked to talk and had this plan in place for quite some time. Since shortly after *Mr.* Spieler died. I don't believe you knew him?"

"Moishe? No, I met Geneva after that, though it sort of feels like I knew him, but no."

The little man chuckled with a twinkle in his eye. "Don't believe everything you've heard. Geneva could tell a tale, couldn't she? Oh, I mean no disrespect. She insisted I call her by her first name."

"I don't doubt it, Mr. Pascha. And please, call me Amelia. Better yet, Mimi."

"Then please do me the honor of calling me Moses." He opened the black leather pouch, pulling a specific sheet of paper with a letterhead I couldn't read. "First order of business, which may seem curious, but I am instructed to tell you to make coffee. In fact, it says I am to insist on it."

"O-kay. Sure, I can make coffee." Relief of sorts hit me, having something to do other than sit with the ache in my chest. Moses and Ethan stood, too.

"Let me do it, Mimi. I know my way around the kitchen."

I held his hand and brushed his rough fingers with my thumb. "Thank you, but I'd like to. Mama was right again. I am better off when given a task."

Max followed me to the kitchen but found some comfort in his kitchen bed. A shiny Nespresso machine intimidated me from its corner nook, so I opted to use the simple, no-electricity-needed French press that sat beside it. Water heated in a kettle on the stove as I pulled mugs from the cupboard, then made a long stretch to reach the top shelf of the left cabinet. A worn fiery orange canister read Aladdin Coffee in bold yellow letters with more modern-day vacuum-sealed bags with the same name stored next to it. The container had seen better days, but it must have meant something to Geneva to keep it all this time.

On my tip-toes, I still couldn't reach it and hopped up on the counter to grab hold of the rusty-edged tin. When I pulled it off the shelf, a sticky note detached from the metal lid and floated to the counter. I recognized Geneva's handwriting. *Aladdin Coffee makes wishes come true.* I chuckled at the woman's theatrics, even with her coffee.

It took a moment to figure out how to open the lid, but once I did, I endured another shock. The water kettle's scream couldn't have been more well-timed to cover the gasp that must have erupted from me. Inside the can, thick stacks of banded one-hundred-dollar bills hid one atop another with two more rolls side by side. The whistle grew louder until I slammed the old tin closed, flipped off the stove burner, and climbed the counter again to grab a bag of Turkish brew on sudden autopilot with my coffee duty.

Who was the enigmatic man sitting in Geneva's dining room? What did he know about the hidden cash stash? I decided to keep that to myself but was eager to show Ethan.

The grounds steeped in the glass carafe on a tray with three mugs and the usual fixings.

"None for me, thank you, Ms. Kanaan. I'm a tea drinker myself."

"I'm sorry. Did I misunderstand? Didn't you ask me to make coffee?"

Moses pointed to the top sheet of paper in a shallow stack. "No, Geneva did. Demanded it, actually. Says so right here."

I twisted back to face the kitchen; pretty sure everything that occurred there had taken place—in real life.

"Everything okay, Mimi? Want to take a minute?"

I had too many questions to slow down now. "No. I'm good. Fine. As well as can be expected. Coffee for you, then?"

"Yes, smells delicious. Rich. Strong."

"Well, it's rich, all right. I'll leave you to pour your own. Now, Mr. Pascha, Moses, why are we meeting like this, and how can we move it along?" Turns out, the can of cash wasn't the only surprise on the horizon.

Thirty-Three

MR. PASCHA'S PRESENTATION WAS quick, efficient, and full of information. That didn't mean my head wasn't buzzing with the deluge of details. Plenty of questions remained and my concerns ranged from the practical to the surreal. And I didn't know how to broach the makeshift piggy bank with Ethan.

"How is it that they can just decide to stop looking? Geneva could be out there hanging onto a piece of fuselage like Rose and Jack and that Titanic door. And can we agree there was definitely room for Jack to get on that thing?"

Ethan pulled me into a hug after we said our goodbyes to the kind if tight-lipped and mysterious Moses Pascha.

"There was definitely room on the door, but I think there was an issue with buoyancy. Whether it could stay afloat given the physics—"

I wrenched my head to level a hard, incredulous stare.

"Ah, rhetorical question. Got it." He frowned. "As for Geneva? The chances are—well, it's not likely. And big commercial airliners go down and never get found. A small private jet? Over the Atlantic?" He held tighter. "Let's hope she went with a glass of champagne in her hand."

Max appeared, nosing his way between our shins.

"You ready for that walk, boy?"

I kneeled to give Max an extra dose of ear-rub love. "You're mine now, buddy. Hope you're okay with that. I'm not sure how Dr. Jaspers will feel about it—actually, I *know* how he feels about pets. Guess we're in the market for a new home. Which is cool because there is nothing else demanding going on in my life. Adding apartment-hunting to my to-do list will help keep things interesting."

"Man, your optimism is inspiring."

"My optimism or my sarcasm?" I wandered to the dining room, where the documents specifying my part of Geneva's end-of-life plans sat on the table. "I can't believe she's gone." I swallowed back the sob that tried to tear out of my throat and focused on the strewn paperwork.

Moses assured us it was a straightforward scenario created so I would not endure any fiscal hardship in taking on Max's care. Silly, given I would do anything for the dog. But caretaker Geneva set up a trust—a pet trust—to provide funds for Max's needs.

Moses and his firm would handle all aspects of the arrangement, including sending me a monthly stipend. Mr. Pascha implied many clients considered detailed discussions as insensitive at best. At worst, vulgar. The contents of the sealed envelope would inform me of the exact monthly payout. That part didn't matter. Max would stay with me no matter what, and Geneva knew it. I replayed the highlights of what little the lawyer told us.

"So, no service of any sort?"

"That is correct."

"And her things? This apartment and its contents?"

"I'm only at liberty to assure you it will be taken care of and that Mrs. Spieler included a clause allowing you to take anything you cared to keep."

My mind jumped to the worn coffee can in the kitchen.

"Surely anything pertaining to your new ward," Pascha continued with a gesture to Max at my feet. *"Movers will empty the residence by the new year, and the sale will cover debts, with the remainder going to predetermined charities. Call my number if you have questions or concerns."*

My finger traced the flowing lines of my name written in Geneva's bold script. How long had she planned for this eventual day?

Ethan's heat warmed my back as he squeezed my shoulders and kissed the top of my head. "How about some fresh air? A walk would do us all good, and I'm pretty sure Max has no plans to leave your vicinity anytime soon."

"I need to tell you something first."

"What's that?"

"It's about the coffee."

"Don't worry about it, Meems. You made it wrong. Turkish coffee is unique, but I'll show you the proper way—"

"This is not about my barista skills, or lack thereof, you java snob." My first genuine grin of the day. "Come with me." I pulled Ethan by a belt loop toward the kitchen.

"This is taking an unexpected, albeit exciting, turn. Have you been eyeing the kitchen island like I've been eyeing the kitchen island? Because I've dreamed about you on this particular slab." He spun me half a twirl and hoisted me onto the counter.

I laughed, enjoying a playful moment. "Rein it in—oh, I used Heffner already. Who's the other guy?"

"Aww, please don't say Larry—"

"Larry Flynt. That's the one."

Ethan hung his head. "You know how to kill a mood."

My ankles locked around his back, and I poked his rock-hard midsection, eager for his smile but met the opposite.

"Sorry. That was inappropriate, given the day."

I pulled him closer, lifting his chin. "Are you kidding me? If anyone approved of indecent flirting and porn publishing mogul jokes on a sad day, it would be Geneva Spieler. You know, she hinted she'd posed once, back in the day. Name dropped her friend Gloria."

"Gloria? As in Steinem? Really? There's a kick-ass journalist. Geneva knew her?"

"Dunno. Geneva tends to speak just vaguely enough to make you wonder. *Tended* to, I guess, is more accurate." More grief sloshed inside me, but I pushed past it. "Hey, do me a favor."

"Name it. Bonus points if it's indecent." He won another grin.

"Reach up to the top shelf of that cupboard and pull down the coffee can."

He looked askance but obeyed, shaking the tin before setting it beside me, still perched on the island. A more quizzical wave rippled across his brow.

"Geneva frequently harangues—pestered me about making coffee. Her coffee. *This* coffee. I've told you I make terrible coffee."

"You weren't joking."

"Shut up. I love coffee, but I'd rather hit a local beanery on a weekend walk or have one of Nora's phenomenal café au laits at work. Not important. But Geneva has been suggesting I 'make coffee' for some time. Now I know why. Open it." I nodded to the vintage can, showing Ethan the Post-it note.

"*Aladdin Coffee makes wishes come true,*" he read aloud. "Clever, I guess. Is that the old ad campaign?"

"Maybe." I shrugged. "*Open* it."

Knowing what Ethan would find didn't keep me from gasping again. He dumped the treasure onto the counter. "Whoa, that's a nearly $100,000 inheritance with your name on it."

"How do you know?"

"This other sticky that says, *'For Amelia Kanaan'* in scrawling script was the big giveaway."

I smacked his arm.

"It also says, *'Trust Moses Pascha.'*"

"That's good to know. How do you know how much it is?"

"Nine stacks of bound one-hundred-dollar bills, plus two smaller rolls—quick math says..."

"Holy cow."

"There she goes, cursing like a sailor again. But what exactly was Geneva into that would have her hiding money in a coffee can?"

Ethan's investigative mind whirred to life in a new way. His curiosity piqued meant he wanted answers, or at least a distraction from the current sullen circumstance.

We returned from our walk and urged Max to eat a treat. No success. Ethan and I shared worried grimaces as the dog wandered down the hall to Geneva's bedroom, only to return with a cocked head and the obvious question, *Where is she?*

My phone rang.

"Hey, Mama. Everything okay?"

"Okay, as Mondays go, I guess."

"Mondays? Huh. It's Monday, isn't it?"

"All day."

Ethan squeezed my elbow, then pointed to the door.

"Hold on, Mama." I pressed the phone to my chest. "You're going?"

"You need to talk to your mother. About all kinds of things. And I need to—"

"Work?"

Ethan couldn't tell me more, so I knew better than to ask. I wondered if the two steps forward, one step back cha-cha we danced, made him ache as much as it did me. I rose on tiptoes to kiss him goodbye, but he hesitated. His forehead pressed to mine.

"Mimi," he whispered my name like an agonized prayer. "I don't think I can kiss you and then go be impartial. It's hard enough to be unbiased just knowing you. But to have your soft mouth under mine? The taste of you on my lips?"

I swallowed hard, willing my legs to do their job. "I think there's a compliment in that somewhere. See you tomorrow?"

He nodded. "And I'll get Max in the morning. After you go. I don't want him to be alone for long."

"Goodnight." I nodded, even more seduced by his concern for my new pet, but forced the phone to my ear to end the day's frustration-foxtrot. "Sorry, Mama. How's your Monday?"

Ethan took three steps before turning one-eighty. "Screw it," he mumbled and grabbed me, planting a deep kiss that burned more like a torrid tango than a wooden waltz.

Thirty-Four

"... SO, I'M THINKING the best thing to do is sit down together, face-to-face, to discuss it."

I'd missed the first part of whatever my mother said and still found it difficult to focus despite her insistence in my ear. The heat from Ethan's mind-numbing kiss still seared from my hair to my toes.

"Uh, okay, and when would you like to do that? Sit and discuss—it?" What did she mean by *it*? The Chastain scandal? Her role in it all those years ago? Her health? The list of possibilities ran long. "Later this week? Wednesday?"

"That'll do. Would you like us to come to you?"

"Us?"

"Winston and me."

Winston? "You want to come to my place? With Winston? You've never been to my home." Darn Ethan and his heart-stopping lips. Whatever I'd missed must be bad.

"About time, I suppose. While I can."

While she can? "Of course, Mama. Name the time."

"Seven o'clock. Have wine. That will help, but I am happy to hear you are open to it. I know you don't like change."

"What?"

"Seven sharp." Mama ended the call.

I dropped the phone in my lap and contemplated wine. Like I needed more mind-numbing.

"Get your head in the game, Kanaan. Your to-do list is growing."

Max lumbered to my side and cocked his head. Another whimper sighed out of him as he rested his chin on my knee.

"Come up here, buddy."

He hopped onto the sofa, turning twice before taking his usual spot.

"Let's make a plan. One. And this is in no particular order. One. See Chastain through recruiting the next class, including Briana Johnson's enrollment. Two. Find a place to live. Three. Make certain I have no other responsibilities regarding Geneva's estate. I don't know about you, Max, but I'm glad to hear Moses and his people seem to have it all in hand. Four. Read the envelope contents and fill out the necessary forms. Five. Talk to Mama and find out: Five A. What she did fifteen years ago. And Five B. What is she up to now? Six. Confirm the staff's holiday gift baskets. Seven. Under no circumstances let Ethan Ledes distract you from numbers one through six."

Max's yawned reply bore an astonishing likeness to the words, "Yeah, right."

"I won't pry," Nora said, "but I'm glad to see you this early in the morning. I didn't know your plan for today, so I have kept your schedule light. Is there anything I can do?" Nora kept close, then bustled around my office, opening blinds and watering the plant.

"Good morning, Nora. Thank you. Geneva Spieler passed away unexpectedly. I needed time to make arrangements for Max and meet with the executor."

Nora already knew. "Yes, and grieve."

"Grieve? Oh, sure. Of course, grieve. That may take more time." I hung my coat, adding item number eight to my to-do list. "After yesterday morning's announcement, I think we should gather the troops. Assure them not much will change without FDR here. Let's get everyone in the conference room after lunch."

"Are you all right, Amelia? About the job?"

"The job hasn't changed as far as I'm concerned. Status quo."

"I'm surprised they didn't announce a replacement. An interim, at least. I'm more surprised the position didn't go to you." A sharp strand of anger laced Nora's words, indignation on my behalf.

"The work is the thing, Nora. Let's get the best class of Mighty Roosters committed to Chastain and worry about job titles down the road. Also, could you get me a lunch with Mr. Pembroke? The younger Pembroke. Tristan. At his convenience, but sooner than later."

"He called for you actually and asks that you return his call." She placed the message slip on my planner.

"Great minds," I quipped. "I'll handle it then. And how are the application numbers looking? Usual Black Friday rush?"

"On par, yes. That rush will dry up in a couple of weeks and surge again January second."

"See? It's *almost* like we've done this before." My wink implied more certainty than was the case, but I read somewhere that bravery begets confidence. Or something like that.

"Does anyone from early decision need the fawning treatment?"

"I thought we decided not to call it that anymore."

"Maybe *you* did. Coffee?" she offered.

The gnawing ache in my chest surged at the word and the image of the Aladdin tin high on a shelf at The Mews. "Yes, thank you."

With one digit to go in dialing Tristan Pembroke, I stopped and hung up my desk landline, half wondering if this new Pembroke number was one I should commit to memory like I had his father's. My business with my fellow alumnus was personal and better conducted on my phone, and I liberated it from its locked drawer. I read the message again and dialed, only to reach his assistant. She instructed me to meet Tristan at noon at The Markham, dashing my plans for partaking in The Roost's famous Taco Tuesday.

No sooner had I decided to test-drive a life change—leaving my mobile phone free from its dark captivity—than a text pinged.

> **The Reporter:** Max hoped to see you for lunch.

> **Mimi:** Just Max? How is he?

> **The Reporter:** Still looking for her. And no, I'll be there too, but merely as his emotional support human. I have a meeting this afternoon. Lunch beforehand?

Mimi: My lunch is already booked, then a meeting with my staff. A cheerleading session, really.

The Reporter: Bolstering morale? I suggest cupcakes. And get extras.

Mimi: Are we in grade school? And why extras?

The Reporter: Everyone loves cupcakes. Including Max and me. Hence the extras.

Mimi: lol Sorry about lunch.

The Reporter: Dinner then. I'll bring it. 12th floor or 1st?

Mimi: 12. @7?

The Reporter: Max says that's too long a wait. Seems pretty adamant.

Mimi: 6:30?

The Reporter: 6:00 it is. See you then.

Out of habit, I placed my phone in the drawer, then thought better of it and slipped it into my blazer pocket. No more missed calls for me.

"I like to see you smile, boss." Nora smiled too. "I don't think it has to do with my coffee, though."

"Your coffee is my life's blood."

"Fine. Don't tell me."

I rerouted our conversation to business. "Do you think you could get me a dozen cupcakes from Alon's delivered for the afternoon meeting?"

"You know I can. A variety?"

"Perfect. Oh, make it eighteen."

"Consider it done." Nora left, closing the door behind her.

The office message bearing Tristan's phone number caught my attention. It wasn't the new digits, but a sight I'd seen many times before, too many to count, dating back to the start of my work in this office. The underlined block letters *NO* in the bottom corner of the slip of paper.

My coffee sip burned like no other when the shocking similarity hit me. The nondescript, everyday initials were identical to the emphatic *NO* on the fake press clipping found at Mama's house.

Thirty-Five

I CONSIDERED SWITCHING MY heels for a more comfortable pair of shoes before my trek to The Markham, but it was The Markham, so heels seemed the appropriate choice. My feet had yet to forgive me for Monday's campus sprints. But aching feet were no distraction from my ricocheting thoughts of Nora's involvement in the long-ago international equestrian story. I pushed it aside to focus on my next task. A personal matter I was eager to cross off my growing list.

Everything sparkled at The Markam, day or night. Low piped instrumental music played, and the soaring glass welcomed the outside in with the day's cloudless sky. Second only to Tristan Pembroke and his one-thousand-watt smile. I returned it with a subtle wave before remembering he knew Geneva. Everything lost some shine at that moment. Alas, Geneva made this meeting possible.

"Amelia, I am so glad you could take the time to meet." He gestured to my chair, then to a nearby server. "A glass of champagne for the lady."

"Oh, no, thank you."

"What? Did I get it wrong? I thought bubbly was your drink."

"My drink?" Who knew so many made notice of what I drank. "Thank you, Tristan. I love a glass of brut as much as the next girl, but noontime on a Tuesday—"

"Hush. Bring us a bottle." As devil-may-care as Tristan presented himself, there was little doubt when he gave an order. The server nodded, then disappeared while I saved my breath from the fight. I had learned to pick my battles long ago.

"And to think I lamented missing The Roost's taco Tuesday on my walk over here." I placed my napkin on my lap. "I'm glad we could meet too. Kismet to find you on my call sheet when I also wanted to speak with you."

"*Kismet*. Now there is a word that needs to make its way into the everyday lexicon. Kismet. And might I say you look lovely, if not a bit tired around the eyes."

I choked on my sip of water at the billionaire flirt's version of a compliment. "What's this about, Tristan? The fancy restaurant? Champagne? Your attempt at flattery, which, not for nothing, needs some work."

He sat back in his seat and busied himself with his napkin as the waiter performed his wine duties. "A dear friend—well, we almost married once."

"Really?" Imagining a monogamous Tristan stretched the mind.

"Depends on who you ask, I guess." He dismissed what sounded like an intriguing story with a grimace and a flick of his hand. "Anyway, she told me I couldn't woo. That I was not a natural *woo*-er. I wholeheartedly disagree, but I'll admit it isn't a muscle I use often. Not in any serious way. But I'm employing it now." He raised his fizzing glass.

Stunned, I emptied my glass in a classless three gulps in the wake of Tristan's surprise declaration.

"It's a party," he cheered and followed my lead, finishing his wine, too.

"Tristan. I'm flattered, but—"

"At least let me make my case, Mimi."

"It's not really a good time—you see. A lot is happening in my life right now. I got a dog and now I need to move. Plus, work is—"

"Yes, work."

"And I don't know if you've heard yet. But I know you knew her. Geneva Spieler died unexpectedly."

"Good lord. But I just saw her."

"Yes, she attended the Fall Ball."

"Was she ill?" Tristan refilled our glasses.

"No. Nothing like that. A plane crash. A private jet over the ocean. No one gave me any details."

"Of course! What a broad, that one. All the more reason to step back and assess life, right? To Geneva!"

We toasted.

"She is actually why I called you. Why I wanted to meet with you."

"You don't say? She is—was a notorious matchmaker. I'm sure you are aware."

"No, not like that, Tristan. I wanted to discuss business of sorts." I sipped my drink again, then pushed it aside to avoid reaching for it again. "Recently, a large sum of money has come my way. Well, large for me. Large for most, I think. It makes me a little uncomfortable—all this cash. And I wondered if you and your philanthropic work would, uh, take some of it. Most of it. All of it. Particularly, if you have anything in the realm of need-based education grants. Obviously, that is an issue dear to me and—"

"No."

"No?" My hand found my champagne coupe again, and I swigged it. "No, you don't have education grants, or no, you won't take my money—*the* money?"

"Yes. But talk about kismet. God, that's a grand word."

I balled my fists and twisted them in the napkin draped in my lap.

"Come work for me."

"Huh?"

"I said I came here to woo you."

"For a job? I thought you meant—"

"*Ha.* Not that it hasn't crossed my mind, but I've seen how you look at that newspaper hack and he at you. I've wandered down that road before. I didn't enjoy the sights."

"Ethan is not a hack." Silverware clanked when my freed fist thumped the table.

"See how you defend him? I'm looking for loyalty like that. Come work for me."

"Why? How?"

"You are smart. You know about non-profits. You work a room effortlessly with a sincerity I don't care to fake. Old rich people adore you. And rich young people will give you money just because you're hot. Professionally speaking, of course. And I would never exploit that."

"No. Of course you wouldn't."

"Seriously, Amelia." Tristan's face said he meant it. "You can deal with the likes of Thatcher Cromwell, and the world is full of them. You understand about need and will treat those in that predicament with gracious respect. Your current staff loves you. I checked. So, I know you can lead. I will pay you more than you think you are worth, but I don't doubt you'll earn every dollar. You can live anywhere because the foundation will provide any necessary transportation."

My mind reeled. Was this possible? Could I leave Chastain? "I'd have rules."

"Of course. Such as?"

"I will never push an agenda I can't commit to."

"Absolutely."

"And while I'm open to persuasive argument, the final decisions will be mine."

"I'll have your back."

"And I can develop my own pet projects. Say, need-based education grants?"

"Sounds brilliant."

"I'll have more questions—"

"No doubt. We can discuss budgets, salary, and benefits. My HR person will send you our proposal that will include all of that language and you and your attorney can comb through it. It'll be in your private inbox by end of business. I'll need that address."

"I don't have an attorney." I scribbled my personal email address on a card and slid it to him.

"Get one. Use your new windfall to place one on retainer, take this job, and then spend my money on worthwhile endeavors and raise some more."

"This is—How much time do I have? When do you need an answer?"

"I promised myself I wouldn't play hardball."

"This isn't hardball?"

He glowered at his beautiful watch. "You have until the next bottle of champagne arrives for a verbal commitment, Ms. Kanaan." Tristan flattened a grin.

"What? You couldn't possibly expect me—"

"I'm kidding, Mimi. I'm all about sober consent."

"And a sexual harassment-free, non-hostile work environment, yes, I see."

"See? Kismet!" He downed his bubbly.

I had little time to cross campus for my admissions staff meeting. My head swirled, buzzing with excitement. Not from champagne. I'm a rule follower, after all, but Tristan's job offer stunned me. Blew my rule-following mind. The unfamiliar smile-induced ache in my cheeks outdid the shoe-induced version in my feet as I hurried through The Markham's lobby to get to campus walk. I'd never imagined possibilities like those Tristan Pembroke offered. And that I could do it from anywhere, that I could do it from Atlanta, made it all the more enticing. Mama and I would be okay. Better than okay.

And then the day took an even more enjoyable turn.

"Meems." Ethan and Max picked up speed to reach me. "Hey, you've got something on your face there."

"What?" I dragged the back of my hand across my mouth. "Shoot. I just—"

"It's a smile, Mimi. And I like seeing it."

I reverted to schoolyard antics, giving Ethan a shove in lieu of fisting his shirt to pull him in for a kiss. Max got my affection instead.

"Hey, buddy." I squatted to meet Max on his level and showered him with kisses and ear rubs. "Your emotional support human is a jokester, huh? I sure wish I could nuzzle him like this in public."

A low growl, just loud enough, rumbled above me. A very human growl.

"Moving on." Ethan breathed deeply, his eyes squinting with a wicked glint. "Must have been a yummy lunch."

"Better than yummy. Your new BFF knows how to show a girl a fun time."

"Is that right? I want to hear more about that—I think. And speak of the devil."

From the building steps, Tristan waved with the enthusiasm of someone who'd drunk the lion's share of a bottle of wine. "Hey. My next appointment. So much adulting today. I'm going to need a nap."

I looked from one to the other. "You two have a meeting? Here? On campus?"

"I have a few questions I thought Tristan could answer. We're going to stroll around campus with Max."

"Stay out of trouble, boys. I have to get to a staff meeting."

"Cupcakes?" Ethan's eyes brightened.

"With extras. For later." I gave a not-so-subtle wink.

"Even better."

"Good lord, you two are cute, but your spycraft sexy time codes aren't particularly clever."

I gasped, heat billowing up my neck. "No. I meant, he meant, *we* meant *actual* cupcakes, Tristan."

"Don't ruin this for me, Amelia. I'm a complete and total Mimi and Ethan stan—as the kids say." Tristan snickered over his shoulder as he walked away.

Ethan and I gave motionless waves goodbye as he backed away, following the puckish billionaire with Max in tow.

Thirty-Six

I FLUNG OPEN THE *12A* door, still flying high on the job offer news with an added bump from cream cheese frosting, a red velvet cupcake, and a well-received meeting with my co-workers. Ethan and Max arrived early, before I kicked off the heels still pinching my feet. That extra three inches came with its perks, putting me face to face with the man I'd daydreamed of kissing much of the afternoon. A breath away from contact, I hesitated.

"Do I smell tacos?"

Ethan raised a super-sized grease-splotched paper bag and leaned in for his reward. But by then, I only had a mouth for overstuffed hard shells with all the fixings. I snatched the bag with giddy excitement.

"How did you know? I swear, given this week, today cannot get any better." I kicked off my shoes and scampered toward the kitchen with my nose in the bag, inhaling the spicy goodness.

Ethan tended to Max's leash and treats he still refused to eat. "Wow. He wasn't kidding."

"Who wasn't kidding?" Despite my eagerness to dive into the aromatic takeout, I stopped.

"Tristan. He suggested the tacos. Said you'd like them. Said you *wanted* them. Thought it was the act of a faithful wingman, but now I wonder if it wasn't some—*cough*—block tactic. But I'm glad to see that smile still firmly affixed."

My smile grew wider. "Tristan's interest in me is purely business. Or didn't he tell you? Maybe with a side order of harmless flirty needling." With a wiggling index finger, I beckoned Ethan, and he proved far more obedient than my new dog ever behaved. "I think I forgot to say hello to you. Give you a proper greeting." On tiptoes, I grabbed his collar to pull him close. "Hi."

"Hi."

The kiss was better than tacos. Better than champagne, a new job, red velvet cupcakes, and tacos combined. That good. But...

Ethan neglected to lock the door. A disadvantage of living in an old building. No automatic lock. The loud rap coincided with the high-pitched *yoo-hoo* of Mrs. Rose Bimah.

"Mimi. Sugar. Don't worry. I'm here now." She stopped to pat my cheek. "And I brought food." Behind her, the woman pulled a wagon. Think Red-flyer, except black, high-sided, and collapsible. It carried a variety of lidded cookware. In the distraction, she snatched the paper sack of greasy goodness from my grasp. "This is not a time for mediocre meals made by strangers. It's a time for nourishment made with care, and I've been cooking since I heard about poor Geneva." Rose helped herself to the kitchen, talking all the way. Louder as she set to work.

"I know this must devastate you, Mimi. Me, on the other hand, I have endured enough heartbreak in my life. Grief just slides off me like hot lard. But you, sugar. You've always been a bit—soft, shall we say? But don't you worry, I will sit at your side for as long as you need me. And don't even think about shooing me away. I know misery when I see it. And hello to you too, Sonny. I see you have taken my advice and upgraded your wardrobe. Well done, you."

I rested my head on Ethan's chest, deflated. The interruption frustrated me, but more than that, it reminded me of the current situation, spurring guilt for having smiled so much throughout the day. How quickly I avoided mourning my friend, instead fantasizing about a new job, a new home, a new man in my life, and all with a dog, too.

"Is this a message from the universe trying to tell me something? Tell *us* something?" I whispered.

"Nope," Ethan answered with speed. "Not a message I have any interest in hearing, anyway."

"I'm serious, Ethan."

"Me too." He held tighter, but not for long. "I guess that is my cue to go."

"No. Stay."

"Yes, Sonny. Stay," the eavesdropping Mrs. Bimah shouted from the kitchen.

"There's more food than I know what to do with, and I have things to tell you. And questions to ask you, and your arms feel really nice wrapped around me, and I was gonna let you rub my feet, plus that kiss—"

"I can't believe I'm gonna say this, but maybe not so much with all the honesty, Meems. At least consider not saying every thought that pops into your head." He chuckled.

"Like you have been Mr. Straight-and-narrow with your kitchen island fantasies. Sorry, not sorry."

"Good. But we are going to have to—let's just say the next months of living with this damn ethical wall between will be—"

"Months?"

"At least. You are seeing Chastain through to the next recruitment class, aren't you?"

I didn't answer. Not to be coy, but because I didn't know. But the fact I didn't know said I was really considering a serious life change more than I'd admitted. Out loud, anyway.

"That's what I thought." Ethan assumed my silence was confirmation. "I'm not running out on you. But I am going to leave you in Mrs. B's capable hands. You know where to find me. And consider—maybe contemplate being a bit less forthright when it comes to—"

"I will not, so don't even ask."

"Oh, thank God."

We held hands on the short walk to the door. Max offered a goodbye sneeze. I couldn't help but think if we had one more second to reconsider, things might have gone another way. But while Ethan's hand turned the old brass knob, the Chen sisters pushed through the doorway, each carrying another version of lidded cookware. The stern face of Lei Chen entered first, while the quietly crying Susu followed. Rose rushed from the kitchen, and the three women held each other in a three-way hug, each emitting their own unique sorrowful sob.

I placed a brief kiss on Ethan's cheek and nudged him out of *12A*, knowing my role in the evening and little of it had to do with *my* grief. I didn't know what to do with my heartache anyway, but I found comfort in helping the others express their own.

The feast spread across the kitchen island, befitting a crowd carbo-loading before a marathon. I flexed and pointed my still sore feet, relieved I wouldn't be running any races that night. But what started as a somber evening morphed into a celebration of friendship in general and Geneva in particular. The stories grew more outrageous the later it got. Moishe was really in the CIA. Geneva was a cigarette girl at a mobster's nightclub in Reno. As newlyweds (the first time), they parachuted into the African savanna and helped birth a water buffalo, at which point, the locals crowned Geneva an honorary African Queen.

These women had braved divorce, cancer scares, the deaths of spouses and parents, connived match-making schemes, and hosted countless tournaments of mahjong. They teased and berated one another, celebrated birthdays, supported each other with advice and unvarnished truths, argued loudly, and even provoked silent-treatment skirmishes that sometimes lasted as long as an afternoon. And now they mourned the loss of one of their tribe. Their family. A sister-in-life. And they did it while downing her best booze. The only way Geneva Spieler would have it.

I watched those feisty women, thankful for knowing them and sad for not knowing anyone like them in my social circle. What social circle? And while they toasted me as their adoptee, an honorary maiden of the Midtown Mews Matrons, I revisited a past regret, wondering if I would ever open up enough to find my own tribe. Then again, maybe I already had.

Thirty-Seven

My knuckles stopped short, inches from Ethan's door. It was seven-thirty in the morning, but even after two months, I couldn't say for sure if the reporter was a morning person. I shrugged off my doubts, hoping the cupcake I brought would earn forgiveness if I woke him.

"Morning," a sweaty man greeted me wearing a cheery smile and Fighting Irish garb I hadn't seen in a while.

"Are you okay? You're—sweating."

"Yeah. Just back from a run. Wanna come in?"

"Yes. Very much."

He stepped aside and gestured for me to enter.

"Is that for me?" He eyed the cupcake.

"Uh-huh."

"Great. Now I don't have to make breakfast."

"Well, I promised cupcakes, and I don't want you to think I'm a tease."

Ethan's exercise-induced flush deepened a shade. "Aww, you're coming out of the gate strong this early in the morning."

"Just trying to soften you up for a favor."

"You'll want to rethink your tactics, then."

My cheeks bloomed too, hearing us cross another proverbial line.

Thankfully, Ethan reined in the runaway innuendo. "What do you need, Mimi?"

"Hm?"

"The favor?"

"Right. I have to go home this evening. To my home. Druid Hills. My mom and her boyfriend—wow, that felt weird to say. Mama and her friend Winston are coming to discuss things."

"What things?"

"Yeah, I sort of missed that part." I chastised myself for my distraction post-kiss, then coughed away a laugh, knowing I'd do it again given the chance.

"You want back-up?"

"No." I paused, thinking how much I would like him by my side, but pushed past the notion and continued. "I can't take Max with me, so I hoped you—"

"You don't have to ask. Max and I can hang. I'm writing today, running down a few things but all from a laptop and phone. I'd love the company and a reason to get up to stretch my legs. You'll be doing me a favor."

"You're sure? Even overnight? It'll be late, so I'll probably stay there."

"Oh."

"Is that a problem? If you have to go somewhere, Max will be fine for a bit, I think. Mr. Colby will walk him."

"No. Max is no trouble. Just thought I'd see you later. You mentioned you had things to tell me, questions to ask." He waved off his fleeting frown. "We'll find time. I might miss your face, is all. Wait. Your mom has a boyfriend?"

"She does. It's new. Well, new to me. Wish me luck. Text if you need me." I backed away.

"Need you?" Ethan grinned.

"Want me—argh, no. You've got my number."

"Yeah, I do." Ethan leered from a flirty lean in his doorway.

I spun, hurrying down the long hall toward the lobby to find a cab. "Eat your cupcake, Ledes," I called over my shoulder.

"Have an awesome day, Meems."

I find solace in the mundane. Making a list and crossing off each item as I complete it brings me satisfaction. And even as issues like the scandal, Tristan's job offer, Geneva's death, and Mama and Winston's impending visit bubbled underneath, I enjoyed finding my routine on the surface. The day flew by in the typical way with phone calls, candidate essays, and thank-you notes for donors. I wrote many of them by hand.

"Taking off a few minutes early, Nora. Mama and her new beau are coming over. Anything pressing before I go?"

"Only that you asked me to remind you to call Moses Pascha."

"Yes. Thank you. I'll do that on my walk home."

"What's with the old coffee tin?"

"Oh, it's how I carry around enormous sums of money these days." I tucked the Aladdin can under my arm like a football.

Nora offered a sad consolation grin, shaking her head. "Sometimes I don't get your sense of humor. See you in the morning."

I hesitated, trying to summon the nerve to bring up the fake news clipping. To ask if I'd been the victim of some older iteration of the fawning treatment. If Nora told some unwitting student minion to spread the lie. Did she know it was a lie at the time?

I shook off that train of thought. Victim? No. The fallout was all mine. I hadn't rectified the rumor. I had shunned Mama. Whatever the context, the blame rested on me.

"Good night, Nora."

I dialed Moses before I reached the stairs. He answered the call on the first ring, and we exchanged pleasantries before I brought up the new issue.

"Someone recently told me to get a lawyer. A lawyer who does the sort of thing I hope you do, Mr. Pascha."

"Please, Amelia. It's Moses. And what sort of *thing* are we talking about?"

It seemed an odd question. Didn't Moses know what kind of law he practiced? Because I didn't, but given how we met, I assumed it included managing financial issues. I squinted at his card in the fading twilight. *Pascha and Associates, Moses Pascha, Esq.* and his phone number. Nothing more.

"I have a friend. No—say, *hypothetically*, I had a friend, and my friend received a job offer." I took special care to keep my two fibs for Wednesday Wine with Mama and Winston. "It's a big departure from her current work. The prospective employer has sent her a proposal of sorts. Job description, salary, benefits, bonus structure, you get the drift. And someone suggested I—*she* should have it perused by a legal advocate. Is that something you do? Hypothetically?"

"Most certainly, not only in the hypothetical. But I should say there are other ways to seek this sort of advice."

"Are you good at what you do, Mr.—Moses?"

"I have been told I am, yes."

"Then if Geneva trusted you, I trust you."

"All right. You will receive an email regarding my retainer and a secure link to upload the offer of employment. I'm sorry, your *friend* will receive said email."

"Oh, Moses? I'm the friend."

"Whatever you say, Ms. Kanaan. I'm your lawyer now."

Thirty-Eight

I DIDN'T HESITATE HITTING *send* to Moses Pascha when I read the offer sent from the Pembroke Institute's human resources but lamented not yet sharing the prospect with Ethan. That seemed like an in-person conversation, not on the phone and certainly not using my thumbs.

> **Mimi:** Is that frosting on his nose?

I swiped through texted photos Ethan sent.

> **The Reporter:** It is, but don't worry. I got Max to eat some kugel first. The rascal somehow ate around the raisins. He spit them out.

> **Mimi:** I didn't know that was an option.

> **The Reporter:** Not a fan? My SIL Nat made a Christmas kugel with cranberries last year. It was a hit.

> **Mimi:** I love that your family has Christmas kugel.

> **The Reporter:** My family would love you.

Mimi:...

The Reporter: Oof. Where's the unsend when you need it? Thumbs got away from me. I'm gonna log off. Hope tonight goes well with your mom.

Mimi: Wait

The Reporter:...

Mimi: C U tmrw?

The Reporter: Hope so.

Mimi: Don't let Max sleep on the bed.

The Reporter: My bed, my rules.

Mimi: Sounds—fair. G'night.

I'd never been more jealous of a dog.

My racing heart skipped a beat with a knock at my door. I regretted missing out on the half glass of wine I'd intended to down to help ease whatever happened next. Then again, Ethan was always a welcome distraction. Better than any wine.

"Hold on, Mama. Sometimes it sticks. Let me give it a hard tug." The door opened with a squeaky *clunk*.

"Good grief, Amelia. What is with your door?"

"Oh, come now, Miss Livie. It's quaint." Winston earned instant points towards winning my heart.

"No, it's not. It's a hassle. And a safety hazard, just like how dark it is out here. Hard to believe we're in the middle of the city." Mama tossed her coat to me and helped herself to the rest of my home. "Well, I don't hate it as much as I thought I would. It's small, of course. But how much room does one person need?"

"Wine? Who wants wine? I do. Winston? Mama? I've got red, white, whiskey?"

"I'll pour. You relax, Mimi. And you, Miss Livie, be nice." He gave me a supportive wink, and his point tally grew.

The couple sat on the sofa, and I curled up in the wingback that would forever be Ethan's sleeping chair.

"Welcome." We all raised our glasses. "So, what brings you here? Are you sick? Is it your heart?"

"What heart?" Mama was funnier than she knew. "I'm healthy as a horse. But this horse needs a new pasture."

The reference to horses jolted me back to the equestrian fake news of my youth. I took a slug of cabernet.

"I don't understand."

Mama pulled out a blue folder emblazoned with a familiar logo. My eyes bulged.

"The progress train is coming, Mimi, and it's better to get on board than to be run over by it. And we happen to be in a better than fine position to profit."

I cussed the name Archie Clay under my breath. "Oh, Mama."

"Don't *Oh, Mama* me like I'm a child."

"Well, that doesn't even make sense, and I don't think you are a child. I think the conductor of your *progress train* is preying on people with lesser means." At least the guy kept to a script. "Progress train," I scoffed. "And while it might sound like he will offer you a nice sum of money for your house, you still need to find someplace to live which will cost as much or more. The only ones coming out ahead on this deal are Mr. Clay and his sons."

"I told you, Winston. My stubborn daughter won't listen to a word I say. That's why you're here. Explain it to her."

"Your stubborn daughter is sitting right here, and I apologize, Winston, if I've been dismissive. I only want Mama to keep a roof over her head. A safe, affordable, comfortable roof."

Winston patted Mama's knee, chuckling. "I'd like to think my daughter and my Beatrice, may she rest in peace, would squabble like the two of you if her mother lived longer. It's a little like music to my ears. And for the record, Mimi, you are not wrong."

I bit back what would have been a sarcastic *Ha,* but relished Winston's slam dunk.

"You best start changing your tune, old man, or you will find the sofa a chilly place to sleep tonight."

That's when I vowed never to call Ethan 'old man' again and wished I could scrub the image of poor Winston in his boxers on my mother's lumpy couch. But Winston's laugh in response to Mama's snappish ire tickled me. The more she groused, the jollier he got, so much so that Mama struggled to keep her resting 'angry' face.

"I'm getting to it, Livie. Hold your horses."

Ugh. More horses.

"Our advantage comes in pooled resources, Mimi. The more we have to sell, the more valuable it is to the developer. Exponentially. It gives them more flexibility if they can—for example—run new sewer lines for three parcels at a time or knock down three structures all at once."

"Sure. That makes sense." It did too. Two parcels would be more valuable to a developer for many reasons. My brain gears picked up speed considering Mama's property and Winston's, but then, remembered the obstacle. "It's a shame the tract next to yours and—"

Mama took Winston's hand. The first sign of affection I'd witnessed between her and—anyone. Ever. My focus stuck to their joined hands. A magical tractor beam, making it impossible to look away. Winston's huge hands engulfed Mama's with a loving squeeze.

She whispered, "She's gonna be mad."

The two kept their heads bent together in not-so-covert conversation.

"Probably so, Livie. Secrets do that," he murmured.

"What's going on, Mama?"

Her entire demeanor changed. Between the sweet handholding and her softened expression, I stiffened, bracing for impact.

"I'll start by saying it was my money. Well, it was *your* money that you insisted on giving to me even when I didn't ask for it. I'm not exactly living *La Vida Loca* here, and you pay the mortgage on my house. Plus, I've earned a few raises over the years, and what the hell else was I going to do with it?"

"Do with what?"

"Don't interrupt, Amelia," she barked.

There's my Mama.

"The cleaning business has picked up over the years, too, and I've watched the *la-dee-dah-ing* of the streets and houses and businesses. I saw the writing on the wall long ago."

"Mama, get to the—"

"Maybe circle around to the point, Livie."

"Fine. So, three years ago, when the Mendozas told me they wanted to move to Sheboygan to be nearer to their grandchildren—I mean, sure grandchildren would be nice, but Sheboygan? I told them the snow would be up to their—"

"The point, Livie—" Winston prodded.

"We made a deal."

"Who made a deal, Mama?"

"The Mendozas and me."

"Who the hell are the Men—"

"Watch your language, young lady."

"Sorry." Even in the heightened confusion, I apologized for breaking her hypocritical no-swearing rule. "Who are the Mendozas?"

"The next-door neighbors. I saved enough for a down payment, the Mendozas held the note, and I bought it. I've been paying for it ever since." She slid the folder toward me. "Considering what it's worth these three years later, it was an excellent deal."

"You own the house next door to you?"

"Yes. Not outright, but yes."

"Holy sh—"

Without weighing everyone down in the minutia, among the three of us, we owned three large lots that in this era could hold as many as four, maybe five McMansions that Clay and Sons bet they could sell for a million dollars or more apiece. Winston's daughter was a commercial realtor in Atlanta high-rises but considered the offer and gave it her daughterly approval.

The contents of the blue folder outlined the deal. But the new lovebirds brought even more news to share.

Using Winston's fix-it skills and small business owner experience (he owned a hardware store in Buffalo) and Mama's cleaning prowess and years of office management, the two were moving to the mountains of North Georgia—a hotbed of vacation homes and Airbnb-type tourism—to start a cleaning and fix-it service for getaway rental properties. A well-thought-out and detailed business plan appeared from another folder.

"This is a lot to consider."

"We have considered it, Amelia."

"Now, Livie. Give the woman a moment. We've had weeks to chew on this deal, make our plans. She's had it less than an hour." More points to the handsome Mr. Bonmanos.

"Let me take this and have—uh, my lawyer, Moses, look at it. Okay?"

"A lawyer? Look at my daughter, Winston. She's got a lawyer." Mama's tone oozed teasing. "Moses? That sounds—"

"Mama," I scolded. "Do not finish that thought."

"What? What'd I say?"

"Hold on a second. If you both plan to sell your homes, does that mean you two will live—"

"Amelia Louise," Mama snapped. "Mind your business."

I pressed my lips together, admonished. But as I busied my mouth with another gulp of wine, I knew Moses Pascha wouldn't only be looking into Clay and Sons. He'd do a clean sweep of Mr. Winston Bonmanos of Buffalo to see what skeletons might be in his closets.

If I had my way, my first call would have been to Ethan. I considered packing another bag to go back to The Mews. Instead, still buzzing from wine, no dinner, and a real estate deal that made my head spin, I called Mr. Pascha to leave a message about the new items to emerge in my decidedly more interesting life of late.

"Good evening, Ms. Kanaan."

"Mr. Pascha. I only meant to leave a message. So sorry to disturb you at this hour." I wondered why this successful, knowledgeable man answered his own phone at any time of day.

"You are not disturbing me. My business takes place in every time zone. When the phone rings, I answer it. How may I help you?"

"I have a couple of questions, and I'm not sure if you are the right person to ask, but—"

"You can ask me anything."

"Thank you, but I'm not sure what sort of law you practice, so…"

"I tell my clients to think of me as general counsel. If I can't help, I will find them someone who will." His answer had a vagueness that, at first, concerned me. It rang familiar, like the ambiguity Geneva often used. Just as quickly, I knew I had called the right man for all the changes in my life. "I would like to say that I have read the offer of employment presented by The Pembroke Institute. Even without our attorney-client privilege or paid retainer, you should consider the job. This is free advice in your best interest from your friend Moses."

Another up and down surge hit my insides. First elation that the opportunity offered by Tristan read legitimate and worthwhile, not that I thought it wouldn't, then concern at hearing he didn't consider me a client.

"That's good to hear, Moses, but does that mean you're not my lawyer and, perhaps more importantly, that you can tell anyone about my job offer?" A twinge of panic tightened my voice.

His quiet hum of a chuckle relieved me. "Certainly not, Mimi. And, if you know nothing else about me, know this. I am likely the most discreet person you will ever know."

We ended the call with a plan for a brief meeting at lunchtime the following day to shore up our new partnership and move forward with the latest events. I thought his insight and recommendations would help and sent him all the details of the issues in question, the Clay and Sons' real estate deal and a sneak peek at Mr. Winston Bonmanos. Fingers-crossed that neither would raise any red flags.

But it wasn't until I climbed into my bed and clung to a pillow that I cried.

A hurricane of emotions stormed out of me. The whirl of so many emotions I had shoved down deep these last few days came to a tearful, snotty head. Frustration and anger toward a broken system I had inadvertently aided from the inside. Joy at a career opportunity that would be lucrative and challenging while doing good. Relief that my mother wisely and so bravely took steps that might truly benefit her in the next chapter of her life. Guilt for feeling an ounce of liberation because of her wisdom and bravery that I admired so much. An overwhelming fondness for a man unlike any I had ever experienced in a way that thrilled and terrified me. And tumbling through all of it, sorrow at losing a dear friend without warning. A friend who'd meant more to me than I knew and wanted more for me than I dared to dream.

Was Geneva the price for my chance at all these unspeakable wishes I never risked imagining?

Thirty-Nine

MY HEAD THROBBED LIKE a tequila morning-after without the hazy memories of loud laughs, louder music, or any table dancing. A crying hangover hit me harder than a booze-fueled version, but I cried dry and woke up, craving the brisk walk to campus I'd been missing since my extended stay at The Mews. But then I got a better offer.

"Sorry for the ambush." Ethan threw a stick several yards into the grand home's side yard. Max tracked it from his spot at Ethan's feet but showed no interest in chasing it down to fetch. Despite his breed, his adoring owner had spoiled any innate retriever instinct out of him.

"Are you kidding? You're my two favorites."

"Did you hear that, boy? We're her favorites."

I don't care what people say. Dogs smile. Even mopey Max with Ethan's rigorous head rub produced the biggest doggy grin I'd seen in a long while.

"I brought coffee. It's in the car. I parked across the street."

"Oh. I was just being nice before, but now you really are my favorite. I think you just saved me a fib for the day." My lips brushed his cheek, but the wall between us felt higher, thicker, two-sided.

"Glad I'm good for something, I guess."

"Hey. Wait a minute. That was a joke. And you're good for lots of things. You've been a lifesaver, if I'm honest. I know this hasn't been great, but I don't want to imagine what these months, or even the last twenty-four hours would have been like without knowing you. If you feel taken advantage of or misled, that's not my intention."

"No, I don't think that."

"Then why so grumpy? Did Max keep you up? Is he a wiggler too?" That earned me a grin.

"Just feeling like I'm always the bringer of bad news. Getting tired of hurting you."

"More bad news? I think I'll take that coffee now."

We settled in Ethan's rental car, warm in the morning sunshine.

"Do you want to go first?" he asked as I sipped the delicious Peachy Bean roast.

"Me?"

"You said you had things you wanted to tell me."

"Boy, do I, but I think you should go first. Is it Chastain related?"

"Not exactly. I have some questions too. The on-the-record kind. About your mom."

"No." The single syllable burst out of me more abruptly than I intended. Max took notice from the back seat, nosing my arm over the console between Ethan and me. I'd known the day would come when investigative journalist Ethan Ledes would want me to speak on the record. It was inevitable but facing it stung worse than I expected.

"Mimi. She's not in trouble, and I won't get her in trouble. You can trust me."

I shook my head. "If there is something you need to know, I suppose I can try to find out, but no, you aren't dragging her into this. I'm sorry, but it will need to be secondhand or not at all."

"Maybe I should get someone else here to do this. A colleague. Someone who isn't—who will be more objective." He gripped the steering wheel, staring into the bright sun.

"I don't want a stranger prying. You won't hurt me. You don't want to hurt me. I know that, so I won't let you. It's a choice, right? I choose not to let your questions hurt me. Okay? Go ahead. Ask."

We took deep breaths in sync before he continued.

"My guess is you don't know the answer, but I'm having trouble connecting the dots. This sort of academic wrangling, the services that parents invest in—"

"The cheating, you mean? Let's call it what it is."

"Yes. The cheating. It—well, it costs a lot of money. At least, the research says it does. Here. California. The Northeast. Everywhere we investigate, the M.O.'s the same, so I have a hard time believing your mother had enough to pay one of these collegiate crooks."

I exhaled, reminding myself I had chosen not to get hurt. "Whoa. You don't know my mother, Ethan, but I kind of hope you do someday. And she may be a lot of things, but she isn't a thief. So, if you think she stole to pay—"

"A thief? No, I think someone took advantage of *her* all those years ago. Someone made her promises, took her money, however much, and then she lucked out when you got accepted to Chastain. And if you hadn't gotten in, whoever the reprobate was would have disappeared with her money, anyway. I think your mom was the victim. Most of the families involved in this nowadays are—of different means. But my *Public Eye* colleagues have also heard stories of grifters taking money from families who don't have it to give, promising results the con artists couldn't possibly guarantee. It's another whole injustice. Not perpetrated by the wealthy, but on desperate parents of—lesser means with dreams of a better life for their children."

My fingers fumbled for the door handle. The blast of cool air hit me, an instant, if temporary, reprieve from the anger boiling my insides.

"Mimi." Ethan grabbed my arm, but I wrenched free of his grip, still belted into my seat. The buckle smacked the passenger side window when I finally unlatched it, and the car door rebounded, slowing my escape to the sidewalk. Ethan called out my name again, sprinting around the car, while Max jumped to the front seat to follow me in a panic.

"I'm fine. I just need air. And a minute. Everything's fine."

"I'm so sorry, Mimi. If I could keep this from you—"

"No. I needed to know, but Mama? Mama can never hear of this. Is that clear? Her pride would never recover. I swear, it would kill her."

"But—" Ethan tugged me to him, but I squirmed to keep my space.

"What do you want, Ethan? A name? A dollar figure? What's done is done as far as she is concerned; it was forever ago. The jerk's long gone, and the amount was too much. Way too much, no matter how small the sum. That year was—it was too much."

"You're right. You are absolutely right. Forget it."

"I'm not trying to make your job harder. This is not some professional maneuvering because we're on opposite sides of this thing. I just want to move on. I just want to move on and protect her." I allowed myself to lean into him when he coaxed me close for the third time.

His low, rumbling chuckle vibrated through me. "I should probably confess that my desire for answers has less to do with my professional interest and more with my growing, aggressive need to introduce the one who did it to a tire iron. Whoever made you cold and hungry."

I held tighter but craned my neck to see him. "A macho thing, huh?"

He rolled his eyes and shrugged. "Something like that."

"Get in line, Ledes. I want first crack."

"I'm on your side, you know. One hundred percent. I support your decision."

"Thank you."

"Now, I've never considered myself a silver linings kind of guy, but can I ask if you looked at the admissions data? The ten-years' worth?"

My frame stiffened in his arms. I hadn't found the time or nerve to look. What if I didn't stack up to the rest? What would I do with that information?

"Silver lining?" I shook my head.

"Well, if whatever your mom did couldn't have influenced the decision, then the deciding factors were all you. Your grades. Your test scores. Essays, interviews. You got in on your own. Now you know." Ethan shrugged. "Silver lining."

I took the easiest breath I'd had in days. Palpable relief. I nodded but didn't want to dwell on the past. Moving forward started now. "Speaking of decisions. I've got a couple more to make and could use a sounding board."

That smile that could eclipse the sun traveled all the way to Ethan's kind eyes, showing me the eager partner I never knew I wanted, never knew I could have. "Fire away, Meems."

We pulled into the back lot of the admissions building and parked. I yammered the entire way to campus, telling Ethan about the job offer from Tristan and the Clay and Sons opportunity. For a man who asked questions for a living, he displayed the patience of a saint.

"Well?"

His smile hadn't quit. "Well, what? You haven't asked me anything yet?"

"What do you think? About both things?"

"Taking the job and selling the property? I think you have a lot on your plate."

"Are you dodging the question?"

"Nope. I have already told you I'd support your decisions. You trust Pascha?"

"I do. But I trust you too."

"Then trust me when I say these are decisions you need to make on your own. They will be game changers for your life."

"Ah. *My* life, huh? No. Right."

Ethan's sunny glow dimmed as his steering wheel grip went white knuckle.

"I'm late for work." I unbuckled, but Ethan caught my hand.

"Wait, what just happened here?"

Max mini-sneezed to remind us we weren't alone.

"Nothing unusual. Just me laying it out there, except that I *asked* for help this time. Something I don't do, like at all. And you weren't up for it. I overstepped. I see that."

"What part of one hundred percent don't you get, Mimi?"

"No, you're right. *My* life. *My* decisions to make. I appreciate your support. I do. But now I'm wondering if maybe you're only all in until the banter stops. When real life happens, you, I don't know—but that brick wall you've accused me of building? You're quite the stonemason yourself. Or maybe that's when you hop a plane. To escape your inquisitive family or venture off to the next story. Is that it? Do you have a plane to catch, Ethan? Cuz, I gotta tell ya, I'm not a big fan of flying these days."

He didn't answer.

"I've got to get inside before Nora calls the National Guard."

"Where are you sleeping tonight?"

"Really, Ethan?"

"I mean, because of M-A-X."

"If this is about the D-O-G, I mean *really* about him, I'll take him off your hands right now. But if it's about wanting to see me later and you can't admit that even when I'm telling—"

"It's not about him. It's about you. It's about us. It's about wanting more than I can ask. More than I *should* ask."

I exhaled, then tilted to kiss his cheek, breathed in his smell, and felt the tickle of his curls on my lashes. "I know. Scary, right?"

A tentative grin appeared. "When did you get so cocky?"

"Welp, see there's this guy and I am totally—bananas nuts for him, and he's been pretty outspoken about things. At least he was for a time. And I'm just following his lead. But maybe he's getting a bit nervous now. The dog that caught the car." I patted his cheek, wanting so much more.

"That's not what this is."

I exhaled. "Go to work. We're fine. We just need to keep talking. And since talking is all we've got for the time being, I'll resist the urge to crawl into your lap and kiss you for all of campus to see. And tonight, we can talk some more."

"So much talking," he whined in fun.

"Like grown-ups."

"Well, I'm really looking forward to being grown-up with you."

I gave his shoulder a stout schoolyard wallop, then Max an ear rub. "Max, take care of this guy today, okay? He's having feelings."

Max yawned in the affirmative.

When I hopped out and rounded the front of the SUV, Ethan lowered his car window.

"Banana nuts, huh?"

I spun on my heel, shielding my eyes from the gleam of the returned full smile and the sun. "Yep. I'm thinking of making t-shirts. What do you think?"

"Pretty sure I'll be thinking of you in nothing but a t-shirt for the rest of the day."

My saucer-sized eyes gawked at him. "And he's back, ladies and gentlemen. Hey, go for a run, Bob Costas. See what I did there? Running? Sports journalist?"

Ethan groaned, "How long have you been holding onto that one?"

"It's been a minute. Not gonna lie."

"Oh, I know."

I waved and took the concrete steps in record time. Sometimes an ugly cry is all one needs to gain some perspective. My foggy future started to clear.

Forty

"I KNOW, I KNOW I'm late." I rushed into the reception area, ready to make my one-stop apology tour despite not having an ounce of regret.

"Did I say anything?" Nora's scowl said enough, and the letter opener she wielded provided an extra layer that eliminated any remorse I had about leaving my Peachy Bean coffee in Ethan's car.

"Then I won't apologize." Having saved a fib, I smiled and headed to my inner sanctum. Nora didn't follow, but she'd already visited my office. The lights were on, and the cascading green of the thriving philodendron still wore droplets from an earlier watering. Plus, the blinds were open, providing a clear view of the back lot where Ethan, Max, and I had been minutes ago.

When I settled into my desk chair, a brief call list sat on my day planner. Dr. Cromwell, Rashida Turner, and Briana Johnson. I added the names of personal calls I needed to make to a mental list: Moses Pascha and Tristan Pembroke. The mix read like a Who's Who of influential people in my life. Nora's message order indicated which she considered most important, but I started from the middle. I pressed two to listen to the message.

Amelia. Rashida Turner here. I had a wonderful meeting with Briana Johnson. Chastain would be lucky to get her, but I don't think you will, and that's a good thing. Feel free to track me down if you have questions. Thanks for the introduction. She might be my boss someday.

I smiled, agreeing with Rashida on all counts, then pressed three for Briana's voicemail.

Hi, Miss Kanaan. Hope you know how hard this is. Leaving a message. You know kids today don't do voicemail. (Briana laughed) *Oh, this is Briana, by the way. Briana Johnson. See? We're terrible at this sort of communication. Anyway, I met Ms. Turner. She was very cool. Totally inspiring, so I guess you were right to pair us together. Thank you.*

Before I continued with voicemail, I skimmed the latest application numbers that accompanied my call sheet. They met expectations. FDR's sudden "retirement" hadn't deterred many potential students from hitting send. But I wondered if the coming revelations would impact acceptances in the spring. A pang of disappointment hit, knowing one of them wouldn't be Briana. Leaving Atlanta on her own terms was the best call for the young woman, and she owed it to herself to take the chance.

Nora entered with a surprise café au lait. "How are you?"

"I'm well. Thank you. Starting to see the forest for the trees, I think. You don't need to worry about me."

"The president will surely offer you the job today." Nora pointed to the list.

"Hm," I hummed with a sip of coffee, savoring the hot swallow. I almost laughed when I realized the only thing I'd likely miss when I left Chastain would be Nora and her barista skills. *When I leave Chastain.* That's when it occurred to me I'd made my decision. I would resign at the end of the spring semester. "I'm surprised you didn't hear. Dr. Cromwell already offered me the title."

"He did?"

"Maybe *offered* isn't the right word. He tried to foist it on me, more like. I did not accept." I punctuated my matter-of-fact reply with another taste of milky goodness.

"Praise Jesus," she murmured.

I caught the spit take before damage was done. "What?"

"My apologies." Nora's more sullen than usual mood improved.

"Why are you sorry? Why are you obviously relieved? Do you doubt I can do the job?"

"I don't doubt you can do anything—except maybe live your life free of other people's expectations."

The laugh I'd held in snorted out of me. "Tell me what you really think, Nora."

"Since you asked, I will." She sat across from me like whatever I had coming had been stewing for some time.

I leaned back in my seat, ready to hear it.

"You have been here too long. Between your degrees and work. Nearly half your life, Amelia. Half. Your. Life."

I opened my mouth to interrupt, but she waved me off and continued.

"If you take the deanship, you will never go. You will wake up someday and realize you have squandered away your best years. And worse, you might find yourself doing things, shady things you never thought you could do. Sometimes you get lucky and get assigned a new boss who sees your worth. Appreciates you and inspires you all over again. But that one boss is one in million."

A fully loaded silence seized the room. Her confession, an apology, and a wordless plea for forgiveness. I processed every unsaid syllable.

Nora continued. "But you've done your time. Not taking this position is one small step toward your freedom. Even if you take some time to figure out an escape plan—"

"I'm going, Nora," I cut her off. "*Escape* sounds somewhat dramatic, but I've worked ten years and—"

"Hallelujah, hallelujah!" Nora threw back her head and raised her hands, hollering in celebration. Rocking back and forth, she clutched at her chest. A gleeful smile took over her entire face. A rare but beautiful sight.

"Glad to know you'll miss me," I joked.

"Miss you? Not here, I won't. You go, I go, and I have been ready to go since Methuselah wore short pants."

"But you don't even know where I'm going." I squinted at the woman, still taken aback by her elated show of teeth.

"Ha. I'm not going *with* you. I'm going home. I'm going to sit on my front porch, snap beans, and yell at my grandbabies."

"You grow beans?"

"I will now. When do we ride, boss lady?" She clapped her hands and rubbed her palms together.

"Ride? Who are you?" I didn't let the question hang long. The time had come to burst my assistant's joyous new outlook. "I'm under contract, Nora. And that contract isn't up until spring recruitment ends. Short of getting fired—"

"I don't suppose a termination on your record will be helpful in your job search." Funny how legally binding employment agreements knocked the wind out of poor Nora's liberation sails.

"Thankfully, the next job has already fallen into my lap. I haven't officially accepted it yet, but my start date will still depend on Chastain," I paused, "and maybe a vacation." The thought of an ocean or mountain view, maybe a pyramid or the Eiffel Tower, made my head spin. The more my foggy future cleared, the giddier I got. My executive chair kept me upright.

"Forget who *I* am," Nora scoffed. "A vacation? Who are *you*?"

"Someone who has some serious planning to do. And it starts with saying yes to the new offer."

"Well, don't let me slow you down." She launched herself from her wingback to leave.

"Nora?"

"Yes, child."

"Any—unscrupulousness, anything shady. If it had to do with me—long ago me? I forgive you. And if you stayed all this time to protect me from it? I thank you. Thank you *so* much."

She bowed her head and left, closing the door behind her.

Maybe someday I'd find a way to ask outright, but if I knew anything, I knew Nora's part came from a place of wanting to help. In my case, to ease the way for a young student out of her element, find a way to acclimate, feel seen, and find a sense of belonging. Beyond that, Nora's actions over the years, whatever thumb she had put on the scale, she likely saw it as her way of leveling the playing field. The only way she knew might help. Was it right? No, but it came from a place of good. Of that, I had no doubt.

I pushed aside the call sheet and pulled out my mobile phone.

"Tell me something good, Mimi, because if you break my heart, it will ruin me, which would be a shame because I'm having a fantastic hair day," Tristan answered on the first ring, full of charm and arrogance.

"Good morning, Mr. Pembroke. You sound in fine spirits today."

"It's the hap, happiest seeeeason of all, Ms. Kanaan. And you heard the part about my hair, right? Also, Mr. Pembroke is my Daddy Dearest. I insist you call me Tristan."

"Even if you're my new boss?"

"Good Lord, you don't know how happy I am to hear that. But if we're being real, I'm a Chastain trustee now. Either way, I'm technically your boss."

"Don't make me regret this mere seconds in, Tristan."

"No. Quite right. But have I mentioned how happy this makes me?"

"Glad to hear it, but as my other boss, technically, you must know I'm under contract. You can't have me yet."

Tristan laughed a sighing laugh, as if I said something funny but tedious. "Really, Mimi. Do I strike you as someone who waits for things I want when I want them now? Meet me at Dr. Cromwell's in fifteen minutes. Thatcher and Janice will expect you."

The *beep, beep, beep* of an ended call sounded in my ear as I wondered what my work life would look like going from the rarely seen, old man FDR to the larger-than-life man-child Tristan Pembroke. I couldn't wait to find out.

Forty-One

Tristan's laugh sliced through the door, but it carried a different tone than what he used around me. Janice gestured for me to enter before she and I could have our usual warm and fuzzy greeting. I don't think either of us missed it.

"Amelia, yes, come in, please." Dr. Cromwell welcomed me as both men stood.

I caught a side eye from Tristan when he gave my chair a slight turn and whispered, "Follow along."

My stomach flopped. Improv is not my strong suit.

Cromwell settled back in his seat. "I was just allaying Mr. Pembroke's concerns. Our newest Board of Trustees member had questions about our admissions department reshuffling."

"Oh, Thatcher, call me Tristan, and my family has been on the Board of Trustees since the first FDR—the U.S. president, not our recently departed dean. Consider me like all the rest, even my father." While it sounded like polite chit-chat, Tristan's message left no doubt who held the better hand. The Pembroke name echoed through these halls for decades and would for years to come. It carried more weight than any university president could withstand. Even at half this president's age, the alpha in the room sat on my side of the desk.

"If you'll permit me," I cut in to break up the mounting staring contest. "The Pembroke connection to the university dates back to *Teddy* Roosevelt, not Franklin." My nervous tell got the best of me, blurting this unnecessary fact.

"See?" Tristan slapped his thigh. "This is why I adore the woman. The things she knows."

"Yes, as I was saying, we are lucky to have her," Dr. Cromwell seconded the praise.

"*Is* that what you were saying?" Tristan raised a single brow, cocking his head.

"My apologies." The already admonished president's ruddy complexion deepened with a tight smile. "If I didn't say it, I was thinking it."

"*Huh.* Because what I heard you say was that you believe the Mighty Rooster admissions process is so well established, such a well-oiled machine that FDR—the second one, not the president—that Franklin Delano Rayburn was tantamount to a figurehead. And the entire department is practically plug-and-play, as the kids say. Anyone could fill those upper-level positions, and it wouldn't affect the work at all. That's what I heard."

The red in my cheeks fired up too. "Did you really say that, Dr. Cromwell? Is that what you think? That *anyone* could do what I do?"

"Oh, we're all friends here, Mimi. Call him Thatcher." Tristan smiled as he reclined in his chair with his bare ankle across his knee, having too much fun at Cromwell's expense.

"I—uh—Tristan, I thought we were backroom talking. You know, as men do."

"Yeah, that was your first mistake. Never assume. I really loathe the old boys' club. *Ring. Ring.*" Tristan pantomimed a phone to his ear. "Oh, it's for you, sir. It's the twentieth century and they want their misogyny back."

"I simply wanted to assure you that—uh, with Amelia at the helm, all would be fine with Chastain's future."

"But she isn't at the helm, is she?"

"*No*, I'm not, I interjected, my defiance on full display.

Cromwell brushed it aside. "Yes, well, I thought we'd rectify that today. It's why my office called hers first thing this morning. There is only a matter of the paperwork."

"It's not only a matter of paperwork," I objected.

Tristan leaned toward the desk, pointing at me. "*She* says it's *not* only a matter of paperwork." He piled on while the president's rigid grin disappeared.

"It's not?"

Tristan turned his attention to me. "I don't know if you know this, Mimi, because, *unlike* me, you are a person of prudence and would never let slip sensitive information. But it seems Chastain might be in a teeny tiny bit of trouble. My old pal, Ethan Ledes—do you two know Ethan? I meant to make introductions at the Fall Ball, but the party got away from me."

The mention of Ethan's name made Cromwell and me sit straighter.

"Anyway, E, that's what I call Ethan, fancies himself a reporter. An investigative journalist, I think he calls it. He says there's a little hanky panky going on behind the admissions woodshed. Not only at Chastain, but other big-name universities too. And well, to make a long story short, FDR caught wind of the scandal discovery and—"

"Oh, come now. I wouldn't call it a *scandal*, Tristan," Cromwell groused. "It's business."

"No? Okay. Do you plan to interrupt me again, Thatcher?" The playful Tristan vanished as quickly as the older man's smile had.

The change occurred in silence, the power shift forcing the president to loosen his tie and clear his throat to fill the void.

"As I was saying, FDR knew the jig was up, as my granddaddy used to say, and flew the coop." Despite his vernacular, Tristan's tone was all business. The frivolous frat boy knew how to wrangle control of a situation when the time called for it. He swiveled back to me. "I believe our beloved president here plans to elevate you just high enough to take the fall when the scandal—I mean, *business*, breaks."

Now I wondered if this had been the topic of Ethan and Tristan's discussion when I'd spotted them walking Max earlier in the week.

"Did—Mr. Ledes, tell you that?" I shouldn't have asked. It wasn't the time or place, but I had mixed feelings about the new BFFs conspiring behind my back, even if on my behalf.

"When you saw us together outside The Markham? No. We spoke about something else entirely unrelated. He may be a dear friend, and I'm not about to air his dirty laundry or do his job for him, but I've been in enough boardrooms to know how this scene plays out. A stooge set up to take the blame. Besides, what old and not-so-old cronies will boast about on a squash court will just as easily titillate as bore you. Someone's buddy's nephew is looking to make the leap to elite academia. Isn't that right, Thatcher? Figurehead, indeed."

The president paled from beet red to a green-gray but kept mum.

"Change in plan, Thatch. Amelia Kanaan is free and clear of her contract. Reasons given, if at all, are up to her. How you fill the holes left by her and Mr. Rayburn is up to you. That's way above my pay grade. Definitely comes under the header 'president problems.' My suggestion? If you like where you sit, you best find qualified replacements. This institution is only as strong as its weakest department. And Ms. Kanaan has done stellar work. If there is even so much as a whisper that she's in any way complicit in these admissions irregularities, I will sic Ethan Ledes on you with all his evidence proving the contrary, and this easily managed blip will become your worst nightmare. E has a reputation for moving mountains for people he cares about, and what can I say? The man idolizes me." The more light-hearted Tristan reemerged.

"How does any of that help me, Tristan? You're leaving me with more shit than FDR's flown chicken coop."

Tristan *tsked* with folded hands as he tilted back, while I leaned in to explain.

"No, Thatcher. I'm leaving you with the ability to rectify this indelicate matter now. Quietly and before the world hears about it. By the time *The Public Eye*—to borrow your *French* despite the venerated board member present—*shit* hits the fan, your pile will be long gone. This practice stops. Whatever it is you knew, sanctioned, or turned a blind eye to, ends now. And to show no hard feelings or concerns about the viability of Chastain's future, The Pembroke Institute will continue to donate to Chastain's endowment in the manner you all have become accustomed. Unless, of course, the new Director of Philanthropy believes she can better spend Pembroke's money elsewhere." I shrugged. "Time will tell."

With a stifled laugh, Tristan gesticulated with an exaggerated point to me, mouthing, "What she said."

"Good Lord, I love the smell of squashed pompous indignation in the morning," Tristan bellowed from the top of the granite steps, then trotted down the stairs to meet me. "Way to 'follow along,' by the way."

"Think it'll do any good?"

"If you have anything to say about it? Without a doubt. I just know I never want to be on the wrong side of Amelia Kanaan. A veiled threat to withhold our donations never occurred to me. Well played, Kanaan. Let me walk you to, well, where do you want to go?"

I gestured to campus walk. "I'm going back to my office. I have things to address. A few loose ends I want to take care of personally."

"Look at you and your ethics. Fidelity, even when this place likely would have scapegoated you."

"I prefer to think this work is about the community we serve, not the higher ups."

We strolled along the brick walkway lined with leafless trees. Even bare, the grounds exuded beauty, but also a complicated history. Despite the chill, students took academic time-outs from studying for the impending exam week. A frisbee toss. A couple jogging the manicured path. A solo studier typing away on a secluded bench, earbuds blocking out his surroundings.

"That's why I am thrilled to have you on board with the institute."

"I don't *officially* work for you yet, sir. I have a counter offer I hope you will consider."

"There is nothing you would dare ask for that I wouldn't give you to know my precious non-profit is in your gifted hands."

"As far as the job is concerned, I don't need anything. Your offer is ridiculously generous, and the work is worthwhile. My lawyer says it'd be a mistake not to take the position."

"Your lawyer, huh? You work fast, Mimi."

"May I be nosy and ask what you and Ethan talked about if it wasn't about the university?"

"It was nothing, really. Little bit of this, little bit of that. He knows I like to fly. Planes. Small engine, private aircraft. He asked about flight plans and manifests. What's required, what isn't. Said it was for another story he was thinking about diving into when this one wraps up. Background research. We didn't speak of you at all. Oh, except a quick mention of your love of tacos."

If I had to guess, Max and I weren't the only ones having a hard time letting Geneva Spieler go.

"So, your *sine qua non*?"

"Yes, there *is* something I need before we get to the work with the Pembroke Institute."

"You mean before we throw all the lavish parties?"

"Yes, before the parties." I shook my head at my soon-to-be boss.

"If it is within my power, it is yours, my fair-haired charitable goddess."

"I need a vacation."

The man didn't skip a beat. "Six weeks, and I'll pay half salary but not a penny more."

"Are you kidding me?" I would have only asked for the time. Getting paid never occurred to me.

"I never joke about vacations. I love vacation."

Too dumbfounded to choke out my agreement, my billionaire boss countered his own counter.

"Fine. You drive a hard bargain, Ms. Kanaan. Eight weeks. Final offer."

"Deal!" I yelped.

Forty-Two

AFTER AN HOUR'S WORTH of shuffling papers, reading a few new applications marked 'special case,' and the last of my handwritten thank-you notes to donors, I ducked out to meet Moses. He wanted an out-of-the-way place. Nothing public. We opted for my carriage house. That home was closer and didn't house the potential distraction of a man and his dog. *My* dog. Our dog?

"I say, I say there, Miss Amelia." Reginald Jaspers III waved to me as he stepped from the broad front porch that stretched the entire front of his home. "How are you on this glorious specimen of a day?"

"Hello, Dr. Jaspers. I'm well and you?"

"Couldn't be finer unless my Great-Grammy still walked this earth."

I couldn't imagine how old that would make the woman, but I took the bait. "Sorry to hear of her passing. A dear friend of mine died recently."

"Naw, Great-Grammy died before I was born and by most accounts was meaner than a rustled hive of hornets."

"You know you don't have to, uh, do the—routine for me."

"Oh, thank heavens. It's exhausting but also somehow automatic. I think I spend more time in character than out of it these days. My husband tells our friends he's married to the

Afro-Caribbean Daniel Day Louis. But I've only got the one accent," he sighed. "Unusual to see you home this time of day."

"I have a—personal meeting."

"Oh, do tell."

"With my lawyer."

"Oh, never mind."

"Actually, this is a happy accident, running into you. The friend who passed away left me her dog. Don't worry, he's staying elsewhere, but it means I will need to move. And soon, I'm afraid."

The professor's eyes widened and shrank.

"Maybe you heard some other news from your friend Dr. Cromwell? About me?"

"I have not, but I glimpsed the news the other day."

"Ah. Well, just between you and me, I'll be leaving Chastain. I got an unprecedented offer, and it's time for a change."

"Can't see Thatcher taking that very well. FDR, then you?"

My lips pressed together between my teeth.

"That's okay, dear." The storytelling southerner resurfaced. "Just between you and me, Thatcher Cromwell can be a real *sum'bitch*, if you'll pardon my crass tongue, and he cheats at golf." Dr. Jaspers winked. "I'll be right sorry to see you go, Miss Amelia, but sure as shootin', it'll be for the best."

I pried open the coffee can, wondering about Moses's reaction. He had none.

"You're sure cash is okay for the retainer fee?"

"Legal tender is legal tender. It might surprise you how many clients prefer to deal with cash—for various reasons. Sign here."

I did and handed him the agreed-upon amount.

"I think what I've done today will please you."

"Done? Already? It's only noon."

"I'm one of those old men who only sleeps four hours a night. And I like to keep busy. A blessing and a curse." He deposited the cash into his briefcase and pulled out a folder. "If you want printed material regarding Mr. Bonmanos, I can provide them. Or I can email the file."

"Or you could just tell me if there is anything I should be concerned about and leave it at that? Do we need a trail, paper or otherwise?"

"We do not. Mr. Winston Bonmanos appears to be who he portends. No criminal record. No bankruptcies. No concerning debt, considering his age. Married once. Widowed. He owns the property outright. No mortgage, no lien. He—"

"That's enough. Honestly, this makes me feel like a creep, but I needed to be sure."

"A background check can be the greatest gift a daughter can give her mother. You cannot be too careful."

"Well, this gift needs to remain under wraps for eternity."

"Noted. Moving on to the real estate deal." Mr. Pascha didn't dilly-dally, opening the file on the coffee table.

"Yes."

"It's an adequate starting offer."

"Starting offer?"

"I can do better for you."

"How's that, Moses?" The sticky note found with the money clung to the inside of the coffee can in my lap. *Trust Moses Pascha,* in Geneva's curly handwriting, stared back at me.

"By doing what you pay me to do. With your permission and that of the other two parties, I will counter." He slid me forms for Mama and Winston to sign. "The only thing I require, once they sign these, is a closing date and where to mail the check."

I stifled a laugh at the words 'mail' and 'check,' two things I told Mama people didn't use anymore. "Can we make it three equal checks? One for Mama, one for Winston, and the third for me?"

"Absolutely. Once you give me the green light, consider it done." He closed the folder.

"Is it really that simple?"

"In my experience, asking the right person for help simplifies most things in life." After a reassuring pat on my knee, Moses closed his briefcase and left.

My workday wasn't done, and I didn't know what day would be my last. The possibilities brimmed from my overflowing cup, and my eagerness to grab that fabled brass ring propelled me around the park on my return to campus. I laughed out loud at my sudden love for abused clichés, finally finding their appeal. The world was my friggin' oyster, and I fingered the fake pearls at my neck in a thank-you to the woman who helped make it possible.

But one prospect didn't appeal to me—getting Mama through the sales process, convincing her to accept Moses's expertise, and all the back and forth of paperwork. I called her to get that boulder rolling.

"Good news, Mama." I lathered on the positive attitude. "Moses Pascha will take on the Clay and Sons' offer and thinks he can negotiate a better deal on behalf of all of us. You, Winston, and me. Now, I know you don't know Moses, but I trust him and think—"

"Great. Let's do it," she interrupted my planned speech.

"Just like that?"

"Did I stutter, Amelia? Winston is here and gives the thumbs up, too. You trust the man, then we do too."

"Uh, okay. He needs you to sign some forms. When can we meet?"

"You mean paper forms? Can't you scan and send them or use some e-sign program? Time to join the twenty-first century, Mimi. Besides, we aren't exactly in town."

"I'm sorry. What now?" Hadn't I just taught her how to Venmo?

The Cleaning Lady and Mr. Fix-it were fitting out their new business office in a storefront rental that Winston's daughter helped them find in a small town in Georgia's Blue Ridge mountains. The progress train was on the move and if I didn't jump fast, I'd find myself left at the station.

"I got a new job too, Mama."

"Is that right? Not on my account, I hope. I've been bugging you for years."

"An opportunity presented itself and I took it."

"How daring, Mimi. And unlike you. Glad you're finally taking after your mama. It's about time."

Once again, I knew a compliment was hidden in there. She thought so, anyway. Mama was Mama and always would be, but she didn't need me. Not like she used to, not like I thought. She did the best she could in circumstances that would have knocked down the toughest, and look where she landed. A self-sufficient daughter, a smart business venture on the horizon, and a business partner who also kept her warm at night. Life was good.

"Mimi?"

"Hm?"

"Don't waste another minute of your life. You only get so many."

"See you soon?"

"We will always have Monday nights. On the phone."

"I love you, Mama."

There was silence on the other end of the line, then she said, "What was that? I-I really need to get back to work, Amelia. Winston is flexing his boss muscles here."

The twosome giggled like a couple of teenagers before she ended the call without even a goodbye.

Whether or not she knew it, Mama taught me another lesson. Not only would I not waste another minute of my life, but I wouldn't hold back saying how I felt, particularly about the people in my life. My feet picked up speed, crossing onto campus as I hailed a cab to Midtown Mews.

Forty-Three

"Hello, Mr. Colby." I ran past him toward the long first-floor hall on my way to the apartment on the far end, but spun, dodging a potted palm, while asking, "Have you seen Ethan? Mr. Ledes, I mean?"

"I haven't, no, but it's been so busy. I trust all's well with you, Miss Mimi?"

I noted the empty lobby again, wondering how the old man defined 'busy.' "Never better, Mr. Colby. Never better." I'd caught my mother's giggle (apparently a trait we shared, but I'd never known until today), and twirled back around, charging off to my future.

Swallowing hard, I steadied my breath before knocking on the door. Silence. I knocked again. Still nothing. Despite knowing he wouldn't answer, I gave a third round of rapping, resting my forehead under the scrolled metal *1B*.

Anticlimactic, to say the least.

I trudged back toward the lobby and the slow elevator, too deflated to take the stairs.

"I've sorted the mail, Miss Mimi. Would you like to take Ms. —Spieler's up with you?" Mr. Colby shuffled to me with a bundle secured with a rubber band. Lost in my own world in recent days, I hadn't noticed the doorman's slower pace or his drooping caterpillar brows. Every floor of the old residence felt the loss of Geneva Spieler.

"Thank you, Mr. Colby. Are you doing all right?"

"Ah, sure. The world is a bit dimmer nowadays, but it keeps spinning."

"Hardly seems possible without her, does it?"

"Our loss is the African savanna's gain, I s'pose."

"I'm sorry. How's that?"

"I think she *really* went into hiding to live out her reign as queen. She told me she might have to one day. Either that or she's reunited with that gangster-turned-CIA-informant husband of hers. Maybe both. Though it's funny, I thought I saw him the other day. Here. In the lobby. With you and yer fella. Then again, some days my shoes don't match, and I eat spaghetti for breakfast." He shrugged and pushed the call button for me. "Either way, I know she's at peace. It just feels better, doesn't it? Knowing that?" Mr. Colby's earnestness brought tears to my eyes and as usual, I let slide the man's peculiar behavior.

I cleared the new lump in my throat. Tried to, anyway. "Yes, Mr. Colby. It certainly does."

The elevator rumbled to open as I squeezed the man's arm in sad solidarity, and I waved goodbye from inside the burled wood box during the prolonged pause, made longer because I thought it rude to press the 'close door' button. Somehow, in the letdown of my Y'allywood-version of the race to the end of a rom-com's final scene, and the sweet doorman's Pollyanna take on dear Geneva's last act, the slower than ever old lift gave me the time to consider new life choices in the prolonged climb to the *12A*.

My chin rested on my chest in the insufferable ascent as I fought not to let a single tear fall, surprised I had any left. But creamy-white furry feet forced the first drop to roll down my cheek when the diabolical sliding doors jerked open the first few inches, then stalled.

"Max?" I squawked through the crack.

"Mimi?" Ethan replied along with Max's *hello* yip.

"Ethan?" I glimpsed sneakers. "You're here." I wiped my eyes.

"We came up for treats after our walk, but someone with paws stubbornly refuses to take the stairs. Up or down. Wait, are you crying?"

"*No.*" Yes, I fibbed, then dropped my bag and mail bundle, trying to pry apart the doors by hand. "Why won't these damn doors open?" I grunted.

"Uh oh, boy. Someone's fired up. Better stand back. Give it a sec, Meems. They'll move when they're good and ready. Not unlike our furry friend here."

"I don't have a sec. I've wasted too much time already."

"What's going on?"

I pressed myself to the brass barricade to see Ethan dressed in the same Notre Dame wear as the day we met. My arm wouldn't fit through the narrow opening. "Don't catch a plane."

"What?"

"Don't catch a plane, not without me, anyway."

"Mi—"

"I took the Pembroke job."

"Congratulations. That's—"

"And I'm selling to Clay and Sons. Moses is brokering the deal."

"Hey, we should celebrate."

"And I'm—well, I'm—*bananas nuts* for you." No, that wasn't what I'd meant to say.

"Yeah," he chuckled. "I've been thinking about the t-shirts all day."

"Screw the damn t-shirts." Okay, I didn't mean to sound angry either, but...

Ethan paused before agreeing with a tentative, "Uh, o-kay. But I think you *are* crying."

I took a beat. "I am crying."

"Why?" His fingers slid in the narrow gap, groping for mine.

I sucked in a deep breath to calm myself. It didn't help much. "I think, I think it's because—Ethan? I love you. I'm *in* love with you. And I didn't think I was capable, like I was love-impaired or too broken, but I do and I know it's too fast or too soon or too—I don't know what, but I am. And I'm ready. I'm ready to go or stay or—go—and why the *hell* won't these doors open? God, I *hate* this elevator."

I kicked the brushed brass obstacle just as the elevator gods obliged us, but I didn't make it out of the contraption. Tripping over my messenger bag and mail, we collided, wrapped in each other's arms. When my back hit the railing, Ethan's mouth pulled from mine to find my cheek, my ear, then his lips found my neck and the jewelry clasped to it.

"God, I *love* this elevator," I rasped.

"Kissing a girl in pearls is my new favorite thing."

"Then shut up and keep doing it."

We laughed into another heated kiss. Hungry mouths and even greedier hands explored, wanting more than our setting would allow. The Portie at our feet reminded us with his usual sneeze.

"It's not, you know," Ethan said, still pressed to me. He stretched his shirt to dab dry my freckles. Freckles he made beautiful.

"Not what?"

"Too soon, too fast. It's not *too* anything. I'm in love with you, too—uh, *also*."

"I know." It could have been a joke, but it wasn't. I knew it for sure.

He gave a cheeky eye roll, then kissed me again.

I held him close as I pulled from his mouth. "Run away with me."

"Aww, I thought you'd never ask. Where to?"

"I'm thinking Indiana, for starters. Max and I want to see snow. Play in mounds of the stuff." Norman Rockwell images of sledding, ice skating, and snowball fights danced in my head. "Plus, what's a better way to really know someone than a twelve-hour road trip?"

"It'll take us longer than that. We'll be making lots of stops." Ethan winked. "With Max and all, you know?"

"I *absolutely* know, um—*Huh*. I've run out of journalists' names to call you. Shoot."

"Oh, darn. Let's get out of this box before we're stuck." He bent to grab Max's leash and my bag and handed me the rolled postal bundle, the rubber band snapped in the exchange, spilling mail on the floor.

"I've got it."

My two favorites strolled down the hall to *12A*.

"Come on, boy. Back to your mom's place for now."

My stomach rose at the mention of Geneva, then stuck in my throat when a postcard appeared in the scattered magazines and envelopes. Vivid colors caught my blurred eyes, and the word *MEXICO* blazed across an illustrated sky of brilliant blue. When I knew I wouldn't fall over, my already goofy grin spread wider, and another trail of tears rolled down my cheeks as I stood.

"Hey, Ethan. Did you know, since 2019, you can drive a dog across the U.S. border to Mexico? With nothing but his up-to-date shot record?"

Ethan smiled as I walked toward him. "I did *not* know that. Why do *you* know that?"

"I read an article—Rick Steves! *Ha-ha*! The game continues."

He stopped my celebration of the bookish name game with a kiss. "God, I really love you." He held me with one arm around my waist as he thumbed away the newest water works, these tears spurred by joy.

"Ever been to San Miguel de Allende?"

"Been to Mexico, but not that exact spot. Why so specific?"

"After ice skating in Indiana, I'm thinking margaritas in Mexico."

"I like the sound of that. You, in a bikini. Me—staring at you in a bikini." His twinkling gaze drifted off in some daydream.

I thumped his arm to bring him back to real life. "I don't even own a bathing suit, much less a bikini."

"Wow, this just gets better and better," he joked with a squeeze. "Still, why there?"

I showed him the beautiful postcard depicting a flowered and lanterned streetscape with a terracotta-colored cathedral in the background, the words San Miguel de Allende printed at the bottom edge of the mailed picture. Ethan furrowed his inquisitive brow, but his eyes grew wide, and his mouth fell open as I turned over the card for him to read the message.

Hola mi hermosa!

Starting over. And there's a man I'd like you to meet...again. Now bring me my damn dog.

THE END

Fingers-crossed, I will have a feel-good holiday story out for you mid-fall 2026. In the meantime, if you haven't read my other books, they are listed below. As always, short, honest, but kind reviews truly make more novels possible. Even a simple star-rating helps. Thank you so much. I appreciate your support.

Other books by Kelly Elizabeth Huston:
Tex Miller Is Dead
A Very Crowded House
A Girl, Stuck
See Sadie Jane Run

Acknowledgments

Readers had to wait an entire year for this book. I didn't mean to tease or exact any sort of power ploy. Nothing was as well-schemed as that. No, I busied myself with an extreme case of imposter syndrome (for a few reasons), some content concerns (publishing can be a wildly dogmatic landscape to navigate), and plumb exhaustion (publishing four 90k+ word books in seventeen months is a lot).

Thank you to the usual suspects. My family for all the attagirls. My editor, Ash, who is always on point and keeps me level-headed while nudging me in all the right directions. My critique partner Kyle, who spotted my problem early on and gave me lots to consider. To Heather, who is an assistant dean at a private southern university, for helping me get the university hierarchy and day-to-day close to real life, and Michaela and Aly who make me feel like I'm a big deal. And a special thanks to Paulette Stout, Dr. Kimberly Varnado, and Dr. Madia Cooper-Ashirifi, three women of color who guided me along the third rail of DE&I and the racial aspects of the story. I breathe easier knowing I passed muster with these three brilliant women who offered their time to help despite their busy lives.

My intent was to write a funny, thoughtful, sweet love story, but I wanted to include some current events. In a time of political divides, with generational, geographical, and socio-economic issues all in play, I still hoped to create relatable characters struggling to navigate these rifts in ways other than building walls. Whether it's protecting your heart or avoiding confrontation, putting up barriers is the easy thing to do, but it only leads to regret and loneliness. Doing the hard things—facing controversy, being vulnerable, walking in another's shoes—will hone us all in the end and *being better* is one of the greatest achievements we can meet.

To keep up to date on what comes next, visit HTTPS://WWW.KELLYELIZABETHHUSTON.COM/ and sign up for Kelly's newsletter

www.ingramcontent.com/pod-product-compliance
Lightning Source LLC
Chambersburg PA
CBHW030349120726
47901CB00007B/1966